T0271522

DEATH ON THE THAMES

ALAN JOHNSON

DEATH ON THE THAMES

WILDFIRE

First published in 2024 by
WILDFIRE
an imprint of HEADLINE PUBLISHING GROUP

2

Cataloguing in Publication Data is available from the British Library

Hardback ISBN 978 1 0354 0344 8
Trade paperback ISBN 978 1 0354 0345 5

Typeset in Sabon LT Pro by EM&EN
Printed and bound in Great Britain by Clays Ltd, Elcograf S.p.A.

Headline's policy is to use papers that are natural, renewable and recyclable
products and made from wood grown in well-managed forests and other
controlled sources. The logging and manufacturing processes are expected
to conform to the environmental regulations of the country of origin.

HEADLINE PUBLISHING GROUP
An Hachette UK Company
Carmelite House
50 Victoria Embankment
London EC4Y 0DZ

www.headline.co.uk
www.hachette.co.uk

To the memory of
Detective Chief Superintendent Brian Dunn
of Greater Manchester Police;
born 1938, died 2011.

PART ONE

1999

1

THE SINGLE SHOT

It didn't seem like anything to worry about – at first. She'd glanced out of her bedroom window that morning and saw him standing on the pavement opposite as if waiting for a car to pass before crossing, except that no car passed, and he hadn't crossed. He just stood looking up at the house for at least a minute. She knew him, and knew he wasn't exactly 'Brain of Britain' ever since the day his poor widowed mother had brought him to her house to ask if she could help find him a job where she worked – at the BBC.

They lived just round the corner. Why should she find anything remotely threatening about him being in her street?

By the time she left the house, pulling the red varnished front door firmly shut behind her, he was nowhere to be seen. On the train into work, she remembered bumping into his mother at the shops one day and being told how much he'd hated the job at Television Centre: the job she'd helped to find for him – the job he'd left after only a few weeks.

'I know he's never been academic,' his mother had said, 'but he does have his talents,' adding pointedly that humping scenery around all day wasn't one of them.

So ungrateful.

And more recently there was the incident outside her house, when he rode his bike straight at her, calling out vile things as he cycled away. Rather than complaining that she hadn't made him a star, his mother should be grateful she hadn't pressed charges.

It was a quiet day at the office, so she was heading home by lunchtime. On the train, an elderly couple asked for her autograph, thanking her for 'everything you do to keep us safe.' The approach wasn't unusual, but it was the first time she'd been asked to sign her name on the back of a pension book. Walking home from the station, along the banks of the Thames, she smiled as she thought of the encounter.

As she turned into her street, she saw him again – fleetingly – crossing the road thirty metres ahead, walking quickly as if there was somewhere he needed to be. She thought that if she bumped into him, she'd be friendly – let bygones be bygones – and demonstrate that, as far as she was concerned, there were no hard feelings, ingratiate herself, try to end this nonsense.

All the same, she wondered, why was he still here? Lurking in her street? He must know about the programmes she made, the connections she had with the police. She was damned if some half-wit was going to frighten her. But, as she covered the last few metres towards her house, she found herself hurrying as if there was danger, on this April morning, on this quiet street, in broad daylight.

She opened her handbag to feel for the big bunch of keys with its plastic Bob the Builder fob. Separating the house key from the rest, she lifted it towards the door. It was then that she heard the footsteps behind her, felt the forceful hand on her shoulder pushing her down onto her knees to receive the single, fatal gunshot.

2

OPERATION INCISIVE

The early April sky was streaked with red. It had been an unusually warm afternoon, now darkening into night. Two plain-clothes detectives sat in an unmarked Rover; part of the twenty-five-officer team deployed on Operation Incisive, a joint Met/Surrey Police initiative to catch whoever was responsible for a string of sexual assaults on women in the Hampton Court area.

One of the police officers – a thickset man with wispy hair and a paunch – was demonstrating a surprising dexterity as his fat fingers picked at the remains of a fish supper. Detective Sergeant Ralph Harrison was an opinionated man, and the opinion he was currently articulating concerned what he saw as the stupidity of young girls dressing inappropriately as they went through the social rituals of a Friday evening.

'I mean, I could understand it if this was the Costa del Sol, or that place in Cyprus, where me and Sheila went on our holidays, but it's not. This is close to the chilly old Thames, and in an area where women have been attacked previously – most often on a Friday night. And this is a Friday night,' he said, lifting a final salt-laden chip, which he consumed prior to his peroration. 'I'm not saying they're asking for it, course I'm not, but for God's sake, girls, just exercise a bit of common sense.'

The young woman sitting next to him behind the steering wheel said nothing. She'd heard this stuff so often during her short time in the Met that she could no longer be bothered to point out that the girls going about their lawful business were dressed in accordance with the culture and fashion of the late twentieth century and it was the job of the police to protect them, rather than offer excuses for those who would do them harm. Detective Constable Louise Mangan was Harrison's subordinate and more pleased than he was to have a role in this operation. She hadn't been a plain-clothes officer for long but had been in the Met long enough to feel that the force was lethargic about attacks on women in general, and particularly so in relation to these incidents in the Hampton Court area.

The assaults had been happening here for three years. The first had been along the towpath on the Middlesex side of the Thames, followed by a second on the Surrey bank. There followed further incidents in Hampton Wick, Bushy Park and on Pavilion Terrace. Low-level stuff at first; a buttock slapped, a skirt briefly lifted as the assailant sped by on a bicycle.

A senior officer had originally suggested that it was a passing trend engaged in by pubescent boys; a bit of mischief that should be left for community officers to deal with. It was only when pressure from the families of the girls, supported by their MPs, forced the Commissioner to insist upon a proper collation of all the evidence that this 'group activity' theory disintegrated, and it became obvious that one person was responsible. For a start, the assaults happened consecutively, never concurrently. Matching descriptions of the perpetrator, whilst not being enough to reveal his identity, disclosed important consistencies – the same yellow reflective polycarbonate cycling helmet, mirrored lens goggles, a drop-handle sports bike, the absence of any lamps back or front, and every victim who heard their attacker say anything reporting the same vicious words spat out as he fled – 'filthy fucking whore.'

The assaults had become increasingly violent. One teenage girl was strangled to stop her crying out; she was lucky to be alive. Another was repeatedly punched when she fought back against her attacker, and the most recent, nineteen-year-old Tiffany Mordaunt, had disappeared on a night out in the vicinity on a Friday night two weeks ago.

A tabloid newspaper, the *Daily Candour*, was now running front page stories on 'The Beast of Hampton Court', but the attacks continued. Whoever was responsible wasn't exactly lying low. The criminal psychologists at the Met felt he had reached the stage where a perverse awareness of the likelihood of being caught made him ever more reckless.

He'd struck again the previous Friday, in Hampton Court Park; pouncing on an older woman, an American tourist walking back towards the gates after visiting Hampton Court Palace. She'd been molested, traumatised, sworn at, her assailant using the same words – 'filthy fucking whore' – on the same sports bike, wearing the same helmet, same mirrored goggles.

The disappearance of Tiffany Mordaunt had at last provoked an adequate police response – Operation Incisive.

Tonight, there were seven police vehicles of one sort or another, from motorcycles to people carriers stationed across the broad area in which the attacks had taken place. As well as the officers in (or on) these contraptions, there were policemen and women mingling with Friday-night revellers, walking the streets, paying particular attention to passing cyclists.

Louise Mangan had only become a detective six months ago, joining Borough Command in Southwest London on her first plain-clothes assignment. She'd badly wanted to be part of Incisive. In part, this had been about combatting the sexism she knew still existed in the department and that she believed would affect this particular investigation. She had experienced some of this herself after the birth of her two daughters (Michelle in 1994 and Chloe in 1996) when some in the department had implied that she needed to choose between being a mother and being an officer, but such experiences had only made her more determined to combat misogyny within the force by proving herself. She'd even had to join as a 'Woman Police Constable', a separate and anomalous designation that was due to disappear shortly. She felt that these small advances mattered.

Detective Sergeant Ralph Harrison, sitting beside her in the car, personified old-school policing. Ralph wasn't a bad person. From the time she'd already spent with him, Louise could recognise laudable qualities of bravery and loyalty and patriotism forged through his many years of service. Louise was married to a police sergeant (a uniformed one), she knew how the hierarchy worked. But Tom Mangan was part of her more enlightened generation, the post-boomer Generation X, better equipped to embrace the impending third millennium than the officer sitting next to her who had now begun pontificating on a different subject. The Macpherson Inquiry into the racist murder of Stephen Lawrence had just been published.

'That all happened six years ago,' Harrison was saying, 'a lot of water has flowed down the Thames since then. I don't buy this shit. Excuse my French, Louise, but that's what it is, about the Met being, you know, intentionally racist.'

Louise muttered something, unwilling to become engaged in this conversation but unable to resist a correction.

'Sorry, what was that?' her sergeant asked.

'The report said the Met was institutionally racist, not intentionally racist,' Louise said.

Harrison reflected for a moment. 'Same thing, isn't it?'

Louise, unwilling to pursue the matter further, agreed it probably was. It was too late at night to champion Macpherson, and Ralph's criticism was mild compared to some of the entrenched bigotry she'd been subjected to by other colleagues.

Harrison and Louise had been occupying this car park on Hampton Court Green for two hours, receiving regular reports from fellow officers staked out across the area, keeping a close eye out for lone females and yellow-helmeted cyclists. There'd been a few false alarms, and one embarrassing mistake when an officer apprehended what he thought was a voyeur in black camouflage, but who turned out to be a local vicar taking a stroll after evensong.

Then, at 9 p.m., the radio burst into life. A girl walking along Lower Hampton Road had been dragged into the scrubland bordering the road. Her scream had been heard by two of the Surrey officers monitoring that patch and their car siren had scared the attacker off. He was last seen cycling fast towards Kempton Park riding a drop-handle sports bike and wearing a fluorescent yellow helmet.

Detective Sergeant Harrison had been outside the car smoking a cigarette when the alert was broadcast. 'Okay, you wait here,' he said to Louise. 'He'll be coming through the park.' He stamped on what was left of his fag, and ran towards Bushy Park behind them.

Alone in the car, Louise examined the map. She could see how easily a cyclist could disappear onto the trails and pathways of the park, but she could also see that he'd have needed to cross the A308. Knowing he was being pursued, she asked herself, wouldn't he be more likely to try to blend in with the many cyclists using this main route down towards Hampton Court? The car park where she and Harrison had based themselves opened directly onto that road. But her sergeant had gone in the opposite direction.

Louise left the vehicle and ran to the road. She needed to walk about twenty metres to a bend in the A308 to get a long view. Even this long after the rush hour, traffic roared past in a ceaseless stream. She could see plenty of bikers on a fenced-off elevated section that was supposed to be a footpath, but had long been claimed by cyclists, a horde of which were currently heading towards her.

Most of the cyclists seemed decidedly un-sporty, using their bicycles simply to get from A to B. Louise could only see a couple of serious bikers with their heads bent low over dropped handlebars, dressed in lycra, and with plastic bottles clipped to their cycle frames. Only one wore a helmet, and it appeared to be red rather than yellow.

Louise realised that the attacker may have gone in the other direction, towards Kingston, but the Surrey guys hadn't seen him, and, in any case, Hampton Court was known to be the epicentre of his activities. She calculated that, given the timing of the attack and the distances involved, if he was cycling in her direction on the A308 he wouldn't get to where she was for another few minutes. She had time to run back to the car, grab the binoculars from the glove compartment and make a proper job of monitoring the approaching traffic.

As soon as she returned to her vantage point and adjusted the focus on the binoculars, she was excited to see a cyclist in a luminous yellow helmet with mirrored goggles on a drop-handled sports bike around three hundred metres away.

Louise radioed the information upstream to the team that had frightened the attacker off and downstream to the officers stationed on Hampton Court Bridge. By the time she'd lifted the binoculars to her eyes once again, the rider had vanished. She tried to concentrate her gaze harder, ensuring the viewfinder was perfectly focused. By now the yellow helmeted biker should have been just a few metres away, at the point where a bunch of riders she'd seen him huddled in with had now reached. But there was no sign of him. Where could he have gone?

Louise's map showed no junctions leading off the A308. On the left were the railings around Bushy Park, on the right the Thames. If he'd turned round for some reason, the officers further up would spot him, but crossing over lanes to change course wouldn't be easy in this traffic and the disruption would still be visible, like the waves left by a boat changing course on a busy river.

Louise returned to the car and was standing by the driver's door chewing over her options, instinctively keen to move towards the spot where she'd last seen the yellow-helmeted rider, when she heard Ralph Harrison yelling from behind. Turning quickly, she saw another cyclist come racing out of Bushy Park and onto the car park heading straight towards her.

'Use your spray,' Harrison shouted, but before she could reach for the canister of CS gas clipped to her belt, the bike was almost upon her and showed no signs of slowing down. Louise took a small step to her left before flinging herself at the bike, hitting its rider sideways on, a coup de grace exercised in a single manoeuvre.

Together, Louise and Harrison managed to restrain the cyclist sufficiently to apply handcuffs. The ruckus attracted an audience. Motorists had pulled over to watch and before long a knot of pedestrian spectators had gathered. The commotion itself was over in minutes and Harrison removed the cyclist's yellow reflective polycarbonate helmet to place him gently into the back of the Rover. But before the two detectives could drive off with their prize, they had to wait a further fifteen minutes for a bigger police vehicle to collect the drop-handle sports bike. In that time the crowd had grown even bigger as word spread that the Beast of Hampton Court had been snared.

When he'd left Louise, just as the alarm was raised, Detective Sergeant Harrison had thought better of simply crashing through the undergrowth, preferring instead to wait in the bushes next to the track through Bushy Park, where he felt the fugitive was most likely to emerge.

'When I saw him bombing towards me, I stepped out and told him to stop. But the bastard managed to ride around me . . . You must have been watching old Fred Astaire movies,' Harrison told Louise admiringly. 'I couldn't do those moves you did.'

'Well, Ginger Rogers was always the better dancer. Didn't she once say she could do all the moves that Fred could do, but backwards and in heels? Excellent metaphor for the more skilful contributions we women make.'

If Ralph Harrison recognised her good-natured teasing, he ignored it. They were crossing the car park towards their vehicle at the police station in Kingston-upon-Thames. It was 3 a.m. and the man they'd captured, Darnell Thomas, a local fitness instructor, was being questioned by detectives from the Flying Squad who had overall responsibility for Operation Incisive. Louise would drop Ralph off at his house in Sudbury before driving home to the flat in Brixton that she, Tom and the girls had recently moved into.

DS Harrison and Louise were due back on duty in six hours' time. As the arresting officers, when they returned, they'd be required to fill in numerous forms once Darnell Thomas had been formerly charged.

'I don't suppose there's any doubt that he will be charged?' Louise asked as she turned the key in the ignition.

'Nah, got him bang to rights.'

'But he says he bolted because he thought you were some thug lurking in the park,' Louise persisted, 'and you do look a bit thuggish.'

'Thanks very much.'

'The point is, he wouldn't have known we were police officers,' Louise continued.

'That's true. I didn't have time to show him my warrant card but there's no doubt he's our man. The girl he attacked tonight didn't get a clear view of his face, but he was in the location, riding a sports-bike, and wearing that distinctive yellow cycle helmet. When the Flying Squad guys have finished questioning him about tonight's attack and the attempted murder of the girl he tried to strangle, they'll begin to interrogate him about the one who's gone missing. Our work is done.'

Louise drove in silence. Her report about the man she'd seen cycling towards her along the A308 had been logged but discounted now that Darnell Thomas was in custody. Nevertheless, she planned to resubmit it to the DCI in charge of the investigation.

As the car pulled up outside Ralph Harrison's house, Louise said, 'I really did see that cyclist in the yellow helmet coming down the main road, Sarge, so there is another suspect. And he was wearing the goggles. Thomas wasn't.'

By now Harrison was standing outside the car. He bent back down so that Louise could hear him without the need to speak too loudly into the soft night air.

'But where the hell did your man go? Given that Darnell's in custody and your guy vanished into thin air, I think the reality is that there's only one suspect here. He probably threw the goggles away because they marked him out.'

'But so did the helmet,' Louise protested.

'True, but he was a man in a hurry, and the helmet takes more time to get off. As I can testify, having removed Darnell's to get him in the car. Now you get yourself home and grab as much rest as you can. I'll see you in the morning.'

Harrison walked off towards his front door but before Louise could put the car in gear he was back with an afterthought.

'The fact that Darnell Thomas is black may lead some people to accuse us of being intentionally racist, but they don't have responsibility for stopping these attacks, we do. Goodnight, Ginger, and well done.'

3

CRIMESOLVE

Four people gathered in a scruffy room at BBC Television Centre in Wood Lane, London W12, with a fifth person expected to join them at any moment. The quartet was responsible for one of the most successful programmes on British television. *Crimesolve*, broadcast monthly on BBC2, had recorded 16 million viewers for its March edition.

Now, as the show's creative nucleus gathered to plan the April programme, they heard the news. The Beast of Hampton Court had been caught. What was undoubtedly of significant benefit to society had been a setback for *Crimesolve*, because they'd been planning to dedicate the entire hour of the next episode to the efforts of Operation Incisive. Interviews had been filmed with some of the girls who'd been attacked (in silhouette, their identities protected), a depiction of the attacker reconstructed, and a profile of Tiffany Mordaunt, the missing girl, prepared. All wasted. The perpetrator was in custody. Now the programme would have to run with one of the other stories they kept in reserve for precisely this kind of eventuality. None of these reports were as well developed as the scheduled item, and with less than four weeks left, they'd need to work hard to have a substitute show of the required quality.

'Jenny will be upset,' said Simon Tait, the director. 'She hates stressful situations.'

'I don't see why she should feel stressed,' said the producer, Carl Burnett. 'We're the ones with all the work to do. All that's required of Jenny is to look pretty while she reads from the autocue.'

Things had been difficult between Burnett and Jenny Daniels – the show's presenter, and the person they were waiting for – ever since a brief romance ended a year ago. The producer was said to be as jealous of his former lover's success as he was of the man who'd replaced him in her affections. Daniels had dumped Burnett with the kind of decisiveness which had characterised her television career.

What probably rankled with Burnett more was that her new beau, Dr Jamie Templeman, was a good six inches taller, about two stone lighter and at least ten years younger than the overweight TV producer. Templeman wasn't just younger than Burnett, he was also three years younger than Daniels herself. And he was a doctor, a proper one: a doctor of medicine, an acknowledged expert in the medical effects of so-called recreational drugs.

The other two people in the scruffy room at Television Centre – Olive Sabatini and Luke O'Sullivan – did all the heavy lifting for *Crimesolve*. As assistant producers responsible for content they worked with a team of researchers to come up with unsolved crimes for the show to re-enact. Once it had been decided which story to run with, it was Olive and Luke's responsibility to produce the script.

Usually, the stories they worked on were heavily dependent on the cooperation of the relevant police force. Indeed, it was the police who usually offered up the story. The one they were now contemplating sending onto the pitch as a substitute for Hampton Court had no such credentials and would represent a new departure for *Crimesolve*. It also happened to involve Dr Jamie Templeman.

There had been a significant increase in the use of illicit opioids and cocaine across London. The *Crimesolve* team had been made aware of the human damage this was doing after being approach by the parents of a young girl who'd died of a heroin overdose, requesting the programme highlight the many personal tragedies caused by the recreational habits of respectable middle-class citizens. These people were fuelling a drugs trade in London that was now one of the most substantial in the world.

Despite a personal appeal by Simon Tait and even some behind the scenes lobbying from the Director General, the Met had refused to collaborate with the BBC on this item, arguing that the issues were too sensitive, and that advertising the easy availability of this stuff could boost demand. But Tait and his colleagues felt the police were simply embarrassed about their failure to get to grips with the problem.

Dr Templeman, who was researching a book on the subject, had told *Crimesolve* about the Brit who had created the criminal network that had made London such a magnet for narcotics. His name was Jack Handysides. This had been passed to the Commissioner's office but only seemed to reinforce the Met's negative attitude. Now, with the Hampton Court story being pulled, the team was again discussing running the item unilaterally, without any police involvement.

'This is one of the best stories we've ever had and, okay, it's more *Panorama* than *Crimesolve* territory – well outside our comfort zone – but it's absolutely consistent with our ethos,' Simon Tait was saying. 'Going solo won't happen often, but we're not a mouthpiece for the Met and this may force them to get their collective finger out. We can use Jenny's doctor chappie to good effect as well. He's telegenic and knows all about the way prescription drugs get used for illicit purposes.'

Carl Burnett's body language conveyed his discomfort with this assessment of the man who'd usurped him in Daniels' love life, but he said nothing.

'But we could still run with the missing girl,' Luke O'Sullivan suggested. 'The link with the assaults in Hampton Court is only speculative and she does remain a missing person.'

'You're right, Luke,' the director said. 'It could just be coincidental that she vanished in the general area where the Beast of Hampton Court has been operating and on a Friday evening, which is when the attacks usually happen, but you know how sensitive the legal people are about prejudicing a court case. We dare not do her while a prime suspect is still being questioned. We can return to Tiffany Mordaunt for the May programme if she's still missing.'

At this moment, twenty minutes after the meeting was scheduled to commence, the door was flung open so violently that it knocked over a coat stand positioned behind it, spilling a couple of jackets onto Carl Burnett's head. Jenny Daniels burst in cursing the traffic in general and the congestion around Shepherds Bush Green in particular.

'An hour and a bloody half to drive eleven miles,' she

exclaimed, throwing her coat over the back of an empty chair and depositing her huge bunch of keys, with their Bob the Builder fob, onto the table.

In her late thirties, Daniels' peaches and cream complexion and short blond hair made her look younger than she was. Her slightly officious tone and cut-glass accent was suggestive of a Head Teacher at a private girls' school rather than a major TV star. Declared 'TV Personality of the Year 1998', Daniels hosted two early evening family shows as well as her monthly appearances on *Crimesolve*. The powder-blue Jaeger coat that she'd slung so carelessly down was a perfect match for the business-like, navy pleated skirt and pink knitted top she wore underneath.

'No worries, Jenny, we'd hardly started,' said the emollient director, Simon Tait. 'I suppose you've heard the news about the Hampton Court arrest?'

'Yes, huge relief for we who live in the area,' Daniels responded, pouring coffee from a silver jug on a side table.

'I thought you were living in Fulham these days,' Olive Sabatini said.

It was well known on set and off that Jenny Daniels had been living with Dr Jamie Templeman at his home close to Fulham Broadway for the past year.

'Okay, I'll rephrase that. It's a huge relief for those of us who have homes in the area which they have to visit occasionally.'

Daniels carried her overfilled cup to her place at the table.

'I went back to East Molesey last night and guess what? Some bastard cyclist nearly crashed into me outside the house.'

'What happened?' asked Tait, keen to get on with the meeting but sensing that this was a tale that was going to be told anyway.

'Well, I'd just got out of my car and was standing on the pavement rooting around in my bag for the house keys when this idiot comes straight at me along the pavement. Fortunately, the lovely old couple who live next door drove up at that very moment. I saw this awful man's face illuminated in the headlights. I looked at him, and he looked at me. You know? Like in one of those movies when everything seems to freeze?'

'And was that it?' Burnett asked, a slight sneer in his voice as Daniels left her audience in suspense whilst trying to find a spoon to stir her coffee.

'No, he swore at me and rode off.'

'What did he say?' asked Olive Sabatini, genuinely interested.

'Oh, I don't know . . . "filthy fucking bitch" or something.'

Sabatini pressed her to remember the exact words.

'You're being a little pedantic if you don't mind me saying, Olive dear,' Simon Tait observed.

'I've just written the script for the Hampton Court piece we were going to do, and the attacker used the same words – "you filthy fucking whore" – every time.'

'That's it, that's what he shouted at me – "you filthy fucking whore" – I remember thinking that at least he took me for a working girl,' Daniels said, hooting with laughter before a gradual realisation descended. 'Oh my God! It must have been him. Thank goodness he's been caught.'

'But you said this happened last night,' Luke O'Sullivan interrupted.

'Yes, before he was captured, I suppose.'

'Not possible,' O'Sullivan continued, 'although the police have just announced that they've caught the guy, they nabbed him three days ago, on Friday night. They haven't given a name yet but one of our contacts at the Met told me the man they've caught is black.'

'Well, this idiot was very white,' Daniels said. 'So white that if his colour had a name, I'd paint my kitchen with it.'

'Was he wearing a cycle helmet?' Olive asked.

'No, just a woolly hat. The headlights from my neighbour's car caught him full on. I'd certainly recognise his ugly mug if I ever saw it again; in fact, there was something familiar about it.'

'Look, for all we know, every perverted nutter on two wheels – and in my experience of driving in London, there are plenty of them – has heard what formula of words this guy was using and is out on the streets screaming those words at every passing female,' Carl Burnett, who hated cyclists almost as much as he hated listening to his former lover's anecdotes, said forcefully. 'Can we please get down to work? There is much to do, and not much time to do it in.'

'But that's impossible,' Olive Sabatini said quietly. 'The police have never revealed what was said. That was to be a major element of our reconstruction – suitably bleeped, of course.'

'Olive, forget it; Jenny may have misheard him,' Burnett insisted. 'It's a common enough expletive used by women-haters through the ages. Hampton Court is binned. Can we please get on with talking about what to replace it with?'

It wasn't until they'd broken for lunch that the subject was raised again, by Olive Sabatini in a whispered conversation with Jenny Daniels as they sat munching sandwiches in a corner of the windowless room.

'You should report what happened last night to the police,' Olive suggested.

'Gawd, can you imagine the bollocks I'd have to go through? The questioning, the paperwork – and me, the presenter of *Crimesolve*.'

'But you saw this man clearly and he must know he'd be recognised if you saw him again.'

'Olive, love, I've got three other shows to do this week and this one's turned into a nightmare. My Doctor Jamie will be delighted that we're now going to cover the subject that he's been banging on about, but it doesn't make my working life any easier. I'm not going to waste my time trying to convince Mister Fucking Plod to chase down a miscreant who they think, with some justification, they've already caught.'

Olive Sabatini was unpersuaded. The man who had attacked Jenny Daniels was a danger to women, even if he was just copying the guy who was now in custody. If Jenny wasn't going to pass this information to the police, she would.

4

A VISIT TO TAGG'S ISLAND

Darnell Thomas was charged with three counts of assault, two of attempted rape and one of attempted murder. Under renewed questioning by the Flying Squad, one of the girls who'd been attacked changed her story. She now thought her attacker may well have been black. It had been dark and difficult to discern the man's ethnicity beneath his helmet and goggles. This girl picked Thomas out at an identity parade.

He had no strong alibi for the evenings on which these attacks took place. A fitness fanatic, as well as a fitness instructor, he was out on his bike every Friday between 8 p.m. and 10 p.m. all through the year, whatever the weather. When he was arrested it was the evening of the week when his wife took the kids to see her mother in Wimbledon. With no school for them and no work for him next day, he'd explained to his interrogators, it had been the perfect opportunity to enjoy his favourite leisure activity.

The previous Friday evening he'd been trying to beat his own fastest time for doing ten laps of Bushy Park, leaving the perimeter road and crossing the park from north to south. In his statement he said that when the plain-clothes officer had accosted him, he thought he was being attacked

– first by a man (Harrison), and then by a female accomplice (Louise). In his statement, he claimed at the time he hadn't even realised the second attacker was a woman, such was the speed at which it all happened.

It emerged that Thomas had been subjected to racially motivated attacks by skinheads when he was an adolescent. This experience had made him determined to become fitter and stronger. The single conviction that had given him a criminal record had been for an incident during the Brixton riots, when Darnell had been one of many young black men who'd gone to the area to see what was happening, but become caught up in the violence. He claimed he'd been fitted up. But that was eighteen years ago, and he'd never been in any trouble since.

No alibi, a previous conviction, a positive identification, apprehended in the vicinity of the latest attack: Operation Incisive was convinced they'd got their man.

And yet . . . whilst Louise Mangan, having completed the paperwork and attended the debriefings, would have preferred to believe that the women of Hampton Court were now safe, the doubts niggled away in her mind.

DS Ralph Harrison had been generous in ensuring she received appropriate recognition for Thomas's capture, likely to be a citation according to a lovely note she'd received from the Deputy Commissioner. Louise was entitled to rest on her laurels. But she couldn't forget what she'd seen that night: a different cyclist on a similar sports bike, wearing the same kind of yellow reflective helmet, coming towards her on a route and at a time consistent with when and where the latest attack had taken place.

And where was Tiffany Mordaunt? The interrogating officers had got nowhere with Thomas on this aspect, which added to Louise's growing conviction that they'd arrested the wrong man. It played on her mind.

Her husband, Tom Mangan, a desk sergeant in Bermondsey, was the only person she could talk to about it. He was equally passionate about rooting out injustice. This shared passion was what had motivated them both to join the Met after leaving university, where they'd met in the late eighties.

Louise had wanted to be a detective since childhood. She could pinpoint the exact age and the two incidents that had sparked this ambition. They happened around the same time. The first was a national news story concerning a young girl of thirteen snatched off the street in Birmingham. Louise, who was the same age, followed every twist and turn of the pursuit, which ended happily when the abductor was tracked down and the girl released unharmed.

At the time, Louise had felt such empathy with the girl that she'd been unable to sleep properly, imagining herself in the same perilous situation. When the girl was rescued, Louise felt such enormous gratitude towards the police that she began to imagine herself as one of them; catching villains, righting wrongs, reuniting terrified children with their mums and dads. Even in adulthood, a case like that of Tiffany Mordaunt sparked the same emotions.

The second incident had felt even closer to home. One terrible night the same year as the young girl was abducted, her father had been mugged whilst walking down a dark lane towards his car close to Guildford station.

She had been in her room doing homework looking out onto their quiet street when her father eventually came home. She saw him step out of his car, stooped and bleeding. Her father was a gentle soul; a chartered accountant who'd never been known to so much as raise his voice. His two attackers had punched him in the face and then kicked him in the groin so hard that he could hardly walk. He'd entered the house that evening blighted by something sinister that came with him into the safe and secure world of their home.

Louise had stood at the top of the stairs long enough to see the defeat and humiliation in his eyes before being ordered back into her bedroom by her mother. But what seemed to be a dark curse on the house was lifted a short while later when a police car arrived. She'd remained confined to her room but had sneaked out onto the stairs, clutching the banister as she listened to the low reassuring voices of the two police officers who she knew would make all the horror go away. She learned later that her father had been robbed of his watch and wallet, both of which were recovered when these two officers caught the hoodlums responsible drinking in a pub not far from the station. From that moment on, while some of her schoolfriends wanted to be popstars and princesses, Louise wanted to be a detective.

So far as this case was concerned, Tom worried that his wife was denying herself the considerable credit associated with helping capture the Beast of Hampton Court but accepted that she wouldn't be able to enjoy her success while doubts lingered about whether they'd arrested the right person.

'Look, Lou,' he'd said to her one evening, 'why don't you go and examine that stretch of road by daylight. You've only seen it at night through binoculars. Who knows what you may have missed? I know you won't be able to do it on duty but if you go early in the morning, I'll look after the kids, and you can at least chew over your doubts in the actual location, rather than worry about it from a distance.'

And so, on a frosty morning a week later, Tom took the kids to their over-priced but flexible nursery in Camberwell while Louise took an early morning train from Waterloo to Hampton Court. Her long slim legs and size 8 feet double-wrapped in socks and leggings beneath a pair of thick chinos; her short, bobbed, auburn hair tucked under a woollen bobble hat borrowed from Tom, its West Ham badge announcing his footballing allegiance, rather than hers. A thick scarf was tucked into her trousers beneath the black quilted knee-length coat that completed her outfit.

'You look like Nanook of the North,' Tom had observed as he'd pulled her close for a farewell kiss before she left the house that morning.

'And you look like the Pied Piper,' she replied, looking down at the two small children waiting to follow him on the walk to Camberwell.

Hampton Court station was at the end of the line. Louise Mangan walked out of the station, crossed the bridge, and turned left onto the A308, where she'd observed the yellow helmeted cyclist coming towards her. It wasn't yet half past seven, and she didn't have to report for duty until eleven. Her long stride was taking her to the location her mind's eye had been focused on ever since the Friday-night encounter. Apart from Tom, nobody knew she was there. She'd not reported her intended visit to Ralph Harrison – revisiting the scene was a moment of unauthorised spontaneity that she knew was bound to be frowned upon by her sergeant. What he didn't know wouldn't hurt him.

Despite the early hour, the traffic was heavy, with lorries connecting to and from the M3, cars commuting from the suburbs where their drivers lived, to London where they worked, and cyclists – droves of them – streaming along the elevated footpath they'd made their own.

Louise walked to where she calculated the suspect cyclist had been that night when she'd seen him through the binoculars. Once at the approximate spot, she turned to walk slowly back, retracing her steps, looking for possible exit channels. There were no gaps in the railings to her left. To her right, on the opposite side of the road, were a couple of big, expensive houses backing onto the Thames; highly desirable properties protected by barriers and security lights that made them improbable escape routes. She could see no access to the river, and knew there was no public footpath along this bank anyway.

Walking back towards the car park on Hampton Court Green where she and Harrison had been stationed that night, Louise noticed something that hadn't registered even when they were poring over maps as part of Operation Incisive. She'd been keeping to the left, the side of the road where the cyclist had been making his way towards her. Now she crossed the teeming road to explore the unexpected gap she'd noticed; a narrow single-track lane leading to the hump of a bridge beneath which flowed the Thames – a bridge leading onto an island.

The maps she had were focused on traffic routes. This turning wasn't marked. She walked down the track for seventy metres or so, a distance that took her away from the maelstrom of the A308, over the bridge and into what felt to her like an enchanted enclave. Facing her was a lavish flower display in the middle of which, on a large, laminated board, she read 'Welcome to Tagg's Island'.

Beneath this greeting was a diagram of the island. Around the perimeter and the inner lagoon were sixty-two houseboats, each represented on the diagram by a blank square. These squares were equal in size, although as she could already see the boats they referenced were not – they ranged from large to enormous. Each square was numbered on the diagram, the numbers correlating to a list of the boats' names in alphabetical order – from *African Queen* to *Xanadu*. After examining this board for a few moments, Louise followed the path that was only prevented from completely circumnavigating the island by the break in the land that allowed river water in to fill the lagoon.

Surprisingly, given the island's proximity to the road on the other side of the bridge, all Louise could hear was the river gently lapping against the shoreline. The frosty air crystalised her breath in momentary puffs of vapour as she followed the path as far as she could. The houseboats were, in the main, set back behind gardens – some ramshackle, others beautifully kept – that ran between the river and the path she was on. Despite these grassy perimeters, Louise could see the dwellings in all their glory. Far removed from her mental image of a houseboat – formed from the barge conversions that she'd seen going up and down the Basingstoke Canal when she was a child growing up in Surrey – these were more house than boat. Big and square, some as high as three storeys, rising from the Thames like prefabricated tiers on a wedding cake.

There was nobody around. Signs everywhere made it clear that this was a 'Private Island' and Louise wondered if she was entitled to be here.

Although she was a police officer, that didn't give her free-rein to trespass. But the sign did say 'Welcome', and all kinds of public services would have to come onto the island – to deliver the post and collect the rubbish, for instance. However, she knew they would have a professional reason for being here, and she didn't. Louise was freelancing.

The cars and motorbikes that transported the residents of Tagg's Island to and from the outside world were parked haphazardly beside the path. And she could see some bicycles chained up against the outside of aquatic homes like lifeboats on a cruise liner, but none of these were the kind of drop-handle sports bike she was looking for.

What was now clear to Louise was that this island was most probably where the man she'd seen cycling towards her that night had vanished to. It was the obvious explanation. She needed to find out more about this place. She'd reached the point where the path disappeared into unkempt grassland. She could hear the river water flowing into the lagoon but had no sight of its channel. The largest and most spectacular of all the houseboats was situated here, blocking the view. Its name – *Navicula* – was displayed across the high security fence, behind which lay a manicured lawn that ran down to what looked like a misplaced country mansion. Still, there was that air of silence, which by now she found discomforting.

She thought she heard something and, turning quickly, saw a cat scooting into the undergrowth. Louise chuckled at how foolish her reaction must have looked.

'Can I help you?' The voice was soft and low. Louise turned quickly once again, her heart thumping, to see a slight young man of around her own age, his hair hanging long and loose round his thin face, and a large knapsack on his back. What she noticed most of all were his piercing green eyes.

'Oh, good morning,' Louise said. 'No, er . . . I just wanted to see this island for myself, you know? Having heard so much about it.'

'Are you looking for anyone in particular?' Green Eyes enquired gently.

Louise wanted to say, 'Yes, someone with a sports bike and a luminous yellow safety helmet,' but, unable to dress up her suspicion as any kind of legitimate authority, she just said, 'No, nobody in particular. Just fascinated by this lovely place. Do you live here?'

'Yes, but only for a few years. My aunt Jane lived here for a long time. She left her houseboat to me in her will.'

Louise expressed her sympathy. Somewhat ludicrously, given that she was talking to a man she didn't know about a relative she hadn't met.

'I've been hiking across Argentina for the last month. My flight back landed at a ludicrously early time and the taxi from Heathrow just dropped me off. You looked like you needed some assistance.'

'This yours?' Louise asked, indicating *Navicula*, the palatial houseboat they were standing in front of.

'Afraid not,' he said, his green eyes crinkling into a smile at the absurdity of the suggestion. 'Mine's a much more modest affair called *Inner Peace* on the other side of the island.'

Louise instinctively liked this man and, seeing him as someone who might have the information she was seeking, asked if there was a café on the island in the hope that she'd be able to take him for a coffee.

'There's nothing on Tagg's except what you see,' he replied. 'No building is allowed on the land these days, although there used to be some magnificent ones. Including a really swanky hotel. Now there's just what you see – sixty-two houseboats with their detritus spread on shore.' He paused before continuing. 'But if you fancy a cup of tea, I can make you one – then you can see what a houseboat looks like from the inside.'

Louise knew she'd be digging herself in deeper by accepting the offer without telling this helpful young man that she was a detective, but she would find it difficult to relate the sequence of events that led to her being there; and she was genuinely keen to know more about Tagg's Island. Surely she should be allowed to do whatever she wanted in her own time. She would go with this pleasant man for a cuppa and a chat. There was no need to complicate matters by telling him what she did for a living or the real reason she was on the island where he lived. The man with green eyes led her towards the *Inner Peace*.

5

A FRIDAY NIGHT OUT

Tiffany Mordaunt listened intently. She couldn't speak because the gag taped across her mouth prevented any sound emerging other than a low 'mmm', which she still emitted periodically in the hope that someone would hear. She couldn't speak, but she could still listen; and what she heard were sounds she'd yet to pinpoint – something familiar but out of context, like birds singing at night.

She thought back to that Friday evening . . . last week? Last month? Yesterday? No, not yesterday. It was further back than yesterday, although she'd lost all sense of time here in the dark, in this room, wherever she was.

She and her two regular Friday night companions – Sally, her cousin, and Natasha, her friend from work – went out every Friday night for a drink. They didn't go clubbing. Saturday was clubbing night. And they weren't on the pull; Sally was engaged, and Natasha had a steady boyfriend. Both were a year or two older than Tiffany, who was still playing the field – except on Friday nights. That was when the three friends got dolled up to impress each other rather than the lads who leered at them in the pubs along the Thames that they usually frequented.

They'd been drinking in The Mitre next to Hampton Court Bridge, gossiping away as usual – confiding in each other the thoughts and feelings that couldn't be expressed to anyone else – and laughing. Taking the micky out of friends and workmates, boys they knew, their parents, grandparents. Discussing the films they'd seen, the TV they'd watched. She had a vague recollection of the music that had been playing in the background; Fat Boy Slim, and a record she loved by Destiny's Child.

Then the atmosphere was ruined by Sally and Natasha's boyfriends making a sudden appearance. It was pure coincidence, apparently; their pub crawl just happened to end up in the one they were in. But an unwelcome intrusion nevertheless – at least for Tiffany.

Her two companions had reached the stage of the evening where alcohol was making them soppy. They always drank more than she did. The guys were hungry, and suggested they all go for a meal. Of course they meant Tiffany as well but she declined. She had no wish to be the proverbial lemon – out of place, listening to the lovebirds cooing. So she told them to go ahead. She'd finish her drink and head home. It was gone ten, the time they'd usually be thinking of going home anyway. After briefly trying to persuade her to change her mind the others agreed to separate. Natasha said something about Tiffany being careful that 'The Beast' didn't get her, and they'd all laughed.

She sat in the bar over her drink for ten minutes after they'd left. A few blokes gave her the eye, including a cyclist who came in just before last orders for a pint of lager to drink outside. Cyclists often used The Mitre. It wasn't unusual although it was a bit late for bikers and this guy gazed at Tiffany for a bit longer than she felt comfortable with. She twiddled with the silver locket that was always on a chain around her neck. It contained a photograph of her mother who'd given it to Tiffany for her tenth birthday. She'd worn it every day since, developing a habit of fiddling with it whenever she was nervous or uncomfortable.

The cyclist went out with his pint and Tiffany left for home shortly afterwards. It was a chilly night, but she had her coat and scarf, and it was less than half a mile to walk to the house she'd grown up in, where her mum and dad would be waiting up for her as they always did. A mist was rising from the river on her left as she followed its course, staying close to the kerb in sight of the passing traffic. There was nobody in front of her and, when she turned to glance back, nobody behind.

A cyclist passed as she crossed a small spur road that seemed to lead nowhere. Tiffany thought it might be the young man she'd seen in the pub, but she couldn't make out his features. The biker was wearing goggles under his yellow cycle helmet and soon disappeared into the darkness.

She walked on for a few more minutes before hearing footsteps approach from behind. Suddenly there was a gloved hand across her mouth. She struggled, unable to escape the grip that kept her silent or the strong force that manoeuvred her in a direction she didn't want to take, down the spur road she'd recently crossed. After that she remembered very little. Something had been administered. A stab to her neck. A vague memory of two men standing over her, talking quietly, removing the tape to give her food and water before replacing it even tighter, the steep irresistible urge to sleep that followed; a deep sleep that she worried she may never wake up from.

But she was awake now, listening. There was a creak-ing sound and suddenly it made sense; she recognised the incongruous noise. It was the sound of water lapping against the walls of her dark room. The realisation came as a shock. She was on a boat somewhere being lifted by a rising tide.

6

THE CRIMINAL CO-OP

'What we know is that London has one of the highest levels of cocaine usage in the world.' Dr Jamie Templeman was talking to camera. Olive Sabatini and Luke O'Sullivan – assistant producers on the *Crimesolve* TV series – were in Dr Templeman's surgery, accompanied by a BBC cameraman and a sound engineer. In the absence of any police cooperation, Templeman was the only figure of authority due to be featured in this episode. It was important to set the scene through his extended contribution.

The testimony of the parents of the young girl who'd died from a cocaine overdose had already been recorded. This was the couple who'd originally alerted the programme to the human cost of the increased supply of Class A drugs in the capital and sparked the director's interest in exploring this as a subject for the show. Its necessary elevation over the Hampton Court story had triggered a desperate rush to have the programme ready for the April edition.

'Our capital city is one of only a handful across the world where cocaine can be ordered and delivered more quickly than a pizza,' the doctor continued. 'We also know that a significant amount of the drugs previously seized by law enforcement officers has found its way back onto the streets. This can only mean that someone on the inside is corruptly helping to place dangerous and addictive narcotics back into the hands of the criminals.'

'Stop!' yelled O'Sullivan. 'Sorry, Jamie, we can't say that.'

'Why not? It can be backed up with evidence.'

'Insufficient evidence according to our legals. I know you're planning to use that in the book you're writing, and your publishers might get different legal advice, but . . .'

'For fuck's sake, do you want to make an impact or not?' Templeman asked aggressively, rising from his chair so suddenly that the mic clipped to his shirt front pinged away, landing somewhere on the studio floor.

'We're heavily dependent on police cooperation,' Sabatini added calmly. 'And we're already pissing them off big time by running this story. Making a specific allegation of corruption is likely to jeopardise the future of the series as well as landing the Beeb with a libel suit.'

'But if we say it's becoming easier to order hard drugs we have to point to a reason,' Templeman pleaded. 'I've done the research for the book. I can explain what's happening and why it's happening. I know who the criminal mastermind behind this operation is, and Jenny told me I'd be able to name him.'

'Jenny presents the programme, but she is not responsible for the content,' O'Sullivan explained, conscious that he was treading on eggshells, given the romance that had developed between Daniels and Templeman.

Luke and Olive had some responsibility for this, having brought Jamie Templeman in as an expert voice to help in a previous episode of the programme. He and Jenny had clicked and within a week the presenter had ended her romance with their boss Carl Burnett and transferred her affections to the handsome doctor.

That had been over a year ago now, but Burnett's emotional wounds were yet to heal. As for this latest show, Jenny Daniels would no doubt receive a full report on what Templeman would describe as O'Sullivan's intransigence.

Olive, grateful for her compatriot's diplomatic intervention, sought to lessen the stress levels further. 'I'm meeting the woman from the Met who we liaise with on the show later. Why don't I run it by her again, making exactly your point and emphasising how determined we are now to go ahead with or without Met approval. This may well be a case of who blinks first. If they think we're going to do the programme anyway I'm sure they'd rather be involved than on the side-lines.'

Olive Sabatini's emollience eased the tension. When filming had finished, the two assistant producers asked Templeman to explain exactly what he'd like to reveal if they could get legal clearance.

'The main character in this – the Mister Big, if you want to use that kind of Hollywood movie jargon – is a man by the name of Jack Handysides. As well as being a ruthless criminal, Jack is a very clever man. Realising that the UK drugs trade is an amorphous mess, he set out to co-ordinate and consolidate the various interconnected players – those bringing synthetic opioids from the Netherlands, cocaine from Columbia, crack from the Caribbean, heroin from Afghanistan – and he succeeded in welding most of them together into a kind of Co-operative Wholesale Society for drugs, with everyone getting a bigger portion of an increasingly lucrative market. The law enforcement agencies, be they police or customs, were inadequately resourced to begin with. Now they're being completely overwhelmed and outwitted by criminals who are collaborating rather than competing.'

'How do you know that this guy Handysides is the mastermind?' Sabatini asked.

'I went native. Pretended to be a dealer. GPs have access to all kinds of drugs, and a fair few have been tempted to dabble in criminality. I used the dark web to advertise the sale of MDMA, more commonly known as ecstasy or "molly". You might not have heard of it yet but believe me, it's going to be the party drug of the millennium. Within days I'd been contacted by one of Handysides' agents and within a week, by the man himself. He poses as a legitimate businessman – a property developer with a side-line in the travel and vacation business. The agent susses out whether you're genuine and once that risk has been assessed by one of the underlings, Jack does the deal. What can you supply, from where, and when and for how much? It's all very smooth. Conducted over the internet with nothing tangible that would be admissible in a court of law.'

'Why don't the police close him down?' Sabatini asked.

'They're hopelessly out of their depth trying to deal with such a huge operation. What you need to bear in mind is that we have nothing to match what the FBI can do in the States. Britain still has a Victorian model of policing in an internet age. They haven't realised what a powerful place cyberspace is, let alone how much more powerful it's bound to become. On a simple organisational basis as we approach the twenty-first century, they still operate to a structure developed in the 1840s and only partially revised once . . . well over thirty years ago! We still have forty-three different police forces, for God's sake, in a small country like England.'

'But there's only one in London, which is where Handysides is concentrating his activities,' O'Sullivan pointed out.

'Yes, but even here we've got the City of London police and around the periphery, county forces in Essex, Kent, Surrey and the Thames Valley. The police have little interaction with Customs and Excise, who are separate from the Inland Revenue. The Immigration and Nationality Directorate is separate from all three and none of them have much to do with UK Visas. You get the picture? The criminals, united under General Handysides, are exploiting these disparate forces of law and order remorselessly.'

'But surely if you know all this,' Luke O'Sullivan pleaded, 'then so does the Met. Why don't they arrest him?'

'Because he covers his tracks and has some of the best legal brains in the country working for him.'

'And that is precisely why we can't name him,' Olive Sabatini said pointedly.

'If we name Jack Handysides on the show, what's he going to do?' Templeman asked rhetorically. 'Do you really think he's going to take us to court? Seriously? A career criminal whose entire motivation is to avoid the courts deciding to get into a high-profile case against one of the most watched TV programmes in Britain. All the various gangs he's managed to bring together will run for the hills if that happens. Trust me, we can name him with impunity. It may not stop his activities, but neither will it kill your show.'

Olive Sabatini was as good as her word. That afternoon when she met the woman she'd liaised with at New Scotland Yard ever since the series began two years ago, she put forward Dr Templeman's argument as cogently as she could.

Latika Joshi listened carefully. It was a grey day, but the non-uniformed Met Communications Officer wore a colourful silk sari that militated against the dullness of the weather. Her kantha-scarfed head nodded sympathetically as Olive explained that without the ability to name Jack Handysides, the show had no proper focus. It would just say what was happening without explaining who was making it happen and why.

'But that is your problem, my dear. Our problem is that we are completely unimpressed by your doctor.' Despite being only a few years older than Olive, Joshi adopted a maternal tone. 'You should think very hard about using him.'

'Why? He's surely someone you should be encouraging, given the risks he's taking to reveal all this stuff,' Sabatini protested.

'But you're conveniently overlooking his admitted involvement in the drugs trade.'

'But that was a necessary subterfuge.'

'Was it really?' Joshi asked.

They were halfway into the hour allocated for their meeting and Olive wanted to use this opportunity to report the attack on Jenny Daniels by the foul-mouthed cyclist, but Joshi's manner disturbed her.

'If you know something about Templeman, can't you tell me in confidence?' she asked.

'My dear, you're making a TV programme in defiance of our wishes, and you expect me to be helpful? It is a foolish thing that you are doing but the Metropolitan Police Service is not obliged to prevent you from making fools of yourselves. The solution is for you to ditch this subject.'

'Leave the programme to one side for a moment,' Olive said. 'You're implying that Jenny Daniels has got herself shacked up with a criminal.'

'I said no such thing, but if I were you, I'd at least warn Miss Daniels of the possibility. Her new boyfriend is obviously expecting to make a lot of money from the book he's writing. Let him take the risk of naming Jack Handysides that way, rather than use *Crimesolve* as a stalking horse.'

Olive could see that she wasn't going to get any further with this. She and Luke were already working on yet another alternative topic, an innocuous consumer piece about avoiding car theft that might have to be this month's story.

'Talking of Jenny,' she said, seizing her opportunity, 'I thought I should tell you that she was attacked outside her house by a cyclist who might be your Beast of Hampton Court.'

'Gosh, poor Jenny. When was this?'

'On Sunday evening.'

'But we caught this man on Friday.'

'Maybe you didn't, is what I'm saying.'

'What kind of attack was it? Was she sexually assaulted?'

'Well, actually when I say she was attacked, I mean the intent was there. Her neighbours drove up just as the cyclist was riding towards Jenny and scared the creep away. He called her a filthy effing whore as he cycled off, which is kind of his signature insult, isn't it?'

Latika Joshi looked concerned as she jotted something down on her desk pad.

'Was he wearing a yellow cycle helmet?' she asked.

'No, but he was riding a drop-handle sports bike. Perhaps he realised that the helmet was a bit of a giveaway and stopped wearing it.'

'Hmm. Well, our guys are convinced that this fitness instructor is our man, and that he knows more than he's letting on about that missing girl. But I'll put this on the record.'

'Jenny says she got a good look at the guy and is convinced she'd recognise him if she saw him again.'

'Does that mean she'll report this herself?' Joshi asked. 'We can't pursue crimes raised by proxy. I presume she asked you to tell me about it prior to her coming in when she's less busy to record it formally.'

'Actually, no, she didn't. I just thought it was important that you knew about this. Like Jenny, I'm a woman living in London. I don't want this arsehole hanging around, whether it's the same one who's attacked all those poor girls or a different one.'

The hour was up and Joshi, putting down her pen, rose to escort Sabatini to the door.

'Well, I'd much rather concentrate on helping Jenny

with this rather than dealing with the unnecessary disruption your programme will cause if you go ahead with the Handysides thing. Who knows? This may be the last time you and I are able to meet professionally.'

They parted amicably enough, the Met comms officer even planting a kiss on her visitor's proffered cheek. As she left the building Sabatini considered the implications of what Latika Joshi had said. What was clear was that the decision as to whether to go ahead with the drugs story would need to be made by someone whose salary reflected a level of responsibility far beyond her own.

7

TEA ON THE *INNER PEACE*

The man with green eyes introduced himself as Sage. There was no clarity as to whether this was a nickname or the one his parents had given him. The name reminded Louise of a TV programme she'd watched as a child in which each animated character was named after a herb: Parsley the lion, a dog called Dill, a policeman called Constable Knapweed. Hadn't there been an owl called Sage who kept falling out of his nest? Louise wondered if she should tell her host that he'd invited a living, breathing version of Constable Knapweed onto his boat, but Sage hadn't asked what she did for a living, so she hadn't told him.

Besides, she was learning an awful lot about Tagg's Island without having to offer up any personal details in exchange, although what she really wanted to know was whether any of its residents rode a drop-handled sports bike and wore a yellow helmet. Sage explained that the island had been known by various names before boat-builder Thomas Tagg arrived in the 1840s. It was Tagg who'd built a palatial hotel, which had often been frequented by royalty. Fred Karno, the famous impresario who'd discovered Charlie Chaplin, had taken ownership of the island in 1912, rebuilding the hotel to include a music hall that thrived well into the twentieth century. Today, there was no single owner and no buildings. The island was run by the boat owners through a resident's association that safeguarded the sparse, unbuilt environment.

'You probably need time to straighten everything up after your time away,' Louise suggested as Sage pottered around, bringing more tea and some stale biscuits. She'd already formed an instinctive fondness for her slight, earnest young host. Considerate and otherworldly, she thought that thirty years previously, he would probably have been going to San Francisco with some flowers in his hair.

Sage told her that one of the advantages of living on a houseboat was that it forced you not to over-complicate your life. He could simply lock up and leave any time he liked. He told Louise that he was a writer who drew inspiration from the tranquillity of what he referred to simply as Tagg's. He told her how his aunt had lived here for many years and been prominent in the resident's association.

'Aunt Jane was very upset about those huge security gates erected at *Navicula* when those dodgy characters moved in,' Sage said.

'How do you mean "dodgy"?' Louise asked.

'I don't really know what I mean. They're foreigners, which raises some people's hackles but not mine. No, for me they just seem out of place. Lots of macho guys come and go from there, swaggering around like they run the island. Marko, who owns *Navicula*, has an export/import business. Apparently, he's going to bring his wife and kids over from wherever they're based.'

'And where is that?'

'Not sure. Eastern Europe – Romania, Albania, some-where like that I guess.'

'They got their own way with the gates, so I presume the other residents weren't as hostile as your aunt,' Louise observed.

'That's right. I used to come here a lot before she died three years ago, and she was forever complaining about the other residents not backing her up. Marko sprayed a fair bit of cash around. Paid to reinforce the bridge, cleaned up some of the unsightly parts of the island, put lots of cash into the coffers of the residents' association.'

Louise and Sage were drinking their tea in the big kitchen looking out onto the Surrey bank of the Thames. Whilst no attempt was made to show her around, Sage told Louise that there were two bedrooms upstairs, but nothing about anybody else living on *The Inner Peace* with him. However Louise couldn't help noticing a black bra fluttering among some clothes on the washing line.

The two essential skills Louise was learning as a detect-ive were interview and interrogation – the former to gain information from people who weren't suspects in a crime and the latter to get information from those who were. She was very much in interview mode with Sage, keen to know what he knew about his fellow residents (or 'live-aboards' as he called them), particularly any who might be keen cyclists.

Over their second cup of green tea (Sage was sorry, he had no other variety and never drank coffee) she steered the conversation in this direction by pretending to be an avid biker herself.

'I've often cycled on the main road past this place,'

she said. 'Last week I was behind a proper cyclist – aero-dynamic helmet, goggles, all the gear – who turned onto that little road that leads onto the island. It was this that nudged me to find the time to come and see Tagg's for myself.'

'That will have been Patrick. He's a fanatic, always out on his bike.'

Louise pressed her luck. 'One of many here, I suppose, given that you'd have trouble getting around London on your boats?'

'Very funny. As you'll have noticed, the boats are all static, although they can navigate the river if they must,' said Sage, 'and you'll also have seen that most of us have cars these days. Mine's that beaten-up old Peugeot you walked past as we came aboard. I'm going to have trouble starting it after a month away. Lots of residents keep old pushbikes as backup, but Patrick's probably the only live-aboard who's into Lycra.'

'He did look like a pro,' Louise said, 'which boat does he live on?'

'Why do you want to know? Did he cut you up or something?'

Louise gave a laugh that she hoped wouldn't betray her trepidation about pushing this too far. After playing for time with a gulp of tea, she said something about an accessory – 'a flashing, rotating rear safety light' – that she'd noticed on the man's bike. She said she'd like to know which cycle shop it came from.

'If you're really interested in discussing your hobby with our resident cycling nut, you should come back this evening and I'll introduce you.'

It emerged that Patrick rented a houseboat called *The Great Gatsby* on the east side of the island, was of a similar age to them both (in his twenties) and worked somewhere in the city as an investment banker, cycling into work early in the morning and returning after dark.

'Patrick's not really my cup of proverbial but he was always very sweet to Aunt Jane, acting as her unofficial financial advisor. She introduced me to him when I was visiting her, so when I moved in after she'd died, Patrick was one of the few people I already knew on the island.'

'What's his full name?' Louise asked, planning to use the Police National Computer to check him out. Realising how officious the question sounded, she added quickly, 'I think he might be a pal of someone I know at the cycling club I go to.'

'Patrick Venn. But I doubt if he's anything to do with your club. He's not very clubbable – I think he only joins things he can control.'

Louise said she'd welcome the chance to pick Patrick's brains about cycling equipment and some arrangements were tentatively explored.

'I've got someone coming to look at the condition of the boat's hull this evening. That needs to be at low tide, so around half-six. Should be finished by half-seven, and by then Patrick should be home.'

Louise thought quickly. She'd be on duty until 11 p.m. but thought she might be able to persuade DS Harrison to allow her to follow up on her hunch, even if it was just to shut her up about it. She was glad she hadn't told Sage that she was a police officer. It was doubtful if Patrick Venn would be willing to discuss his hobby with a copper;

in any case she doubted if Sage, with his counter-cultural lifestyle would have much affinity with the Metropolitan Police Service. Louise felt guilty about misleading him and determined to end the deception as soon as she could.

'I look forward to seeing you again this evening,' Sage said as they walked across the wooden gangplank, through the little latched gate and back onto terra firma. It was still cold, but the clear light of an April morning was by now reflecting off the water, flecked with the shadows of overhanging branches.

As they strolled towards the bridge, two large SUVs crossed onto the island, their blacked-out windows looking incongruous against the tranquil backdrop. Sage eyed the vehicles suspiciously.

'I presume they're the "dodgy characters" you were talking about,' Louise said.

'Yes, on their way to *Navicula*.'

They stepped to the side to let the convoy go past.

Louise could see a cloud momentarily pass across her host's green eyes. It vanished as they said their farewells. Something about Sage's quiet demeanour made her feel tactile towards him. Louise had only known him for ninety minutes and yet she reached out for a farewell hug. She suspected it had something to do with the guilt she felt about gleaning information under false pretences.

'What on earth are you doing?' she thought to herself. 'You're a rookie detective not Sherlock bloody Holmes.' She feared this would be the last time she and Sage would be pals: that when she came back that evening and revealed all, it would be the end of a beautiful friendship.

8

HARRISON IS HELPFUL

When Detective Constable Louise Mangan got to work, she was called immediately to a case conference about winding up Operation Incisive. There were around twenty people in the room at Kingston police station. The few seats available had been nabbed by those who'd arrived early. The rest stood around, notebooks in hand, waiting for the meeting to begin. Louise stood next to Detective Sergeant Ralph Harrison who was showing off a handheld contraption.

'Where's your notebook?' Louise asked.

'This, my girl, is the future.'

Harrison demonstrated how, by scrawling on the screen of his device with what he insisted was a laser pen attached by a coiled rubber cord, he could take notes that would never erode and always be retrievable.

'It'll never catch on,' Louise said, smiling down on her sergeant, who was a good two inches shorter.

'That's what they said about female detectives,' Harrison replied, attracting a blow to the arm from Louise's notebook.

The final participant to arrive was Detective Chief Inspector Sean Meredith from New Scotland Yard, who was leading the operation. The room fell silent.

'Right,' Meredith said, 'I don't think this need detain us for long. We have our man, Darnell Thomas. He's yet to confess and still protesting his innocence but there's nothing unusual about that. His wife told us that she suspected he was having an affair, and sure enough, it's emerged that he was. With a glamorous colleague at the fitness centre.'

Louise wondered how this was in any way relevant to the case, let alone incriminating evidence. She was the only woman in the room. This, together with her lowly rank, made her loath to raise objections with Meredith, although she felt her heart rate rise as she contemplated the prospect. However, by the time she'd composed the intervention in her mind the moment had passed.

'Thomas fits the description, has no alibi, was picked out at an identity parade and was in the vicinity of the last attack when he was apprehended . . .'

'By Louise here,' Harrison called out to his colleague's consternation.

'Indeed, well done to her,' Meredith said, prompting a little burst of applause.

'Any progress on finding Tiffany Mordaunt?' asked a large detective standing at the back.

'Nothing yet, but she could have been one of Thomas's victims. He was out on his bike that Friday night and by his own admission was in the general area of the route she'd have had to take to walk home. We've questioned everyone we can find who was in The Mitre that night. According to a bartender who knew her vaguely, she didn't get into any other company after her mates went off and she left alone.'

'But she's been missing for too long for Tiffany to be one of Thomas's victims surely?' the large detective responded.

'Well, you're working specifically on the case, Harry,' Meredith said. 'You know my theory. The so-called Beast of Hampton Court liked a bit of slap and tickle to liven up his bike rides, but he never attempted abduction.'

'But he did attempt murder,' Louise heard herself say, almost unconsciously.

'Yes, Detective Constable, he did – which is why that's one of the charges against him. But he only strangled that girl to try to shut her up—'

DCI Meredith stopped mid-sentence, becoming aware of Louise Mangan's horrified reaction and realising he needed a different word formulation.

'What I'm saying is that all his victims have lived to tell the tale, and none of them were taken hostage. Of course, we all hope that there's an innocent explanation for Tiffany vanishing. But if not, it's perfectly possible that there is no connection between her disappearance and the series of assaults in that vicinity. Our mad randy biker doesn't have a monopoly on crime in this area.'

There were amused smiles and nodding heads around the room as Meredith concluded his remarks.

'In any case, I've decided to separate the Mordaunt case away from Operation Incisive. Harry and his team will continue the search for Tiffany under my command, but we have the so-called Beast of Hampton Court so Operation Incisive can be disbanded, and you can all move on to other things. Darnell Thomas is due in court next week for the plea hearing. It should all be straightforward. Anyone here from comms?'

A thin man in a shabby suit put his hand up.

'Anything to say before we wrap this operation up?' asked the DCI whose time was obviously precious.

The thin man ran through the media arrangements. The most significant would be an exclusive interview that Meredith would give to the *Daily Candour* later that afternoon.

'Excellent,' said Meredith. 'We must keep the tabloids happy. Anything else?'

'Only that I've been copied into a rather worrying email from Latika Joshi, who handles all the arrangements with the *Crimesolve* programme. It says that Jenny Daniels was unsettled by a cyclist in East Molesey, near where she lives.'

'"Unsettled"? What does that mean?'

'Apparently the assailant was on a sports bike and rode straight at her. He was frightened off by Daniels' neighbours arriving in their car,' the comms man explained.

'Well now, we wouldn't want to see the lovely Jenny unsettled in any way, would we?' said Meredith to a murmur of lascivious agreement. 'But this may have been Darnell Thomas on the hunt for more victims.'

'The attack was on Sunday night, Thomas had already been arrested the previous Friday. That's the gist of Ms Joshi's email,' the thin man said.

There was hardly a moment's reflection before the DCI responded. 'What we appear to have here is a famous TV personality almost being crashed into by one of the cyclists who pedal too fast, using the pavement instead of the road. Pass her on to whoever's responsible for tackling this new offence the government has come up with – what's it called?'

'Anti-social behaviour,' someone called out.

'That's the one. Sounds like an obvious example.'

Meredith, displaying pleasure in his drollery, prepared to bring proceedings to a close, but the timid comms man had more to say.

'According to Jenny Daniels' testimony, her would-be attacker used the exact words that have been reported by every victim.'

Meredith remained unimpressed.

'It's not an unusual phrase,' he said. 'So, this guy called her a "filthy fucking whore"? Perhaps he was one of the many former lovers we hear Jenny has had.'

Laughter rippled round the room. But Louise wasn't laughing. She was furious and about to speak out when she felt a hand on her shoulder.

'Easy, tiger.' Ralph Harrison, standing next to Louise, wasn't laughing. Instead he was exercising gentle restraint. 'Discretion is the better part of valour and all that,' he whispered softly.

Louise was angry with herself for failing to speak up although she appreciated the sagacity of her sergeant's advice. Countering the embedded culture of casual misogyny would require concerted effort rather than an angry outburst.

As for the case itself, her concern that she'd helped to arrest an innocent man was now intensified by what she'd just heard. Her report about seeing another cyclist on the A308 that evening had been dismissed by Meredith as vague and insubstantial – and he was right; it was both of those things. She could hardly have used this forum to relate her unauthorised trip to Tagg's Island that morning, let alone throw in the name of Patrick Venn – Sage's neighbour – as a potential suspect, given that she had no evidence whatsoever.

When DCI Meredith had gone there were some administrative formalities to complete before the meeting broke up and Louise was able to nab the thin man from comms.

'What are you going to do about the Jenny Daniels issue?' she asked.

'I've done my bit by raising it. If the DCI in charge doesn't think it's relevant to the case, then it's not relevant to the case, simple as that.'

'Can you forward the email to me?' Louise asked.

The Met was just becoming familiar with electronic forms of communication. There'd been some resistance to what many saw as a rather flimsy record of events compared to the solidity of a proper cardboard file with notes held together by a treasury tag.

'If you're not on the copy list, you're not supposed to see it. So, no, I can't.'

The comms man's forehead was creased into what seemed to be a permanent frown as he continued to pack away his papers, placing them haphazardly into an old leather briefcase that looked as if it may have predated the creation of the Metropolitan Police.

'I was the officer who caught Darnell Thomas,' Louise said. 'I think I should at least be allowed to see that report.'

Her plea caused the comms man to stop shuffling his papers and pause for thought. 'Well, at least someone's taking it seriously, I suppose. I thought for a moment that Meredith was about to shoot the messenger. Look, I daren't copy you into the email, but I've worked for Latika on liaising with *Crimesolve*, and I happen to know where this information came from. There's an assistant producer on the show, a young woman by the name of Olive Sabatini. Why don't I give you her contact details and you can follow it up with her direct?'

By mid-afternoon Louise had arranged to meet Sabatini the next day, telling her over the phone, simply and truthfully, that she'd been part of Operation Incisive, and was keen to know more about Jenny Daniels' traumatic experience.

She now had time to focus on her return visit to Tagg's Island later that evening. There wasn't much else to occupy her mind. As Incisive was winding down, she and DS Ralph Harrison were being lined up to investigate a safe-cracking heist at a bank in Streatham but that couldn't get underway until forensics had finished examining the crime scene. Louise was keen for Harrison to go back to Tagg's Island with her in order to turn her amateur sleuthing into a proper police investigation.

But first, she had to level with Harrison about what she'd been doing that morning. They were both on the same twelve-hour shift until 11 p.m., so Louise couldn't return to the island in her own time, and she badly wanted Sage to introduce her to Patrick Venn, his cycling fellow Tagg's Island resident. She seized her moment to talk to him about it as they sat drinking coffee in the Kingston police station canteen that afternoon.

She was beginning to like Ralph Harrison. Almost twice her age, he was set in his ways. And those ways were the product of a working life spent in uniform, first with the army and for the last thirty years, the Met. For the last decade he'd been in plain clothes, but he saw the

M&S suits he invariably wore simply as a different kind of uniform.

Ralph was conservative with a small 'c' and, as Louise soon found out when she began to work with him, a big 'C' as well. A devotee of the woman he always referred to reverentially as Mrs T, Ralph thought the country had gone downhill since her demise, that Britain was ruled from Brussels and that two culprits by the name of Mr Health and Mr Safety were threatening England's entire way of life.

But Louise quickly perceived that what played most negatively on Harrison's mind was the prospect of retirement. His entire adult life, since joining the Army aged sixteen, had been regimented. He'd once told Louise how much he valued order and hierarchy; how lost he'd be without the shape that the military and the Met had given him. He and Sheila – his wife – had one grown-up daughter, and a grandson who Ralph doted on. Despite having the opportunity to retire on a full pension since turning fifty a couple of years ago, he'd chosen to remain in post, basically because retirement terrified him.

Louise was comfortable around men like Ralph. There were lots of them in the Met: a bit reactionary but possessed of a fundamental decency that underscored everything they did. And she trusted Ralph, particularly after the support he'd shown that morning – trusted him enough to tell him all about her clandestine visit to Tagg's Island and to urge him to go back there with her that evening.

'If we go back officially this evening we can question this Patrick Venn character, perhaps interview him under caution.'

'No, we cannot, Louise. We have nothing to caution him about.'

'Yes, we have, Sarge. Leave aside the other cases; I'm referring to the incident with Jenny Daniels. It's a case that hasn't been investigated so we can legitimately use it as an excuse to interrogate him. Don't you see? We nab him on that one, and then steer the interview onto the other stuff; in particular the Friday night attack that Darnell Thomas has been charged with. If I'm right, it was him cycling down the road towards me while you were thrashing about in the bushes.'

Harrison looked out thoughtfully through the steamy window of the canteen. 'Did Daniels report the incident to the police?' he asked.

'Not officially, no. But one of her team spoke to someone at the Met about it. So in that sense, it was reported.'

'No, Louise, it was not. Without Daniels personally reporting something like this, there is no crime, no crime number, nothing we can refer to that gives us any legitimacy to question this guy. We're a police force, Louise, not a bunch of vigilantes.'

Louise knew her sergeant was right. She herself was a great respecter of rules. Conscious that she was acting completely out of character, she nevertheless continued to advocate her cause.

'So, Meredith ignores the distinct possibility that we've arrested the wrong man, and you support him?' she said.

'No, I'm not supporting him. I actually think you may be on to something, but neither of us can act on this unless Meredith gives us the go-ahead. That's what I'm saying.

You don't have enough evidence to persuade Meredith of this theory at the moment.'

'But to get enough to persuade him, I need to question Patrick Venn. And this evening, I have the perfect opportunity.'

Harrison sat hunched over the table stirring his coffee mechanically, deep in thought.

'Tell you what I'm going to do,' he said eventually. 'You've got a real interest in local history, right? You went to that island this morning because of your fascination with the geology of the Thames.'

Louise looked quizzically at her sergeant.

'Bear with me, Detective Constable. I'm saying that you've approached me concerning this passion you have for geology . . .'

'Don't you mean geography?'

'Whatever I mean, it starts with "g-e-o". There's an opportunity tonight for you to be shown around Tagg's Island by one of the residents, so I've let you off for a few hours because we're not busy and you'll be on call if there's an emergency.'

'So, I can go this evening with your permission?'

'Christ, do I have to spell it out for you?' Harrison pleaded in exasperation. 'I'll cover for you if any questions arise.'

'But you won't come with me?'

'No. I'll drop you off at a suitable distance and pick you up again later but if you think about it, you're likely to get much more by pursuing your interest in geolography alone than you would if I was with you. Me being there would expose you as a copper. Unless you intend to introduce me as your dad or something.'

'That wouldn't be a bad idea. You're certainly old enough,' Louise joked as she mulled this over for a moment, sipping her coffee. 'Although without you there, I'll struggle to ask the questions I could have put to him if we were involved in a proper investigation.'

'Sure, you'll need to find an angle to discover if he was riding his bike on that Friday evening, for instance, but there again, the more off-guard our Mr Venn is, the more likely he'll say something useful to you. Think of it as working undercover.'

'And what comes after that?' Louise asked.

'That depends on what you find out, but here's the second part of my plan. I'll look up Patrick Venn on the Police National Computer, see if we've got anything on him AND I'll come with you to see that TV woman tomorrow. With a bit of luck, we'll then have enough between us to make a case to DCI Meredith. Either that or we'll know we're paddling our canoe up the wrong creek.'

9

A UNITED NATIONS OF CRIMINALITY

Early evening on Tagg's Island. The owner of *Navicula*, Marko Rockov, was in conference. Some of the men he was talking to had arrived on the island that morning in the SUVs with blacked-out windows that had driven past Sage and Louise. Others resided permanently on the houseboat as Rockov's personal guard. Their boss was a physically big man. Once a boxer in the former Yugoslavia, he'd been hired as an enforcer for a Serbian drug cartel in the early eighties after the fragile alliance that had held the Balkans together disintegrated following the death of President Tito.

Noted for his brains as much as his brawn, Rockov had a successful import/export business based in Greece and the Balkans. But an illicit trade in drugs had soon become the main source of his considerable income. He had all the skills required of a drug dealer; the Serb could motivate, negotiate and network. So when Jack Handysides began to amalgamate different narcotics gangs in London to form a single lucrative enterprise, Rockov had been one of the first to sign up.

He'd purchased this place on Tagg's Island principally because of its superb access to the Thames. Rockov loved rivers and messing about in boats. Now he delighted in living onboard one. And there were practical, professional advantages. *Navicula* had an important strategic position, situated as it was on an important marine drugs highway. If the Thames was the Mediterranean, *Navicula* would be its Gibraltar.

Having been here for two years, the Serb was now arranging to bring over his wife, her septuagenarian mother and his two teenage children to make *Navicula* their family home. The NATO bombing aimed at forcing Serbian militia to withdraw from Kosovo was making life increasingly dangerous for Rockov's loved ones in Belgrade. He resented the UK's involvement in the current war against his homeland, but not enough to sacrifice the good living he was making in London.

The men who had come to *Navicula* that morning were all Serbian, apart from Rockov's chief of staff, Jeremy Van Wyk, a South African. Slim and wiry, Van Wyk was smartly dressed in a three-piece suit, and looked more like a bank clerk than a gangster. He'd originally been a chemist in Cape Town before becoming involved in the narcotics trade, which took him to Belgrade where he and Rockov had met. They'd formed a partnership there that was sometimes referred to by rivals as Brawn and Brain. They were a perfect match in the drugs trade because whilst the South African was an expert on the drugs, the Serbian was an expert on the trade. Van Wyk's nationality may have been unusual at *Navicula*, but in the new Handysides empire Rockov worked with people of all nationalities, Mexican, Albanian, Columbian, Russian: a United Nations of criminality.

Now, in the spacious, glass-fronted living room that

overlooked the Thames, they awaited Jack Handysides' arrival.

Rockov was like a Town Hall mayor preparing for a royal visit. He fussed over the layout of the room, where Handysides should sit to get the best view of the river, what refreshments were available – no alcohol, Handysides was strictly teetotal – whether to have music playing in the background or not.

Rockov had worked with Handysides for two years now, but this would be the great man's first visit to Tagg's Island. The welcoming party knew when Jack was due to arrive, but not the method of that arrival. Nobody ever knew what mode of travel Handysides would use. He never rode in limousines, and always travelled alone – no driver, no bodyguards, no entourage. Anonymity was his greatest protection. Most of those who worked for him didn't even know what he looked like. There were no published photographs and Jack never socialised – ever.

Like all the other agents, Marko Rockov would be contacted via an innocuous text message about where to meet in person to receive instructions. This was the occasion this evening: a meeting in person on Tagg's Island.

At 5 p.m. the bell attached to the security camera on the gate was pressed. Nobody on the floating mansion had heard a car pull up, and Rockov's man on the bridge watching out for Handysides had remained incommunicado. The most powerful criminal in London had seemingly stepped off a bus, strolled past the lookout without attracting a second glance, and materialised at *Navicula*.

Van Wyk rushed down to the gates to greet this distinguished guest and show him up to the conference room.

Jack Handysides was of average height, with a pale complexion and thick red hair. He wore glasses and, despite only being in his early thirties, looked middle-aged. He was determinedly nondescript. Wearing a beige gaberdine raincoat over a dark suit, the most flamboyant thing about him was the tartan scarf looped untidily around his neck. It was a chilly evening with mist already hovering above the Thames.

Greeting Handysides as he entered the room, Rockov knew it would be futile to try to engage in any small talk. Jack had no interests outside his work. He also seemed devoid of ego or any desire to show off the enormous wealth he must have accumulated. The most successful criminal in London conducted himself with a modesty that enhanced his quiet authority. Handysides was a man who was respected rather than feared. Yet his very ordinariness made those who did have cause to fear him more worried than if they'd upset a more obvious tyrant.

Within five minutes of his arrival the guest of honour was addressing the five men gathered round him.

'There will be another big consignment of cocaine transported by barge along the Thames tonight. The police plan to transfer it onto a truck at Maidenhead, and from there it will be taken to the incinerator on Slough Trading Estate. So, usual arrangements, but much bigger scale. Which is why I wanted to speak to you this evening. These are the drugs that were captured in that high-profile seizure in Southampton last year. Came by ship from Chile via an outfit that has yet to join our business venture. Unfortunately, these wholesalers got caught. They were mainly Mexican but with some British bumpkins on board as well. Customs apparently had some inside information. The haul was retained pending trial. Now that's over and a guilty verdict has been secured the drugs are due to be destroyed – as they will be, all bar forty wrapped packages that will be unloaded as the barge comes past Tagg's Island in around eight hours' time. I know you've done this before with smaller amounts dropped on your doorstep, so to speak, but this was the biggest consignment ever seized in the UK, so our cut is that much greater. It will take longer to offload and needs to be distributed through our network more quickly. It's too dangerous to have such a large amount stored. This stuff needs to hit the streets by tomorrow lunchtime. Any questions?'

Rockov and his men were familiar with the 'usual arrangements'. The inconspicuous barge coming up the Thames from Blackfriars would steer close to *Navicula*, and a few parcels of drugs would be offloaded as it passed. The houseboat was perfectly situated at the mouth of the lagoon, the side from which the drugs would be thrown and collected hidden from prying eyes on both banks of the river. The difference tonight would be that the barge would have to anchor in order to offload so many parcels, but it wouldn't be for long, and the operation would be no less secluded.

'I only wonder why we're taking such a small part of the consignment?' one of Rockov's men asked. 'If we've got people we're paying on the barge, why don't we take the lot?'

'Because, my friend, this way we don't kill the goose that lays so many golden eggs. The forty packages contain over two hundred kilograms worth, £15m to us. Sure, it's only ten percent of the drugs on board but taking more would jeopardise the entire operation. If they discover what's happening the police would be bound to change the method of transportation and we'd lose the ongoing opportunities that your strategic location presents.' Handysides' indeterminate North of England accent became stronger as he emphasised the final words.

'How come they don't notice so many missing packages?' another of Rockov's men asked.

'Since the transportation of this stuff to the incinerator was contracted out to a private security company, we've managed to get our people on the inside. They found a way to doctor the paperwork they receive so that with this assignment, for instance, they'll reduce the number of packages taken on board by forty so that when the cargo is counted off at Maidenhead, it tallies.'

'So, privatisation really has made us richer, just like your Mrs Thatcher said it would,' Rockov joked.

When the conference finished, Rockov asked if Handysides would stay for something to eat.

'Thanks, Marko, but I have things to do. You've got this sorted – nothing can go wrong, and if it does, you know how to contact me. I need to be off, but there is one other thing I need to tell you about.' Handysides motioned the Serbian to a corner of the room where they could speak privately away from the other men.

'You know that television programme about crime? The one with Jenny Daniels?'

'I know, of course I know. That woman is interfering in my country's affairs.'

'Marko, I'm aware you have a grudge against her for presenting that TV appeal . . .'

'She was saying my president, Mr Milosevic, is forcing people from their homes,' Rockov interrupted. 'Is not true.'

'Okay, you need to forget about that because Jenny Daniels may be about to do something far more relevant to us . . . and far more damaging.'

'What?' asked the surprised Serbian.

'That doctor boyfriend of hers, Templeman, who's been prying into my affairs is apparently going to name me on national television, exposing me as the man behind a powerful London drugs syndicate.'

'We can't let that happen,' Rockov said darkly.

'I knew that would be your reaction, but you need to leave it to my lawyers.'

'And if they fail? Who should we target, the doctor? Daniels?'

'Nobody,' Handysides said firmly. 'You will not target anybody. I do not want you or anyone else to fight this battle for me.'

'But if they name you, they will soon name me. I have my wife and children coming here. I can't risk that happening.'

'I've constructed this business to make sure nothing can happen like that. This is not a house of cards. Even if I am named it won't impact on you. I will make sure it's all resolved. I don't need you to do anything. Understood?'

There was a steeliness in Handysides' voice that had a moderating effect on the Serbian.

'Our discipline is our greatest strength,' Handysides said. 'I didn't want you to hear about the programme or even be watching it when my name is revealed, if it should come to that. I don't want you getting a nasty surprise. Whatever happens, I will deal with it.'

Handysides had his hand on Rockov's shoulder and was looking intently into the Serbian's dark eyes. His authority was absolute. Marko Rockov, tall and powerfully built, fell into line as quietly as a small child being restrained by a teacher.

'Funnily enough, I hear Miss Daniels lives just across from here in East Molesey,' Handysides said, congenially. 'You might bump into her in Sainsbury's.'

After Handysides had left an hour later Rockov addressed his men.

'My friends, you have been in the presence of greatness. Jack Handysides is a genius. He's just delivered millions of pounds into our hands and you'd have thought he'd come to read the gas meter.'

'You may be star struck by him,' said Jeremy Van Wyk to Rockov after the others had gone, 'but in my view Handysides is now a liability. I hear that he specifically instructed Captain Crazy not to harm an informer he'd found in his organisation.'

Captain Crazy was the nickname of a South African drug smuggler known and admired for his violent temper.

'It's Jack's way, and it works. The Captain would have done something stupid and done it incompetently. What Jack did was ship the informer to Russia where he can't cause any damage. After a few months the guy will be wishing Captain Crazy had killed him.'

'Or maybe he comes back and tells the police everything they want to know.'

'He won't come back from where Jack has sent him – to Siberia to oversee a little operation we have acquired there. Stick to your medicine, Jeremy, and let me handle the dangerous bits.'

Van Wyk gave a sigh of exasperation.

'But that's what I want to do,' he cried. 'You're much better at dealing with the difficult stuff than Handysides. He's too passive, too unthreatening. He can't do "the dangerous bits", as you say – but you can. Jack has built us the vehicle; you should take over driving it.'

At that moment, the man they were talking about was walking back across the bridge connecting Tagg's Island with Hampton Court Road. A woman was walking in the opposite direction, deep in thought, her eyes lowered. It was a narrow pavement, and they almost collided.

'Sorry,' said Jack Handysides.

'No, my fault, I should have been looking where I was going,' said Detective Constable Louise Mangan.

After a momentary pause, they walked on in opposite directions: Louise onto the island, Handysides away from it.

As she reached the crown of the bridge the Detective Constable's two-way radio came to life. It was Harrison asking what fish she wanted from the chip shop he would be visiting just prior to picking her up later. Jack Handysides had walked on too far to hear what was said, but he had heard the unmistakeable crackle of her two-way radio.

10

LOW TIDE

When Louise Mangan arrived back at the 'Welcome to Tagg's Island' sign, having placed an order for cod and chips with her sergeant as she crossed the bridge, the island was as quiet as it had been on her first visit. She'd almost walked into a man crossing the bridge, but apart from him there was no one around.

Detective Sergeant Harrison had allowed three hours for Louise to pursue these extra-curricular activities, arranging to pick her up at 10 p.m. from the car park near where they'd been stationed on the night of Darnell Thomas's arrest. When she got to where the *Inner Peace* was moored, Louise saw two men crouched at the river's edge, illuminated by an arc light. She recognised one of them as Sage. He cut an almost biblical figure, bent over the water in a pure white sweatshirt, his long hair hanging loose around his thin shoulders.

Low tide had almost grounded the boat to the extent that only about half a metre of water lapped against its hull. Alerted by the sound of the latch on the gate being lifted, Sage greeted Louise more like an old friend than an acquaintance he'd made only that morning.

The man with him, standing in the water wearing thigh-high waders and a three-quarter length coat, continued to inspect the hull without looking up until, realising that the hem of his coat was in danger of getting soaked, he made a little ceremony of taking it off, and folding it neatly over a plastic garden chair.

Sage made no introductions. Leading Louise away from the water's edge, he told her that the inspection had started later than expected and was taking longer than he'd hoped. He'd take her round to meet the cyclist, Patrick Venn, as soon as this was finished. But that wasn't likely to be for another couple of hours.

'Colin has found a couple of things that have to be sorted out straight away,' he concluded.

'Colin?'

'Oh, sorry. I'll introduce you in a moment,' Sage said quietly. 'Wouldn't want to disturb him just as he's got going.'

He told Louise that Colin Brown, the man working under the arc light, was a godsend for the residents of Tagg's Island.

'He's not the sharpest knife in the drawer,' Sage whispered, 'but he knows everything there is to know about maintaining these boats, and not just the exteriors. He knows about the flushing systems, the Calor gas supplies, the electric distillers that ensure clean drinking water – everything.'

'Does he live on the island?' Louise asked, her voice lowered to Sage's level.

'No, he's not a liveaboard, but he's not far from here. Lives with his mum in East Molesey. Been in trouble with the police. Mainly low-scale stuff from what I hear, although he did disappear off the scene for a while a few years back. People said he was serving a prison sentence. Aunt Jane thought that giving him work would help his rehabilitation, bless her. But Colin has real expertise, which is why he's in great demand here.'

It was cold and dark away from the heat source of the lamp. Sage asked his visitor if she wanted to wait onboard in the warm kitchen, explaining that he needed to stay outside to deal with any queries, but Louise said she was well wrapped and content to remain where she was.

It was an hour and a half before Brown finished and walked over to join them straight away. He was a small muscular man with a high forehead that made his short dark hair look like a skull cap. He spoke to Sage as if nobody else was there.

'Your old aunty Jane had nothing done to this boat's hull for years,' Brown said pointing unnecessarily to the *Inner Peace*. 'If it was fibre glass that wouldn't matter much, but fungus spores thrive and multiply on water destroying any wood they come into contact with. That's why I told your aunt to have the hull varnished with marine spar or epoxy years ago, but she never did. Said she would but never got round to it.'

'She was probably worried about the cost,' said Sage. 'Can you do it now, or has it gone too far?'

Brown scratched his chin, staring hard at the boat. 'It's not too late. I can do it. Clean it, seal it with resin, paint it. Come up lovely, it will.'

'How much?'

Sage's question provoked more chin scratching.

'You go to a specialist – well over a thousand quid. Me? I'd do it for five hundred, how's that?'

'Brilliant – when?'

'Need to get it done quick. You must be due your out of water inspection soon. As things stand, you'll fail it and probably lose your licence, so needs to be in the next couple of weeks.'

When the transaction had been completed Sage finally introduced his visitor.

'Colin, this is my friend Louise. She's a cyclist, and I'm taking her to meet someone on the island.'

There was a limp handshake, and Louise noticed how Brown avoided eye contact to the extent that she wondered if he somehow sensed being in the presence of a copper as many petty criminals claimed they could.

Just as Sage and Colin were discussing details of when the work on the boat would be carried out and what materials would be needed, two men appeared on the other side of the latched gate that led down to *The Inner Peace*. Sage whispered to Louise that these were two of Rockov's men from the floating mansion on the lagoon. One, tall and muscular, was wearing a tight-fitting tee-shirt despite the evening chill, his tattooed arms on full display. He was one of the 'heavies'. The small, neat man with him, wearing a three-piece suit, was Rockov's second-in-command, Jeremy Van Wyk.

'Hey, Colin,' he shouted. 'You coming round to finish those jobs?'

'Yeah, I'll drop by tomorrow, 'bout midday.'

'Is this your girlfriend?' the muscular man asked, gesturing leeringly towards Louise. 'What's she doing on the island?'

Sage looked at the two men with undisguised hostility.

'That's none of your business,' he asserted.

'Everything that happens on this island is our business,' the tattooed man said.

Louise was calculating whether to continue being a passive observer. She could see that Brown felt intimidated by these men.

She decided on engagement. 'Who says?' she asked. 'And what gives you the right to poke your nose into my affairs?'

The men seemed taken aback by her aggression.

'Sorry,' said Van Wyk, 'we work for Mr Rockov at *Navicula*. He's anxious to ensure that his neighbours feel safe and secure. These boats can attract thieves, so he asks us to check around every so often. I apologise for my comrade here. He was only joking. Sage, why don't you introduce us to your friend?'

Before Sage could respond, Louise introduced herself.

'My name is Mrs Mangan, I'm nobody's girlfriend. And if you must know, I'm helping Sage prepare his boat for its out of water inspection. Now, if you don't mind, we'll get back to work.'

Louise had only heard the term 'out of water inspection' a few minutes before, but she calculated that it was better to give these men a reason for being on the island than invite unwelcome speculation.

'Sorry to disturb you,' the South African said, steering his colleague away and back on to what seemed to be their evening patrol.

'Do those characters come round regularly?' Louise asked once they were out of earshot.

'Yes, and I have to say my neighbours generally appreciate their presence. It's part of the way Rockov has ingratiated himself with the residents' association.'

'They're okay,' Colin added, which seemed a strange response given his obvious apprehension when the two men had appeared. 'I do lots of work for them over at *Navicula* and although the one in the tee-shirt takes the piss out of me, I don't mind, because Rockov pays well.'

Sage and Louise left Colin tidying up his stuff while they went across to the other side of the island to meet Patrick Venn, the keen cyclist who was Louise's reason for being there that evening. She was conscious that they were running late and there was only another thirty minutes before Harrison was due to pick her up.

'Why did you tell them you were here regarding the out of water inspection?' Sage asked as they walked towards *The Great Gatsby*.

'Oh, I just wanted rid of them, and I figured the best way was to give an actual reason for my presence.'

Louise thought she detected a hint of suspicion in her companion's green eyes.

Several minutes after their encounter with Louise, Jeremy Van Wyk and his colleague were back at *Navicula* briefing Rockov on the mystery woman who Jack Handysides had alerted them to after hearing the crackle of her radio when they'd passed on the bridge.

'She works for a boat maintenance company, so I guess she needs to stay in touch with her technicians,' Van Wyk said.

'She could do that by mobile phone. Boat repairers don't use walkie-talkies to conduct their business, the police do,' Rockov responded. 'And if she's here in connection with the boat, why is she on foot? Why not in a van with all her equipment.'

'I think you're being paranoid, boss,' the second man said. 'If she's here to keep watch on us, what is she doing with that idiot Colin and our resident hippy?'

'And if the police were on to us, surely they'd send more than one policewoman on foot,' Van Wyk added.

The men were standing on the immaculate lawn that inclined gently down to the houseboat itself. Rockov was smoking a cigarillo, his head back blowing smoke up towards a full yellow moon. 'I don't like it. This will be our biggest haul from the operation, and suddenly there's a stranger on the island with a two-way radio? As it's over four hours until the barge passes, I doubt she's here in connection with that. But I want her watched. Let me know when she's left the island.'

A voluptuous blonde in a loosely tied dressing gown answered the buzzer attached to the fence post outside Patrick Venn's houseboat. Sage introduced her as Vicky, Patrick's partner.

No, she said, when Louise asked, Patrick wasn't home yet. The blonde thought he must have gone out with friends for a drink. She had no idea when he'd be back. They'd need to come another time. Louise was disappointed that she'd wasted an evening, but given that her sergeant was due to pick her up at ten, she couldn't hang around.

All was quiet on the island as Sage accompanied her on the short walk back to the bridge.

'How are you getting home?' he asked.

'Same way I came – on the bus.'

It was another lie, which she could moderate by calling it a 'white lie' or a fib. But a lie was a lie, and one of the central tenets of her Christian faith was honesty. She hated being dishonest to this gentle soul who was being so helpful, but she could see no alternative. Louise was convinced that she'd helped arrest an innocent man and that the guilty party, the man who'd assaulted all those women, the man who may well be responsible for Tiffany Mordaunt's abduction was somewhere on this island. She had to continue the pretence, at least for now.

Sage and Louise said their farewells after agreeing that they should try to catch Patrick Venn at home over the weekend. Sage's determination to have no means of telephonic communication meant that making precise arrangements with him was difficult. But, as he pointed out, given that he spent most of his time on the *Inner Peace* writing, she could just drop by whenever it suited her.

Crossing the bridge, Louise stopped, captivated by the shimmering image of the full moon reflected on the water below. She caught a fleeting glimpse of someone behind her ducking quickly into the shadows. Back on the main road, she waited at the bus stop and boarded a number 68 towards Richmond, radioing Ralph Harrison to pick her up from two stops further on. There'd been nobody at the stop and looking back after boarding the bus, there was no vehicle behind. Whoever had been following her had only wanted to ensure she'd left the island.

'Your fish supper will be cold,' Harrison said when she got in the car. 'I've eaten mine.'

'Typical, take a girl out for dinner and then scoff yours before she arrives.'

'So, what's with all the Secret Squirrel?' Ralph asked.

'I was being followed and it was important that I wasn't seen getting into this car. I was supposed to have arrived on the bus and I needed to leave the same way.'

'Any news about the cyclist?' Harrison asked.

'Not yet, but this supper isn't the only fishy thing about this evening,' Louise said, 'there's a bunch of thugs on that island who we need to be investigating.'

'Not tonight, Josephine. I'm taking you home. Tomorrow we'll go to see that TV producer and take things from there. Now eat your chips.'

The tide had turned and carried upriver on its swell came the low flat barge. Red lights winked from bow and stern as it made its noiseless journey through the moonlit water. It was 1 a.m., and most residents in the desirable Thamesside residences it passed were asleep. Anyone watching the river would hardly notice a type of vessel that had worked these waters for hundreds of years – congruous, anonymous.

Approaching Tagg's Island, the barge slowed and then anchored across the inlet to the lagoon. In a burst of feverish activity, forty parcels, tightly wrapped in cellophane, were thrown from ship to shore.

Three bargemen in hooded anoraks did the throwing from the starboard side of the boat; catching them were Rockov's men, still dressed in tee-shirts despite the cold.

Within fifteen minutes the operation was complete. The parcels of cocaine lay under a sheet of tarpaulin in the back of a builder's van. They were then covered in rubble ready for the journey to a warehouse in Battersea, to be distributed across a network of gangs, all of whom were ultimately controlled by Jack Handysides. The retail part of the trade would be in place by noon with considerable financial returns beginning to flow back to *Navicula* by early evening.

An observer from the Surrey bank would have seen only the port side of the barge where there had been no activity. Anyone watching from the Middlesex bank would have had their view blocked by the island. There was only one vantage point from where *Navicula*'s contact with the barge could have been observed. This was on Tagg's Island itself, close to the lagoon – a marshy spot where nobody went but which gave a clear view of the cargo being unloaded.

It was from here, unseen, that Sage watched the entire operation.

Tiffany heard the creak of footsteps on the stairs heading down to where she lay, strapped into a wooden bed, a gag still taped across her mouth. She'd already eaten. Whoever it was wasn't coming to feed her.

Two shadowy figures were framed in the doorway; the straps on her bed unfastened; the blanket pulled away, exposing her nakedness. One of the men caressed her while the other looked on. She wanted to scream, but couldn't. All she could do was cry, tears coursing down her face. All she could do – cry and try to remain aware.

Her abuser said nothing until after it was over, and the two men were leaving. He had his back to her, directing his words over his shoulder as if articulating an afterthought.

'Filthy fucking whore,' he said.

11

A VISIT TO WHITE CITY

Ralph Harrison kept his promise, convincing DCI Meredith that it would be wise to follow up the report of an attack on Jenny Daniels by visiting the woman who'd made it: the assistant producer of *Crimesolve*, Olive Sabatini.

As Harrison had argued, if the TV programme felt that this attack on their star presenter was being ignored, they could make life difficult for those in charge of the investigation. In any case, it was a line of enquiry that had become particularly pertinent following another sexual assault that had taken place at around half-ten the previous evening. Eighteen-year-old Darcy Kramer had been walking home after a night out with friends, taking a route that skirted Richmond Park. A cyclist had drawn level, before forcing her to the ground. The attack was thwarted when Darcy's screams attracted the attention of a couple walking their dog.

All she could say about her attacker was that he was white, wore mirrored goggles, had a stubbly chin and wore one of those open-faced balaclavas popular in cold weather. He wasn't wearing a safety helmet. He had shouted something as he cycled away but the poor girl was distraught and unable to say what it was, although her dog-walking rescuers thought that it might indeed have been 'filthy fucking whore'.

'Well, we know that Darnell Thomas didn't attack this girl because he's still in custody, but have they done a DNA check yet?' Louise asked Harrison as they discussed this latest development on their way to the BBC.

A potential breakthrough was that the attacker broke a fingernail clawing at Darcy's clothes. Forensics had found it caught in the fluffy material of her jacket. This would provide a DNA code which could be checked against a database that had been growing gradually since being established in the mid-nineties. The potential of this nascent technology was expanding all the time, but its importance had yet to permeate throughout the force.

'Don't know if they have or not,' Harrison replied. 'I presume the material is safely stored somewhere as evidence. All this technical stuff is a mystery to me. Why don't you ask your friend Meredith?'

Louise dismissed Harrison's facetious comment with an ironic, 'Ha ha. Very funny.'

DCI Sean Meredith had remained implacable about refusing to reopen the wider investigation, insisting to Harrison that the attack on Darcy Kramer had been unconnected to the Beast of Hampton Court investigation, just like the 'mild transgression' (as he described it) against Jenny Daniels.

Meredith argued that the main feature of the series of attacks that led to the arrest of Darnell Thomas was that the perpetrator had worn a distinctive cycle helmet. In neither of the two recent incidents was the attacker wearing any type of safety helmet, let alone the luminous yellow one that Thomas had on. As for the use of similar profanities, the *Daily Candour* had now reported 'Darnell's catchphrase' (again, a Meredith description) and gone on to say that, 'other toe-rags were trying to muscle in on his notoriety.'

'Ah, I see,' Louise said sarcastically when Harrison relayed all this back to her. 'It's a copycat attack because he uses the same obscenities but it's nothing to do with the other attacks because he wasn't wearing a yellow cycle helmet. Surely any copycat nutter would have replicated everything. Perhaps a better explanation is that this guy realised that the helmet marked him out and so stopped wearing it. Isn't that more feasible?'

'Calm down, Louise,' Harrison cautioned. 'The prosecuting authorities don't seem to have any doubts that Darnell Thomas is our man. Sean knows what he's doing and what he's doing is giving us the go-ahead to talk to the TV producer who reported the Daniels incident and for other members of the old 'Incisive' team to investigate the Darcy Kramer attack. That's not a bad outcome.'

'I'd still like to know that the DNA is being checked. And why on earth isn't Meredith scaling up Operation Incisive? Why is he continuing to shrink it? Tiffany Mordaunt is still missing, and now there's been another attack. Even if we ignore what happened to Jenny Daniels there's enough to justify intensifying the investigation,' Louise mused as she navigated the traffic on Wood Lane leading up to Television Centre at White City. 'Does this new incident mean we're not going to be moved onto that safe-cracking case?' she asked as they pulled up at the security barrier.

'No, it doesn't. You'll soon learn that it's only in crime novels that detectives are allowed the luxury of dealing with only one case at a time. We'll go to the BBC now and then get over to Streatham in the next few days when forensics have reported on the crime scene at the bank. You'll need to put your one-woman crusade on hold for now.'

Olive Sabatini was in a meeting when the two plain-clothes officers arrived outside her workroom at Television Centre. The door was way back on its hinges, which made Louise suspect that the man Sabatini was talking to had burst in uninvited. Waiting outside, Harrison and Louise could hear every word that was being exchanged.

'For fuck's sake, Olive, this has the potential to be the biggest story *Crimesolve* has ever done. But it's worth nothing if you don't name Jack Handysides.'

'I'm sorry, Jamie, it's way above my paygrade. You need to talk to Carl or Simon. I'm just a cog; they're the wheel.'

Her protagonist seemed to regain control of his temper as he said, a little less loudly, 'Jenny thinks we should name him. Surely she's the wheel. Neither Simon or Carl will speak to me – which is why I had to come to you.'

'Look, I'll go back to them,' Olive promised in a conciliatory tone, 'but you have to understand that it's not just a case of the Met refusing to co-operate on this; they are actively opposed to doing so, and will be pulling strings right up to Director General level. They claim that naming Handysides now will jeopardise the solid case they're trying to build against him. Simon and Carl can't ignore that kind of representation.'

'Well, you'd better tell the Met that I won't be able to ignore their utter incompetence as I finalise my book,' Dr Jamie Templeman said defiantly as he turned to leave the office, striding past the two waiting detectives without seeming to notice them, his handsome features set stern.

'Sounds as if you've got some tensions to diffuse there,' Harrison said as Sabatini shepherded him and Louise into her office.

'We only do one programme a month and you wouldn't believe the hassle we've had with this one. We were going to do a piece on Operation Incisive until you guys rather inconveniently reported that you'd caught the perpetrator. Then Jenny and her boyfriend – and in case you didn't realise, incidentally, he's the man who just left my office – wanted to do something on the surge in hard drugs on our streets. But that's also been blocked by your guys. The way it's going we may have to do something about parking fines in central London.'

'Who's this Jack Handysides fellow we heard you arguing about?' Louise asked as she and Ralph Harrison settled onto a battered sofa in Sabatini's rather threadbare office.

The BBC assistant producer gave her visitors the background to the drugs story that *Crimesolve* wanted to feature, her elfin features contrasting with the tale of exploitation and addiction she was relating.

'I've never been involved with our narcotics squad,' Harrison said when she'd finished, 'but if the Met is counselling against naming this guy Handysides, it must be because they don't want their plans disrupted.'

'Well, they're certainly disrupting mine,' Sabatini said before welcoming her visitors' interest in the report she'd made about the attack on Jenny Daniels.

'I don't think Jenny will be best pleased with me if she finds out I blabbed to you.'

'But we can't do much unless she's willing to report it herself,' Louise explained. 'She has to verify what happened that night.'

'There's even less chance of that happening now than when I reported this to your liaison woman,' Olive announced.

'Why? Surely she wants this guy caught?' Harrison said, unable to disguise his frustration at what he saw as a bunch of luvvies being precious.

'She doesn't need you to track him down because she's now confident that she knows who attacked her and she doesn't want him prosecuted.'

Olive Sabatini told the two surprised police officers that Daniels had a strong imprint of her attacker's features scorched onto her memory, and such a clear impression of having seen him before that she'd been spending sleepless nights trying to remember who he was. A few days ago, she'd told Olive that it had all fallen into place: in the mid-1980s a woman living a few streets away had contacted Jenny to say that her adult son had always wanted to work in television. He hadn't had the easiest of lives – the woman having struggled to bring him up alone – and she wondered if Daniels could meet mother and son to offer some advice.

'Being the kind-hearted person she is – and given that they were practically neighbours in East Molesey – Jenny agreed, and arranged for the woman to bring her son round. That's why she was so sure she'd seen him before; he'd actually been in her house.'

'So, if this was over a decade ago, how old is this lad now?' Harrison asked.

'Jenny reckons he'll be well into his thirties. As I said, she's even less likely to report the attack now that she knows who carried it out. She told me that she did try to help after the guy's mother had brought him to see her. Jenny got him a six-month trial as a scene shifter at the Beeb, but he only lasted for half that time. Apparently, the guy is a fantasist who believes he's the reincarnation of Elvis Presley. He has a particularly low IQ and was on prescribed medication. Jenny still has his mum's number, and she rang her yesterday. The son is still living at home, and does lots of odd-jobbing around the area, which gives him an income and a measure of self-esteem. The mother confirmed that her son had run out of his serotonin prescription for a few days recently, and Jenny thinks that's when he attacked her. She thinks he's basically harmless.'

'If she had reported the attack, Elvis might be doing a bit of jailhouse rock, and it might have prevented an attempted rape last night,' DS Harrison said sternly. 'Let's have this guy's name. We need to speak to him about last night's assault so we might not need your star presenter's cooperation, but it would have helped.'

Sabatini hadn't heard about the latest attack and news of it shocked her.

'You've done the right thing, Olive, even if Jenny Daniels hasn't,' Louise said, adopting a more conciliatory tone than her sergeant. 'We'd have never known about this if you hadn't had the gumption to tell us – but we do need that name.'

Olive said she'd written it on a memo pad and began sifting through the chaotic tangle of papers on her desk.

'Ah, here it is,' she said eventually, handing a piece of paper with a name scribbled on it. 'Colin Brown.'

The Police National Computer had produced nothing on Patrick Venn but revealed much about Colin Brown. A suspended sentence for two counts of indecent assault in 1981, followed by a three-year sentence (of which he'd served half) for the attempted rape of a woman in Richmond the following year. Nothing since.

Louise told Ralph Harrison how she'd met Colin Brown on Tagg's Island the previous evening, but that he'd left her company in plenty of time to be able to make the attack on Darcy Kramer at 10.30 p.m. She hadn't known he rode a sports bike, and thought about contacting Sage to find out more about the man who'd come to check his boat. However, given that her new friend had neither land-line nor mobile phone, it was a futile notion. In any case she was still reluctant to risk their friendship by revealing that she was a police officer.

A 'Colin Brown' piece would fit neatly into the Hampton Court jigsaw. He lived in the area, had a record of assaults on women and, presuming he was the man cycling towards Louise along Hampton Court Road that night, knew Tagg's Island well enough to have taken refuge there. Perhaps there'd be no need to speak to Patrick Venn now. But Darnell Thomas was about to be prosecuted for the attack that night and five other charges including attempted murder.

Harrison went to see DCI Meredith, who gave the go-ahead for Brown to be brought in for questioning under caution, but only in connection with the Jenny Daniels and Darcy Kramer incidents.

'Why?' Louise reacted angrily. 'What will it take for that man to see sense? Perhaps he'd order more stringent questioning if Colin Brown was black.' But Harrison defended his DCI.

'Sean's thinking is perfectly logical. Just because you've arrested someone for housebreaking doesn't mean that the next time you arrest a housebreaker you assume he's responsible for every other burglary in the area, does it? Same thing here – there's more than one bastard with a propensity towards attacking women. Sad but true. In any case we have ways of finding things out irrespective of whether the DCI authorises our line of questioning or not.'

Louise found this cryptic comment reassuring. She was learning a lot from DS Harrison, including how in the absence of direction from above, they could plot their own course.

They went to the address in East Molesey where Colin Brown lived with his mother. It was just past one o'clock. Nobody was home, but a neighbour told them that Mrs Brown had gone to collect her pension from the post office, and would be back after she stopped for a bit of shopping on the way, as she did every Thursday. Colin would be working nearby, the neighbour said, mentioning the various odd jobs he was known to undertake.

It was then that Louise remembered the conversation she'd witnessed between Brown and the *Navicula* duo the previous evening, specifically the arrangement they'd made for the next day. She knew exactly where Colin Brown would be.

12

COFFEE ON THE *NAVICULA*

The morning was unfolding slowly at *Navicula*. Its occupants had worked deep into the night, and most were still not back from distributing the cocaine offloaded from the barge that had passed by in the early hours. Only Marko Rockov and his main henchman, Jeremy Van Wyk, had remained on Tagg's Island. By nine o'clock, they were taking calls from various agents, completing the transactions that would seal the success of this lucrative venture. At ten o'clock, the two people who handled domestic arrangements at *Navicula* arrived. One began mowing the lawn, the other cooked bacon and scrambled eggs which Rockov and Van Wyk sat down to eat in the lavish kitchen half an hour later.

'What time is that half-wit due to arrive?'

It was unusual for Marko Rockov to show any great interest in someone performing menial tasks around his riverside estate. But the Serbian was particularly anxious to talk to Colin Brown who was coming to fit new carbon monoxide detectors on the boat. Rockov was still suspicious about the woman who'd come onto Tagg's Island the previous evening, even though she'd been followed off the island, and the transfer of drugs from ship to shore had gone ahead without a hitch. Handysides had warned

Rockov not to drop his guard, and, as an ex-boxer, the Serb knew the wisdom of this advice.

'He's supposed to be here around midday,' Van Wyk replied. 'I can tell you're still not completely satisfied about what that woman he was with was doing on the island. Do you want us to dig a little deeper?'

'No need. This guy isn't blessed with a great brain,' Rockov countered. 'But there's no reason why he wouldn't tell us what we want to know about that woman without you having to use the kind of persuasion you're so good at. Besides, Jack is coming back soon to make sure everything's okay. He'll be very angry if we've risked attracting attention by beating up a local resident.'

Instead, Rockov suggested an alternative approach, which involved him and Colin Brown taking a coffee break together on the open roof deck of the enormous houseboat. The early morning mist had cleared by the time Brown arrived and the sun was hauling itself up to its April pinnacle in the cold, blue sky. The handyman had been reluctant to join the boat owner for coffee, but Rockov's associate had made it clear that rejecting the invitation was inadvisable.

By noon the two men sat holding mugs of steaming coffee, the host effusive, his guest defensive.

'I just want to thank you for all the work you do around this place,' Rockov said. 'My guys say I should put you on the payroll permanently. Is that something you'd want?'

'Oh, I'm okay doing stuff when you want me, thanks all the same.'

'You and I must be around the same age – in our thirties?'

Brown nodded. 'I'm a couple of years younger than Elvis was when he died.' Sensing his host's puzzlement, he said, 'I'm a recognised expert on the life of The King. Been invited to Graceland many times.'

'That's interesting. And my guys tell me you have a girl-friend. They saw you with her last night. That's why I was thinking it's time you settled down and got a steady job.'

Colin Brown shifted uncomfortably, spilling coffee on his wicker chair.

'I ain't got no girlfriend,' he said.

'So, who was that you were with last night?'

'What, her? Down at Sage's place?'

Rockov nodded.

Despite his nervous state, Brown found the suggestion amusing enough to give a snort of laughter. 'She ain't my girlfriend,' he said.

'Who is she, then?' the Serbian asked coldly.

'I dunno. She come along while I was looking at Sage's boat. Said to your men that she was something to do with the out of water inspection, but she weren't. She didn't know nothing about boats.'

'We think she might be a cop,' Rockov said, watching the handyman closely to gauge his reaction. Brown became more disconcerted.

'A policewoman?' he exclaimed, replaying the events of the previous evening in his mind to fix them against this new information.

The surprised reaction seemed genuine and his inter-locuter didn't think Brown had the guile to disguise his emotions. Colin told Rockov how he'd been doing main-tenance work on the *Inner Peace* for years, since well before Sage took ownership. Last night was simply a continuation of that long involvement. He thought the stranger was one of Sage's friends.

Rockov, hearing Brown say categorically that this woman had nothing to do with inspecting the boat, was anxious to take his charm offensive further. A second cup of coffee was ordered, and a plate of chocolate digestives emerged alongside.

Colin Brown was sufficiently beguiled to relax a little. He now felt that Marko Rockov had a genuine interest in his welfare, hence the job offer he'd made earlier. Colin felt appreciated.

'So, what makes you so sure this woman last night wasn't there in connection with the boat's inspection?' Rockov asked after a few minutes more of amiable chatter.

'I could tell. For a start she never said what Sage had to do to stop the hull being eroded any further. It's simple stuff but it was left to me. Secondly, she never said when the inspection was due. In fact, she said nothing at all about the work I was doing – showed no interest – she was standing too far away to clock anything. Nah, she weren't nothing to do with the inspection.'

'And you've been doing this stuff all your working life?' Rockov asked, trying to establish his employee's level of expertise beyond question.

'Yes, but I done lots of other things. Worked in the record industry, been in films, worked for the BBC.'

Rockov would have preferred a straight answer rather than this drift into fantasy. Nevertheless, he felt obliged to indulge his guest a little further.

'Who did you work for at the BBC?'

'That *Crimesolve* woman,' Brown replied.

'What, you worked for Jenny Daniels?' Rockov asked incredulously.

'Yeah, Jenny Daniels – I hates her, I do,' he said as if trying to impress through the force of his disdain.

'Why do you hate Jenny Daniels?' Rockov asked quietly, his interest in Brown intensifying.

The handyman recounted how he'd wanted to work for the BBC as a presenter or perhaps a newsreader; how his mum had approached Jenny Daniels who lived a few streets away and taken Colin to meet her.

'All she done was make me hump around scenery at White City – night and day, carrying stuff around like a slave. Takin' the piss, she was.'

The Serb, mildly amused by Colin Brown's assumption that Daniels oversaw the entire British Broadcasting Corporation, didn't reveal his own hostility towards the famous TV personality. His guest was left to chatter aimlessly whilst simultaneously munching his way through the plate of chocolate biscuits.

When they were finished, Colin went back to fitting the carbon monoxide detectors, leaving Rockov to reflect on their conversation.

Van Wyk arrived for a debrief, and Rockov told him that it was extremely doubtful their mystery woman was involved in boat maintenance as she'd claimed. Handysides had been right to be suspicious and they needed to keep a close eye on the *Inner Peace* and its long-haired owner.

'You know him better than the rest of us. Weren't you supplying him with medication when we first came here?'

'Not for him,' Van Wyk responded, 'but for his aunt, who used to live there. You remember? The one who was always objecting to things we wanted to do?'

Rockov confirmed his recollection, and the conversation moved on. The reference Brown had made to Jenny Daniels wasn't mentioned. Rockov needed more time to think about a plan he was formulating as a result of this fresh information. He wasn't prepared to see his lucrative business destroyed through an exposé of Jack Handysides on national television: all he had worked for, the risks he had taken, the enforced separation from his family, the reputation he'd built and maintained, the potential for greater rewards from this opulent and strategic position on the Thames; all in jeopardy because of one TV presenter who'd revelled in the destruction of Rockov's homeland and was now poised to enhance her own reputation at the expense of Jack Handysides.

Jack had said he'd pay another visit to Tagg's Island soon, but the plan being formulated in Rockov's imagination wouldn't require executive approval. Jack Handysides' name and activities had to be protected with or without his consent.

DS Harrison and Louise decided against arresting Colin Brown at *Navicula*. It would take a little longer, but waiting for Brown to leave via the only route available to him was better than causing a very public rumpus on the island itself.

If he started work at twelve noon, as Louise remembered Brown saying the previous evening, then he was unlikely to finish much before one-thirty. If they went now, they shouldn't have long to wait before he appeared.

They parked in the turn-off close to the bridge and an hour later Brown cycled across.

'So, he does have a sports bike,' Harrison remarked as he and Louise left the unmarked Rover to arrest him.

When accosted, Brown thought he'd fallen into a trap and that Rockov had something to do with it. His confusion was understandable given that he'd been questioned at *Navicula* about a woman he knew nothing about, only to be apprehended by that very woman as he left Tagg's Island. Harrison made the arrest and administered the necessary caution, but it was Louise who Brown directed his hostility towards.

'You ain't got no right to do this, you . . . you—'

'What am I, Colin? A filthy fucking whore, perhaps? Is that what you were about to call me?' Louise asked calmly.

Although the arrest was carried out with the minimum of fuss, word soon got back to Marko Rockov. One of his minions had been returning to *Navicula* as the handcuffed handyman was being helped into the back of the Rover, while a second, marked vehicle picked up the cycle. When he was told that one of the detectives was a woman, Rockov guessed that it would be the same one who'd come onto the island the previous evening.

This information was immediately conveyed to Jack Handysides. Problem solved. The police's interest was in Colin Brown not *Navicula*. They could relax.

Rockov said nothing about the idea he'd been formulating to deal with Jenny Daniels. Jack had enough to worry about. No need to trouble him with more information than he needed to have. In any case, Rockov knew the plan might need revising if Colin Brown remained in police custody. For it to work, he needed Brown to be released back into the community.

13

THE GOOD DOCTOR

All was not as it seemed with Dr Jamie Templeman MD, MBBS, MRCGP. The exposé he was writing on Jack Handysides was set for publication in the autumn. But, whilst he was contracted to produce 70,000 words by May to meet this deadline, he'd written only 10,000, and it was already April.

As for his relationship with Jenny Daniels, it seemed to be a match blessed by the gods. Since she'd moved into his terraced house in Fulham a year ago, the glamorous television star and her tall handsome beau had become fixtures on the social scene, photographed together at film premieres, charity functions and award presentations. The previous summer they'd been snapped amongst the Centre Court spectators at Wimbledon sitting next to Hugh Grant and Liz Hurley. The tabloids went into a frenzy, convinced the two couples had attended as a foursome; that Hugh and Liz and Jamie and Jenny were close friends. But, alas, their proximity was due simply to a random allocation of the seating arrangements. They'd hardly exchanged a word with the famous film star and his glamorous girlfriend.

Jamie and Jenny had become engaged in January, and were to be married in September at around the time the book was due to be published. But while Jenny Daniels was devoted to her fiancé, this devotion wasn't entirely reciprocated. Templeman had always found monogamy difficult. He'd been married before to another doctor. The marriage had lasted for two years until Jamie had been discovered in flagrante delicto by the then-Mrs Templeman at the surgery where they both worked. She had returned earlier than expected from a pharmaceutical conference abroad, popping in to pick up some medical notes on her way back from the airport. The surgery had been in darkness, but noticing a light on in a rest room, she'd found her husband on top of a half-naked medical student of Spanish extraction. As Mrs Templeman told her friends, Jamie always had liked to do it with the lights on.

The marriage finished, but the affair did not. Over the intervening seven years the medical student – Sarah Sanchez – had qualified, married (to a cardiothoracic surgeon rather than Templeman) and had two children. Dr Templeman left the practice and worked hard to become a specialist in prescription drug addiction and its ramifications for society.

It was in this expert capacity that he'd acquired a national profile, appearing as a talking head in documentaries and on the TV news and writing learned articles for *The Lancet*, the *Health Service Journal* and the broadsheets. Much had happened over those years, but he and Sanchez had never lost touch. They'd meet up for lunch intermittently, as they had on this April day in 1999. Invariably they'd end up, as they had now, in a hotel room making slow languorous love – with the lights on.

Sanchez knew all about Templeman's engagement to Jenny Daniels, well beyond what had been reported in the gossip columns. She'd become increasingly resentful of the hold that Jenny seemed to have over her cavalier lover. Jamie had never contemplated a future with Sarah. She was his confidante and whilst he found comfort in telling her his troubles, it had never been a two-way process. He'd never considered a future with Sarah, but Sarah dreamed of a future with him. When the engagement was announced she was distraught. Sure, she had married, but it had been for financial security rather than love. Her heart remained with Dr Jamie Templeman.

As for Templeman, nothing had changed since the escapade that had led to his divorce. The reason the good doctor struggled with monogamy was that he found unfaithfulness so thrilling. The risks were real, but they enhanced the pleasure. And there was pleasure – pleasures of the flesh, yes, but also the pleasure of conducting a secret existence. He was genuinely fond of Sarah Sanchez, but fondness was as far as it ever went for him – with his lover, and now with his fiancée, Jenny Daniels.

'For a man with a lot on his mind, you've not lost your touch,' Sarah said when the sex was over. She was sitting on the bed propped up against the pillows wearing only a blouse. Her lover stood by the window, half dressed, reading a message on the pager that had just burst into life, buzzing and vibrating on the bedside table. He'd told Sarah all about the BBC's stand-off with the Met on the *Crimesolve* episode he'd fronted and the difficulties he was having writing the book.

'It's very good of you to review my copulatory performance,' Templeman responded, 'but I might have pleased you even more without all this on my mind.'

'That's my boy – always looking to up his game. But surely you'll be given time to finish the book. They'll simply delay the publication date.'

'That very much depends on the reaction of the guy who just paged me.'

'Who's that?' Sarah asked.

'I haven't got time to explain and it's probably best that you don't know anyway,' Dr Templeman said, bending to kiss his lover goodbye.

'Farewell, Templeman.' Sarah always referred to her lover by his surname. 'Don't forget to get in touch the next time you get writer's block.'

He took the stairs down from their fourth-floor room, glancing again at his pager as he exited the hotel through its revolving doors. The message said, 'Meet me at six – usual place. J'

Templeman took the tube to Covent Garden, walked to a small bar off Long Acre and waited for Jeremy Van Wyk.

Jamie had told Sarah Sanchez more about himself than he'd ever told anyone – but he still hadn't told her everything. He'd told her about the research he'd done for his book; how he'd posed as a GP interested in selling prescription drugs to clandestine networks interested in distributing them . . . but he hadn't told her about his continuing links to organised crime.

It had all started a couple of years ago. Jamie had been at Bart's Hospital for an event involving three patients who'd become addicted to painkillers. They were presenting to an audience, composed mainly of clinicians, explaining the route to addiction, how to spot the signs and how best to find a way back to normality.

During the coffee break, a man had approached him saying that he represented a major American pharmaceutical company interested in working with Templeman. The rewards would be considerable, the man had stated confidently, before handing Jamie a card without a name – only an embossed London telephone number. 'Just ring the magic number,' the man had said.

Templeman, at this point, needed money. He no longer had the secure foundation of a regular practice, having had to leave the one he'd worked at with his former wife and branch out alone. He was now seeing only private patients, which was technically lucrative, but the divorce had been expensive and he'd rented a surgery in South Kensington that ate into his earnings. He badly needed to supplement his income with more than the modest fees he received for the odd magazine article or TV appearance. So he rang the magic number.

It was answered by a well-spoken woman who introduced herself as Rita. All he had to do was provide some blank prescription forms, and Rita would do the rest. It was a small-scale operation, but it earned Templeman enough cash to buy a better car and rent a nicer flat.

Two years ago, when he rang Rita's number for a second time, it had been answered by a man who told the doctor that Rita had retired and sold her business to a larger organisation. This outfit seemed to have more pharmacies involved and more clinicians dealing in controlled Class A drugs as well as anabolic steroids, hallucinogens, opioids and benzodiazepines. Templeman was drawn in deeper and deeper, soon providing drugs as well as blank prescription forms.

While the good doctor always claimed that it was in order to research his book that he'd become a drug dealer, it had happened the other way round. Having become so deeply involved in this illicit trade – including selling MDMA, as he'd said in the *Crimesolve* film – he'd accumulated enough material for a book and saw writing it as the only plausible way out of the mess he'd got himself into.

But he still couldn't escape the clutches of the man he was waiting to meet. The contact who'd replaced Rita had himself been replaced, twice. The criminal network had expanded, and Templeman's earnings increased accordingly. He could now afford a highly desirable house in Fulham, holidays in exotic locations and dinners at the swankiest West End restaurants.

Eighteen months ago, he'd rung the magic number to hear a new voice, with a South African accent. Jeremy Van Wyk took a much closer interest in Dr Templeman than the previous contacts, arranging to meet every few weeks in this Covent Garden bar, confiding in him about how the organisation worked; explaining how various small businesses had merged into a much larger organisation able to pay providers like Templeman more in exchange for greater productivity. According to Van Wyk, Dr Jamie Templeman was the most important provider of all. The higher his national profile, the greater his value to the organisation.

At first their relationship had been good; convivial even. The two men got on well. Jamie liked Jeremy's urbanity, his smooth professionalism, and the way he made drug dealing seem like any other form of commercial activity. When the press reported that the doctor had signed a book deal, Jeremy offered to help. It was Van Wyk who told Templeman about Jack Handysides, giving him all the information he needed to expose the man responsible for making London the epicentre of the international trade in illegal drugs. Contrary to what he'd said on camera, Templeman had never met Handysides. All Templeman knew about the man came from Van Wyk.

The South African felt that now Handysides had fulfilled his function of amalgamating the various gangs, it was Jeremy's boss, Marko Rockov, who had the ruthlessness necessary to maximise the opportunities this fusion presented. Van Wyck conceded that Rockov himself didn't see things that way, but he would, once Handysides was out of the way.

Van Wyk was clear he would much rather see Handysides removed by being arrested than run the risk of internecine warfare that would arise should someone try to assassinate him.

The book should do the job of exposing Handysides nicely, but Van Wyk was aware that Templeman hadn't written much of it, and this lethargy had created tensions that made their relationship less chummy.

The *Crimesolve* episode was now a better option for achieving these goals, but Handysides had got wind of it and told Rockov to simply sit on his hands and hope for the best. The South African saw this as a perfect illustration of why Handysides was too weak to run the empire he had created.

'Can't you persuade your boss that it's in his interest to help get Handysides banged up?' Templeman asked as they sat in a quiet corner of the near-deserted bar.

'No, I can't. And your girlfriend fronting the programme makes it more difficult.'

'Why?'

'That's best explained by one of the many Serbians I work with. That Kosovo appeal by Daniels infuriated them.'

'I hope your boss understands that Jenny is just a presenter. She doesn't commission these programmes,' Templeman said.

'There's a lot that needs to be explained to Rockov, and the reason I wanted to see you was to say that you need to be the one who does the explaining.'

'Me?' Templeman asked a little too shrilly.

Van Wyk put his finger to his lips. 'Yes, my friend, you. I've kept your involvement in our organisation to myself. It's time you came out of the shadows.'

'Hang on, Jeremy, I told you I don't want to get involved any deeper.'

Van Wyk took another slug of beer from the bottle he was holding and drew himself closer to the good doctor.

'You're up to your neck already, my friend. Since taking over your little portion of the business, I've kept a note of every transaction we've made, recorded every phone call. I've even arranged a few surreptitious photographs of us together. There's a lot more I could make you do if I chose to. All I'm asking is that you meet Rockov. That's not too much to ask, is it? I'll take you over to Tagg's Island. I'll tell my boss all about what you've done for us, and all you could yet do. You might begin by apologising for your girlfriend's appeal broadcast, and promising him it won't happen again. After that, we can go on to the main agenda item. I know Rockov as well as I know anyone. If we get him on board and persuade him of the advantages of dispensing with Jack Handysides, which means he's helping rather than hindering that process, I'm certain it will work.'

'And if I refuse?' Templeman asked.

'Somebody is going to get exposed here, Jamie. You need to make sure it isn't you.'

14

MANGAN IS TAKEN OFF THE CASE

Detective Chief Inspector Sean Meredith watched through the two-way mirror as Colin Brown was being interrogated by DS Harrison and DC Louise Mangan. It was Louise's first experience of attending such an event as a detective asking the questions rather than as a uniformed officer guarding the door. Meredith couldn't help but be impressed by the professional way she was conducting herself, speaking clearly, patiently repeating the many points the suspect claimed not to understand, maintaining steady eye contact despite Brown's shifty demeanour. There was a preternatural calm about the detective constable that seemed to be having a tranquillising effect on the normally volatile Detective Sergeant Harrison sitting beside her. Meredith was still insisting that Brown only be questioned concerning the attack on Darcy Kramer the previous evening and on Jenny Daniels ten days ago. Told that Daniels had identified him, Brown's illogical hatred of the TV presenter bubbled to the surface. He couldn't deny that he'd sworn at the TV star after having almost crashed into her. But this was of little importance given Daniels' refusal to press charges. Questioning turned to the latest incident. On this Brown was floundering, unable to say where he'd been at half-past ten the previous evening. His lawyer complained that her client would need more time to collect his thoughts, that he was being harassed. But this complaint was difficult to sustain against Louise Mangan's unthreatening serenity. Exuding sympathy, Louise told Brown to take as long as he needed before answering.

Harrison asked if Brown had a bike. He did. Was it a drop-handle sports bike? It was. Had he been riding it yesterday evening? He had been.

Meredith, watching through the window, felt a break-through approaching. A charge in connection with Darcy Kramer would be enough to keep Brown in custody, perhaps giving more time for him to be questioned over the other attacks, although Meredith remained confident that this most recent attack was a reproduction and that Darnell Thomas was responsible for the originals.

Once again Harrison asked Colin Brown for his where-abouts the previous evening, provoking an even greater look of confusion on the suspect's thin face.

'She knows where I was,' Brown said eventually, point-ing at Louise. 'She was there as well.'

DCI Meredith moved closer to the mirror, his interest intensified by the revelation that DC Mangan and the reprobate she was interviewing had a connection.

'I was with you until around 9.30 p.m. We're keen to know where you were an hour later.'

Brown looked around the room, as though he might find a suitable answer somewhere on the cream walls of the interrogation suite.

He lifted a glass of water to gulp a couple of mouthfuls. 'Er, I don't know. Asleep, I suppose,' he muttered eventually.

'Got him,' thought Meredith. 'No alibi, a record of assaulting women, rides a sports bike with drop-handlebars and the presenter of *Crimesolve* no less can identify him.'

But his triumphalism was premature. The suspect was thinking, eyes closed, brows knitted.

When he spoke again, it was as if a fog had lifted. 'I know where I was. I was with Sage on Tagg's Island, that's where I was.'

Under further questioning Brown explained that when he'd reached his house in East Molesey, he'd remembered the coat that he'd left neatly folded on the plastic chair. He'd gone back to Tagg's Island immediately. Sage's partner had invited him in for a cup of tea. Sage had joined them, and they'd nattered away until half-eleven.

'His bird was there as well. So two people can say where I was last night at the time you're asking about.'

Louise gave a passing thought to this reference to a female occupant of the *Inner Peace*, which confirmed the suspicion she'd formed after seeing the bra on the washing line. A woman who obviously hadn't gone abroad with Sage to Argentina, and hadn't been around when Louise had gone round for tea.

They'd check out Brown's story, of course, but it seemed that they'd need to look elsewhere for the man who'd assaulted Darcy Kramer. It was certainly Brown who'd contemplated attacking Jenny Daniels, but that attack had been averted and Daniels hadn't even reported it. Colin Brown was in the clear.

When Harrison and Louise left the interview room they were confronted by a furious DCI Meredith who wanted to know who the hell Sage was and what Louise thought she was up to by visiting him 'on that bloody island' the previous evening. Harrison stepped in immediately to deflect the attack, explaining that he'd arranged for Louise to take an hour or two off to go to Tagg's Island.

'Why did you want to go there?' Meredith asked Louise. There was an awkward silence.

Neither Harrison nor Louise felt it wise to mention her suspicion that Meredith had charged the wrong man and that she was following a theory already dismissed by her DCI as a fantasy.

'Tom and I are thinking of buying a houseboat,' Louise announced suddenly. 'I went early yesterday morning before coming on duty to look at a couple of nice ones that are up for sale and Ralph let me pop back to see this guy Sage who'd promised to give me more info on how house-boats are serviced and inspected. Colin Brown happened to be working on Sage's boat. Not sure yet if we'll buy one, but me and Tom have always fancied a life afloat.'

Louise Mangan felt guilty. She'd told another lie.

DCI Meredith made it clear to Harrison and Louise that their work on the Beast of Hampton Court case was over. They must now concentrate on finding the Streatham safe-cracker. Operation Incisive had been disbanded, and if Louise wanted to visit Tagg's Island she should do so on her own time not the Met's. Ralph Harrison received a dressing-down but as he told Louise afterwards, it was painless and left no scars.

Colin Brown's alibi would be checked and verified, and in the meantime Brown's solicitor had worked through the dates of the other Hampton Court attacks, producing credible explanations for where her client had been on three of the dates in question.

At the time of the Bushy Park attack in early March, when the girl had almost been strangled, Brown had been on an outward-bound course in Scotland arranged by his probation officer. Meredith had taken great delight in travelling over to Streatham to convey this information in person to Harrison and Louise at their new location.

'But he definitely attacked Jenny Daniels,' Louise said in response to this news, a bit too defiantly for her own good.

'You mean he engaged in a bit of horseplay,' Meredith replied calmly. 'And Miss Daniels has sensibly refused to take it further.'

No woman would have described what Brown did and said as 'horseplay', Louise thought before pressing her point further. 'But we don't need her to press charges in a case like this,' she pleaded.

'In a case like what? Presuming his alibi checks out, Colin Brown didn't attack Darcy Kramer the other night. And he's not guilty of the attempted murder in Bushy Park. Darnell Thomas will go to trial in September for that assault and five others. We don't know who attacked Darcy Kramer, only that it wasn't Colin Brown. At a time when we need to concentrate on finding the person who kidnapped Tiffany Mordaunt and attacked Darcy, you want us to waste time on a petty criminal whose fantasies are probably the most dangerous thing about him. No, Louise – NO. We'll keep Brown's name on file, but we won't waste any more time in the blind alley that you've tried to lead us down.'

*

'Well, he does have a point,' Tom Mangan said, twisting another mouthful of spaghetti onto his fork. He'd suggested taking Louise out to dinner on this precious evening when neither of them was working, and Tom's mother had been available to babysit.

In the early years of their relationship, they'd resolved not to discuss work when out for dinner, but that resolution had long fallen victim to circumstance. As their careers developed, they had fewer opportunities to relax together and when they did, work surfaced as the natural topic of conversation – the thing that they most wanted to talk about apart from their children. Tonight, Chloe and Michelle had been discussed over the starter followed by a bit of cursory chatter about a software problem known as the millennium bug that, it was predicted, would shut down police computer systems at the turn of the century. By the time they were tucking into their Spaghetti Bolognese (for Tom) and Chicken Milanese (for Louise) they were well into the subject of work.

'What do you mean, "he has a point"?' Louise asked, eyes flashing confrontationally, as she reached for her wine.

'I mean precisely that. Sorry, love, I agree with you about attacks on women not being taken seriously enough, but Meredith isn't dropping the case. He's just putting you and Ralph onto other work. He could have disciplined you both for that trip to Tagg's Island.'

'Darnell Thomas wouldn't be in custody if we hadn't apprehended him,' Louise reminded her husband. 'But the evidence against him is so superficial. I can't understand why the DPP is still pursuing it.'

'Except that one of the victims picked him out in a line-up,' Tom pointed out.

'Having never previously mentioned that her assailant was black,' Louise said dismissively.

'But Thomas was wearing that distinctive cycle helmet.'

'So was the guy who I saw turning onto Tagg's Island that night.'

'No, Louise, you didn't see him turning onto Tagg's Island. You saw him cycling towards you along the A308 and assumed that's where he went.'

'But Meredith's treating the Tiffany Mordaunt case as if it's unconnected.'

'Love, you know the statistics; someone goes missing every ninety seconds. The fact that Tiffany went missing on a Friday evening in Hampton Court doesn't mean she's a victim of the barmy biker.'

Husband and wife chewed their food in silence for a few minutes.

'Oh, I don't know, Tom. I just think it's all too pat,' Louise said after this reflective pause. 'It took ages for the Met to take these attacks seriously and when they do, hey presto, they charge a black guy – the Met's two biggest weaknesses, women and ethnic minorities.'

'If the Macpherson Report doesn't lead to change, nothing will,' Tom said. 'We need more black police officers and more women. At least they've scrapped the WPC title.'

'They can change all the titles they like, it's the culture that needs to change. Let me tell you what happened to me at Kingston yesterday. Some greasy git of a Detective Inspector asked me if I could help him do up his flies because he'd heard I'd been working on the Hampton Court problem. Get it? Hampton caught?'

'Did you report him?' her husband asked angrily.

'Tom, you really have no idea. All his mates, including the senior officers, were laughing like drains – I knew exactly what response I'd get – "It's just a bit of banter Louise, can't you take a joke?" I told him to fuck off and you know what, Tom? I'm more likely to be disciplined for saying that to him than he is for saying what he said to me.'

Tom reached for his wife's hand.

'Things must have been bad for you to swear,' he said soothingly. 'It'll change, Lou, believe me – it will change.'

They held hands across the table until Louise broke the silence.

'I realise this will come as a shock, and please don't ask me to explain. But if you run into Sean Meredith, you need to tell him that we're thinking of buying a houseboat.'

15

THE STREATHAM BANK ROBBERY

Back at work in Streatham the next day, Louise tried to put Tagg's Island out of her mind, but it nagged away like a sore tooth.

Colin Brown was bound to tell Sage that she was a police officer, which wouldn't have mattered so much if she hadn't started to consider the man with green eyes to be a friend who she'd deceived for longer than was necessary.

She also felt that she had unfinished business on the island, namely Patrick Venn who rode a sports bike and was out riding on the night Darcy Kramer had been attacked. It was a piece of loose soil from a furrow that Louise had ploughed alone. She talked about it to Ralph Harrison, asking if he thought other members of the Operation Incisive team could be persuaded to follow it up. She also wondered if there was a way she could make a formal submission about the suspicious activity at *Navicula*. But Harrison pointed out that whilst her report about seeing another cyclist that night remained on file, the investigation was dormant, and the latest attack was unlikely to resuscitate it; not while DCI Meredith was convinced that all previous assaults were the work of Darnell Thomas. As for Tagg's Island, she needed to move on.

'But the guys in that huge houseboat are so obviously

dodgy characters, strutting around like extras in a Sylvester Stallone movie.'

'Dodgy characters seem to be attracted to your island, Louise,' Harrison said. 'And your mate is one of them. Who says *he* wasn't the biker you saw?'

'Sage would have had to have cycled from Buenos Aires,' Louise replied airily.

'But you only think he was in Argentina because he told you that. The first rule of being a detective is to set aside assumptions. What matters are facts and the fact is that you know very little about Sapphire or whatever his name is.'

Louise knew Harrison was right. She needed to put Tagg's Island out of her mind.

'I know how you feel,' Ralph told her. 'When I was younger and more idealistic, I'd obsess about cases I was involved in. But I soon realised that if you want to be a good detective you have to insulate yourself against all that. And you, Louise, have the potential to be a very good detective. Right now, you need to concentrate on today's job, not yesterday's.'

Again, she accepted that her Detective Sergeant was speaking sound common sense. Meredith had ensured that their only remaining connection to Hampton Court was as the arresting officers, which required only the formality of a court appearance when Darnell Thomas came to trial. For now, however, he expected them to focus on the job in hand – a job that had its own fascination.

Louise had never been involved in a bank robbery investigation before. The team that she and Harrison joined was led by Detective Inspector Damian James, who specialised in robberies of this kind. His main assistant was another specialist, police staff member Iris Theakston. She'd been recruited direct from academia, primarily for her civil engineering qualifications, and was introduced by DI James as his Senior Service Engineer.

'Sounds like an expert in cigarette production,' Harrison quipped quietly to Louise.

They were attending a case conference at Streatham police station, sitting on threadbare canvas chairs in a stuffy room with a single-bar electric heater. Nine or ten other personnel assigned to the case were milling around when James began the meeting. He told the team that the heist had been so well planned that he thought they could all guess the likely suspect.

'The precision, the know-how, the sheer audacity – it all points to Basil,' the DI said as if chairing a committee deciding on an awards presentation.

Louise nudged Ralph sitting next to her.

'Basil who?' she whispered.

'Basil Brush,' Harrison replied, earning himself a dig in the ribs.

The Streatham branch of Lloyds Bank announced the importance of its function through the grandeur of its architecture. The fine old building occupied a corner of Streatham High Road at the junction with Streatham Hill. After DI James's introduction, Iris Theakston took centre stage, explaining that in the week prior to the robbery the area around the bank had been disrupted by road works; a common feature on this main route into central London. Workmen had begun digging up the road outside

Woolworths, about a hundred metres down from the bank on a Monday morning.

Affected shops had been visited by a tall, well-dressed, distinguished-looking man in his early forties who flashed an identity card and explained that there'd been an issue with submerged power cables. He claimed that his men would work around the clock to fix the problem, and expected it to take three days at most. All the necessary legal notices were posted on lampposts and telegraph poles, barriers were erected and, beneath a canopy at the centre of the site, the promised intensive effort to fix the problem had begun. The distinguished-looking man in charge was obviously prepared to get his hands dirty, attending daily, dressed in overalls and protective equipment and working beneath the canopy.

'They tunnelled to a spot immediately below the bank's strongroom,' Iris Theakston explained to the team, 'and then burrowed up using hydraulic shovels.'

'Didn't they trigger any alarms?' Harrison asked.

'No,' DI James pronounced bluntly before his colleague could respond. 'A less audacious thief would have broken in at the weekend when the bank was closed. They'd have grabbed whatever they could and left in a hurry before there was a response to the alarms. But Basil knew that on a working day there'd be too much staff activity for the internal alarms to be switched on.'

'That's right,' said Iris Theakston, seizing the narrative again. 'The thieves broke in sometime on Wednesday morning. They used a jackhammer to break open over a hundred safe-deposit boxes, taking cash and items with an estimated value of two million pounds back with them through the tunnel they'd made. The strongroom was left looking as it had before they broke in; all the safe-deposit boxes were closed, and a heavy piece of metal shelving had been pulled across the hole they'd arrived through.'

'But all those strongrooms are monitored by CCTV,' one of the detectives said. 'Wasn't anybody watching the screens?'

'They were, but our Basil seems to have developed a new piece of wizardry,' DI James interjected before his colleague could draw breath. 'We still don't know exactly how he did it, but the CCTV was turned back by a week so that the footage on the screens that day was from the previous week, when all was as it should have been in the strongroom.'

A stillness descended as the team of detectives, all of whom – apart from Harrison and Louise – were experienced in this line of police work, engaged in a collective moment of quiet admiration.

'So given all that, how can we be so sure that the robbery took place on Wednesday morning?' Louise asked, breaking the silence.

'We only know because the disruption to traffic ended at Wednesday lunchtime,' DI James said. 'The workmen tidied everything up, loading all their equipment, together with the traffic barriers, into a white transit van. The van was also, of course, a useful vehicle for transporting their loot. There are currently no cameras along Streatham High Road so we don't have the vehicle registration. But we can piece together the sequence of events from the testimony of several local shopkeepers. The gang leader – that tall, well-dressed gentleman who used his charm so effectively – apparently waved a cheery farewell to a bus inspector who'd taken a particular interest in the progress of the repairs.'

'The robbery wasn't discovered until 4 o'clock that afternoon,' Iris Theakston added, 'when staff entered the strongroom for a routine deposit.'

'No fingerprints?' asked an overweight detective standing by the door.

'Nope. The professor here is one of our top guys on forensics. He can tell you himself.'

DI James gave the floor to a middle-aged man of Asian descent whose silver-grey hair was brushed back neatly, away from his bushy eyebrows.

'We did a full sweep of the strongroom as well as each individual safe-deposit box. There were no fingerprints. Whilst that's not unusual – assuming this was a professional gang, of course – we had hoped to find some DNA. It's a new science, and even the most experienced villains have struggled to understand how minute droplets from a sneeze, for instance, can identify an individual with an amazing level of accuracy. But there were no droplets, no saliva, no strands of hair – nothing.'

'Sorry, I should have introduced Professor Assem Bukhari properly,' DI James said. 'He's one of the Met's leading experts on DNA. He led the team that set up the database, didn't you, Prof?'

The professor smiled demurely.

'But here's the thing,' the DI continued, 'although we've had that DNA database for four or five years, the chief suspect in this case, Basil Bennett, isn't on it. The last sentence he served ended in 1990, well before DNA samples were taken routinely from prisoners, so even if we did find DNA samples, we couldn't have checked them against Basil's.'

'But we can arrest him for this, surely?' DS Harrison suggested. 'If he was the guy who spoke to the shopkeepers, they'd recognise him. Leaving the theft of two million quid to one side, we can charge him with deception, or fraud, or giving false information.'

'How about for digging up the fucking A23?' the overweight officer by the door suggested.

'Basil will have looked very different,' DI James responded. 'We know how good he is at disguise. The bus inspector said the man in charge of the roadworks had a full head of dark hair, and a nose like Cyrano de Bergerac's. The last image we have of Basil Bennett is of a bald man with a conk that can't even be described as prominent. We've already questioned some of Basil's known associates, all of whom have strong alibis, as will Basil. The time lag between the theft and its discovery leaves plenty of ambiguity to exploit over where he was and what he was doing.'

'You have to admire the cunning old sod,' said one of the other detectives.

'Yeah, he's an artiste, is our Basil,' the DI said.

'I can see that you chaps have a lot of admiration for Mr Bennett, but he is a thief. A very clever thief, but a thief, nevertheless,' Iris Theakston said vexatiously. 'This all sounds a bit matey to me.'

DI James rolled his eyes to convey to his colleagues the quiet fortitude required of him in working with this woman.

'Perhaps we "chaps" have a better understanding of the

criminal mind than a wet-behind-the-ears girl who's fresh out of college and knows nothing about policing,' he said.

'And perhaps you don't,' Louise called out as Theakston's cheeks flushed with embarrassment. 'Iris has made a perfectly reasonable point. Why don't you answer it instead of treating us to the kind of sexist bigotry that we women in the force are sick of listening to.'

DI James was visibly taken aback. He'd read enough circulars from the Met's personnel department to understand how attitudes were changing regarding something called 'employee diversity' and the need to treat women in the force with respect.

'What's your name?' he asked.

'DC Louise Mangan. Sir.'

'Well, DC Mangan, I'll tell you what I'm going to do.' James spoke slowly to suppress the angrier response he'd have preferred to make. 'We know where Basil Bennett lives – in a nice suburban Romford semi with his wife and two kids. I'm sending you and Harrison to arrest him.'

'But I thought we didn't have enough on Basil to charge him,' said the fat detective by the door.

'We don't. But who said anything about charging him? We only need a bit of superficial to arrest him – and, if I'm not mistaken, we are fully entitled to take the DNA of those arrested but not charged. We might not get Basil today, but at least we'll get his DNA.'

'So, you think I was wrong to remonstrate with James.' Louise asked, breaking the silence as she and Harrison drove towards Romford. It was more of a statement than a question.

'Listen, Louise, I think you were perfectly entitled to be cross about the way he was performing, I just don't want you getting a reputation as some kind of women's lib agitator. You're at the beginning of your career, not the end. If people like Meredith and James take against you, you'll be back in uniform before you know it.'

'But if I stay silent at moments like that – and God knows I've held my tongue enough times already – it just feeds the culture that everyone from the Home Secretary to the Commissioner say needs to change.'

They'd driven a few further miles before Harrison responded.

'I just worry for you, that's all. It's fine for me. Having a gobby DC working with me has its advantages.'

'I take offence at the "gobby", but how do you mean?'

'Well, there is no doubt that if it wasn't for your outburst, one of the more senior detectives would have been assigned to make this arrest. Thanks to you, instead of being stuck at Streatham shuffling paper, I'm on my way to meet the legendary Basil Bennett.'

'So, you think he sent me to make the arrest as a punishment?' Louise asked.

'No, as a penitence. Your intervention struck home. You do have to concede that arresting Bennett to get his DNA onto the database is a masterstroke,' Ralph replied. 'Or should that be "mistress-stroke"? At least it's taken your mind away from Hampton Court.'

'Not entirely,' Louise said ruefully. 'I had a chat with Professor Bukhari about DNA before we left. It was easy to turn the conversation from us going to arrest Basil to get his DNA to my suspicion that an important piece of evidence in a serious assault case hadn't been checked for DNA.'

'You mean the material from Darcy Kramer's jacket?'

'Yes, and Professor Bukhari is going to check it out personally. He's pretty high up in forensic circles, and says that it's been difficult to ensure that all relevant items are tested as a matter of course and if there's been an oversight it needs to be corrected.'

'Didn't they get a fingernail from the attack on Darcy Kramer?' Harrison asked. 'How long does this stuff last before it fades away?'

'I asked the same question. The Prof says it depends on the conditions it's been preserved in. The forensic team will have recognised its significance and hopefully the guys they passed it on to will as well. If not, we may never find it. That's where the problems occur apparently, between the stuff being found at the crime scene and it being logged and filed. He's going to give me a call to let me know in the next day or so.'

'Won't Meredith find out that you're interfering in a case he's removed you from?'

'I told the Prof I had Meredith's full authority and if this comes to anything it must be reported to him direct. Even Sean can't complain about the correction of an oversight which may produce valuable evidence?'

Harrison, who had no answer, nodded sagely.

As Harrison and Louise pulled up in their unmarked Rover outside Basil Bennett's house, the man they'd come to arrest was mowing the lawn. When Louise had asked Ralph earlier why they were going to arrest such a notorious criminal without any backup he'd told her that Bennett had never been known to use force. The absence of violence was why his crimes were classified as burglary rather than robbery.

'Mr Bennett?' Harrison shouted, having to make himself heard above the noise of the petrol-fuelled lawnmower. The tall man, dressed in brown corduroy trousers, carried on cutting the grass whilst turning his head to address his visitors.

'To what do I owe this visit by Her Majesty's constabulary?' he asked.

'Can we go inside?' Louise asked, presuming that Basil's long criminal career had enabled him to spot a cop car regardless of whether it was marked or not.

'I don't want to be unhospitable,' Bennett said, 'but I do wish to complete the tasks set for me by Mrs Bennett. She would be mollified if she thought I was slacking.'

Louise had been told about Basil's strained relationship with the English language and how, to appear more articulate than he was, he used a vocabulary that contained many words that were either inappropriate or non-existent.

After the formal introductions, Harrison proceeded to make the arrest, citing the bank robbery in Streatham and reminding Bennett of his rights in the specified way but still having to shout over the putt-putt of the machine. Basil finished cutting the final strip of the large well-kept lawn before turning to address his captors.

'It will be my absolute pleasure to accompany you. I only ask that we go to Romford nick to do this rather than one further up town. I need to get back to my chores as quickly as possible.'

Harrison agreed and arrangements were made for Bennett's solicitor to meet them there. As Louise drove with the prisoner sitting on the back seat next to Harrison, Basil began a conversation with her.

'My twelve-year-old daughter has just started to talk about her ambitions in life. She says she'd like to join the Metropolitan Police; do you think it's a good career choice?' he asked.

'Yes, definitely. We need more women.'

'And may I ask if it was always your vacation?'

Louise, resisting the temptation to correct him, said that she did consider it to be her 'vacation'.

'But doesn't it trouble you to be so dishonest?'

'I don't think we are dishonest,' Louise responded.

'But you're being dishonest now, aren't you? I've only been to Streatham once in my life and that was when I was a teenager. I took a girlfriend on a date to the ice rink there – lovely girl, she skated while I sat in the café drinking hot chocolate. It was not a happy afternoon.'

Bennett didn't come back from this reverie to finish his point until they were almost at the station.

'You have no evidence that I was involved in that bank robbery, and I doubt you'll even bother to question me. It's my NDA that you're after.'

He may have mixed up the initials, Louise thought, but the wily old goat has got us bang to rights.

16

TEMPLEMAN MAKES HIS CASE

It was raining when Jeremy Van Wyk met Dr Jamie Templeman at Hampton Court station. An April shower beat against the stretched fabric of the umbrella that Van Wyk held as the two men left the shelter of the concourse. The early evening return of commuters was at its zenith, and nothing was said until they'd crossed the Thames and were clear of the crowd.

'I've rolled the wicket,' Van Wyk stated as they turned onto Hampton Court Road. 'Marko is looking forward to meeting you. I've told him that you're crucial to the decision as to whether the programme goes ahead or not and that you're keen to hear his side of the argument. It will just be you, me and him – and don't forget to pretend to be sympathetic to the Serbian cause, even if you're not. He needs to know that Jenny Daniels was only doing what she was paid to do with that appeal. Tell him it's not something she feels strongly about – it was a charity appeal not a party-political broadcast.'

'Is it that important? Shouldn't I just concentrate on the *Crimesolve* episode?' Templeman asked.

'He's obsessed about what he regards as a personal attack on his homeland. And I worry that he's planning something nasty for your girlfriend.'

'What do you mean? Surely he wouldn't do her any harm?' Templeman pleaded.

'There are plenty of Serbian nationalists around him who would; and there's a guy who does odd jobs around the place that Marko's suddenly spending lots of time with. I keep coming across the two of them whispering in corners. Currently he has two complaints against Jenny: that she's insulted all Serbians, and is about to expose Handysides. We need to convince him that on the first, he's wrong, and on the second he's misguided.'

'Okay, I'll do my best. Anything else?' Templeman asked.

'He has to understand that Handysides is too weak to hold the alliance together; that naming him would be in his own best interests. Remember, he believes that you have inside knowledge from the police and security service, as well as from other criminal networks here and abroad. He's convinced that you're a world leading expert on the drugs trade.'

'I probably am,' Templeman pleaded plaintively.

'Don't believe your own propaganda, or the rubbish that your publisher is no doubt preparing to put on the cover of the book. I'll bow to your knowledge of medicine . . . But on the rest? You only know what I've told you.'

Jamie Templeman's handsome features were drawn, his eyes bleary and bloodshot. He was labouring under an even greater weight of anguish than usual, as prior to this meeting, Jenny Daniels had finally found out about his womanising. Arriving home from work the previous evening he'd been ambushed with a question delivered quietly and calmly in the enormous kitchen of his house in Fulham. Was it true that on Tuesday, 13 April he'd had lunch with a woman and then spent the afternoon with her at the Regent Hotel?

It had been like a courtroom scene, with Jenny as the prosecuting barrister. He'd issued an emphatic denial, claiming to be offended that she could even contemplate such treachery. But Jenny produced the signed restaurant bill and hotel receipt.

He'd quickly concocted a lie – that after lunch with a client he felt so ill he'd been forced to check into a hotel to rest and recover. He knew how she worried about his health, so had kept it to himself. It was the best he could come up with on the spur of the moment.

The scene of what followed was still playing in Templeman's mind like a VHS tape. Jenny's raised voice as she recited the charges against him, standing in that spacious kitchen, her sharp words pinging off the hanging copper pans like bullets. Two words in particular. A name: Sarah Sanchez.

Jenny knew all about Sarah, and nothing he said could retrieve the situation. Sarah was a former colleague, he explained; she was married; yes, he'd met her for lunch, but no, she hadn't gone with him to the hotel. He felt he'd done enough to extricate himself, but Jenny seemed to have inside knowledge.

Who from? Not Sarah herself surely?

When the argument was at its most heated, he'd accused Jenny of spying on him, which made things worse. She'd screamed her denial and resentment at Templeman trying to turn the argument against her. In the end she admitted her source – Carl Burnett, the *Crimesolve* producer and Templeman's predecessor in Jenny's affections. Carl Burnett must be in cahoots with Sarah Sanchez; how else would he have gained possession of the hotel and restaurant receipts?

He'd have liked to have questioned Jenny further, but his fiancée had packed a bag and returned to her house in East Molesey. She'd been blocking his calls all day. While he was over this way, he was determined to go round to see her after his meeting with Rockov – to appear on her doorstep, dripping wet in the rain; contrite and pathetic, hoping she'd take pity.

These thoughts occupied Templeman's mind as the two men walked along Hampton Court Road, crossed the little bridge onto Tagg's Island, and took the path that led round to *Navicula* on the inner lagoon.

The meeting was to be held in Rockov's office – a small, masculine space on the lower deck, all mahogany and dark leather. As Templeman and Van Wyk entered, another man was coming out.

Templeman had never seen Colin Brown before, and so was unaware that he was passing the man who'd terrified his girlfriend just a few days earlier.

Marko Rockov stood up from behind a large desk that took up half the floorspace, to welcome his guest. 'Jeremy has told me all about your contribution to our business, Dr Templeman,' he said, ushering the doctor towards a chair opposite. Then, rather than resuming his seat, he placed his backside on the edge of the desk so that he loomed over his visitor throughout the interview. He asked if the *Crimesolve* programme on Handysides was likely to go ahead.

'Can't be sure yet,' Templeman responded. 'The April programme is due to air in . . . let's see, today's Friday, the programme's monthly slot is on a Tuesday, so it's due to be broadcast in eleven days' time, on the twenty-seventh. The Beeb is still paranoid about upsetting the Met, and the legal people are in a tizzy. But I remain optimistic; mainly because I think professional pride will trump fear of the establishment. The BBC has a choice, we either go with a broadcast that will make the front pages or we screen an insipid programme about car theft.'

'And Jeremy here tells me that you think it would be in my best interests if it went ahead?'

Templeman took his cue, launching into the arguments he'd concocted with Van Wyk, mixing fact and fantasy. He told Rockov how Handysides had been brilliant at bringing the various criminal gangs together, but that he was less adept at the day-to-day running of the vast organisation he had created. He cited several incidents where, had Handysides been more ruthless, problems could have been resolved rather than allowed to fester.

This last argument struck a chord with Rockov – as Van Wyk had told Templeman it would – because Handysides had specifically instructed him not to intervene in trying to prevent the programme being broadcast.

Templeman went on to assert that if Handysides was still in charge when the police and crime agencies eventually got their act together, the entire project could be swept away because Jack didn't have the determination to defend it as aggressively as Rockov would.

Templeman flattered his host shamelessly. He talked about the need to knock heads together within the organisation. 'Jack is too squeamish. He's not a violent man and the time will soon come when violence is going to be necessary. His obsession is with protecting his anonymity, not with taking this powerful consortium to the next level. If this TV programme isn't broadcast, your business faces a period of slow decline with Jack at the helm. If it does go ahead, the ship sails on under a new captain capable of navigating the stormier waters ahead,' the good doctor concluded, pleased with his peroration.

Jeremy Van Wyk gave a discreet thumbs-up to Templeton as his boss removed his buttocks from the edge of the desk, and walked round its perimeter to resume his normal seat.

While Rockov had pretended to be impressed by the arguments, in reality he was unmoved. In fact, he was now even more determined that this episode of *Crimesolve* should never be broadcast. Nothing the doctor said had changed his mind.

Sure, Rockov knew Jack Handysides could hardly be described as ruthless but the extraordinary alliances he'd made succeeded in the main because of Jack's unthreatening approach rather than in spite of it.

If Handysides went, those lucrative voyages down the Thames to the incinerator would go with him, as would many other projects for which Jack was personally responsible. But beyond these arguments lay one essential fact; Marko Rockov no longer wanted to be top dog. The flame of ambition that once burned so fiercely in his heart had died. All he wanted now was to share his peaceful aquatic existence on Tagg's Island with his family once they arrived from Belgrade.

But in addition to being unpersuaded by Templeman's arguments, Rockov continued to harbour a grudge against the doctor's girlfriend.

'You live with the presenter of this television programme, I believe?' he asked, having authorised Van Wyk to pour the whiskies.

'With Jenny Daniels? Yes, I do – did – do,' Templeman stuttered, painful memories from the previous evening suddenly resurrected, but anxious not to reveal his domestic upheaval.

'Jeremy tells me she had nothing to do with the film about my homeland.'

'Yes, that's right. It was a charity appeal that she was asked to present. She really has no animosity towards Serbia and doesn't understand the Kosovo situation. Jenny just read the script that had been written for her. Indeed she . . .'

Rockov had raised his hand to silence his guest. 'I know, I know. It was stupid of me to be so resentful. I want to send her some flowers. Can we have her address? She lives with you, no?'

'She's had to go back to her own house just up the road from here in East Molesey for a week or so. Best send them there,' Templeman said, scribbling the address on a notepad that Rockov had pushed across the desk to him.

The three men drank their whiskies in an atmosphere so convivial it convinced Van Wyk that his mission had been accomplished. And he said as much to Templeman as they parted an hour later.

'Marko only gets the whisky out for special occasions, and only drinks when he's happy. Thanks to you I think Handysides just lost an ally.'

It was still raining and the South African offered to get one of Rockov's minions to drive Templeman home, but the good doctor declined. He said the train would be quicker given the congestion at this time of night, but he actually intended to walk to Jenny Daniels' house nearby.

They parted on the bridge. Van Wyk returned to *Navicula* where he found Colin Brown ensconced once more in Rockov's office. The two men were talking conspiratorially, heads close together. Their conversation ceased as soon as Van Wyk appeared. Rockov took something off the desk quickly, placing it in a Tesco carrier bag that it had probably emerged from.

'Not now, Jeremy,' Rockov said. 'Can't you see I'm busy?'

Van Wyk withdrew, closing the door behind him. His boss must have assumed that he'd walked Templeman back to the station and that he'd have longer to take advantage of his absence. It was fifteen minutes before the door opened again and the South African, who'd been having a second whisky in the lounge area above, was summoned. Colin Brown and the Tesco bag had gone.

'Your doctor friend made a good case,' Rockov said as his chief of staff entered. 'Make sure he tells us as soon as he knows if Handysides is going to be in the next episode of *Crimesolve*. In the meantime, Jack is going to pay us that follow-up visit he's been promising.'

'That's if he hasn't had his cover blown by then, I presume,' Van Wyk observed.

'He'll be coming over next Saturday; a week tomorrow. According to Templeman, the TV programme will be shown a few days later, on the Tuesday – so it should be alright. We need to spend next week preparing ourselves, because Jack tells me there'll be another consignment of goodies coming up the Thames on the barge that evening.'

Van Wyk was worried, firstly because Rockov's attitude was not that of a man preparing to take command of the Handysides empire, and secondly because he'd caught a long enough glimpse of the item that had been so speedily placed in the Tesco bag to recognise it as a gun.

Templeman tried to ring Jenny to inform her of his imminent arrival, but she was still ignoring his calls. He tried the landline, to no avail. When he arrived at her house it was in darkness. Jenny obviously wasn't back home yet.

Templeman decided to wait, grateful for the umbrella that Van Wyk had pressed upon him. He spent thirty minutes walking up and down the street, pausing every so often under a lamppost almost opposite Jenny's house. A car pulled up, Jenny's car, out of which she stepped – his fiancée . . . and someone else. There was a man with her.

Templeman stepped back into the shadows with the umbrella low across his head, hiding his face. He watched as Jenny and her passenger crossed the pavement, coats held over heads to protect them from the downpour. It was only when they went into the house and turned on the light in the passage that he could see the man she was with. It was Carl Burnett.

The door was shut; curtains were drawn. There would be nothing more to see and nothing more he needed to see.

Templeman could only wonder at the speed with which the woman he was engaged to had recruited a replacement. What to do next? He thought about knocking on the door and making a scene but, in a rare moment of introspection, realised that it was his unfaithfulness that had created this mess. He had always known Jenny wouldn't stand for any nonsense; she'd told him often enough about how highly she valued fidelity and how intolerant of any transgression she would be.

The rain stopped. Templeman walked away, as distraught about the collapse of a relationship as it was possible for him to be.

17

A VISIT IS CONTEMPLATED

Basil Bennett, having been questioned for two hours, had been released and returned to his Romford semi. He claimed to have been with his family at their caravan in Walton-on-the-Naze on the Wednesday when the bank had been broken into. A small collection of timed and dated items had been produced to prove it: a parking receipt, supermarket bill paid with his credit card, and a photo taken on the seafront with Mrs Bennett's new digital camera. There was even footage of Basil lingering in front of the only CCTV camera known to exist in the small Essex coastal resort.

None of this evidence meant that it was impossible for him to have been in Streatham when the crime was committed, but owing to the lack of precision about when that actually was, it proved to be enough. On top of this, there was the personal testimony of several neighbours on the caravan site, all of whom seemed to be exceedingly friendly with the Bennetts. A swab from the inside of Basil's cheek placed him on the DNA database, despite the fact that in respect of the Streatham bank job, nothing had yet been found to compare it with.

Harrison and Louise's only role had been to bring Bennett in for questioning and take him home again afterwards. The interview itself had been conducted by DI

Damian James accompanied by another senior detective. As Louise had observed acidly to Harrison, for DI James and the rest of Basil Bennett's fan club, his appearance in Romford must have seemed like a royal visit.

'*Guten Tag*, my friends,' Basil said as Louise and Ralph dropped him off. 'It was a pleasure to converse with you on your fool's errant.'

After her interlude of excitement Louise was consigned to the more mundane aspects of the investigation; working with insurance inspectors and bank employees to identify what had been in the safe-deposit boxes – detailing the gold and other commodities, the value of any jewellery, the serial numbers of the notes.

Other detectives in the team had been assigned the more satisfying work of finding the employee who'd provided the gang with inside information and tracking down known associates of Bennett to see if they could be placed at the scene of the crime. It seemed to Louise that this was a major operation in which she was playing a very minor role. She presumed that Harrison was as well, but they'd been separated the day before and she had no idea where her sergeant had been despatched to.

One afternoon, while she was ploughing through reams of paperwork, Louise was contacted by a fellow Detective Constable who she'd worked with on Operation Incisive. He'd been sent to Tagg's Island to check out Colin Brown's alibi and was calling to pass on a message from Sage.

'Bit of a weirdo, if you ask me, but he insisted I tell you there's no hard feelings and he'd really like to say that to your face.'

'When was this?' Louise asked.

'Couple of days ago. Sorry, been busy and all that.'

'That's okay. I know what it's like. Did he say anything else?'

'Yes, he said he was planning to go away again so don't leave it too long.'

'Thanks, mate. I presume he confirmed Brown's story.'

'Between him and his girlfriend? Yes, they did. She was there when Brown arrived to get his coat and they were both able to confirm what time Brown had left. So Colin's off the hook, at least for that one.'

Louise wondered who Sage's girlfriend was, but still felt remorse more than curiosity about the way she'd exploited his helpful nature. Not revealing her occupation was at best deceitful and she'd always considered herself to be an honest person. She could surely go to see the man with green eyes as a private citizen but felt she needed to tell DS Harrison, who came back into the incident room at Streatham later that afternoon.

'So nice to see you,' Louise said acerbically. 'I feared you'd been kidnapped.'

'We sergeants have other functions to perform. Did you want something?'

Louise told him about the phone call, and explained her intention to visit Sage on Saturday as a private citizen.

'You should know by now that you can't do anything as a private citizen. A police officer is always a police officer. We don't have the luxury of ever being completely off-duty,' Harrison responded flatly.

'I know, Ralph. I did pay attention at Hendon; all that stuff about us being "permanently representative of the civil authority of government".'

'Well, it was you who said you were going there privately,' Harrison pointed out.

'What I mean is, I want to be able to pay Sage a visit as a friend, not as anything to do with the Hampton Court stuff.'

'But it will be in connection with it,' Ralph said. 'You're only going because an officer working on that case passed on the message.'

'But I'll be going in my own time.'

'That's what you said last time, and look where that landed us.'

'Ralph, I know what I saw that night and nothing that has happened since has disproved my theory that an innocent man is in custody and the bastard responsible for these crimes is still out there. How many more Darcy Kramers do there have to be before Meredith realises he's made a mistake? And you won't like this, Ralph, but it's typical of the way that crimes against women are downgraded, as if sexual assaults are somehow trivial. I accept that we're off that case now, and I only want to go back to thank a man who's been more than helpful, and to apologise for misleading him. He knows now that I'm a copper. Can you imagine what a creep I feel for not telling him? That he had to hear it from Colin bloody Brown or the officers who went to check his alibi?'

They talked it over for a little longer before Harrison conceded defeat.

'I know that nothing I say is going to stop you going,' he said, 'but be careful. Don't go snooping on that other fellow, what's his name?'

'Patrick Venn?' Louise offered.

'Yes, that's him. I remember how keen you were to question him. It's up to Meredith's team to follow that up, not you. Get this straight, Louise, you go on that island on Saturday to see your mate Sage for an hour or so and you come straight off again afterwards, away by early afternoon at the latest.'

Louise nodded her consent and made for the door, her shift having ended. But Harrison hadn't finished.

'Incidentally, Louise,' he said as she passed, 'that isn't advice, it's an order.'

Louise had been looking forward to a rare weekend off but if she didn't make her peace with Sage on Saturday she never would. She wondered how to tell him of her impending arrival. In the absence of any telephonic communication with the *Inner Peace*, she did what the Victorians would have done and sent a postcard, thinking it would give Sage a few days' advance notice of her visit. Acquiring some up-market stationery, she wrote something that she hoped would strike the right tone of apology without being over-affectionate. After all, she hardly knew the man, and felt that her deviousness had been in the interests of legitimate police business, albeit she knew that DCI Meredith wouldn't see it that way.

Before she'd left work, Professor Assem Bukhari had rung to say the material from Darcy Kramer's fluffy jacket on which the fingernail was snagged had been retained, but hadn't been submitted to forensics for examination. This error was now being rectified, and the professor wanted to thank Louise for bringing this to his attention. It had been a serious oversight that he was determined should never be repeated. As well as reporting to DCI Meredith's team, he said he would ensure that Louise was told if anything of interest was discovered on the material.

It was the least he could do.

Olive Sabatini hadn't exchanged a word with Latika Joshi, or anyone else from the Metropolitan Police Service, since Joshi had warned her against using Jack Handysides as the theme for the April edition of *Crimesolve*. There had been further exchanges with the Met on the subject, but all were conducted between people much further up in the hierarchy than Olive and Latika.

At one point Sabatini suggested that a possible solution was to refer to Handysides simply as 'Mr X' or even 'Mr H' so that the story of how the criminal gangs had been welded together could be told without naming the welder. They could expose much of what was known about Jack Handysides – his modus operandi, that he owned a property development company, his holiday and travel business side-line – without using his name. But this idea was vetoed by Dr Templeman who insisted he would only put his name and reputation behind a proper exposé, not a half-baked compromise.

With less than a week before the programme was due to go out, its content still in doubt, the BBC switchboard was paging Olive Sabatini to tell her that a Mrs Joshi was on the line.

'Latika! Long time, no hear,' Olive said when the call came through. 'What can I do for you?'

'This may come as a shock, my dear, but I'm calling to tell you that the Metropolitan Police no longer have any objection to the programme on Jack Handysides going ahead.'

'No objections provided we do what?' Sabatini asked, unable to quite believe this sudden change of heart.

'No objections and no conditions. Indeed, I know it's late in the day, but if we can be of any help, please do let me know.'

'Oh, we've got everything done. We weren't bluffing when we said we'd be going ahead with or without your approval.'

'And we weren't bluffing when we said that the wrath of the Met would cover you in fire and brimstone – but no need to be playing "Call My Bluff" any longer; the crisis has passed, we are no longer at loggerheads, and you and I can be friends again.'

When Olive passed this news to the rest of the team there was suspicion as well as jubilation.

'They were implacable the day before yesterday when the DG had lunch with the Commissioner. They even threatened to rope in the Home Secretary, claiming that the programme would undermine their efforts to tackle organised crime,' the director, Simon Tait, said.

Olive's fellow assistant producer, Luke O'Sullivan, wondered if the Met was setting a trap. 'Maybe they know that Jack Handysides is ready to sue the arse off us and want to teach *Crimesolve* a lesson,' he suggested.

'But in that case why not let the programme go ahead without their blessing?' Olive said.

'Because,' Luke responded, 'they don't know if we're going to do Handysides or car theft. By withdrawing their objection, they ensure we jump into the trap.'

'Luke does have a point,' the producer Carl Burnett said. 'Best ask Latika Joshi for something in writing so that we have some of their skin in this game.'

'Will you let Jenny know the good news?' Tait asked Burnett, knowing that he had been reunited with their star presenter.

'I doubt she'll think it's good news,' the producer replied. 'It will raise the profile of Dr Jamie Templeman, and that's the last thing Jenny wants right now. She's devastated about what that bastard did to her.'

What Carl Burnett neglected to tell his colleagues was how instrumental he'd been in ensuring that Jenny Daniels had all the sordid details of her lover's betrayal. He'd not worked in investigative journalism for twenty years without learning how to acquire information, and Jamie Templeman had been his special project ever since the handsome doctor had stolen Jenny Daniels away.

It hadn't taken Burnett long to learn about the collapse of Templeman's marriage. The lurid details were contained in the divorce papers. He'd contacted Templeman's ex-wife on the premise that the BBC wanted to check if there were any skeletons in the doctor's cupboard before offering him a contract. The former Mrs Templeman had been delighted to tell him all about Sarah Sanchez. When he went to see Sanchez, however, it was without any knowledge that she had continued her affair with the doctor. She was a respectable married woman, the wife of a leading surgeon. Burnett had cast himself as the vanquished lover of Jenny Daniels – which he was – and said he was checking Templeman's character for a possible BBC profile piece – which he wasn't. The two soon became allies in a quest to scupper the planned wedding of the doctor to the television presenter.

Sarah Sanchez had always made a point of insisting that any evidence of her ongoing carnal relationship with Templeman should be kept in her possession. She had as much to lose as he did if their respective partners discovered their secret, and Jamie was untidy, careless and prone to keeping bits of paper that should have been destroyed. If Sanchez gave the evidence of their most recent erotic interlude to Burnett it would scupper Templeman's wedding to Daniels. When things had settled down again, Sarah was confident that she and Templeman would get back to their *'liaison dangereuse'* with Jenny Daniels returned to the arms of her television producer.

'Right, we know what we're doing now,' Simon Tait said, rallying his troops for a few days of intense activity. 'I'll let the DG's office know. Olive, you get back to the Met for something in writing; Luke, you need to get our comms people working on pre-ads and promotion; and Carl, you need to ensure that all is well with the lovely Jenny. Tell her she doesn't need to work with Templeman anymore – we've got all the footage we need. But she does need to be ready to speak his name in her presentation, preferably not through gritted teeth. Oh, and someone needs to tell the man himself. Templeman may be a love rat, but he's the star of this particular show.'

18

SATURDAY MORNING

Jack Handysides arrived on Tagg's Island late on Saturday morning. It was a miserable day, the bleak grey sky reflecting on the Thames like corrugated iron.

He'd come to satisfy himself that all was in place for the drug consignment due to be travelling up the Thames to Maidenhead that evening. The visit was largely cosmetic – the *Navicula* operation was by now well-oiled – and his only function would be to rally the troops in advance.

There were, however, worrying developments elsewhere that should have taken priority, if only he could think of any way he could influence them. The television exposé was due to go ahead. If his legal representatives failed in their eleventh-hour intervention, his cover would be blown. In three days' time, the name 'Jack Handysides' could be all over the media.

Confirmation of this had come from Marko Rockov who'd been given the information first-hand by one of the principal participants in the programme – a man who was also, apparently, working somewhere in Handysides' organisation, and had been for years.

The grim irony of this brought a thin smile to Jack's lips as he crossed the little bridge dressed – as on his previous visit – in the beige mac. But as a concession to the spring weather, he wore it without the tartan scarf.

Louise Mangan was almost ready to make her way to Tagg's Island. The sensitive nature of her meeting with Sage had been drummed into her repeatedly by Ralph Harrison right up to the end of her shift on Friday evening.

'If I let you go to that island to meet this guy, Saffron, it's under strict conditions,' he'd announced.

'It's Sage,' Louise said. 'His name is Sage, and you know it is. Please be serious.'

'Oh, believe me, Louise, I am being deadly serious. I just got my herbs mixed up. What time did you agree to meet him?'

'One o'clock.'

'Okay, so you go onto that island at one, make your peace, and then you're away by two – agreed?' Harrison was emphatic. And although Louise was mildly resentful about the way in which her private life was being dominated by her occupation, she knew that her Sergeant could have put a stop to this visit by bringing in DCI Meredith. The risk she was taking by poking her nose back into a case it had been ordered out of had been made even clearer by her husband the previous evening.

'I know I was the one who encouraged you to go snooping around,' Tom had told her, 'but I wish you'd never discovered that bloody island or the hippy you're so entranced with.'

Louise laughed. 'Entranced? I'm not entranced, Tom. That's such a funny thing to say. What, do you think I've got a crush on him or something?'

'Well, you always liked the skinny boys at university,' Tom said, smiling.

'If that were true, I would hardly have hitched up with a fat lump like you.'

They spent the next few minutes having a mock wrestling match, in which the kids gleefully participated. Later, when the children were in bed and the couple were drinking tea together snuggled on the sofa, Louise returned to the subject.

'Sage says there's no hard feelings and he wants to say that to me in person. I feel guilty about telling him so many lies. I need to say sorry to his face. It's as simple as that. You planned to take the girls to your mum's anyway, so it's not as if we'd have been spending the time together.'

Her husband knew that once Louise had made up her mind, she rarely changed it on any counsel other than her own.

On Saturday morning, after kissing the children and hugging her husband she watched them depart for Bedford, where Tom's mum lived. The two women had never got on. Louise always believed that her mother-in-law thought she wasn't good enough for her son; a thought doubtless shared with many mothers of married sons who probably disguised it a little better than Tom's did.

Soon after their departure, alone in the flat, Louise had received a call from Professor Bukhari. His team had taken a DNA profile from the fingernail of Darcy Kramer's attacker, and had found a match on the DNA database.

'That's wonderful. Have you informed DCI Meredith's team?'

'Of course. Do you think I would breach protocol?'

Louise worried that she'd offended the professor, but his voice remained warm and friendly when he said, 'The fact is, young lady, without you we wouldn't have this important evidence and I was sure to tell DCI Meredith's team that as well.'

I bet Sean was ecstatic when he heard that, thought Louise.

Professor Bukhari expected an arrest to be made over the weekend.

'What's his name?' Louise asked.

'You'll know that such details do not concern me. I'm a scientist not a policeman; but since you ask, the match was with a sex offender from Watford by the name of Ian Escreet.'

'And do you know if the police have released the man they have in custody?'

'Once again, my dear, you are taking me beyond my responsibilities but the answer to your question is not yet, but I expect they will. You know how difficult it is to get things done at weekends.'

This conversation put a spring in Louise's step as she left Hampton Court station on what she expected to be her final visit to Tagg's Island.

Jamie Templeman woke up that Saturday morning with a throbbing head and a mouth like a sandpit. A moderate drinker, he'd spent Friday evening home alone, drowning his sorrows in a bottle of Rioja followed by several treble brandies.

When he'd been given the news a few days ago that all was now plain sailing for the *Crimesolve* programme, he'd been buoyed by a sense of optimism. This episode would lift his profile and fatten his bank balance. It was Olive Sabatini who'd given him the good news, although she also said that while there would be an intensive effort to ensure the programme was 'screen-ready', as she put it, his contribution was already 'in the can'.

So all Templeman had to do was liaise with the press people at the Beeb about media opportunities, of which Olive was sure there'd be plenty. She'd touched upon his rift with Jenny, passing on the message about them not having to do any more work on the episode together. He was concerned that Olive seemed to know all about his domestic difficulties, but realised that as Carl Burnett – the man responsible for that rift – was her boss, her interest was inevitable. Templeman had never been good at taking responsibility for his own actions.

He hadn't expected to be missing his fiancée quite as much as he did, and her rejection of his attempts at reconciliation had surprised him. The doctor had a strong belief in the power of his charm to beguile any woman he fancied, but Jenny Daniels wouldn't let him get close enough to subject her to it. His calls were blocked, his emails, texts and pager messages ignored. What was he supposed to do? Accost her in the street?

He'd passed on the good news about the programme to Jeremy Van Wyk, and hoped this would be their final conversation. He needed to get away from the South African, and he also needed to get back together with Daniels; this *Crimesolve* episode was key to both ambitions. It would separate him from the criminal world he'd entered by demonstrating that his motive all along had been its destruction. He'd even convinced himself that this was true.

Sure, Van Wyk had all that evidence against him, but would he dare to use it? And even if he did, Templeman would just need to stick rigidly to the undercover hero narrative that the programme would create for him.

As for Jenny? He envisaged them being reunited by the programme's success. Perhaps even attending the BAFTAs together to collect their award.

He'd taken some tablets for his throbbing head, showered and was contemplating how best to spend his solitary Saturday when the police arrived.

Marko Rockov called Van Wyk into his office. 'Trouble,' he said succinctly.

'What kind of trouble?' the South African asked.

'I just heard from Mateo, my lawyer. Good Serb guy, who knows everything. He tells me that the police are on their way, lots of them, coming here to Tagg's Island where they will search every boat for drugs.'

'It's just as well that they have such poor intelligence. And that we got that consignment off the island so quickly,' Van Wyk observed.

'Mateo may not have all the details right, but he has warned me that Jack is on his way as well.'

'How long have we got?' Van Wyk asked.

'Mateo says they'll be here this afternoon. It's ten o'clock now.'

'Okay, I have things to do,' his chief of staff announced. 'I'll see you later.'

After he'd gone Rockov made a phone call.

'Colin?' he said softly into his mobile. 'There is no change to the plan. Do it Monday, and do it good.'

He rang off and was gathering some things together in his office when one of his tee-shirted minions put his head round the door.

'Mr Handysides is here,' the man said.

19

SATURDAY AFTERNOON

Sage was looking out for Louise, standing just inside the latched gate, his long hair tied back in a ponytail. They shook hands limply before crossing onto the *Inner Peace*. After a few awkward attempts at polite conversation while they waited for the kettle to boil, Louise cut to the chase.

'I'm so sorry for misleading you, Sage. I should have been upfront and honest from the start, particularly as you were so kind to me.'

Her host waved away her protestations. 'I understand, Louise. You had a job to do and couldn't be sure if I was friend or foe,' he said soothingly. 'I hope you now accept that it's the former.'

'I never thought of you as anything else – that's why I was so upset about the deception.'

There were more exchanges in this vein, each of them trying to mollify the other before Sage told Louise that he had some important information for her.

'If I'd known you were a detective, I'd have told you about some strange goings on at *Navicula*,' he said before describing what he'd seen on the evening when the barge anchored across the inlet to the lagoon.

'I don't know what was being unloaded but I don't

think it was their groceries. Aunt Jane was right – there's something evil behind those gates.'

Louise thanked him for what she said was extremely useful information that she'd follow up on, already anticipating how delighted Harrison would be that at least she'd come back with what seemed to be important intelligence.

'I'd appreciate not being part of any further proceedings. This is a small community, and I wouldn't want my involvement to be widely known. But if your colleagues keep a careful eye on *Navicula* they'll find plenty of evidence without my assistance, I'm sure.'

Having got this out of the way, he insisted that Louise have some lunch with him. It was as if the work was over, and he could now relax. Soon they were tucking into home-made mushroom soup with slabs of crusty bread.

'So, what's this about you going away?' Louise asked through a mouthful of food.

'Well, you know how much I love to travel, and I want to do more of it while I'm still in my twenties.'

'Where to and for how long?' Louise asked.

'To wherever the fancy takes me . . . and for as long as I'm enjoying it. I'm lucky. No ties, no commitments, and, thanks to Aunt Jane, no financial worries.'

They went on to talk about all kind of things – President Clinton's recent impeachment, the forthcoming millennium, the recipe for the mushroom soup. Louise suddenly noticed it was gone 2 p.m. She needed to go.

'I thought you might still be interested in Patrick Venn,' Sage said as his guest gathered her things, preparing to depart.

'Why? Has something happened to him?' Louise asked, unable to resist the lure of unfinished business on the island.

'He seems to have done a runner,' said Sage, who explained that Venn's partner was distraught, and anxious to talk to Louise.

'When the police came to talk to us about Colin Brown's alibi, she told me how she wished she'd told them about Patrick then.'

'Well, she should have. How long has he been gone for?'

'Since we called that night, I think, but she says that he often goes off, so it's nothing unusual.'

'I hope you reassured her that I only wanted to talk to Patrick about his bike,' Louise said.

'Well, that is what you said at the time, but she wondered if it might be in connection with that biker who assaulted all those women. I told her that it couldn't be because you've caught him. Anyway, you can tell her yourself.'

Louise, conscious of Harrison's decree, said she really didn't have time to go over to *The Great Gatsby*.

'No need for you to go anywhere,' her host said, 'I suggested she come here – she should be here soon.'

At that moment there was a buzz on the bell attached to the latched gate and a woman's voice was calling Sage's name as a prelude to coming aboard.

Jack Handysides had stayed for longer than he'd wanted to. Every time he thought about leaving *Navicula*, a new message would come through, necessitating another phone conversation with an associate from a different part of his organisation. All the calls brought bad news.

A warehouse that stocked prescription drugs raided in Croydon; a sophisticated cannabis distribution system around Hampstead Heath broken up by undercover cops; the main hub of his heroin network in Bethnal Green captured.

By 3.30 p.m. on Saturday, it was clear that the actions against Handysides' empire were coordinated, concentrated and devastating. The intricate spider's web he'd created was falling apart. It seemed as if every police officer in London was involved, such was the scale of the attack being ranged against his organisation.

Marko Rockov had given Jack exclusive access to his leather furnished office from where he could monitor the disaster that was unfolding. The Serb, who knew about the reverberations if not the eruption, came into the office looking anxious.

'I sent three of my men to scout around and make sure we can get off the island quickly if we need to,' Rockov announced. 'They haven't come back, and we can't contact them. We need to leave – now.'

Outside, in front of *Navicula*'s huge black gates, a convoy of three SUVs were lined up ready to leave, a couple of tattooed men in each.

'Where are we going?' asked Handysides, surveying the scene.

'I have a safe place in Greenwich we can go to,' Rockov explained. 'But you and I, we go by the river not the road.'

*

'Louise, this is Vicky West. Vicky, this is Louise.'

As Sage performed the introductions, Louise immediately recognised Vicky as the full-busted blonde who'd come to the door when they'd called at *The Great Gatsby* to speak to Patrick Venn a week and a half ago. She looked very different from the drab, dressing-gowned, rather dowdy woman they'd spoken to that night. Dressed in a polo-necked sweater and short denim skirt, and with a full face of make-up, Louise observed that Vicky was a pretty girl not long out of her teens, but with eyes that looked older.

Vicky sat down opposite Detective Constable Mangan, as Louise had introduced herself, and explained how she'd met Patrick Venn at a pub in Richmond the previous summer and fallen in love with him, eventually moving into *The Great Gatsby*. She'd been there ever since.

'Nine months now we've been together. But it's more like eight, because he's not been home for a month now.'

Venn wasn't answering his mobile phone and although Vicky knew he worked somewhere in the City, she didn't know where. Louise was told how much Vicky enjoyed being a 'liveaboard', how she'd upset her parents by dropping out of a dance and drama college course she'd been doing, and how idyllic life had been in those early days with Patrick last summer. She knew he was a keen cyclist, but had wondered why, on warm summer evenings, he would go out on his bike again, having already cycled to and from work.

'We'd be having a quiet evening drink on the boat, looking out over the river, all calm and tranquil, when he'd suddenly dash off on a bike ride as if he'd just thought of somewhere he needed to be.'

Having described their domestic life afloat for longer than was necessary, Vicky's narrative moved from the deck to the bedroom. Lowering her voice and leaning closer to Louise she said, 'He had big problems, you know? Doing it.'

'What do you mean?' Louise asked, a little irritated by Vicky's coyness. 'Was he impotent?'

'Yes, he had that thing, you know, where he couldn't get a hard-on.'

'Do you mean erectile dysfunction?'

Vicky nodded.

Sage, who'd been standing at the kitchen range listening intently, intervened. 'I think that what Vicky's saying is that, if you put all that together, the cycling, the going off suddenly in the evenings, his problems in the bedroom, his disappearance . . .'

Louise had already drawn her own conclusions but was keen for Vicky to speak for herself rather than have it said for her by Sage.

'So, he's not been back since he went to work on the day we called round?' she asked gently.

Vicky nodded her assent.

'That's the evening Darcy Kramer was attacked. And you've heard nothing from him since?'

Another nod.

Louise asked where Patrick kept his cycling stuff and was told there was a shed in the garden of *The Great Gatsby* but there was nothing in it now because Venn had the bike with him. Vicky knew he wore a cycle helmet but couldn't recall the colour. And, yes, she said, he always wore goggles, and they were 'the ones you could see yourself in'.

Louise was confident that Patrick Venn was the man she was looking for, the cyclist she'd seen coming towards her down the main road on the night that Darnell Thomas had been arrested.

'Was Patrick ever violent towards you, either physically or verbally?' she asked.

Vicky's eyes were cast down as she struggled with what was obviously a sensitive question.

'Things got a bit rough,' she said eventually, 'you know, when he was trying to do what men are supposed to be able to do.'

'But did he hit you or swear at you?'

'No, he never hit me, and he only swore when he was getting excited, you know? Sexually.'

'What did he say,' Louise pressed.

'He seemed to enjoy swearing at me, calling me a whore, just to help himself get off.' She lowered her eyes demurely and Louise glanced at her watch.

It was almost 4 p.m., way beyond the time Louise had pledged to be away from Tagg's Island. She asked Vicky if she'd be prepared to relate all she'd said on the record as evidence for Operation Incisive. She said she would. Louise left Vicky sitting over a fresh cup of tea and departed. Sage insisted on showing her out.

'By the way,' she said to Sage as they passed through the little latched gate, 'according to Colin Brown, his alibi could be verified by you and someone he referred to as your girlfriend. It's none of my business but I was just curious to know if you live here alone.'

'Oh, that was the night Vicky came over, a little while after we'd called on her. She was worried that Patrick still hadn't come back. Colin was confused as he often is,' Sage said, smiling at the misunderstanding.

The SUVs drove out of *Navicula*, round the island and onto the bridge. They could get no further. Three police vehicles appeared in front of them, and when the drivers tried to reverse another two blocked their retreat. Armed police shouted gruffly at the tee-shirted men inside to leave their vehicles and put their hands on their heads.

Three of the men managed to escape, scrambling down onto the riverbank and disappearing into the dense foliage. The rest were lined up, four tattooed Serbs to add to the three already captured.

Neither Marko Rockov nor Jeremy Van Wyk was amongst them. Also missing was Jack Handysides.

Louise left the *Inner Peace* just as the SUVs were speeding towards the bridge. She felt as if she'd walked onto a film set. Helmeted, body-armoured police officers were everywhere carrying semi-automatics, their faces masked. Looking through the open gates of *Navicula*, she saw three men running across the manicured lawn to a speedboat tied against the jetty.

Her instinct was to try to prevent their escape, but as she ran through the gates determined to turn thought into action, she was grabbed by one of the armed officers who pushed her against the gates.

'Why the fuck can't you do as you're told at least once in your life,' said a clearly exasperated Detective Sergeant Ralph Harrison.

The speedboat was on its way downriver to London. Marko Rockov was at the controls. Sitting nervously on a bench seat behind him were Jack Handysides and the still besuited Jeremy Van Wyk.

Looking back, they could see the marooned SUVs on the crown of the bridge. There was intense police activity all along the Middlesex bank but the river itself was quiet.

'Don't worry, Jack,' Rockov shouted over the noise of the engine and through a cloud of river spray. 'I'll get you to safety.'

Jack said nothing, he just nudged Van Wyk, and pointed dolefully to the sky, where a police helicopter had appeared to keep them company.

It wasn't until the early evening that they found Tiffany Mordaunt. At first it looked as if an old blanket had been discarded on the piece of marshy land close to the lagoon. The police had been busy searching *Navicula*, completing the paperwork necessary to arrest their four captives, looking for others who may still be on the island. A police-woman noticed a corner of the blanket rise in the strong breeze, revealing what looked like a foot.

The medics calculated that Tiffany had only been dead for a few hours. Four at the most. She'd been injected with thallium and left entirely naked. As her distraught parents noted when they went through the harrowing process of confirming their daughter's identity, her killer had even removed the locket with her mother's photograph that Tiffany had always worn around her neck.

Whoever killed her had obviously been in a hurry. They must have been attempting to put the body in the water but had been disturbed. Presumably the killer had hoped the Thames would have washed away the substantial DNA on the blanket that covered the body. Unfortunately for him, it all matched the profile of one man, a sex offender from Watford called Ian Escreet.

20

BRUNCH IN BELSIZE PARK

It was Sunday's headline news. 'Met Makes Biggest Drugs Raid Ever' announced the *Sunday Telegraph*, whilst the *Sunday Candour* led with 'Cops Beat Robbers'. By all accounts, Operation Zeus was the biggest, most widely co-ordinated police offensive in the history of the Metropolitan Police.

Arrests were made right across London, north to south, east to west; in the City of London, and the suburban commuter belt, in Petticoat Lane and Millionaires Row; and all within a ten-hour time frame. Although there were plenty of guns, no shots were fired either by the police or those they apprehended. Such was the element of surprise and the number of police involved, most of the eighty-seven arrests were of villains too shocked to react. The Home Secretary, Jack Straw, was all over the broadcast media saying that the illicit drugs trade in London had been destroyed in 'the biggest blow against organised crime this century.'

'So that's why you've been sneaking off over the past week,' DC Louise Mangan said to DS Ralph Harrison as they drove towards Kingston where they'd been called in to do some routine work that Sunday morning.

'Had to attend special training sessions, but I couldn't tell you anything about it.'

'I can understand that. What I can't understand is why I wasn't involved,' Louise responded.

'The officers used had to have firearms training, or have given five years unbroken service,' Harrison said.

'Well, I've not had firearms training, but I must have done more than . . .' Louise began to say while working out the mental arithmetic that brought her to a shocking conclusion. 'Surely they didn't count my maternity leave against me?'

'Unbroken service means what it says,' Harrison said unsympathetically. 'Anyway, if I were you, I'd leave it there, seeing as you did get involved, sort of, didn't you, DC Mangan?'

Louise, who had indeed become inadvertently caught up in the offensive, decided it would be best to leave it there. Ralph had already reminded her how, whilst sworn to secrecy, he'd tried hard to ensure that she was away from Tagg's Island before that part of the planned operation began.

He went on to tell her about *Navicula*'s role in recycling drugs that had been seized and were due for incineration. Louise mentioned what Sage had told her about watching the process take place from a vantage point on the island, but it was hardly revelatory. The police knew all about the activities at *Navicula*, and what she thought was fresh information didn't seem to be fresh at all.

She'd been ordered to come in on what was supposed to be the second day of her weekend off, as had Tom. There was so much work to do covering for colleagues seconded to Operation Zeus, and a lot of procedural stuff in respect of the eighty-seven arrests. Louise wondered why her husband hadn't been roped into the operation, and then discovered that he had been. She thought he'd spent the night in Bedford with his mother and the kids, but when she'd spoken to him that morning, he confessed to leaving the girls at his mum's so that he could join a team sent to apprehend a gang of drug mules at Luton Airport.

'It was a top-secret operation, Lou,' he'd pleaded. 'We weren't allowed to say anything, including to our nearest and dearest.'

Louise knew he'd done the required thing by not telling her, but it still hurt. She could accept Ralph not trusting her enough – but Tom? Her husband? Louise couldn't help seeing it as a breach of faith.

The news about Operation Zeus received so much coverage that the discovery of Tiffany Mordaunt's body was only reported in a couple of paragraphs on the inside pages of that day's papers. The immediate assumption was that the Beast of Hampton Court must have been working at *Navicula* as one of Rockov's gang. The attacks on women in the Hampton Court area coincided with the Serb's arrival on Tagg's Island. Darnell Thomas had been released. This was now a murder inquiry.

Louise had written a report about what Vicky had told her regarding Patrick Venn, and wanted to submit it immediately. DS Harrison had advised her to wait until Monday, arguing that a bit of ambiguity around precisely when she secured this information wouldn't go amiss.

'Everyone's focused on our great triumph at the moment, and Meredith certainly won't want to hear that you spent your weekend on a case he considered to be closed. I'm not saying you shouldn't say anything, I'm just suggesting that you leave it for a day or two.'

Louise decided to ignore her sergeant's advice and submitted her report straight away. It would be strange for her to be reprimanded for going to Tagg's Island to pursue her suspicion that the Met had arrested the wrong man just as that suspicion proved to be correct.

'So, that's why New Scotland Yard gave us the nod to go ahead with the programme.' Simon Tait was addressing his colleagues at a hastily convened Sunday morning gathering over brunch at a North London café, or brasserie as it liked to call itself – all soft furnishings, tables too low to eat off properly, and with Sunday broadsheets scattered around to demonstrate the intellectuality of its patrons. Tait and his producer, Carl Burnett, were both locals, but Olive and Luke, the assistant producers, had come all the way from Balham and Stepney respectively.

'The Met knew that by the time we were due to air the exposé, it would be meaningless anyway.'

'With a few tweaks we can make it a revelation rather than an exposé,' Olive Sabatini suggested.

'Yes,' Luke O'Sullivan added, 'Olive and I were talking last night when the news broke. It's the hot topic and we're perfectly placed to tell the story behind the headlines.'

'Not with Dr Jamie Templeman, we can't,' Carl Burnett interjected. 'He's in custody. Jenny found out last night.

Apparently, he's been up to his eyes in drug dealing for years.'

Olive sprung to Templeman's defence. 'I'm sure that his only involvement was to uncover the criminality, not to profit by it.'

'That's a nice way of phrasing it, Olive,' Simon Tait said, 'it would sound good in the script. But, true or not, we can't use our doctor for this programme while he's banged up. Can you imagine the ordure that would descend upon us?'

'How is Jenny?' Luke asked whilst reaching for his fifth pastry, determined to maximise his benefit from this rare expenses-paid breakfast.

'She's fine. The media is bound to make a thing of the Templeman situation and her association with him, but she can honestly say that she'd already dumped him. It seems to me that our choice is simple,' Burnett continued. 'We either don't put a *Crimesolve* programme out this month, or we switch the subject to our alternative, which is car theft. We ought to be able to get that into shape by Tuesday.'

'But that would be awful. With the entire country transfixed by what happened yesterday, only for their trusted *Crimesolve* to ignore it,' Olive pleaded.

Simon Tait swallowed a final forkful of scrambled egg before summing up.

'We are two days away from transmission. We cannot go on air with the programme we've prepared because without the Jamie Templeman segments, we have virtually nothing. And we can't expose Jack Handysides because he's been exposed already and the police have him in custody.'

'That's not right,' Olive mumbled through a mouthful of toast from the other end of the table.

'What's not right?' asked Tait, irritated at having his words of wisdom interrupted.

'That last bit is wrong. I checked with Latika. They didn't catch Jack Handysides, or the two guys with him, who the police thought were a Serb and a South African. Apparently, the speedboat they were in was being tracked by a police helicopter, which was in turn guiding several units of the Specialist Firearms Command. They were trying to predict where the men would come ashore when their vessel suddenly diverted off the river into St Katherine's Dock. An armed unit got there within five minutes of the boat reaching the jetty, but there was no sign of Jack Handysides or his colleagues.'

21

THE HOLIDAY MAKER WHO MISSED
THE PLANE

The next day – Monday, 26 April 1999 – saw Harrison and Louise Mangan return to the routine work they'd been assigned to at Streatham in pursuit of the safe-cracking gang.

Louise couldn't help feeling as if she was the holiday-maker who'd missed the plane. Tom had arrived back with the girls on Sunday night to find her unusually quiet. They hadn't argued – they rarely did – but Tom was bursting to tell a story that Louise found herself not wanting to hear; how he'd spent weeks as part of a scratch unit of officers who were authorised and trained to carry arms; how they'd been deployed not just to catch the drug mules taking large quantities of swallowed heroin onto various planes, but to catch the men who'd deployed them. The drug mules were small fry; the men who'd coerced, threatened and forced those couriers into subservience were the big fish. Thanks to the quality of the intelligence, the entire criminal enterprise had been destroyed – all under the banner of Operation Zeus.

'Tell me something,' Louise asked as Tom talked on excitedly over their Sunday roast, 'did you arrange to take the girls to your mother's as part of the plan to get you close to Luton Airport?'

Tom was forced onto the defensive. 'Well, they were due a visit to Bedford anyway,' he said.

'That's not what I asked,' Louise said coldly.

'Yes, I suppose so. When I was told that our muster point was Luton and given that I couldn't tell you anything, I did think it would be convenient – two birds with one stone and all that.'

Louise was annoyed with herself. She understood that there were police operations so sensitive that they couldn't be spoken about to anybody. Yet she couldn't help finding Tom's circumspection upsetting and indicative of a lack of marital trust. And the subterfuge around the visit to his mum's made it worse, as if Chloe and Michelle had been forced into colluding against her. It was irrational but its irrationality didn't make it any less painful.

Now, on this mild Monday morning in Streatham, Ralph Harrison was equally keen to bathe in the glory of Operation Zeus. *Why shouldn't he be?* Louise asked herself. It had been a massively successful police operation that was making news around the world. At this stage, the papers reported, attempts to catch the criminal mastermind behind the drugs trade in London had failed. Jack Handysides had apparently just faded into the throng moving around St Katherine's Dock and up onto Tower Bridge. The two men with him were seen running through the crowd but no one had dared apprehend them.

Harrison rattled on about the intricacies of the operation, how well organised it was and how he and his fellow officers wondered how such accurate intelligence had been obtained.

Louise listened patiently to her sergeant, wishing that she could have been part of Operation Zeus, and still resentful that maternity leave had been used to exclude her.

'Do you know what really disgusts me?' Louise announced. 'If we hadn't been so wrong about finding the bastard who attacked all those women, we might have got to the truth much sooner and poor Tiffany Mordaunt might still be alive.'

'Fair enough, Louise . . . although you must be the only copper who has worked their socks off to prove that the guy they'd caught was innocent,' he observed quietly. 'Furthermore, you've managed to humiliate a Detective Chief Inspector in the process. Sean Meredith will be incandescent.'

'And an innocent man has been released,' Louise said calmly.

'God knows what it's going to cost the force if he gets a good lawyer to pursue the inevitable claim for wrongful arrest.'

'Ralph, are you seriously suggesting it would have been better to leave things as they were?'

The two officers were drinking tea at the desk they'd been allocated in Streatham police station. There was a surly silence from Harrison before he said, 'So, where does that leave us in respect of suspects in that case we're not involved in anymore? The press is speculating that it was one of Rockov's men.'

'Maybe, but only if one of Rockov's men was a sex offender from Watford called Ian Escreet,' Louise responded.

'Haven't they picked him up yet?' Harrison asked.

'No sign of him apparently. There must be a chance that Patrick Venn is actually Ian Escreet. The age profile fits. From what his girlfriend says, all the evidence points to Venn. He was even fond of calling her "a filthy fucking whore" when sexually aroused. Hopefully they'll follow up on the report I've just submitted and make the link. We may not be involved anymore but I hope our superiors realise that amongst all the celebrations of Operation Zeus, there's unfinished business for Operation Incisive.'

Harrison nodded. 'So much going on,' he said. 'Goodness knows what Jenny Daniels will be talking about on *Crimesolve* tomorrow night.'

'Is it tomorrow?'

'Yes, I made a note of it as soon as we got back from White City that day. I feel as if we've contributed so I told Sheila to video it if I'm out. Perhaps our names will be in the credits,' he joked.

'Well, if you recall, they were going to do the Beast of Hampton Court originally, until we messed their plans up with that arrest. Now I suppose they can revert to Plan A,' Louise said.

'Bit soon,' Harrison said. 'The news about the DNA discovery won't be public for a day or two.'

'Yes, and I doubt if the Met will want them to focus on a wrongful arrest.'

'Does it matter what subject they pick?' Harrison asked rhetorically. 'Most men I know only watch the programme to gaze at Jenny Daniels.'

Louise smiled and the two officers finished their tea in silence.

It was fifteen minutes later, at 11.30 a.m. when the news began to filter through that Jenny Daniels had been shot through the head on the doorstep of her Southwest London home.

PART TWO

2019

22

THE HOUSEBUYER

There was nothing suspicious about the purchase of the property. The house had been on the market for almost a decade in a part of London that developers had shown little interest in. It didn't even qualify for the epithet 'once fashionable' – 'never fashionable' was a more accurate description. The district had always been stubbornly utilitarian – a bleak industrial estate, some brick-built warehouses and a few domestic properties that the occupiers who could, soon moved away from.

The last occupier of this particular house had been an old lady whose family had once owned a paint factory on the industrial estate. The factory had been sold long ago, but the spinster had continued to occupy the family home until she died at the age of ninety-one. The house was a detached four-bedroom with a huge garden, and in the ten intervening years there had only been a few potential purchasers, attracted by its most compelling feature – a gradually decreasing sales price.

The man who eventually bought the place insisted on paying in cash, but this raised no suspicions. The vendee, an elderly gentleman who looked the image of respectability, explained that he'd always mistrusted banks and had squirrelled money away throughout his life. Not a fortune, but enough to buy and repair this house. The estate agent was relieved to be shot of the place, and once the serial numbers of the notes had been checked, the sale had gone ahead, and the new owner was able to begin the Herculean task of renovation.

If the neighbours had feared that the house had been purchased as an asset which would be allowed to sweat in all its decrepitude, their concerns were soon allayed. Within a fortnight of the 'For Sale' placards coming down, a team of workmen arrived to begin the restoration. An armada of empty skips then came, departing a few days later full to the brim with masonry, old floorboards and earth, lots of earth, as the substantial garden increasingly became the focal point of the renovation in work that continued night and day.

An immaculately dressed man was often seen on site supervising the work. He made known the owner's intention of creating a basement extension with an underground complex that would include a home cinema amongst its features. The neighbours were delighted. They'd read about such subterranean extensions being added to properties in more salubrious parts of the city, usually by Russian oligarchs or ageing rock stars. Why not here? It would lift the status of the area. No suspicions were aroused. What was there to be suspicious about?

The cash processing centre on the trading estate nearby didn't advertise itself. Even those living in the vicinity knew nothing about the serious quantities of cash stored inside its grey concrete walls. There was no reason to believe that this had anything to do with a house being renovated at least two hundred and fifty metres away, and well beyond the boundary of the trading estate.

It took five months, but the tunnel from the house to the cash processing centre was almost complete, with the final push timed to take place on a Sunday. There would be no activity on the trading estate that day although, even if the place was as busy as a Moroccan bazaar, nobody could have disturbed this operation. The tunnel had been created by craftsmen. Criminal craftsmen, for sure, but craftsmen nonetheless.

Basil Bennett, the smartly dressed supervisor, sometimes described himself as an 'uncivil engineer'. He could tunnel his way into any forbidden place and once there, crack any safe, disarm any security device, remove anything that stood between him and his bounty. This particular job – planned meticulously and implemented expertly – would not require any safe-cracking. It wouldn't even need any security gates to be opened. Using inside information gleaned from somebody who had recently worked at the centre, Basil intended to tunnel up through the concrete floor of the main cash-holding area. His calculation was that the heist would be worth ten million pounds, making the outlay on equipment and the purchase of the house a profitable investment.

On this Sunday in January 2019, Basil Bennett was briefing five associates for the final stage of the operation, telling those due to enter the saferoom with him how important it was to make a tidy retreat. It was 11 a.m. and freezing cold, although here, underground, where the weather couldn't permeate, it was hot and clammy. The track-mounted excavating machine used to burrow from the garden of the house to this spot beneath the trading estate now stood redundant; a host of carts snaked on the tracks behind it.

For five months these carts had been used to remove debris. Today their task was to carry batches of cash back to the house where the rest of the gang waited to help in its dispersal. Next to the excavator, water jets stood ready to reduce the dust that was bound to accumulate when the concrete floor was breached.

Basil, like his compatriots, was dressed in overalls with goggles protecting his eyes below the brim of a baseball cap. He'd removed his breathing equipment in order to give these final instructions.

'Okay, it's time to tunnel up,' he said, distributing a set of pneumatic hand tools. 'It'll be tight but there'll be a 48-inch diameter that will allow three of us skinny buggers through. We'll throw the money sacks down and you guys here will need to get them on the carts and back to the house. From there we'll load them into the trucks and get the hell out of here, but at a sedentary pace.'

He meant 'sedate', but those working with Basil had long grown used to his mangled vocabulary. In his attempts to demonstrate the breadth of his lexicon he sometimes succeeded only in confusing those he'd meant to impress.

'You know where to meet – we'll divvy the money up there and go our separate ways, content with a job well done and considerably richer than we were before the job commenced.'

There was a general chorus of approval, muffled through the breathing apparatus that the men had already fixed in place. Basil then took charge of the hand-tunnelling. This final process took the best part of three hours before the debris fell away and Basil could see the striplighting across the ceiling of the money vault. He was the first to hoist himself up, emerging through the dust to begin the task of collecting the tightly wrapped wads of cash stored on shelving all around what was previously thought to be an impenetrable enclave.

It was a matter of seconds before Basil Bennett realised there was a welcoming party. Six uniformed police officers were pointing their SIG MCX firearms towards him. From behind them stepped a tall woman who Basil recognised despite her protective headwear and bulletproof vest.

'Basil, how lovely to see you again,' said Detective Chief Superintendent Louise Mangan.

'Mrs Mangan, as I live and breathe. I thought you was with the higher-ups these days.'

'Well, you were wrong. I'm back on the tools.'

'But this is catamount to entrapment,' Basil pleaded.

'The word is "tantamount", and you, Basil, are not only entrapped, you're also nicked.'

23

MANGAN'S DILEMMA

'Gosh, it was so exciting to catch them red-handed like that. How did we know that they'd emerge today?'

DCS Louise Mangan was being driven back to New Scotland Yard by her young and inquisitive apprentice, Detective Inspector Alexandra Cornelius, who, to Mangan's slight irritation, tended to overuse the word 'gosh'. All senior detectives were being required to mentor a graduate. Alex had been allocated to Louise.

'Well, you already know how we became aware of the gang's activities.'

'Yes, I do. It was a Police Community Support Officer who alerted us.'

'And that's an important history lesson for you, Alex; some of our colleagues treated PCSOs with contempt – calling them "toy coppers" and worse,' Mangan explained.

'I used to hear those things,' said a voice from the back of the car that belonged to Detective Sergeant Rushil Din. 'It was received opinion when they started to be recruited into the Met. People used to say they were useless because they don't have the power of arrest. But it's precisely because they're never distracted by the time and bureaucracy involved in that kind of procedure that they're able to concentrate on their main function.'

'Which is?' Alex asked.

'Which is to know what's going on in their community. To be on the streets all the time and not diverted away by having to go to court – as arresting officers are obliged to do – for ages.'

'Not many PCSOs left these days,' Mangan reflected. 'But thankfully the one working in that borough noticed that there was very little work being done on the house, and that all the renovation work seemed to be concentrated on the garden. The workmen told her that they were building an underground complex, but the speed at which they were working reinforced her suspicion that something wasn't quite right, which was why she alerted us.'

'And the timing?' Alex asked as she swung the car too quickly round a tight bend.

'Steady on, Lewis Hamilton, we're really in no hurry,' her boss advised. 'I know you're fast-track, but I didn't think it literally required you to drive like a maniac.'

DCS Mangan liked the young woman she'd been asked to mentor. Alex Cornelius was a five-feet-five ball of energy with a disarming smile that intermittently illuminated the serious expression on her oval face. Like DS Din in the back seat, and Mangan herself, Alex had been recruited straight from university. But unlike Din – whose father was a shopkeeper in Walsall – Alex was from grander stock. She was the daughter of a High Court judge and had been educated privately.

'Gosh, sorry,' she said, slowing the police Jaguar to a safer speed as Mangan resumed her explanation.

'Okay, so on timing, unknown to Basil and his gang we've had them under close surveillance for weeks. Using thermal imaging equipment, we followed the direction of the tunnel towards the cash processing centre and, given how close they'd got by Friday, it didn't take a genius to figure out that, with nobody working at the centre on Sundays apart from external security, this would be the day they'd drill upwards towards the money.'

'I might be being a bit naïve here, but couldn't you have nabbed them ages ago rather than wait until the last minute?' Alex asked.

'Good question, Alex. We could have but the house was purchased legitimately, by an elderly gentleman who had no criminal record. Although he must have been a front for Basil's outfit, we have no proof of that. He claims he hired Basil to do the conversion work and they could have argued that they were preparing the underground extension that was an essential element. The most we could have done them for would be pre-empting the planning permission that the meticulous buggers had actually applied for. More importantly, catching them in the act has saved us a lot of procedural time.'

'You seem to have a good relationship with Mr Bennett, Chief,' DS Din observed.

'I've developed a soft spot for Basil over the years,' Mangan replied.

'But he's a robber,' Alex exclaimed.

'Technically, he's a burglar,' Mangan said. 'You should know the difference between a robbery and a burglary by now.'

'Sorry, I forgot. To be described as a robbery, force has to have been used, right?'

'Correct,' said Mangan. 'You'll have noticed that whereas our guys were armed, none of Basil's people were. He never resorts to violence, which is why the prison terms he's had were shorter than they might have been. He goes inside, serves his sentence and probably spends the time planning his next heist. He must be in his sixties now, but it's an addiction with him and he happens to be very good at it.'

'Wasn't Basil involved in Hatton Garden?' DS Din asked, referring to the theft of fourteen million pounds from a deposit box in the London street famous for its jewellers.

'Probably, but that was four years ago. And we've never been able to prove that he was one of the old codgers who masterminded it. However, it did have all the hallmarks of a Basil Bennett operation.'

A few minutes later Mangan said, 'You were right to chastise me for speaking about Basil as if he was a friend, Alex. It's the way you get when you've been a cop for a long time. I remember twenty years or so back when I also felt that the senior officers were being too admiring of our Mr Bennett.'

'Gosh, you've been dealing with him for that long? That's almost my lifetime.'

'Thanks for reminding me, Alex,' Mangan said jovially. 'Basil's daughter is a copper, by the way.'

'You don't say,' said Din. 'I didn't know that.'

'Yup, joined us about ten years ago. Basil sent me a letter saying that he encouraged her to pursue a career in the police after talking to me about it. I can't remember the conversation, but apparently I can claim credit for the recruitment of PC Bennett, who is now a traffic cop with Essex Police.'

Alex brought the car to an unnecessarily abrupt halt inside the security gates of New Scotland Yard. Mangan told her to go home and enjoy the rest of her Sunday whilst she and DS Din ensured that all the required paperwork was properly processed. Basil Bennett and his collaborators were being distributed to various prisons to be held on remand pending trial. None of them was likely to be released on bail given their previous records.

Later that day, as Louise Mangan gazed out of her office window across the icy expanse of the Thames, she felt a deep sense of satisfaction. Days of triumph like today were rare. As the detective who'd led the operation, she'd receive plenty of accolades, although not from the new Met commissioner.

Commissioner Irvine had retired last September, a year after he and his wife had experienced a brutal encounter with a contract killer in the Lake District – an encounter in which two of his protection officers had been killed. This terrible event had undoubtedly been a factor in George Irvine's decision to go a year earlier than he'd planned. The promotion of his deputy, Karen Dale, to the top job was entirely predictable but it presented Louise with a dilemma. She'd never been happy as an Assistant Commissioner. The position had been just about bearable under Irvine, who'd been the one who promoted her. But while Mangan had loved being a detective, she hated being an administrator, which was how she thought of her role as Assistant Commissioner. Under Karen Dale as the new Commissioner, she knew her job would become intolerable.

The two women had known each other for years but the longevity of their relationship had no bearing on its quality. Louise found Karen humourless and dour, while Karen considered Louise to be glib and facetious. They were of a similar age – Karen was younger, but only by eight months – and had both encountered all the travails of being a woman in a profession that was taking longer than most to come to terms with gender equality. Both had been subjected to appalling incidents of undiluted misogyny. But rather than bind them together, these odious attitudes became another source of tension between them. Louise thought that Karen mimicked some of the authoritarian traits of the men, while Karen thought Louise used her femininity as a weapon to stir up unnecessary internal conflict. The two women had nothing in common, shared no interests, and had no mutual friends.

Louise recognised the significance of a woman being appointed Met Commissioner for the first time. It was historic, a real breakthrough for women in the Force – for women in general. She could recognise the achievement without being enthusiastic about the person who achieved it. There was nothing essentially unpleasant about Karen, she reflected, they just didn't get on and never would.

Both women knew they'd hate working closely together, which was why Louise never even contemplated applying for Karen's old position of Deputy Commissioner, as many colleagues urged her to. At least if she'd stayed where she was, she'd be one of four Assistant Commissioners – but as there was only one Deputy, if she took on that role, she'd inevitably be forced to work with Karen all the time. Louise knew that another option to avoid working with Karen was that she would soon be eligible to retire on a full pension. But she didn't relish that option either. Long years of solitude with no work to absorb her interest wasn't a compelling prospect.

To Mangan's relief Commissioner Dale had come up with a solution. The stringent cuts in police numbers in 2011 had led to a shortage of coppers at all ranks but particularly amongst senior detectives. The government had reversed its policy, and was frantically trying to recruit again. But so many long-serving officers had gone that a third of officers had less than three years' service, and even if they managed to restore police numbers to their previous levels, they'd have novices in positions where there used to be veterans.

This situation allowed Dale to offer Mangan the chance to revert to being a detective, stepping down three grades whilst retaining the same pay, ditching the admin and going back to proper police work as a Detective Chief Superintendent. Louise knew that this would be the most fulfilling way to spend her remaining time with the Met. Her professional dilemma had been sorted, but a personal one remained, and it was on this that Mangan reflected as she gazed out of her office window.

The two issues were related only in so far as the personal one could have a bearing on whether she'd choose to retire in August 2020 when she'd reach fifty years of age. The Met would be keen for her to stay, and Louise had once envisaged remaining rather than face the lonely, meaningless existence that awaited her in retirement.

But that was before she met Petros Diamantapoulis.

Divorced from Tom for eight years, she hadn't expected to fall in love again. But she had – with a Greek policeman she'd worked with in Crete. She'd been sent there to liaise after a British government minister had been reported missing whilst hiking across the island. Petros was a captain in the Hellenic Police.

Now, fifteen months after it began, their love affair was struggling to survive. Petros was a divorcee with a severely disabled daughter which tied him to Athens; Louise had a job she enjoyed in London that would pay a full pension if she remained in it for a while longer. The distance between them was becoming a challenge emotionally, as well as geographically.

Throughout the course of their relationship, they'd been together only three times. Petros had come to England, met Louise's two daughters and stayed for a fortnight. Louise had been to Athens twice and met Delia, Petros's little girl. Given that Delia could neither speak nor hear it hadn't really been a meeting – more an observation during which Louise had felt guilty about her own discomfort. But she saw how much Petros adored Delia, how they seemed to communicate through tactility, and it made her love him all the more.

But the tide of phone calls and text messages between them had ebbed. Louise was desperate not to lose Petros the way she'd lost Tom, her ex-husband, through a slow and gradual deterioration of their relationship. Once again work was at the heart of the problem, but she didn't know how to resolve it. She had been prepared to go to live in Greece in 2020 when she retired, and had made a few vague plans with Petros to this end. But as she looked out towards the South Bank on this gloomy Sunday afternoon, Louise wondered if their love affair could survive for one year, let alone two.

24

A VACANCY AT THE MET

'I heard on the news this morning that we've just had the sunniest December since 1962,' Alexandra Cornelius announced cheerily as she tucked into her fried egg on toast. She had seized a place at this table in the New Scotland Yard eatery, despite not knowing any of the three officers who were already breakfasting together and the availability of empty tables elsewhere.

'Just the kind of thing you long to hear on a shit January morning,' Detective Chief Inspector Mark Barry said, irritated by the unwelcome intrusion.

Alex, oblivious to his hostility, ploughed on. 'Oh, I think this is how January should be – cold and dank. Are you chaps all based here?' she asked, waving her knife vaguely in the direction of her fellow diners.

'No, we chaps aren't,' replied the acerbic DCI Barry.

'We're a team of UCs formed to tackle gang culture,' Detective Constable Grant Traore, sitting next to Barry and directly opposite Alex, explained more amicably.

'Oh, I've heard about you lot. Undercover Cops, right?'

'Give that girl a coconut,' Barry said dryly.

'What about you?' the third diner, Detective Sergeant Roger Neil asked.

Alex told them that she'd left university the previous

year and was now being mentored as a fledgling Detective Inspector. This information was not well received.

'Another fucking virgin birth,' exclaimed DCI Barry. 'I had to slog my way through the ranks. Took me five years just to get from constable to sergeant and you walk straight in only one rank below me already.'

'I suppose I am a bit of an immaculate conception,' Alex said, flashing her most endearing smile at the darkly brooding officer opposite. 'I completely understand how you chaps must feel about it, but it really isn't my fault. The offer was there, I took it. I'm working with Detective Chief Superintendent Mangan.'

'You've got a good mentor there,' Grant said, continuing his role as peacemaker.

He was the youngest of the three officers and Alex was immediately attracted to him. He was more smartly dressed than the others. Whilst they were in jeans and zipped jackets, he wore stylish trousers and a white long-sleeved polo shirt with the top button done up. Alex had always liked a fashionably dressed man. A smart green sweater was draped over the back of his chair, temporarily removed in the uncomfortably hot staff restaurant that users stubbornly continued to refer to as 'the canteen'.

'Yes, she's a wonderful teacher to have,' Alex said as the others drained the dregs from their cups, preparing to depart.

'That must be why she was demoted,' growled Barry, moving away from Alex without a farewell.

Alex, left to finish her breakfast alone, was reflecting on the fact that her boss obviously had at least one detractor in the Met, when Grant Traore returned to retrieve the sweater he'd left behind.

'Take no notice of Mark,' he said, placing the garment casually across his broad shoulders, 'we need more bright youngsters on the force. He's just miffed because he's no longer young and he was never bright.'

They chuckled conspiratorially before Grant turned to depart once more, stopping suddenly as something occurred to him.

'Look, if you want to have a chat one evening about things, you know, over a drink or something . . .'

'What kind of "things" would we have to chat about?' Alex responded teasingly, playing hard to get.

'I'm black and you're a woman. Look around you, you'll notice there aren't many like us here,' Grant said earnestly. 'We could talk about that.'

'Oh, a drink one night would be fab,' Alex said, a bit more gushingly than she'd meant to. They exchanged mobile numbers.

DI Alex Cornelius was a few minutes late arriving at the conference room where Mangan's senior team were receiving a presentation on rising levels of violence against women and girls. Somebody from the mayor's office was giving a slide presentation at the front of the room.

'Good of you to join us,' whispered Rushil Din as Alex slipped into the seat beside him. Louise Mangan was sitting at the front next to the man giving the presentation.

Alex thought her normally pristine boss was looking a little dishevelled. Her long brown hair was bunched at the back. A bright plastic hair claw made it look as if some huge red insect had landed on her head. A few strands of hair hung loose, as if she'd put her hair up in a hurry, disinterested in the outcome. There were dark rings around her eyes, and she looked even paler than usual. Her tall slim frame was clothed in a no-nonsense, blue trouser suit, the pink blouse underneath buttoned to just above the cleavage.

No smile of acknowledgement was directed towards the latecomer, but Alex could see that Louise was deeply interested in the subject under discussion.

The Mayor of London's representative was reciting some worrying statistics. 'As you can see, rape offences are up by fifteen percent, but if we take the rolling total over the period since 2016 there's a twenty-seven percent increase. That's just the average across London, in some boroughs it's up by much more, in Hammersmith and Fulham for instance, the increase is a hundred percent over the same period.'

Mangan interrupted to point out that there was still an under-reporting problem with many victims of sexual assault failing to report their experience.

'But that won't alter the statistics,' the man from the mayor's office said, 'because under-reporting in the base period means we're comparing like with like.'

'I didn't suggest it would alter the stats, although the crime survey suggests that the problem of under-reporting is growing rather than declining. What I'm saying is there are a greater number of assaults on women than even these figures reveal.'

'So get stuffed, knobhead,' Din whispered to Alex.

The meeting had been convened to discuss an action plan worked up between the Mayor and the Met and due to be implemented across the twelve Basic Command Units (BCUs) of the force. It was being explained to the twenty members of Mangan's specialist detective unit which was available to any BCU that had a particular need of their expertise. The problem was that every unit was under-resourced and what was supposed to be a specialist asset was becoming a general pool of labour that each Command Unit was keen to draw upon. Mangan expressed her frustration with this situation when the meeting was adjourned for a mid-morning coffee break.

'What we did yesterday in catching Basil Bennett red-handed is a good example of what we should be doing. Nobody in the BCU had much idea of what to do when that PCSO reported her suspicions. So we get called in, given the time and resources to do the job, and as a result Basil and his mates are in custody. We need to be given a project and left to get on with it.'

'Such as getting better at tackling the rising number of sexual assaults?' suggested Rushil Din.

'That doesn't need a specialist detective unit,' Mangan said, 'it needs a change in attitudes right across the force and the criminal justice system. Half of the cases we detect are NFA'd.'

'That's "no further action",' Din interjected, in case Alex didn't know.

'And a quarter of the cases that do make it to the Criminal Prosecution Service are rejected on evidential grounds. Is it any wonder that so many cases go unreported and unpunished?'

'I wouldn't be quite so despondent. Attitudes were much worse thirty years ago when we joined the Met,' said the fourth coffee-drinker. DCI Harry Kosnich was an experienced, ex-Flying Squad officer who Louise had asked to be her second-in-command. He was a bulky, bearded, bear of a man with a gravelly voice. He and Louise had joined the Met within weeks of each other, and she trusted him.

'They were, Harry,' Mangan said, 'but when things are bad it's not much comfort to know they used to be worse.'

After a short pause in the conversation, Kosnich spoke again. 'As for our unit being pushed and pulled across the force, the main problem is surely that we answer directly to the Deputy Commissioner and there currently isn't one.'

DCI Kosnich had raised an issue that was a major source of controversy at New Scotland Yard. Karen Dale's former position had yet to be filled following her promotion. The names of the likely candidates were being bandied around the building regardless of whether they'd applied or not; there was an Assistant Commissioner interested, a guy from counterterrorism, Sandra Smith, the Chief Constable of Lancashire Police, and even, so it was rumoured, a senior Australian police officer from Melbourne.

'Are you not tempted to apply?' Kosnich asked Mangan, knowing what the answer would be.

'No way,' she replied. 'Alex has a better chance of being appointed Deputy Commissioner than I do.'

'She'd do a better job than Karen ever did,' said Kosnich, who'd become a bit of a father figure to Alex.

'I'll get my application in today,' Alex announced with a grin.

25

A FIRE ON THE THAMES

Early the next morning a fire burned ferociously, its flames mirrored on the placid surface of the Thames. Despite the hour, and the freezing weather, a crowd of spectators had gathered on the Surrey bank. A houseboat was ablaze on Tagg's Island, close to Hampton Court. There was concern that it would ignite a fire trail across the other houseboats packed round the island like suckling pigs at a sow's teats.

The boat on fire was a *pied-à-terre* mooring, a dwelling worth hundreds of thousands of pounds. Its owner was an ageing hippy known as Sage, who'd lived on Tagg's Island for as long as anyone could remember. A recluse who spoke rarely, even to his closest neighbours, it was said that he lived on inherited wealth which included the houseboat that was now ablaze, the *Inner Peace*. By now the vessel had broken into several pieces after an explosion had ripped through its upper deck living quarters, spewing debris out into the river.

The firefighters were battling valiantly to stop the fire spreading to other boats, which had become their priority once the *Inner Peace* became unsalvageable.

Nobody knew if the boat's owner was on board when the blaze broke out, but given the hour and his hermit-like existence, it was assumed that he had been. The morose knot of observers on the island itself, the 'liveaboards' and their guests, had been evacuated from their vessels. A few were still in nightclothes and dressing gowns, but most had managed to grab a coat as protection against the chill night air. One of them claimed to have seen Sage's face at a window in the stern. But others who were also watching said that this must have been an illusion caused by smoke and flame because they'd seen nothing. The occupier was likely to have died quickly, suffocated by the fumes, a view which was first expounded by a thin man in a duffle coat who sounded authoritative. It quickly turned into a consensus. A vicar appeared along with two church volunteers distributing blankets.

Nobody seemed to know much about Sage despite the length of time he'd been living there. He was said to be a writer, although no one had ever seen or heard of any book he'd written. Someone thought he'd once shared the boat with a lady friend, but this was disputed by another onlooker who'd heard that he'd been in a gay relationship with another man. Nobody really knew. Most liveaboards rented for a few months and moved on. The only institutional memory resided in Rosemary Tillman, the Secretary of Tagg's Island Residents Association (TIRA) and Miss Tillman was abroad, unaware of the horror unfolding in her domain.

And so, the evacuated residents milled around, talking in hushed tones as if at a funeral, stamping their feet and hugging themselves to keep warm.

Nobody tried to rescue Sage. The fire had caught hold so quickly that any attempt by resident or firefighter was bound to be futile. Neither had the man aboard made any obvious attempt to escape. Like the captain of a stricken liner, Sage was left to go down with his ship.

Louise Mangan learned of the fire when she read the overnight situation report in her office at New Scotland Yard the next morning:

> *Fire destroyed a houseboat at Tagg's Island on the Thames near Hampton Court. The owner is missing presumed dead.*

That was all that was recorded at the end of a detailed synopsis of every notable event in the Met's geographic area of responsibility. She was still pondering this information when DS Rushil Din came into her office ten minutes later.

'Anything interesting, Chief?' he asked, placing a cup of black tea on her desk.

'Usual stuff, assaults, burglaries, a cash machine ram-raided in Peckham. No stabbings, thankfully.'

'Nothing requiring our attention?'

'No. I think the team can concentrate on tying up the final details of the Basil Bennett case and helping roll out the action plan on violence against women and girls that we discussed yesterday. But there is one thing you can do for me straight away. Can you get me the name of the houseboat that caught fire on the Thames last night and the resident who's missing, presumed dead?'

'No problem. In a nautical mood this morning, are we?'

'Not really,' Mangan said, thumbing distractedly through some paperwork. 'I knew someone on the island where the fire happened. Did a job there years ago.'

Din, sensing that his joviality had been misplaced, said he'd get on to it straight away.

'Where's Alex?' Mangan asked.

'Having breakfast so far as I know. Shall I go and get her?'

'No, leave her be. She'll probably learn more in the canteen than she would in here with me this morning.'

When DI Alex Cornelius walked into the staff restaurant that morning, she was pleased to see Grant Traore sitting at the same table he'd been at the day before. And, once again, the seat opposite him was vacant.

She carried her tray across, but before she could put it down, DCI Mark Barry assailed her.

'No, thank you, not today,' he barked.

Alex froze, bemused as Barry continued to berate her. 'We're having a high-level discussion that needs to be in confidence – so go and have your brekkie somewhere else.'

'Well, surely you should be having your discussion somewhere secure rather than in the middle of the canteen?' Alex asked, genuinely perplexed.

'These college kids are such smart arses,' Barry announced to the room at large. 'Listen, Tinkerbell, I'll decide where to have my meetings – just take your tray and fuck off to somewhere you won't be a nuisance.'

Alex turned in confusion, the tray balanced precariously. Blushing with embarrassment she retreated to a table near the door and sat alone, feeling as if she'd been punched in the stomach. She'd never experienced such snarling contempt from anyone, let alone a senior police officer. Nobody had intervened on her behalf. Even Grant, with whom she was due to fix a date for a drink, had just sat and watched.

Appetite suddenly diminished, Alex cut up her beans on toast and was pushing segments around the plate, sipping tea and staring at the blank wall when Mark Barry sauntered by towards the exit, his entourage in tow. To her horror he placed a meaty hand on her shoulder and leaned in close to her ear to say sotto voce, 'Toughen up, Tinkerbell. If I scare the shit out of you now, imagine the state you'll be in when you meet a proper villain.'

Alex was left wondering if she should report the incident to Louise but decided that it would reflect badly on her, making her seem brittle and over-sensitive. Barry's exhortation to 'toughen up' had its intended effect. She felt somehow responsible for the humiliation she'd been forced to endure.

26

RESTRICTED INFORMATION

Later that morning Rushil Din reported back on the houseboat fire. The man who was missing presumed dead was known as Sage; the houseboat was called the *Inner Peace*. Louise Mangan received this information with a sorrowful expression that worried Din. He thought he saw a tear in her eye and asked if she wanted him to leave the room so that she could reflect in private on what was obviously bad news.

'No, I'll be alright. It's just that I have some fond memories of that guy and of Tagg's Island where his boat was moored.'

Louise thought she'd better explain in case Din thought she was pining over a former lover. She knew it might help her to talk about the events of twenty years ago, and Rushil was always a sympathetic listener. As a keen Met historian, he always showed great interest in his boss's anecdotes. So Mangan told him about Operation Incisive; how she'd originally met Sage on Tagg's Island in pursuit of her theory that the wrong man had been arrested as the so-called Beast of Hampton Court; how her theory had eventually proved to be correct, leading to the release of Darnell Thomas who she and her sergeant had been responsible for apprehending, and how, by that time, they'd both been taken off the case.

'But surely you were put back on the investigation after your hunch proved to be correct?' Din asked.

'No way. The DCI in charge of the case wasn't best pleased, and neither was the Met. Darnell Thomas sued for wrongful arrest and the case was settled out of court for hundreds of thousands of pounds.'

'But didn't it blight the DCI's career?'

'It didn't used to work like that. Sean Meredith retired ten years later as a Commander. I'd say that back then an officer accused of malfeasance was more likely to be lauded than lambasted. The general approach seemed to be that at least officers like that did the business. The innocence of those they did it to seemed to be a mere technicality.'

'If this guy who sued for wrongful arrest wasn't the Beast of Hampton Court, who was?' Din asked.

'I don't think Operation Incisive ever led to a prosecution. The DNA evidence that led to Thomas's release was a breakthrough. It matched that of a sex offender on the database. I can't remember the name, but I had a strong suspicion that one of Sage's neighbours on Tagg's Island was the culprit. But I didn't have any further involvement. The last time I saw Sage he was about to go hiking in the Hebrides. I was moved to a different unit, and was never involved in the case again. One of the victims was found dead on Tagg's Island as it happens, so it was a murder inquiry and they do usually lead to a conviction, but so far as I know there were no arrests or any further attacks.'

'You obviously liked this guy Sage, and it sounds as if there were plenty of loose ends to tie up – shall I get you the file?'

'I'm not sure that's strictly ethical given that I have no

involvement now and was often sailing close to the wind regarding authorisation even back then.'

'Chief, can I just remind you that you're now a Detective Chief Superintendent with a roving brief. Nobody's going to accuse you of impropriety for showing an interest in an unsolved murder.'

Not for the first time, Mangan thought how lucky she was to have DS Rushil Din supporting her. His wisdom was remarkable for one so young, as was his diligence. She'd known him for four years, ever since Rushil and his great friend and colleague Geoff Tonkin had been assigned to her as Detective Constables on a case involving the assassination of a Russian oligarch at the Strand Hotel. The two had been known colloquially in the Met as Torvil and Dean ever since they'd forged a friendship at Hendon Police College, and although they'd gone their separate ways when Tonkin transferred out, they remained close friends.

'Okay, have a flick through the file for me,' Mangan said, 'and let me know if the DNA match ever came to anything. But don't get bogged down in the Jenny Daniels stuff.'

'Jenny Daniels! Were you involved in that?'

'I knew that would get your juices flowing. No, I wasn't involved, but it happened around the same time, in the same vicinity and there's a bit of overlap. Her awful murder probably distracted attention from the Hampton Court assaults. There's plenty of armchair detectives looking into the Daniels case. I'm interested in what happened to the girl who was killed, what was her name? Tiffany something. Her, and now poor Sage, of course, so focus on the murder investigation and the details of what happened last night if you would, please.'

'Your wish is my command,' said Din, leaving Mangan's office straight away.

Alex couldn't shake off the humiliation she'd suffered that morning. Reporting to DCS Mangan's office shortly after it happened, she'd been relieved to be told that her job that day was to be the Chief Superintendent's eyes and ears on the taskforce dealing with the rollout of the Violence Against Women & Young Girls action plan. She felt it was best not to be working too closely with her mentor that day because Mangan was bound to notice the subdued mood she was in, and she didn't trust herself not to reveal what had happened in the canteen. Knowing her boss, she'd be bound to intervene, which would make Alex look and feel even more pathetic than she did already. The irony wasn't lost on her. She had experienced verbal violence perpetrated by a senior police officer in the head-quarters of the very force that was leading an initiative to protect women and young girls from precisely that kind of behaviour. And Alex, who'd committed to encourage women and girls to report their abusers, had stayed silent – miserably and spinelessly silent.

Her father had warned Alex there would be days like these, when her background would become a restraint. He'd wanted her to follow in his footsteps and those of her older brothers by studying law. The Honourable Mr Justice Cornelius had failed in this desire because his daughter felt it was more important to be involved in catching law-breakers than convicting them. Her father and brothers could only ply their lucrative trade, she'd argued, because police officers often risked life and limb to provide them with court fodder.

'That's very true, my dear,' her father had retorted, 'but we're also the ones who protect the innocent – the people who should never have been brought to court in the first place.'

He'd gone on to warn her that her family background would be an asset in the legal profession, but a millstone in the Met.

'A public-school education, a posh accent and friends in high places are not unusual in my profession. In the police, however, they're vanishingly rare and they will make you a target.'

Her mother and father had divorced when Alex was ten, but she'd hardly been affected by the rupture as it happened while she was ensconced at boarding school. Holidays were shared between her father in Cambridge, where Alex had been born and raised, and her mother, who went to live in London with the doctor she'd left her husband to be with.

Alex's determination to join the police had never faltered. She considered this unwavering ambition to be the only thing she had in common with Louise Mangan, a woman she revered.

Leaving New Scotland Yard that evening after a day of tedious office work, Alex still hadn't shaken off the effects of that morning's altercation. She had a flat in Victoria and was walking sullenly towards it along Bird Cage Walk, looking forward to the large gin and tonic she planned to pour herself when she got home. Engrossed in her phone she suddenly heard her name being called from the other side of the dark road. It was Grant Traore, who began to cross towards her.

'Do not speak to me,' Alex commanded, walking faster in her determination to ignore the UC officer.

'Hang on,' Grant implored, running to catch up.

'You heard what your friend said to me and yet you said nothing in my defence and so I have nothing to say to you,' Alex said loudly.

The heads of several pedestrians turned, trying to discern in the dark where the raised voices were coming from. Alex walked on but Grant quickly caught up, falling into step beside her.

'He's a bastard. I told you that – him and Roger, both as bad as each other.'

'So why didn't you say anything?' Alex asked, choking back tears as the trauma she'd endured became all too vivid again.

'For the same reason you didn't – firstly I was shocked by what he said and secondly, he's my boss and if I'd intervened against him, I'd be taken off this work. You need to understand that what I do isn't traffic control or marshalling a crowd at a football match. It's undercover work, sometimes really dangerous. But it's the most exciting and rewarding work I've ever done, and I would be gutted if I was dropped from the team.'

Alex strode on but slowed her pace as the initial burst of anger ebbed away.

'Look, he says awful things to me as well – little snipes about my colour, like when I said I was going on holiday to Spain, and he says, "Well, you can't be going for the suntan, ha ha." He once told Roger a joke in front of me about Stevie Wonder being asked what it was like to be born blind. "It could have been worse," Stevie Wonder replies, "I could have been black." And the two of them are honking with laughter, with me standing there like a spare part. It's like I said to you the other day: me and you have to jump hurdles that are never placed in the way of most of our colleagues; they can just sprint the course.'

The two police officers had stopped walking. Alex was poised to turn off towards Cockpit Steps, the stone staircase she needed to ascend to continue her journey home. She stared down at the pavement, unsure how to respond to Grant's little speech. As she hadn't reported the incident herself, she could hardly blame him for being equally remiss.

Grant broke the awkward silence. 'Did you know that these were the very steps that Pitt the Younger walked up with his seconds on his way to a duel with a fellow MP who'd taken umbrage at something Pitt had said in a parliamentary debate? The amazing thing was that Pitt was Prime Minister at the time. That's how they used to deal with work problems in those days.'

'Bring me some pistols and I'll have it out with that bastard you work with,' Alex said, her face breaking into a slow smile.

'Forget the duel. There's a lovely little pub up there,' Grant responded. 'Let me take you for a drink instead.'

*

Rushil Din emailed Louise that evening to tell her that he'd accessed the file but that it was heavily redacted. Information on much of what had happened on Tagg's Island in the spring of 1999 could only be seen on the specific authority of the Commissioner or Deputy Commissioner. However, Din's email had gone on to say that there was some interesting information that hadn't been redacted and he had also acquired more information on the houseboat fire. All this was the subject of an early morning discussion between Din and Mangan the next day.

'I had a long chat with the forensics guys who're working on the Tagg's Island fire,' Din said. 'The *Inner Peace* was destroyed. All that's left for our people to work on is a blackened hulk where the boat used to be moored, and a few scraps of flotsam retrieved from the river. I'm told there's an extremely fast current in the Thames, so whatever remains of Sage will by now be somewhere in the Thames Estuary or – more likely, given that the fire was over forty-eight hours ago – somewhere out in the North Sea. The Marine Accident Investigation Branch has been asked to determine the precise cause of the blaze.'

'What's the working assumption on how the fire started?' Mangan asked.

'Houseboat fires are surprisingly frequent,' Din responded. 'Calor Gas explosions, candles left alight, smokers being careless with their cigarette butts. And, get this, there's now a craze for creating woodburner stoves out of old gas cylinders. Crazy or what? – it's a wonder these fires aren't even more common. Although the newer boats are made from fibre glass and steel and so much less

213

ALAN JOHNSON

likely to catch fire, most are still the old wooden ones like the *Inner Peace*. Nobody I spoke to suspects foul play.'

Din went on to talk about the unredacted bits of the 1999 file; the arrest of Colin Brown and his subsequent release after an alibi had been established, the DNA profile that cleared Darnell Thomas of being the Beast of Hampton Court. There was a report on the Met's interest in Patrick Venn and how he'd vanished from the rented houseboat on Tagg's Island, but nothing on *Navicula* or the Serbian gangsters who had resided there.

Mangan told Din that the last time she'd seen Sage was on the very day that the Met launched its biggest and most successful initiative against the drugs trade in London and that Sage had witnessed an element of that trade being pursued on Tagg's Island.

'Are you telling me that you were actually involved in Operation Zeus?' Din asked incredulously.

'Well, sort of,' Mangan said, reluctant to reveal her chagrin at being excluded because maternity leave had constituted broken service. 'Tagg's Island was where some of the impounded drugs were offloaded as they were being transported up the Thames for incineration.'

'I see what you meant when you said there was a bit of overlap with the Jenny Daniels murder,' Din remarked. 'It happened a couple of days after Zeus, and Colin Brown became the main suspect.'

'Yes, he had an irrational grudge against Jenny and had made an aborted attempt to attack her a few weeks prior to her murder, which was why my sergeant and I arrested him over the Hampton Court stuff. It was actually Sage who provided Brown with an alibi in respect of one of the assaults. And as for the aborted attack, Daniels refused to press charges.'

'Were you involved in the Jenny Daniels murder investigation?' Din asked.

'I've already told you – I wasn't. I know as much about it as you do. Probably much less because I wouldn't be surprised to hear you've read every book on the subject.'

'Most of them,' said Din, making light of his reputation as a swot. 'We all know she was shot once through the head after being forced to her knees on the doorstep of her house in East Molesey; that the gun was a 9mm short calibre semi-automatic, thought to be a replica or a workshop conversion. But I didn't know Brown had attacked her previously. It makes you wonder why it was over a year before he was arrested for her murder.'

'I remember thinking that at the time,' said Mangan, 'but given the original guilty verdict against him was overturned on appeal, perhaps it's not so puzzling – they just didn't have sufficient evidence. Nobody saw him anywhere near the scene of the crime, and the only solid evidence against him was some gunpowder residue in one of his pockets, which could have been placed there by the other main suspect, Marko Rockov . . .'

'The so-called Serbian warlord who managed to escape when most of his gang was captured as part of Operation Zeus.'

'You do know your stuff, Rushil,' Mangan said admiringly. 'Was there anything about Rockov in the file?'

'Nothing. I presume it's part of the redacted stuff. There's plenty of speculation online about him returning to Serbia after we failed to nab him. The theory is that he murdered Daniels or put Brown up to it before leaving the country. We know Rockov died of cancer in a Belgrade hospital in 2001, taking his secrets to the grave.'

'Anything on the file about Jack Handysides?' Mangan asked.

'No, but I know a lot about him. Operation Zeus and the way the Handysides empire was destroyed is the stuff of legend in the Met. A bit embarrassing that we weren't able to apprehend the man himself. Perhaps that's what led to the redactions.'

'I did worry that you'd get bogged down in the big stuff – the Daniels murder and Operation Zeus – when my only interest is in the Beast of Hampton Court and that DNA profile.'

'Sorry, Chief, my bad. The profile matched a guy by the name of Ian Escreet who assaulted a woman in Watford in 1992 and got a six-month prison sentence. It was in the early days of DNA profiling, so we're lucky it was on the database.'

'Ah yes, I remember. Did they arrest this guy Escreet?'

'No, they didn't arrest him because they couldn't find him. In those days there was no Sex Offenders Register and this Escreet fellow was allowed to wander off to God knows where. The file shows we tried to track him down early in 1999 when the DNA match was established and subsequently made a more strenuous effort later in the year as part of the Tiffany Mordaunt murder investigation, but to no avail. They ended up flagging the profile and hoping that this character's DNA would crop up again, but it never has.'

'We've let poor Tiffany down again then,' Mangan said. 'If that dimwit Meredith hadn't been convinced that he'd got his man, we might have found Tiffany in time. Then, after her murder, we failed to find the killer, even with a DNA match.'

'The report says she'd only been dead for a couple of hours, and that she died near where she was found on the island. The suspicion was that she was being held on one of the boats and only killed when it was clear the police were closing in. Tiffany would have been chucked in the river if the perpetrators had had more time, is the theory on the file. As it was, she was found on a piece of bogland close to the water.'

'Okay, thanks for that, Rushil. Now I suppose we'd better get down to work.'

'What are you going to do about the redacted bits of the file?' Din asked.

'I wasn't going to do anything. It sounds as if the fire was an accident, which is why it's one for the Marine Accident Investigation Branch and not the Met. If Commissioner Irvine was still in situ, I'd think about making a request to see the redacted bits just out of interest, but Karen Dale is unlikely to do me any favours and they haven't filled the Deputy position yet.'

'The rumour is they're going to appoint the Aussie, which won't go down well. They have a very different culture over there.'

'Yes, it's the Mayor's idea, apparently, and the government's gone along with it because they always feel that bringing someone in from outside is the answer to every public sector problem,' Mangan observed. 'But if the Australian gets it, he's even less likely to authorise me to see the complete file. I presume it's restricted because of the overlap with Jenny Daniels – to ensure that we don't feed the frenzy of speculation that's become an industry since that poor woman was killed. Or maybe, as you say, the Met is being over-sensitive because of their failure to apprehend Handysides . . . or, for that matter, Jenny Daniels' murderer.'

'Yes, I suppose you're right, Chief. Colin Brown won substantial libel damages from the *Daily Candour*. I guess we have an obligation to ensure that whatever we know remains strictly confidential.'

'And I have Harry Kosnich coming in any minute to give me a counterterrorism briefing, so be gone – and thanks again.'

DS Din rose to return to his office through the connecting door but stopped at the threshold.

'Bit of a coincidence, though, isn't it? A guy who witnessed what Handysides was up to and knew Colin Brown well enough to give him an alibi gets fried alive on his houseboat. There are more overlaps here than in a Formula One Grand Prix.'

27

AT THE TWO CHAIRMEN

The Two Chairmen pub was packed when Grant and Alex arrived. In the summer, drinkers would happily spill out through its narrow door onto the pavement, joining the smokers whose regular domain that was. But this was the kind of cold winter's evening when even the most dedicated nicotine devotee would be reluctant to venture outside.

Grant, who'd been puffing on a roll-up, threw what remained of it into the gutter before pushing open the door to enter the brightly lit Nirvana within. He nabbed two tall chairs nestled round a high table and went off to queue at the bar for his pint of IPA and his companion's double gin and tonic.

Alex, removing her thick coat, hoisted herself up onto one of the chairs. From there she watched Grant push his way back, the drinks largely intact, and climb onto the seat beside her. She liked what she saw.

They were still perched there two hours later having eaten burger and fries – which Grant had insisted on paying for – and consuming three more rounds of drinks. By now the pub had almost emptied of its regular clientele; worker ants from various government departments, research assistants from the parliamentary estate and civilian staff from New Scotland Yard.

Alex had told Grant about working with Louise Mangan, how much she admired the woman, loved the job and needed to escape the 'fast-track' label to prove her worth as a detective.

Grant told Alex about his Senegalese heritage, how his father had come to England as a boy in the 1960s, met Grant's Scottish mother at the Hammersmith Palais and bonded over their shared passion for ballroom dancing; how he and his three sisters had enjoyed a happy childhood although Grant had been in a bit of trouble at school.

'It was fighting mainly – at my comp, the boys had to stand up for themselves if they wanted to avoid being bullied.'

His father had pushed him towards a career in the police, convinced that it would provide the ethical imperative his son needed – and a decent pension. Unlike Alex, Grant had served his time as a uniformed constable. A keen sportsman, he'd represented the Met at athletics and cycling, as well as football and cricket. It was through these sporting contacts that he'd been approached and asked if he wanted to work in the less publicised areas of the force such as surveillance and undercover operations.

He wasn't allowed to talk about the work he did beyond mentioning that he was currently based in Manchester and that being a heavy drinker was part of his 'legend', the backstory devised for every UC officer before they were deployed. Grant told Alex how different this pub was to the Brickmakers, where he currently had to spend a lot of his time.

'It ought to be called the Troublemakers,' he told her, 'given the reputation of most of its clientele. Although to be fair, they generally behave themselves. If you want a quiet night, go to the pubs the criminals use. They tend not to tolerate disturbances.'

He told Alex that he was only back in London for a week to 'touch base' with the team led by DCI Barry.

'But doesn't Manchester have its own force?' Alex asked.

'In this line of work, the Met goes everywhere,' was all Grant would say in response.

Alex told him about her own sporting prowess, and had no qualms about pointing out the two false teeth she'd acquired after being smacked in the mouth with a hockey stick.

'People don't realise what a terribly dangerous sport hockey is,' she chortled happily, the trauma of that morning's clash with DCI Barry no longer dominating her mood.

Grant liked Alex's lack of pretentiousness, her stunning smile and the way her lips pursed when she was listening intently. Alex liked lots of things about Grant – his quiet demeanour, elegant hands, broad shoulders and soft brown eyes. He asked for her address.

'Why?' she asked, smiling broadly. 'Are you going to write me a letter?'

Grant joked that she may get a Christmas card if she was lucky.

'In my line of work phone numbers are an unreliable method of staying in touch; they change all the time. An address is more permanent . . . And who knows? I might rock up at your front door one day.'

As she watched him write the address down, Alex was surprised to realise how much she wanted him to know where she lived. She decided that, should he walk her home that evening, she'd invite him in, and then who knows what the night might have in store.

She was contemplating this erotic scenario, wondering how tidy her flat was and whether she'd made her bed before leaving that morning, when the atmosphere suddenly changed. Alex's attention was drawn to a man who'd just walked into the pub alone, a slim, middle-aged, red-haired man in a pin-striped suit. Grant had his back to him, but Alex noticed this man staring across at them.

Her companion, realising that Alex's attention had wandered, turned to follow her line of sight. The red-haired man was by now talking to the barman, but hadn't noticed that Grant had clocked him.

'I'm sorry, Alex, I need to leave now,' Grant announced. 'You stay here and keep drinking as if you're waiting for me to come back from the toilet.'

With that he slipped away from the table as if heading for the Gents, which was downstairs. Red-Haired Man turned to watch but, distracted by the barman giving him his change, failed to see Grant walk past the stairs leading down to the toilets and slip quickly through the narrow door onto the street. Alex sat sipping her gin and tonic through a straw, Grant's half-emptied pint glass undisturbed beside her. After ten minutes the man with red hair came over to her table.

'Excuse me,' he said putting a small tumbler tinkling with ice on the high table and taking the chair that Grant had vacated. 'That man you were talking to when I came in, he looked very much like an old friend of mine. Has he gone?'

'Yes,' said Alex. 'He had to be somewhere.'

'Do you know him well?' the man asked.

'Not at all. We just struck up a conversation in here this evening.'

'Does he live local?'

'I really have no idea.'

The man said nothing more. Putting his drink down, he hurried out of the Two Chairmen.

When Louise Mangan got home that evening, she lay in a hot bath reflecting on her conversation with Detective Sergeant Din. She thought about Sage, about his startlingly green eyes and peaceful disposition. He'd led such a quiet life beside the Thames and come to a violent end on the boat he adored. She thought back to the last time she'd seen him, with that woman – what was her name? Tilly? Jilly? Louise remembered that he was about to go back-packing, but had arranged for the girl to come to the *Inner Peace* to tell Louise about her boyfriend, Patrick Venn.

The file had confirmed that the DNA matched someone by the name of Ian Escreet. But if a convicted sex offender wanted to reinvent himself in the days before the Sex Offenders Register, surely the first thing he'd have done was change his name. Indeed, it was something that happened all too often even today. It only cost about forty quid to do it by deed poll, was perfectly legal and some convicts even did it whilst still serving their sentence. Ian Escreet could easily have changed his name to Patrick Venn.

Everything pointed to Venn as the Beast of Hampton Court. The guy she'd seen cycling towards her on the A380 had, in all probability, turned off at Tagg's Island where

Venn lived; Venn rode a sports bike; his girlfriend had not only admitted that he could become violent when sexually frustrated, but also that he would utter the precise words of abuse that the Hampton Court attacker shouted at his victims.

Venn's girlfriend had been courageous enough to report all this to Louise on Sage's houseboat that Saturday afternoon, and yet there was no evidence that the woman had ever been formally interviewed.

What was her name?

Louise had kept a diary ever since she'd begun her career with the Met twenty-seven years ago. Her aim was to capture the daily events in what she was convinced would be an exciting life worth recording. The diaries were stored haphazardly in a cardboard box at the back of the utility room in her Brixton flat. When she'd still been with Tom, he'd remonstrated with her about copying in sections of her police notebook, arguing that such information was the property of the Metropolitan Police Service, and not hers to duplicate. She'd pointed out that the police notebooks were destroyed after six years, and she was fully entitled to ensure the bits that were an integral part of her life survived.

'But you'll never read them,' Tom had claimed, and he was right; she never had. As she rose through the ranks finding time to do the diary became more difficult and by the time of the divorce, she'd given up trying. But she now needed to consult one diary from twenty years ago to see if the name of Patrick Venn's girlfriend had been recorded, and she felt this provided retrospective validation for all the effort that Tom had questioned.

After a long soak, she poured a large glass of Sauvignon Blanc, dragged the cardboard box into the living room and began the process of trawling through the accumulated Boots 'Page-A-Day' diaries. It took a couple of hours to find the diary for 1999, not because it was difficult to locate, but because she couldn't resist thumbing through diaries from other years.

She'd been more assiduous in the earlier years, the entries gradually changing from full detail to sketchy out-line as her responsibilities increased. And the personal was mixed with the professional, the happy with the sad: the joyous holidays in Crete with Tom and the girls, Michelle's first birthday, Louise's mother's dementia. Fortunately, the break-up with Tom and the pain of the divorce came after the diary-keeping had ended, otherwise she'd have been masochistically tempted to relive that awful experience.

Eventually the ticking clock forced her to concentrate on the information she'd set out to find. Petros had committed to ringing her from Athens at 9 p.m. (11 p.m. his time) and he was always very precise in keeping to these arrange-ments. She and Captain Diamantapoulis were planning a May weekend together in Barcelona and he would be call-ing to finalise the details. What had begun as a passionate romance had settled into a comfortable cycle of monthly telephone conversations with occasional physical contact that they both knew wasn't frequent enough to constitute a meaningful relationship.

She found the diary entry she was looking for. On that momentous day in April 1999, she'd met Sage and – here, the girl's name was written clearly in her elegant script – Vicky West. She'd gone on to record how, upon leaving the *Inner Peace* later than expected, she'd walked straight into the police raid on *Navicula* that was part of Operation Zeus.

That monumental blow against the illegal drugs trade, followed quickly by the murder of Jenny Daniels, undoubtedly distracted police attention from the assaults in Hampton Court and the investigation into the death of Tiffany Mordaunt.

The file suggested that there'd been an inconclusive effort to find Ian Escreet. The Met had his DNA profile and, thanks to her report, the testimony of Vicky West which clearly pointed to Patrick Venn as the perpetrator. Yet Tiffany's murder remained unsolved. And now Sage was dead.

Surely, as Din had implied, there was enough overlap to at least provoke a renewed effort to find this man Escreet, who was, perhaps, the missing cyclist, Patrick Venn.

The more she thought about it the more convinced Mangan became that the best way to prove that misogynistic attitudes in the Met had changed would be to authorise a cold case review into the murder of Tiffany Mordaunt. She certainly felt she could have done more to find Tiffany's killer. If only her younger self had been more assertive. Sure, she had been moved on to other work, but she had the vital testimony from Vicky West. Knowing how lax the force was concerning attacks on women, she should never have restricted that valuable information to a report that probably ended up on Sean Meredith's desk. He would still have been trying to justify the arrest of Darnell Thomas.

Even twenty years later that arrest made Louise blush with embarrassment, knowing that she was one of the officers who had arrested him. She needed to see the Deputy Commissioner urgently. The successful candidate was due to be announced tomorrow. Mangan would seek an early audience.

Her phone rang, as scheduled, at nine o'clock. She and Petros talked like friends rather than lovers. He told her about a murder investigation he was involved in, and she told him about catching Basil Bennett red-handed. When they eventually got round to the reason the call had been arranged, Petros told her he was no longer free to meet her in Barcelona on the dates they'd agreed. He was sorry to have to tell her that he was now obliged to attend a police conference in Thessaloniki.

28

FINDING DETECTIVE CONSTABLE TRAORE

Alex didn't know what to do for the best. She'd tried to call Grant Traore on the number he'd given her only to hear the high-pitched whine of a disconnected phone. A subsequent text failed to send. Through the course of a largely sleepless night, she resolved to contact DCI Mark Barry next day.

Despite the head of Grant's unit being so obnoxious towards her, she needed to assure herself that Grant himself was okay. She'd considered consulting Louise Mangan but decided this would only be passing the buck. This was her issue to pursue and, daunting though the prospect was, she needed to tell Barry about the curious incident in the Two Chairmen.

She looked in the canteen as soon as she got to New Scotland Yard but there was no sign of Barry or any of the men he was usually with. Alex went straight to reception to ask where she might find Detective Chief Inspector Barry and, once she'd established her entitlement to receive such information by telling a white lie about acting on DCS Mangan's behalf, was given a mobile phone number, which she rang straight away.

A gruff voice answered with a single syllable – 'Yes?'

When the voice confirmed that Alex was indeed speaking to Mark Barry, she relayed her account of the previous evening; how she and Grant had gone to the Two Chairmen for a drink; the arrival of the red-haired man in a pin-stripe suit; Grant's obvious consternation and rapid departure; how the red-haired man had approached her to ask where her companion had gone and left hurriedly, apparently in pursuit.

'I tried ringing and texting the number Grant gave me, but it was disconnected,' Alex said in conclusion.

'Are you the blond bird who invited yourself onto our breakfast table?' Barry asked.

'No,' Alex said firmly, 'I'm the Detective Inspector with fair hair who sat at the same table as you the other morning. I wasn't aware that I was an egg-laying vertebrate or that tables in the canteen could be owned.'

She was immediately annoyed with herself for being so curt when the pertinent issue wasn't Barry's attitude but Grant Traore's welfare. But she'd approached the conversation determined not to be cowed by this man. There was silence at the other end broken only by the noise of passing traffic. Barry was obviously out on the streets.

'You won't have got through to Grant because he uses burner phones,' Barry said eventually, 'he's probably gone through two or three since giving you that number. He shouldn't be using them to chat up birds and he shouldn't be frequenting pubs around Westminster.'

There was another pause before Barry said, 'Listen, Tinkerbell, you've done good to tell me, but Grant can look after himself. I wouldn't worry about it. I've got your number now so when I see Grant, I'll tell him to get in touch or I'll ring you myself to let you know that he's fine.'

Alex didn't have an opportunity to respond before Barry rang off.

'What's up with you?' Rushil Din asked when Alex walked into the outer office of DCS Mangan's department. 'You look as if you've won the lottery but lost your ticket.'

She responded with something about not sleeping properly, having already decided not to say anything about the incident in the Two Chairmen to any of her colleagues. Her phone call with Mark Barry had been difficult, and Alex considered his response unsatisfactory, but at least she'd alerted Grant Traore's boss to the worrying events of the previous evening. It wasn't as if she was entitled to expect a call from Grant. They hardly knew one another. His job, working undercover in Manchester, wasn't exactly a nine-to-five occupation. He was bound to be difficult to contact – she'd hear from him eventually, she thought . . . she hoped.

There was only one topic of conversation in Mangan's office that morning - the new Deputy Commissioner. The appointment of the Australian, Bob Statham, had just been announced. According to the press release, Statham had 'built a fearsome reputation by taking on the powerful local mafia in Melbourne and severely curtailing it's influence and activity.'

His appointment was the subject of much debate amongst Mangan's staff. Din thought it a mistake not to promote the Assistant Commissioner who'd applied from within the Met; another detective on the team had been a vociferous advocate for Connor O'Farrell from Counter Terrorism, but Louise said she'd once worked with him and thought he was already over-promoted. During a coffee break in the canteen later that morning, she expressed her view that not appointing Sandra Smith, the Chief Constable of Lancashire, was a missed opportunity.

'It would have sent an important message to counter the perception that we're a boys' club. I know there are those who believe that having a woman Commissioner and Deputy Commissioner is unthinkable, but they're the type of people who thought that two women newsreaders on *News at Ten* heralded the end of civilisation. I suspect that the only reason Sarah didn't get the Deputy job was because Karen became Commissioner – the system could just about cope with one woman at the top but not two.'

The only person who spoke up for the Australian was DCI Harry Kosnich. 'The Aussies I've spoken to reckon he's mustard,' he said, dipping a custard cream into his large mug of black tea. 'I don't buy this "grow your own" theory. If we can get the best footballers in the world into the Premier League, we should be able to get the best coppers in the world into the Met. In any case he emigrated to Australia: he was born here. From all I hear, Bob Statham speaks our language – in more ways than one.'

'Well, let's hope he does,' Mangan said, bringing the discussion to a close, 'because I've asked his office for an early meeting.'

'To discuss violence against women and young girls?' Alex asked.

'Yes, violence against them now and twenty years ago.'

When the break was over, but before the team dispersed, Mangan asked Din to step into her office.

'I've thought about what you said yesterday regarding Sage, and I think you're right about there being too many unanswered questions.'

Din had guessed that her reference to seeking an early meeting with the new Deputy Commissioner was connected to those parts of the 1999 file that had been redacted.

'Good call, Chief,' he said. 'Can I come with you when you see Mr Statham?'

'We'll see. It might be better for me to see him alone and you might have retired by the time I manage to break into his diary anyway. But there is something you can do right now.'

Mangan told her Detective Sergeant about her suspicion that Ian Escreet, whose DNA matched that found in the Tiffany Mordaunt case, and Patrick Venn, the cyclist who, like Sage, had lived in a houseboat on Tagg's Island, were one and the same person.

'When I see the Deputy Commissioner, I will ask to see the redacted bits of that file, but my priority will be to convince him to instigate a cold case review into the murder of Tiffany Mordaunt. When I last spoke to Sage twenty years ago, Venn had already done a bunk, so he won't be easy to find. Making him a prime suspect in a re-opened murder investigation will help. That last conversation with Sage was also when I spoke to Venn's partner, whose name I only remembered last night. Vicky West was a principal witness, the fact that she didn't even warrant a mention on the file shows how rudimentary the investigation into Tiffany's murder must have been.'

'To be fair, Chief, they were looking for Ian Escreet not Patrick Venn.'

'But I submitted a report of my meeting with Vicky. You'd have thought her testimony would have sparked sufficient interest for her to at least be questioned. They didn't do that then, but we need to do it now. I need you to trace Vicky West. She may have a married name by now, of course. All I can tell you is that she was a pretty blonde with a full figure who looked as if she was just out of her teens, so she'd be around forty now. She'd been on a dance and drama college course somewhere in Richmond, Surrey. Oh, and while you're at it, get me all we know about Ian Escreet.'

'You've got a great memory to retain all that stuff about Vicky West from a conversation twenty years ago,' Din said.

Mangan thought it best not to reveal the transcription of bits of her police notebook into her diary, feeling that her conscientious assistant would be bound to disapprove, and so just smiled sweetly, saying, 'I was young and hadn't lost so many brain cells back then. I'm just sorry I can't give you more to go on.'

'That's okay, with your authority I can scan all the usual files, census information, council-tax payers, etc., including the ones that only officers of your rank can see. Given that we've got his DNA, there must be a case file on Escreet.'

'Do your best, Rushil, and get Alex to help. It would be good for her to at least get to know her way around the Police National Computer.'

'I'm a bit worried about her,' Din said, getting up to leave. 'She's very subdued, has been since yesterday – as if she's had some bad news.'

'Okay, I hadn't noticed but there again I've not seen too much of her recently. I'll have a quiet word to see if she wants to talk about it. Can't have our Alex subdued, it would be like having a power cut.'

That evening, as Alex Cornelius passed the Two Chairmen on her way home, she decided to pop in for a drink. She knew she wouldn't find Grant Traore there, but she fancied a drink, and it was a nice pub that contained some pleasant memories from the other night. The cramped atmosphere, those tall chairs and high tables, the smell of burger and chips – it would all remind her of the serenity she'd felt in Grant's company.

Alex was still concerned about his sudden disappearance. She'd given up trying to contact him since her conversation with Barry, but she continued to worry about what might have happened to him. The next best thing to sharing an evening with him would be to return to the place where she'd last seen him and worry about him there.

She pushed her way to the bar. It was around the same time as they'd arrived the previous evening, and the pub was just as crowded. Alex couldn't help scanning the room in the illogical hope of seeing Grant. Then she began looking for the red-haired man whose entrance had put her companion to flight. He may well be someone who frequented the place regularly and she concluded that she ought to try to find him if she wanted to solve the mystery of Grant's disappearance. *You're a detective*, Alex told herself, *for God's sake do a bit of detecting.*

Everybody in the pub seemed to be in the company of friends, from couples talking furtively in corners to gaggles of workmates filling all the available floor space and emitting great gusts of laughter that became louder with each round of drinks.

Rain began to lash against the pub's leaded glass windows as an evening storm made the prospect of leaving even more unattractive. Once she got herself served at the bar, Alex continued to push her way through the melee, protecting her tall glass against the crush, scanning the faces of her fellow drinkers. She made her way outside to peruse the smokers huddled in the shelter of an overhanging balustrade and then back into the pub to examine the diners who'd found a table on which to rest their plates.

It was then that she saw him. He was coming in from Dartmouth Street, wearing a different suit, but was unquestionably the same red-haired man. Not wanting to be seen standing alone, Alex started speaking to some people close by.

'God, this place doesn't get any quieter, does it?' was enough to spark a conversation and make it seem as if she was in company. The red-haired man brushed by her making his way towards the bar. Looking round he paused, looked back and returned to where Alex was standing, staring at her intensely.

'Oh, hello,' Alex trilled. 'Did you find your friend?'

'No, have you seen him anywhere?'

'No, I haven't, but I'm just someone he was chatting up, you seemed to know him very well.'

'Can I get you a refill?' the man asked, having to shout above the hullabaloo.

'I'm in a round with my friends, but if you insist, I'll have a G and T – Hendricks gin, Fever Tree tonic.'

When he came back with the drinks, they moved towards one of the high tables, but not before Alex said a profuse farewell to three bemused drinkers who hadn't a clue who she was. The red-haired man introduced himself as Martin. She calculated he must be in his early fifties, much older than her. He wore a wedding ring, had an expensive watch strapped to his wrist and the suit he wore was blue worsted, probably not off-the-peg from Primark. He told Alex he was a businessman from Manchester who'd come to London for a conference at the Institute of Directors. Alex mentally filed away this information. But she needed his surname and so asked for his card, which was freely given.

MARTIN CUTLER
Managing Director
MODERNATE

was printed in embossed gold on thick white card, along with an address in Salford and two telephone numbers – landline and mobile.

Modernate was a management consultancy that 'specialises in finding digital solutions to analogue problems', as Martin explained before asking about Alex. She surprised herself by inventing a persona on the spot. She was Alex Maddison, a civil servant working in Her Majesty's Treasury. Cutler didn't ask for a card, but she'd already prepared to tell him that she wasn't of a sufficiently high grade to have one. He did ask for a mobile number which Alex gave him, calculating that it was a risk worth taking if it would help to find Grant.

They talked for ten minutes without getting to the point, until Martin said, 'Sorry about last night. I could have sworn the guy you were talking to was an old friend who I haven't seen in years.'

'Did you catch up with him?' Alex asked.

'I wasn't trying to.'

'I thought you were, the way you left so quickly,' Alex said, struggling to retain the light-hearted nature of the exchange.

'Did he tell you what his name was?' Martin asked.

'Yes. What was the name of your old friend?'

'Philip Geddes.'

'I've forgotten his name already, but it wasn't that. I'd know if you said it.'

Alex could tell that Martin Cutler was just as keen to glean information from her as she was from him. This was no casual encounter. He must have come to the pub in the hope that she'd be there. They were playing a game. She didn't trust Cutler and was certain that he didn't trust her.

However, both of their stories were plausible enough. Alex could have been chatted up by a guy she'd never seen before, and Martin Cutler could be a legitimate business-man who'd travelled down to London for a conference and thought he'd seen an old friend in a Westminster pub. They were both playing their parts well enough to maintain the charade.

Cutler offered to take her to dinner, but Alex decided not to push her luck. He had learnt nothing about her apart from a mobile number, whereas she had a name, a business address and two telephone numbers, all of which may well have been genuine . . . unlike the surname she'd given him, and the guff she'd made up about a civil service career.

So, concluding that she'd better quit while she was ahead, Alex told Martin she needed an early night, left the pub and headed for home.

She knew she'd be followed. Despite the bonhomie and the light-hearted way each of them had explained their brief encounter the previous evening, the mutual distrust lurked like an iceberg just beneath the surface.

Why had Martin Cutler come back to the same pub if it wasn't to see if Alex was there? And whilst Cutler may have believed it feasible that Alex was telling the truth about Grant Traore chatting her up, she'd spent a long time last night making it look as if he'd just popped to the loo. Why else if not to disguise his early exit?

Alex wasn't scared about being followed; far from it – she was thrilled. It made her feel like a proper detective, even if she was the pursued rather than the pursuer.

The rain outside had stopped but a thick curtain of misty darkness was descending as she left the Two Chairmen. It didn't prevent her spotting him as she walked along Petty France on her way up to Victoria Street. A slow-moving taxi provided a clear reflection of who was behind her as she paused ready to cross the street. Cutler was too close and too ginger not to be noticed.

She cut down Palmer Street, past the rear entrance of St James's Park tube station and, as she walked, she held her mobile in front of her as if conducting a FaceTime conversation. But the camera was in selfie mode, and she could see him bobbing along behind her. By the time she got to the House of Fraser department store on Victoria Street she'd formulated a plan of evasion. She took the escalator to the first floor – women's clothing – to spend a few minutes rummaging through a rack of dresses. She held one of them in front of her as if checking how it looked in the full-length mirror, whilst observing her pursuer, loitering sheepishly in the lingerie section. Alex put the dress back on the rack and took the up escalator to the second floor. There she sprinted the twenty metres to the down escalator, as if tearing along the wing in a hockey match. She calculated that she'd be back on the ground floor before her lumbering pursuer had reached the second.

It was ten minutes before a bemused Martin Cutler came hurrying out of House of Fraser, phone in hand, frantically looking up and down Victoria Street for his quarry. Alex watched from the window seat of the Starbucks opposite as he half walked, half ran towards Victoria Station. She finished her cappuccino and set off in the opposite direction to her flat on Howick Place.

When she arrived home, Alex texted Detective Chief Inspector Mark Barry with a full account of the evening's events and a photograph of Martin Cutler's business card. She ended the text message by emphasising that she didn't expect to receive any details of Grant's mission but would appreciate a simple reassurance that his whereabouts were known and that he was safe. There was no response.

29

MANGAN MEETS THE MAN FROM MELBOURNE

It was three weeks before DCS Mangan met the new Deputy Commissioner. She considered this to be remarkably speedy, given her low expectations. The gossip in New Scotland Yard was that Bob Statham had insisted on starting with the Met straight away. He'd convinced the State Governor of Victoria that the sooner he left Australia the better and the Governor had agreed to waive the notice period that he could have insisted on. Far from being resentful of one of their senior officers being poached in this way, Statham's transfer had evoked a sense of national pride Down Under, summed up in one Australian newspaper's headline 'Once They Sent Us Their Convicts – Now We Send Them Our Police'.

The word on the street was that Statham had told the Met that he didn't need time to bed in domestically and wanted to get on with the job. He hardly had any family commitments anyway. Statham was divorced and his two kids were being raised by their mother in Adelaide. A fortnight after his appointment was announced he was in London, occupying the big, but rather dismal Deputy Commissioner's office on the top floor with its wonderful view of the river.

The gossip-mill continued to churn; Statham had turned down a lavish housing allowance, preferring instead to occupy a modest flat in Kennington; he'd warned the Mayor of London, whose idea it had been to appoint him, not to intrude into operational matters; asked Commissioner Karen Dale to cancel the posh cocktail reception at a hotel in Westminster she'd arranged, saying he'd prefer to meet his senior team in a pub close to Trafalgar Square.

Louise Mangan could confirm this last piece of gossip as fact, having received the invitation to attend the reception at the St Ermin's Hotel, and then the email informing her of the event's cancellation.

She'd gone to the pub near Trafalgar Square and observed Karen Dale swanning around introducing Statham to the various senior coppers in attendance. One wag said it was like Rod Hull guiding Emu, so closely did Commissioner Dale stick to her new Deputy, a pale man of medium height with a saggy double chin. He'd wedged his uniform cap in his left armpit leaving his bald head exposed.

Mangan was one of the last to be introduced.

'This is Detective Superintendent Mangan, who until recently was an Assistant Commissioner. She's helping us with some detective work prior to retirement, aren't you, Louise?'

Statham took Dale's cold introduction in his stride and Louise thought she sensed a countervailing warmth in his response.

'Hopefully, you won't be retiring until we've had that meeting you've been asking for,' he'd said, looking at her as if she was the most important person in the room, a knack that others had already told her he possessed. Louise was delighted that her request for a meeting had registered. It was set to take place four days after that encounter in the pub.

She had asked if DS Din could attend with her, but Statham made clear he wanted this initial meeting to be one-to-one.

'If we need to record any action points, we can do it easily enough without a minute-taker,' the Deputy Commissioner explained as he guided Louise towards the nest of straight-backed chairs in a corner of his office. 'The value of these meetings for me is to get to know the organisation I'm working for through building a relationship with its senior officers. Sometimes, having other people present militates against openness and honesty, and these are the things I value most in the people I work closely with.'

On his otherwise sparse desk, passed on their way to the nest of chairs, Louise noticed two files, one marked 'Violence Against Women and Young Girls – Policy', the other 'Murder of Tiffany Mordaunt – 1999'.

'I like what you're doing,' Statham announced as soon as they'd sat down. 'And everything I've heard about you.'

Louise had been told that the Deputy Commissioner's manner was typically Australian, direct and to the point.

'Was Karen correct when she said you were about to retire?' he asked.

'I suppose when a copper is approaching fifty, with thirty years of service, he or she is always "about to retire" in one sense.'

'Yes, in a sense. But what makes no sense whatsoever is for us to lose a bloody good detective. I need people like you to stay on the force.'

Louise said she had no immediate plans to retire.

'Bit of tension between you and the boss?' Statham said.

Mangan wasn't sure if this was a question or an observation. Whilst Statham had retained his English accent despite the many years since he'd emigrated, he had acquired the upward inflection common in the way Australians spoke.

'I didn't think I was a very good Assistant Commissioner,' was all she eventually said by way of a response.

'Listen,' Statham continued, after a few seconds of intensely observing Mangan's features as if trying to memorise them. 'I want you to go to town on this violence against women issue. I don't need to tell you that it's an internal as well as external problem. Externally, the most important thing is to be serious about stamping out domestic violence – that's the breeding ground; men who think it's perfectly acceptable to knock their wives and girlfriends around; sons who grow up watching their fathers beat their mothers and think the behaviour is linked to masculinity. As for the internal problem, some idiots in our ranks still classify women being assaulted by their partners as nothing to do with the police. Others are simply violent bastards who think that way because they're fond of indulging in a bit of domestic violence themselves. I was pleased to see you have a training programme written into the strategy, but this has to exist alongside of getting rid of the rubbish in our ranks – identifying the misogynists, not just launching some misguided belief that they can have the misogyny trained out of them.'

He went on to recite some of the problems that had been encountered trying to tackle these problems in Australia and how the attempts to counter what they termed as 'family violence' went hand in hand with a major programme of police reform.

'Strewth, Louise, I'm subjecting you to a lecture here. I didn't mean to punish you with a bloody speech.'

And then he said, 'Looking at the file it doesn't seem to me as if my predecessor did very much on violence against women and young girls. I want you to know that I regard it as *the* central issue in the Deputy Commissioner's brief.'

She was shocked. His predecessor was Karen Dale. Louise decided to say nothing, and Statham moved straight on to the other issue she'd come to talk to him about: the cold case review request.

'I don't see how we can demonstrate our determination to tackle the issue of violence towards women when a man who murdered a woman twenty years ago and assaulted many others is still free as a bird. Go to it, Louise.'

'Thank you very much. Does this mean you're giving me the authority to see the redacted bits of the file, sir?' Louise asked.

'Enough of the "sir" bollocks. You call me Bob and I'll call you Louise. Look, I don't know what's been redacted and I haven't had time to check with Karen just how sensitive this file, is but so far as I can see, those redacted bits relate to something different – a big push you guys had back in the day against drug trafficking. You don't need to see those bits to get on with the cold case review, do you?'

'Well, there is a bit of an overlap, as my sergeant puts it, with another unsolved murder that's more high profile.'

'Yeah, I know. Jenny Daniels, right? That was a big story all around the world, but where's the overlap?'

Louise explained about *Navicula*, Marko Rockov and Colin Brown. Statham listened intently.

'I'm not authorising you to re-open the Jenny Daniels case because my understanding is it was never closed. If there's any part of the redacted stuff that you specifically feel you need for the cold case review, you come and see me, right? There's nothing restricted about the murder of Tiffany Mordaunt. You get on with that and we'll see how things develop.'

As he showed Louise to the door, his hand on her elbow, Statham repeated his admiration for her skill as a detective. Louise was thinking this was just a bit of insincere flattery, but as if reading her mind, the Deputy Commissioner's parting words were, 'I don't do bullshit, Louise.'

30

TRAORE'S DILEMMA

Detective Constable Grant Traore had dedicated two years of his life to one project – infiltrating and destroying the gang responsible for a significant percentage of all serious crime committed in the Manchester area. Now the first objective had been achieved and the second was in prospect.

A security operative at Manchester Airport who knew all there was to know about airside operations, had told her lover about a consignment of valuable diamonds due to be stored in a warehouse close to Terminal 3, before being shipped out on a private plane to Abu Dhabi. Unbeknown to the security operative, her lover was a career criminal – part of the gang that Grant's undercover police unit was determined to demolish. Six men had been recruited by the gang for this airport job. Grant Traore, or 'Philip Geddes' as they knew him, was one of them.

The gang was known colloquially as Blue Moon because of an allegiance to Manchester City FC. It was by far the most successful criminal enterprise in the northwest, as well as the most vicious. They were responsible for at least four murders and numerous cases of GBH. Whilst most of the gang's foot soldiers were familiar to the police, little was known about the man in charge; only that he was a powerful individual who was good at sacrificing infantry to keep the General safe.

The Met had been working with Greater Manchester Police to put Blue Moon out of business by capturing the leader as well as his followers. Grant had spent two years in Manchester being Geddes, a cockney who'd served a prison sentence in Strangeways and had remained in the vicinity after being released. He was unable to return to London, he told all and sundry in the shady haunts he frequented, because he'd made too many enemies there.

Grant's undercover role was working well. His availability for the kind of work Blue Moon wanted done was floated on an information channel that the Met and GMP had gained access to, a sort of Job Centre Plus for criminals. His fictional prison sentence in Strangeways had been realistically established and contacts made with the criminal fraternities of Salford, Moss Side and Trafford. Geddes' 'legend' had been skilfully established.

Eventually, he'd been approached by an agent of Blue Moon to do some mundane stuff such as drug couriering and a bit of surveillance work which established his credentials and eventually led to him being approached for this airport job. Within a week of being recruited he'd been invited to attend a meal in a private dining room above an Indian restaurant on the Curry Mile in Rusholme. In two hours over biriyani and naan bread, Philip Geddes (Grant) had been briefed on the heist that was planned for a month's time. The guy giving the briefing had introduced himself as Raymond Sillars. He was a local businessman, and his girlfriend was the security operative whose pillow talk had been so revealing. Sillars had told the gathering that she had now been invited to join the planning team, making it clear that her acceptance of this invitation wouldn't be entirely voluntary.

Grant had been told by his boss, DCI Barry at New Scotland Yard, that Sillars was the man they were after; that Sillars was the respectable businessman who ran Blue Moon but remained well out of sight, behind the scenes. Grant had become less sure of this as the evening progressed. For a start, if he was the man behind the scenes, what was he doing here at the restaurant on full display. Apart from 'Philip Geddes', the crew consisted of a heavy known as Stitch Maguire, a Rastafarian called William, a geriatric safe-cracker referred to as Arnold, a Polish thug who spent the evening telling anyone who'd listen how feared he'd been in Warsaw, and a young, weasel-faced, skinny Manc in a baseball cap.

Sillars outlined the plan. Three of them were to use whatever force was necessary to access the warehouse, where Arnold would crack the safe and relieve it of its content. 'Philip' and Stitch would be responsible for the getaway. Questions were asked and answered, suggestions made before the outline plan was in place ready to be fine-tuned over the coming weeks. All of this had been recorded by Grant who'd gone to the restaurant with recording equipment taped to his upper torso underneath the fashionable hooded top he was wearing.

Perhaps Raymond Sillars was the overlord that Barry thought he was, Grant reflected. But there was something about his demeanour; a reticence, an indecisiveness, a meekness, that convinced Grant that they were in the presence of the monkey rather than the organ-grinder.

After the gathering had dispersed, coming downstairs a little while after the rest of the crew, having paid a visit to the toilet to readjust a wire that he feared was in danger of becoming visible, Grant saw Sillars going into the main restaurant. The rest of the gang had left the building. Grant wondered why their host would go into the restaurant. He surely couldn't still be hungry, and the bill had been called for and paid upstairs. Grant waited a few minutes before following. Raymond Sillars was sitting at a table near the door deep in conversation with a red-haired man. An attractive woman was with them, picking at food, uninvolved in the conversation.

Sillars seeing Grant, stood up quickly. 'Philip,' he said, 'the toilets are upstairs.'

'I know,' Grant said. 'I just want to make a reservation for next Saturday, my girlfriend's birthday. Such good grub here.'

'Good to know we're attracting cockneys to Manchester,' said the red-haired man without looking up.

'Philip's exiled here from London,' Sillars explained. 'Bit too naughty for the capital, weren't you, son?'

They laughed awkwardly. It was obvious that Raymond Sillars wasn't going to do any introductions so Grant went to the reception desk where, raising his voice, he made a reservation for two for Saturday in the name of Philip Geddes. Grant could sense that the red-haired man had been watching him with a studied intensity, but as he walked back past him, lifting a hand in a gesture of farewell to Sillars, the man with him was paying close attention to the menu.

*

Grant Traore was called back to New Scotland Yard two days later for what DCI Barry had described as a 'feedback session'. Although the jewel robbery wouldn't happen for weeks, Grant felt it was dangerous for him to disappear from Manchester and risk being seen in London. He said as much to Barry, who made light of his concerns.

'Listen, Grant,' the Detective Chief Inspector said, 'we've got the tape you recorded at the restaurant and the case is building nicely but this will probably be our last chance to get your feedback face to face, and to ensure there are no cock-ups when we move in to arrest your buddies. Follow three rules and you'll be okay. Rule one: no going back to your old haunts. Rule two: no chasing pussy. And rule three: no frequenting the fleshpots of London. Spend your evenings alone with a pizza in your room at the Premier Inn. You're not even allowed to go to the pub for a pint, you understand?'

'Yes, boss,' Grant replied, using Barry's preferred form of address.

'Oh, and one last thing. Don't go near any dealers in London. That's a sure way to advertise your presence.'

This was a reference to what Grant realised was a serious vulnerability. On a previous mission to bust a drug-smuggling cartel, it had been necessary for him to pretend to be a user. Unfortunately, he'd pretended too well and become addicted to cocaine. The Met had taken a sympathetic approach, recognising their culpability, and had put Grant on a rehabilitation course. Only DCI Barry knew that it hadn't worked. Grant didn't know how he knew, but he did. Barry had sidled up to him one day and whispered, 'A little bird tells me you've gone back to Charlie.'

Grant had mumbled something about being determined to overcome the addiction, to which Barry had simply given him a pat on the back and walked away. Nothing more was said, but Grant knew that his boss was content to use this addiction as a Sword of Damacles, to guarantee his loyalty.

When the red-haired man had come into the Two Chairmen, Grant knew he had to get away fast. Their encounter at the Indian restaurant had been recent enough for this friend of Raymond Sillars to remember every detail. Once outside the pub, hurrying back to Euston for a train to Manchester, he reflected on whether the man had actually seen him. Not just glanced casually in his direction, but actually seen him enough to know that Philip Geddes – the Manchester villain supposedly estranged from his home city – had been drinking in a London pub. Grant calculated that he'd got out in time. He was keen to find out who the red-haired man was, suspecting him of being part of Blue Moon. Hence his apparent closeness to Raymond Sillars. Perhaps he was the actual leader of Blue Moon, and Sillars his subordinate. But the Two Chairmen wasn't the place to make further enquiries. And he'd been having such an enjoyable evening with Alex, who he was confident would cover his back long enough for him to get to Euston.

Grant Traore was back in Manchester by eleven-thirty that evening, and made a point of appearing in his usual insalubrious haunts around the city, even to the extent of having a loud altercation with a barman in a Deansgate pub. Not his regular, but one equally notorious for its criminal clientele. Grant complained loudly about being short-changed. While no punches were thrown, his language was violent enough to get him forcibly ejected – which was exactly what he wanted. He also managed to acquire a different outer layer, taking somebody's black coat from the overhead rack on the train in an attempt to look different to how he'd looked in the Westminster pub – just in case any Blue Moon associates were being asked to report sightings.

Not much had been left behind in his room at the Premier Inn, just some toiletries, underwear and a couple of shirts. He'd thought about alerting the team at New Scotland Yard to pick them up but that would necessitate explaining what had happened; that he'd been in a pub, with a girl, and may well have been seen by the prominent criminal he was supposed to be helping to catch. Best say nothing. The room was paid for. Premier Inn was welcome to his stuff.

He could bail out of this assignment at any time. There was a phone number, all he had to do was dial it, give a code and the mission would be aborted. It was a last resort, and one that Grant calculated he wouldn't need. He'd been back in Manchester for two days now; nothing had happened; nothing would happen so long as he stayed calm. If the guy in the Two Chairmen had recognised him, Grant would have known by now. He was safe. Safe to continue being unsafe as a UC on an entrapment operation.

Tonight, he was in a transit van with the crew member who he'd be working with on the getaway. They were parked up by the perimeter fence watching the airside warehouse where the diamonds were to be stored. On the night itself, Sillars' girlfriend would ensure that Grant and his oppo could access the site in a stolen FedEx vehicle, picking up the other crew members who would emerge from that warehouse with the diamonds. Tonight's purpose was surveillance. Grant was working with Stitch Maguire – so named because of the faint scars left by the stitches that had saved his life following a gangland attempt to cut his throat, a botched attack fifteen years ago that had given Maguire an aura of invincibility.

What Stitch didn't know as they continued to observe the target, was that on the night of the robbery, he and Grant would be detained behind the wheel of the stolen van while their colleagues were being arrested inside the warehouse. These provisional arrangements had been finalised at the briefing session in London.

'Heard you got thrown out of the Rose and Crown the other night,' Stitch said in his gruff Mancunian accent as they began their reconnaissance.

'Given how bad the beer is in that shithole, being thrown out is better than being thrown in,' Grant responded, pleased to know that the disturbance he'd caused had registered in the right places.

They continued watching, taking notes like two ornithologists quietly observing a nest of rare birds. As they were driving away Stitch told 'Philip' that someone wanted to see them; a very important someone; the man who Stitch spoke of as 'the Top Gun'.

'Raymond Sillars?' Grant asked.

'I mean the real boss,' Stitch clarified. 'He wants to run through the plan with the crew, make sure everything's in place.'

'Where do we meet?'

'Fuck knows. Hasn't told me yet. Somewhere out of the way, I should think, a kind of company awayday.'

'Why will the boss be there? I thought he kept well out of the way.'

'Maybe he's there to tell you off,' Stitch suggested, 'for getting chucked out of that pub. You shouldn't be drawing attention to yourself this close to a major job.'

Grant thought Stitch was joking, although it was difficult to tell. He pressed his colleague again on why the Top Gun was due to join them.

'It is unusual. This guy stays well away from the dirty end of the business. There again, this is a high-value job, so I suppose he's entitled to make sure all the ducks are in a row. You should feel honoured. I've worked for Blue Moon on and off for ten years now and I've only seen Top Gun twice. You join the crew and get to see him straight away.'

'Does he have red hair?' Grant asked.

'He does as it happens,' said Stitch.

'I think I might have already seen him at the restaurant we went to,' Grant said.

'Well, I never saw him there.'

By now Stitch was pulling up next to the Brickmakers Arms from where he'd picked his passenger up earlier that evening. When Grant, a.k.a. Philip, asked when and where the meeting Stitch had told him about would happen, Maguire just said he should expect to be picked up over the next few weeks, probably from this venue.

Grant knew that this was the opportunity he'd been waiting for, to get beyond Blue Moon's foot soldiers such as Stitch Maguire and the rest of the guys who'd been at the Indian restaurant and identify their commanding officer. The man who, as Stitch had confirmed, wasn't Raymond Sillars.

31

RETURN TO TAGG'S ISLAND

It was raining heavily as the car carrying Louise Mangan drove across a narrow bridge onto Tagg's Island. Alex was driving, Louise was in the back. On the other side, they parked up, left the car and, under the shelter of a huge umbrella, walked through a little latched gate to stand in silence at the water's edge. All that was left of the *Inner Peace* was its fire-scorched hull.

Deputy Commissioner Statham had given Mangan authority to pursue the cold case investigation into Tiffany Mordaunt's murder, and this allowed her to commence enquiries here, where Tiffany had been found, on the island that held so many memories for Louise. The principal reason for today's visit was to question the residents and discover if any of them remembered Patrick Venn and his girlfriend, Vicky West.

The fire on Sage's boat was peripheral to the investigation, but provided a useful focus. Mangan had deployed four officers from her unit to make enquiries boat by boat, ostensibly about the fire, but actually to learn more about the couple who'd occupied *The Great Gatsby*. Unfortunately, many of the boats were empty through the winter, *Gatsby* being one of them.

Navicula, the grandest vessel on Tagg's Island – where

Rockov and his men had plied their illegal trade – was now owned by a businessman and was empty for most of the year. As they passed its grand facade Louise thought it looked much the same as it had twenty years ago, although the huge security gates had been replaced with scaled-down versions that were less forbidding.

Mangan asked Alex to oversee the quartet of officers who were due to visit all sixty-two boats on the island, suggesting that she also did some of those visits herself.

'Make sure we don't treat this as a box-ticking exercise. Patrick Venn is the prime suspect in a murder investigation. Did he reappear on the island? How long did Vicky West stay at *The Great Gatsby*? Use the fire as an excuse to ask about Sage. I know he went backpacking all those years ago, but I don't know when he came back. He was good friends with Vicky. Did she continue to visit him on the *Inner Peace* after he returned? Remember, our best chance of finding Patrick Venn is to find Vicky West. And if we find Patrick Venn, we also find Ian Escreet, who I suspect is one and the same. While you're at it, ask if Colin Brown is still doing odd jobs around here. He probably doesn't need the money with all the compensation he's received, but we know he still lives in the area. I'm trying to get authority to question him as part of this investigation but it's sensitive given all the Jenny Daniels stuff.'

Mangan could always tell when Alex was listening intently, because her lips pursed in an involuntary sign of complete concentration.

'She seems more like her old self,' Rushil had said of Alex before they'd left the office. 'Did you have that quiet word with her?'

'No, but I will. There's something going on between her and Mark Barry. When I was going home the other day, Elizabeth on reception asked me if I'd got hold of DCI Barry. Apparently, Alex used my authority to get Elizabeth to give her his personal mobile number. I didn't tell Elizabeth that I had no wish to talk to Barry, just played along with it. I've been waiting for Alex to talk to me about it, but she hasn't. Not a word.'

'Do you want me to look into it?'

'No, Rushil. Don't say anything. I'm planning to have a little heart to heart with her myself. You get on with trying to find Vicky West, while Alex and I pay a visit to Tagg's Island.'

It was ten o'clock in the morning.

Left on her own after Alex had departed with the umbrella to catch up with her four colleagues, Louise felt a surge of sadness. The rain was easing, and she was staring at what was once the *Inner Peace*. Being by herself was something she was used to. She wasn't one for self-pity, but she did worry that this was her destiny – to be alone.

Since their phone call the other evening, there'd been no further contact with Petros, her Greek policeman. Their weekend together in Barcelona hadn't happened, and now that he'd been promoted, she doubted there would be any more weekends together. Her hope of them both retiring together was fading.

Her morose mood wasn't helped by being on the island, in the rain, next to where Sage had lived – and died.

It felt as if she was standing by an open grave at a burial service. The slow rhythm of the water lapping sombrely against the shore seemed like the drum beat of a funeral march. She remembered her first visit to Tagg's Island on a morning not dissimilar to this, when she'd been startled by Sage coming up suddenly behind her, breaking the morning silence with his soft voice. As she dwelt on this memory, Mangan suddenly sensed that there was somebody close by. It gave her a peculiar sense of déjà vu. Twenty years ago, when she had felt this way, Sage had spoken, but this time the presence was silent.

She turned quickly and emitted a little gasp of surprise when she saw a man standing only a few metres away. He was wearing a dog collar.

'Sorry to startle you,' the man said. 'I'm Stephen.'

He held out his hand apparently confident that his attire was sufficient explanation for his presence. DCS Mangan introduced herself and, making the natural assumption that she was there in connection with the fire, the vicar told her he'd been providing pastoral care to a sick parish-ioner on the island when it broke out.

'It was good of you to administer to the needy at two in the morning,' Mangan said, genuinely impressed.

'It was two-thirty actually,' the Reverend said, as if such compassion was more natural at half-past the hour. 'And God's work isn't done in shifts.'

Mangan told him why she was there and a little bit about her past association with Sage.

In turn the man who'd surprised her said that he was the Reverend Stephen Marsh based at St Mary's in the parish of Hampton. He'd also known the deceased.

'Sage was such a spiritual man,' he reflected, 'although never remotely religious. Like everyone on Tagg's Island he was a bit eccentric. Living on a houseboat is a rather eccentric thing to do, don't you think? Sage just had a different type of eccentricity, a kind of other-worldliness.'

The rain had stopped, and the Reverend Marsh put his umbrella down without interrupting the flow of his conversation.

'Did you know that Fred Karno, of circus fame, once owned this island? Built a hotel here called Karsino which was very successful a century ago. I always imagine that the people who run off to join a circus have a similar motivation to those who choose to live their lives afloat – a desire to escape reality.' The vicar gave a thin smile, amused by his own observation.

'Sage told me all about the history of this island,' Mangan said. 'How Fred sold up when the hotel's popularity faded, and how the island is now owned by its residents.'

'Yes, that's right. It's a tiny part of my parish of course. The only time I come here is to give comfort to the sick and frail, as I was doing on the night of the fire. I actually gave pastoral care to Sage's aunty Jane, who lived here before him. In fact, that's how I got to know Sage.'

'Do you know anything about a man by the name of Patrick Venn?' Mangan asked. 'He rented *The Great Gatsby* over on the other side of the island.'

'Afraid not. I'd love to help the police with their enquiries, as they say.' The thin smile broke through once more. 'But, to repeat, this place is a mere thumbprint of my domain. The person you need to talk to is Rosemary Tillman. She's not only the secretary of the residents' association, she's also the island's institutional memory.

Fascinating woman: was a mezzo-soprano with the Royal Opera and the only person on this island who comes to church regularly. She's at St Mary's every Sunday when she's at home.'

Louise didn't say anything about her own regular church attendance at another St Mary's, the one in Brixton.

'Sounds as if Rosemary could be of enormous help to me. Where do I find her?'

'Her houseboat is *The Bounty*, but she's away in Spain at the moment.'

'Do you know when she's back?'

'Due back by the end of this week. She knows all about the fire because I texted her. Didn't want Rosemary to be shocked upon her return, but there again I didn't want to spoil her holiday, so all she knows is there was a fire. She doesn't know about poor Sage yet.'

Reverend Marsh stared reflectively across to the Surrey bank of the Thames. He was a short man with a kind face and more hair on his eyebrows than his head. He carried an air of melancholy, that seemed entirely appropriate to his profession – and Mangan's mood. Louise thought how good it would be to have him as the regular priest at her church rather than the succession of temporary shepherds sent to tend the dwindling flock that she was part of.

'I'm just a little puzzled about what you're doing here,' the reverend said. 'Surrey police have already spent a lot of time on Tagg's, why is the Met involved?'

'I apologise if I wasn't clear enough. We're here as part of our investigation into the unsolved murder of a young girl back in 1999. That's why I asked you about Patrick Venn. He's a prime suspect.'

'I see,' the vicar said. 'So you're not here in connection with the fire really. You accept that it was a tragic accident?'

The way he posed the question seemed to suggest he took a different view.

'Why?' she asked. 'Do you think someone might have started it deliberately?'

'Goodness me, no, of course not,' Reverend Marsh said emphatically. 'There's no enmity here. The residents of Tagg's Island are mostly artistic people; musicians, writers, painters; people who have an eye for beauty and a dread of anything confrontational. You could say that Sage was a typical resident. Why don't I take you to see Rosemary when she's back, give you an introduction so to speak? She'll be able to tell you more about this place than I can.'

It was late afternoon when Mangan was reunited with Detective Inspector Alex Cornelius, who had coordinated interviews with half the residents of the island. The task should be completed in the evening, Alex suggested, because of the number of boats whose residents seemed to be at work during the day.

'Even where there was somebody at home, they didn't have anything important to say,' Alex continued. 'There was nobody at *The Great Gatsby*, and I couldn't find anyone who lived here when Venn was renting it. Only a few people seemed to know anything about Sage. One guy who knew him said he always seemed distracted. He told me that if he'd been asked to bet on a boat catching fire, he'd have put his money on it being *Inner Peace*.'

'And Vicky West?'

'Nope, drew a blank on the name and description, although one of the arty-farty types did say he remembered seeing a young woman sunning herself on the *Gatsby* once, but it was a long time ago.'

'Lots of artistic people on the island, I'm told,' Mangan said.

'Painters,' Alex exclaimed. 'Lots of painters. One chap, old enough to be my grandfather, said he'd like to do my portrait. He's a proper artist, had a canvas on an easel and everything.'

'You should have accepted,' Mangan joked.

'Thought about it but the old goat would probably have asked me to do it *au naturel.*'

Mangan smiled, but her fondness for Alex Cornelius was tempered by the knowledge that her young assistant was hiding something to do with DCI Barry. And following her conversation with the Reverend Stephen Marsh earlier, she had a strong suspicion that he was keeping something from her as well.

32

ALEX MAKES A BIG MISTAKE

'Here's what we know about Vicky West.'

Rushil Din was reporting back to Mangan on the task he'd been given. Alex Cornelius, who had helped to trawl through a cascade of computerised information, was sitting next to him in Mangan's office at New Scotland Yard.

'Nice, well brought-up girl from a respectable family, mother was a teacher, still alive. Local police have interviewed her, but she claims Vicky has been estranged from the family for years, and so she has no idea of her whereabouts. Father was a businessman. Died four years ago, and the mother claims his anguish over Vicky contributed to his illness.'

'She may not have been a good daughter,' Alex added, 'but she was never in trouble with the police – nothing whatsoever on the PNC.'

'I never thought there would be,' Mangan said. 'Vicky's not the suspect. Her boyfriend is.'

'Sure,' said Din. 'But you did ask us to check, and Alex here is now a world expert on the police computer.'

The two officers smiled but Louise Mangan seemed to be in no mood for joviality.

'Okay, carry on, Rushil,' she said brusquely.

'Vicky had a passport. Used it for visits to Spain, Greece and Turkey but she hasn't travelled for a while. She's in this country somewhere.'

'What about HMRC?'

'There are a fair few Vicky Wests paying income tax, but none who match our Vicky's profile.'

'Council Tax?'

'Ditto. She may well be using a married name, but we found nothing in the Registrar's records. She could be living with a man whose surname she's adopted. And that man may well be Patrick Venn, although, as you know, we can't trace him either.'

'What about Ian Escreet?' Mangan asked.

'One offence as a twenty-one-year-old – attempted rape in Watford, the town where he lived. Young girl walking home late at night, Escreet bundled her into his car, drove her to some woods and tried to rape her. The girl screamed and fought him off. Another couple who were parked up in the area intervened. The bloke was a squaddie, and he gave Escreet a good hiding. You should see the mugshot, both eyes closed, broken nose, swollen lip – got a right pasting and then an eighteen-month sentence.'

'What else did you find out about him?'

'Parents divorced. Both professional people, both dead now. No siblings. Must have changed his name because we can't find any reference to him after he left prison. The probation service lost touch with him and his last known address in Watford is now a Vets for Pets.'

'It's as if three people have vanished into thin air,' Alex reflected. 'Patrick Venn, Vicky West and Ian Escreet.'

'The photo of Escreet may not be of much use to us, but do we have any photographs of Vicky West?' Mangan asked.

'Yes, we've got a passport photo, but it's from a while ago,' Din said.

'And am I right in thinking that Vicky doesn't pop up at all in the case file we're reopening?'

'Only through officers following up your report in 1999 who visited *The Great Gatsby* to talk to her. There was nobody home and they left a note asking her to contact them.'

'Nothing more?'

'No. Once they got the DNA match to Ian Escreet they were after him rather than Patrick Venn.'

'Did they by any chance also go to see Sage in response to my report?' Mangan asked.

'Yes, on the same day as they called on Vicky. He wasn't home either but that's no surprise. You said he was going backpacking in the Hebrides or somewhere, didn't you?'

'Could she and Sage have gone together?' Alex asked.

'Maybe. She was with him on the night when Colin Brown went back to get his coat,' Mangan said quietly, almost to herself, 'and I suspected that Sage had a girl-friend. I saw a bra on his washing line.'

'Gosh,' said Alex. 'A *ménage à trois*.'

'In Walsall we call it a threesome,' said Din. 'So you think Vicky was hooked up with Patrick Venn *and* Sage?'

'Yes, but Alex is right, we need to focus on the people we actually know exist – or existed in the case of Sage. Venn is nothing more than a name.'

'Where do we go next re Vicky West, Chief?' Din asked.

'I'm not sure but I've got an idea.'

There was an expectant silence until Mangan said, 'I need to speak to a priest about it first.'

Mangan had been waiting for the right opportunity to interrogate Alex about obtaining Mark Barry's contact details under false pretences. The chance presented itself later that afternoon. Alex had asked to see her about taking some annual leave and – after asking Din to prevent any interruptions – Mangan ushered her mentee into her office. Instead of showing her to the soft furnishings where they would normally sit, she directed Alex to a chair opposite her desk, like a headteacher preparing to admonish a pupil.

'I have two questions for you,' Mangan said immediately as Alex sat down. 'Question One, what's been upsetting you lately? We've all noticed how subdued you've become.'

'Oh, it's nothing. Just been a bit down lately, that's all. That's why I want to take some time off. Feeling a bit better now.'

Mangan let the reply hang in the air for a few moments before asking Question Two. 'When exactly did I ask you to get me the number of Detective Chief Inspector Mark Barry's personal mobile?'

This had the intended effect. Taken by surprise, and too guileless to invent something, Alex spilled the whole story, accompanying it with tears of anguish and embarrassment. Within half an hour Mangan had been told the complete answer to her second question, and could thereby discern the more accurate answer to the first.

Alex told her about sitting with Barry and his men at breakfast; about Grant Traore being keen to make a date; how she, equally keen, went to sit with Grant the next morning; about the abuse Barry had subjected her to; about meeting Grant on the way home; their visit to the Two Chairmen; how Grant had left quickly when the red-haired man walked in; and, finally, about how she'd acquired that man's contact details the next night before passing them on to DCI Barry, and Barry telling her that Grant used burner phones which was why she'd not been able to get through to him.

'I didn't want to go anywhere near him after the way he humiliated me, but I had to ensure he knew about this man, Martin Cutler. So I needed Barry's number. I could only get it if I said I was acting on your authority.'

By now Alex was dabbing at her eyes with a twisted paper tissue, sniffing noisily between sentences.

'You should have told me what Barry said immediately,' Mangan said in a tone harsher than Alex had heard her use before.

'I'm not reporting it to you now,' Alex insisted. 'I feel very strongly that if I report him, it will make Grant's predicament even worse.'

'And if you don't report him, Barry will continue to be the pathetic excuse for a copper he's been ever since he joined the force.'

Alex sat continuing to torture the diminishing tissue between her fingers, looking down to avoid Mangan's accusatory gaze.

'Our priority has to be to ensure Grant's safety, so I'll see Mr Barry about that before I pursue the formal complaint about his behaviour that you, my girl, are about to submit.'

'Oh, Grant's okay now. That's why I'm not as upset anymore – I heard from him yesterday.'

'Really? How?'

'A WhatsApp message – look.'

Alex held up her phone to show Mangan the exchange.

> Sorry about leaving you like that in the Two Chairmen. Just wanted to let you know I'm back in Manchester. How are you? X

> Much better now I've heard from you. Lots to tell you about old ginger-nut. Ha, ha, Speak soon. Alex x

'And this was yesterday?' Mangan asked.

'Well, last night. Why are you looking at me like that?'

'Because Alex, this can't be from Grant because you can't WhatsApp from a burner phone. Did you say you gave your phone number to this man, Cutler?'

Alex nodded and began trying to explain why she'd done that, but Mangan was already up and striding towards the door.

33

THE SATURDAY ROUTINE

'Pint of the usual?' Liam, the young barman asked.

Grant was following his usual Saturday routine – have a drink, place a bet, grab a cheeseburger from McDonalds for lunch. It had been two weeks since Stitch Maguire had told him about the awayday at which the crew's commander-in-chief would be in attendance. He wasn't expecting a formal invitation. It would happen like this: a car would stop beside him, a door would open, he'd get in, and off they'd go – to God knows where.

'Do you want anything with that?' Liam asked.

Grant knew the barman wasn't asking if he fancied a packet of cheese and onion crisps. This pub was his regular supplier of the thing he needed most of all, his cocaine supply. It was quiet enough for the deal to take place across the bar; a plastic pouch containing three grams was pushed his way in exchange for two crisp fifty-pound notes travelling in the opposite direction.

'Better spent on this stuff than waste it on the gee-gees,' Liam said, pointing to the copy of the *Racing Post* that Grant had placed on the bar while he completed the transaction.

'Oh, so now you're my fucking financial advisor?' Grant said cheerily.

Liam was a student at Manchester University who'd been sucked into the drugs trade as a way of supplementing his student loan when he became a barman at The Brickmakers Arms. Grant liked Liam; considered him to be one of the few genuine friends he'd made in Manchester and, despite his role in the drugs trade, a basically honest person in the nest of thieves that was the Brickmakers. He'd told Grant that his degree subject was Criminology, and that working here was a vital component in his education.

Walking away from the bar, Grant placed his drink on a table by the window to better catch the light – and to keep an eye fixed on the street outside. His hunch was that this Saturday would likely be the day. By following his regular routine he'd made himself easy to find. Grant realised he could be walking into a trap, that the man with red hair may well have arranged this awayday to discover what 'Philip Geddes' had been doing in that Westminster pub.

But having returned to Manchester so quickly and covered his tracks so well, he felt he'd retrieved the situation. If Top Gun – as Stitch had called the man in charge – had been so certain he'd seen him in London why would he wait weeks before taking any action? Grant had decided that it would be too dangerous to risk being wired for sound on this occasion. For a start he didn't know when they might come for him, and he didn't fancy going round Manchester day after day like a mobile radio station. He also felt that it would be taking too much of a risk.

But he had taken the precaution of bringing a tracker device disguised as an innocent-looking lighter that he now placed on the pub table along with his tobacco pouch and his pint. In this pub at this time of day there would be no attempt to enforce the 'smoke free' legislation – and the lighter did actually work. As long as he opened the window, Grant could enjoy a smoke with his pint and his paper. The two other customers were both smoking, and there would be no complaints from Liam behind the bar.

Grant flicked the little wheel on the lighter to ignite his cigarette. He then flicked the wheel in the opposite direction knowing this action switched on the tracker. Once activated, it had a battery life of several weeks. Now he was ready to write out his bet.

Feeling for the biro in the inside pocket of the long black overcoat he'd acquired on the train, he touched the letter that he'd been meaning to post. He'd written to Alex, reassuring her that he'd got back to Manchester with no obvious ramifications, and thanking her for covering his back.

He was still beguiled by the volatile blonde; impressed by her, intrigued by her. He badly wanted to see her again.

Texts, calls and emails from any device could be monitored, and this message was personal. So writing to Alex at the address she'd given him was the safest and most discreet channel of communication. The trouble was that he'd been carrying this letter around for the past fortnight intending to affix a stamp and post it, but arriving home every evening with it still in his pocket. He wondered if he should just tear it up. Alex Cornelius was a busy police officer who'd probably forgotten all about their evening together by now. In the absence of any news to the contrary, she'd assume that everything was alright anyway.

But on the other hand, the written word didn't come easily to Grant and there were sentiments in this letter that had taken a long time to compose and that he wanted her to read.

In the midst of these tender thoughts, as he looked out onto St John's Street through the pub window, he noticed a car pull up a few metres down the road. A black Mercedes with Stitch Maguire at the wheel. Out of the front passenger seat jumped the skinny lad with the baseball cap who he'd seen at the curry house. He was coming into the pub. Grant could see another man in the car behind Stitch, indistinct apart from his red hair. The young man in the baseball cap walked straight to the table where Grant pretended to be engrossed in his racing selections.

'Mr Geddes,' he said politely. 'Your car's outside.'

Grant folded his paper and was beginning to gather his odds and ends when Baseball Cap grabbed the lighter.

'No inflammables allowed in the car,' the lad announced, tossing the lighter into a metal bin next to what was once a period fireplace. Grant, invited to follow him out, pretended to be finishing writing out his bet whilst scrawling the Mercedes number plate, MA19 BXX, on the back of the envelope addressed to Alex Cornelius. He approached Liam at the bar.

'Just need to get this bet on,' he called to Baseball Cap who was swaggering towards the door.

Grant passed the envelope across the counter, along with a twenty-pound note.

'Do me a favour, Liam,' he said softly. 'Put a stamp on this and post it for me.'

'Christ! Is that how much a stamp costs these days?' Liam joked.

'Very funny – keep the change,' Grant said, hoping his friend would be better at posting letters than he'd been.

Grant may have had his tracking device confiscated, but he hadn't been frisked before getting into the car, so the Glock 17 pistol he'd tucked into the waistband of his chinos when he got dressed that morning was still there. He could feel its reassuring presence under his sweater. The black overcoat had been taken from him by Stitch and placed in the car boot whilst he was shepherded into the back next to the red-haired man; the man he'd seen in the restaurant and at the Two Chairmen pub. There was no greeting.

The man with red hair remained glued to his iPhone throughout the journey. As soon as one call ended another began. Neither Stitch nor Baseball Cap acknowledged Grant's presence, either. The continual phone calls demanded silence.

Grant had to restrain himself from asking questions such as: Where were they going? Why was he being honoured with a place in Top Gun's car? Where were the rest of the crew?

They drove through the centre of Manchester, doubling back on themselves several times. It was clear to Grant that they were taking precautions to shake off any vehicle that might be trying to follow them.

Still the phone calls continued, incoming and outgoing. The contributions from the back of the car were mainly monosyllabic – 'yes', 'fine', 'good' – with the occasional flourish, 'that would be great', 'it has to be Friday', 'I'm not budging' and, as the finale to one conversation, 'tell him to get stuffed.'

After half an hour of meandering back and forth they seemed to be on their way somewhere. Stockport was signposted and then Buxton. Now they were on a country road with fields all around before the Mercedes drove up a single-track lane to what Grant assumed was their destination. The red-haired man, phone still fixed to his ear, was the first to leave the car, striding towards some open French windows. Stitch and Baseball Cap were suddenly at the rear door helping their passenger out, like a couple of paramedics guiding a geriatric patient into A&E.

It was quick and it was deft. In fact, Grant didn't realise anything had happened until he felt the back of his sweater, searching for the comforting shape of his gun. It wasn't there. Neither was the burner phone that had been in his back pocket. The guy with the baseball cap looked pleased with himself. His blouson jacket bulged.

34

SHOWDOWN

Detective Chief Superintendent Mangan was with Alex Cornelius in the office of Deputy Commissioner Bob Statham. Mangan had asked Statham to use his authority to launch a search for Detective Constable Grant Traore and get him to safety if necessary, even if that meant scuppering his undercover mission. She explained how Grant had probably been spotted in a pub in London when he was supposed to be confined to Manchester. The man who'd seen him was a Manchester businessman known as Martin Cutler, strongly suspected of being surreptitiously involved in organised crime.

'DI Cornelius here was with Grant in the pub when Cutler appeared. Grant left immediately, and hoping he hadn't been seen. But Cutler had Alex's mobile number and he used it to trick her into confirming that Grant had indeed been the person with her in the pub. So the entire undercover operation has been compromised.'

Statham had put a call out for DCI Barry to join them. The atmosphere in the room was tense. Louise could tell that the Australian didn't appreciate this intrusion, and she completely understood his desire to have Barry in the room before discussing it further. It was only fair for the officer in charge of this covert operation to be involved in any decision to abort it. She'd already tried calling Barry herself, only disturbing the Deputy Commissioner when she'd been unable to make contact.

Mark Barry arrived five minutes later. Statham asked Louise to state her case again, which she did, diplomatically emphasising that DCI Barry would not have seen the WhatsApp messages and that she'd tried to speak to Barry before resorting to the Deputy Commissioner.

'If the WhatsApp message didn't come from Grant Traore, it must have come from Martin Cutler who now knows that Grant was definitely the man he saw in the London pub,' she concluded.

When the Deputy Commissioner invited Barry to respond he spoke like a man struggling to suppress his fury; a volcano that was about to erupt. 'That text to her,' he said, pointing dismissively at Alex, 'what mobile number was it from? We have Cutler's number. Was it his?'

The question was directed at nobody in particular but Louise took it upon herself to answer.

'No, of course it wasn't. He knew that Alex has his number. He was pretending the message was from Grant: of course he didn't use his own number. It was Alex who got his calling card and passed the details to you. That's the only reason you have his number.'

Barry, having asked the question, ignored the unwelcome answer and continued his angry cross-examination. 'What Cutler said to her was absolutely true. We've checked it out. He was down from Manchester for a conference at the Institute of Directors and staying in a hotel close to the Two Chairmen. Martin Cutler is a leading businessman in Manchester. Modernate is just one of his many companies. Just because he was trying to chat her up doesn't mean he was up to no good.'

'Why was he asking all those questions about Grant?' Mangan asked.

'Because he'd met him a few days before he travelled to London. Grant reported that he'd seen Cutler in an Indian restaurant he'd been to in Manchester. Grant thought he was the leader of the outfit we're after, but he's wrong. The man behind Blue Moon is a businessman by the name of Raymond Sillars, and we're on his trail.'

'Why did Cutler follow me that night?' Alex asked.

Barry suddenly seemed to be making an even greater effort to control his temper. 'I'm not sure he was following you – you have no proof of that. Since Grant raised this spectre of a red-haired man, we've spent time and effort checking him out.' DCI Barry was now addressing his remarks to the Deputy Commissioner. 'We know all about him now. You'll have Knights of St Gregory in Australia?' he asked.

'Of course. It's the highest order in the Catholic church.'

'Precisely. Bestowed by the Pope – a papal knighthood. Well, Martin Cutler has been ordained as one for his philanthropic work in Manchester. He's almost sainted.' The DCI paused for a few seconds to give his statement maximum effect, before carrying on.

'Going back to that WhatsApp message,' he said, as if acting out a courtroom drama. 'Even though she doesn't know if it came from Cutler, my colleague here is somehow convinced it didn't come from Grant Traore.' He turned to face Louise. 'Why?'

'Because Grant uses burner phones and burner phones can't access WhatsApp,' she answered.

'This is what happens when people with no knowledge of covert operations poke their nose in,' Barry said, turning towards Statham again, addressing his comments to the only other man in the room. 'If Grant Traore was in any kind of imminent danger I'd know about it,' he declared. 'I don't know how it works in Australia, but I don't imagine it's much different. There are procedures that can be activated immediately to abort a mission if the officer feels he's in imminent danger. What's more, each officer is armed and able to defend themselves. As for phones, our people don't always rely on burners, they often acquire mobiles that aren't registered to them and can't be used to trace them. From what Tinkerbell here tells me about Grant, he'd be keen to let her know he's okay – that's what he's done—'

Mangan intervened. 'Please refer to Detective Inspector Cornelius by her name, not your patronising epithet. Do you understand?'

Barry, taken aback by the vehemence of this reaction from an officer senior to him, looked to the Deputy Commissioner for support.

Statham spoke quietly. 'Her name isn't Tinkerbell, Detective Chief Inspector,' he said. 'Why use such a demeaning term?'

Barry was forced to back down.

'Sorry, sir,' he muttered diffidently.

'But he only contacted Alex after she'd given Cutler her number,' Mangan observed. 'If Grant was concerned enough to reassure Alex of his safety, why wouldn't he have done that straight away? Why leave it so long?'

Barry continued to address himself to the Deputy Commissioner as if the two women weren't in the room. 'Traore is a good officer but he has a weakness,' he said before suddenly switching his attention back to Alex. 'You told me when you reported that incident in the pub, that you'd bumped into Grant on Birdcage Walk that evening. Where do you think he was coming from? Not this building obviously. He was walking towards it; you were the one walking away from here.'

'How would I know where he was coming from?' Alex said, sticking her chin out defiantly.

'You don't know, but I do. It was dark? And you were walking alongside St James's Park?' Alex nodded. 'He'd have been coming back from meeting his dealer in the park.'

'His dealer?' Statham exclaimed. 'You mean this officer has a drug habit?'

'He does, sir,' Barry said. 'He acquired it in the line of duty, and we're doing our best to wean him off, although it does add to his credibility with the people he's mixing with in Manchester. Once we get this mob banged up – and that day isn't far off if we're allowed to get on with it – we'll get Grant properly fixed, but in the meantime . . . it can make him a bit unreliable at times with us, so I'm sure it must have an effect on his personal life as well.'

The Deputy Commissioner stood up, signifying that he'd heard enough. 'You obviously believe that DC Traore sent that message and that he's as safe as he can be on this type of mission,' he said to Barry.

'That's it in a nutshell, sir. As well as being able to abort the mission at any time and being armed, he has a tracking device which means we always know where he is. At the moment it's telling us that he's exactly where he should be, moving around central Manchester in accordance with his mission.'

'Okay. I know how important this undercover work is. If we intervene, this entire operation will collapse. I'm not willing to risk that. You can carry on, DCI Barry, but I'll expect regular reports and firm evidence that our guy is still operational and not in the kind of trouble that DCS Mangan understandably feared he was in.'

There was a smug look of satisfaction on Barry's face as he passed Mangan on his way out of the Deputy Commissioner's office.

As Mangan was about to leave, Statham called her back inside and, after making sure the door was shut, asked how she was getting on with the cold case review.

'It's going okay, sir, given the problems we were bound to have asking questions about something that happened so long ago.'

'Less of the "sir", please. I'll call you Louise if you call me Bob. Is that agreed?'

Louise said nothing. The stress of the encounter she'd just had with Barry was still permeating the room. She suspected that Statham had asked about the review in an effort to ease the tension between them.

'Let me tell you something, Louise,' Statham said. 'I've met lots of tosspots like Mark Barry in my time. You must have, too. Weak men in powerful positions who use their authority as a licence to bully and humiliate.'

'Yes, I have, sir, and you know what? They're still there despite all the expressions of solidarity I've heard from senior officers like you. If I can persuade DI Cornelius to submit a complaint about the disgraceful way she's been treated, we'll see how serious the Met is about enforcing their own guidelines.'

'Sure, go ahead, Louise. But in the meantime he's commanding an important unit on a dangerous operation and I have to ensure that our focus is on fighting crime, not each other. I've not been here long enough to understand the reasons behind the various personality clashes, but I do know that I'm second-in-command to the first ever female Commissioner of the Metropolitan Police Service. Surely that counts for something?'

Louise, still hoping he was right, despite her previous experience of working with Karen Dale, nodded in acknowledgement but said nothing.

'Talking of the Commissioner, somebody sent her a letter which impacts on your investigation.' As he spoke, Statham led Louise gently towards a seat.

'As you know, we got our press and publicity people onto this re-opened murder case, and they did a good job in getting the news media to report it. As a result, this woman – a Mrs Olive Burnett – wrote to the Commissioner saying she had something important to contribute.'

The Deputy Commissioner handed over a file on the

face of which was a memo from Dale's office which was in a typeface large enough for Mangan to read as it was handed across.

'This woman apparently worked with Jenny Daniels on the *Crimesolve* TV programme twenty years ago. Her observations may well be helpful in the Mordaunt cold case review.'

The memo had obviously been drafted by someone in the correspondence team who dealt with all letters addressed to the Commissioner. Mangan doubted if Commissioner Dale had even seen it.

'The letter is on this file which is yours to read at leisure,' Statham said. 'I've had a glance through and asked for a copy to be sent to whoever was responsible for the Jenny Daniels investigation, which this touches upon.'

'I know that the Daniels case remains open, but there's been no serious investigation since Colin Brown was found guilty,' Louise told him.

'But that was overturned.'

'Yes, it was. Six years later. But the feeling was that there was nothing left to investigate.'

'Speaks volumes about what the Met thought about his conviction being overturned,' Statham said. 'But I know how determined you are to avoid being diverted onto the Daniels case and this letter specifically refers to the sexual assaults around Hampton Court at the time. We'll have a catch-up on this in a few weeks' time if that's okay with you.'

'Thank you, sir,' Louise said as she got up and moved towards the door.

'I'll say it again: call me Bob.'

'I'll call you "sir" for now if you don't mind,' Louise said, making it clear to the Australian that first-name terms was a prize that needed to be earned.

Mangan opened the file as soon as she got back to her office. The letter, hand-written in a neat almost copperplate script, read:

> *Dear Commissioner,*
>
> *My name is Olive Burnett (nee Sabatini) and I worked as an assistant producer on the TV programme 'Crimesolve' twenty years ago when its presenter, Jenny Daniels, was murdered. My late husband, Carl Burnett, produced the programme and was in a relationship with Jenny Daniels until not long before she was killed.*
>
> *This letter is not about the Daniels tragedy.*
>
> *Carl spoke to the police many times about that and was, I believe, instrumental in revealing the involvement of Dr Jamie Templeman in the events leading up to the murder. I still work in the media, albeit in local radio rather than national television, and saw your press release about the cold case review into another murder, that of Tiffany Mordaunt in Hampton Court at around the same time, and in the same general vicinity as the Daniels case. My late husband was first and foremost an investigative journalist, and in the course of his research into the Daniels murder, he developed a particular interest in an island on the Thames close to Hampton*

Court. It's called Tagg's Island, and it's where Marko Rockov, who was a prime suspect in the murder, was based.

Colin Brown, who was famously convicted and then found innocent of killing Jenny, fixed boats for many people on the island, including Rockov. As the Met will know, Brown was a suspect in the Tiffany Mordaunt case until an alibi and subsequently a DNA sample proved his innocence. So, Colin Brown definitely wasn't the so-called Beast of Hampton Court. But in the course of his investigations my late husband learned some things that may be pertinent to your reopened investigations.

Please may I come to speak to you or the senior officer in charge of the review.

Yours sincerely,

(Mrs) Olive Burnett

There was a printed letter heading with an address in Mortlake, and other contact details.

Louise showed the letter to Rushil Din who, as usual, was still bustling around the office at 7 o'clock on a Friday evening.

'On Monday I'm going to Tagg's Island,' she told him. 'The vicar I met is taking me to meet the secretary of the residents' association. In the meantime can you arrange for Mrs Burnett to come in to see me as soon as possible.'

'Will you be taking Alex with you on Monday?'

'No. I've agreed to give her a couple of weeks off. That's what she wanted to see me about; says she needs to rest a bit. Didn't she tell you?'

'No,' Din said. 'Actually, she blanked me when she came back down from your meeting with the Deputy Commissioner. Just grabbed her coat and left.'

'Alex is in a place I'm very familiar with,' said Mangan. 'It's a town called Disillusion.'

Louise had arranged to have a drink with Harry Kosnich after work that evening. In a long police career, she'd had many close colleagues but few friends. Harry, however, was one of those friends. They'd arranged to meet well away from the Yard, in a small pub they often used for after-work chats. It was tucked away in an alley connecting Pall Mall to St James's Street and, as usual, Mangan was the one who arrived first. By the time the big, grizzled frame of DCI Kosnich appeared round the door she was already on her second drink. Harry had been out of the office all day, and knew nothing of Louise's meeting with the Deputy Commissioner.

'Mark Barry's a plonker but I can't see how Statham could have taken your side against him,' he said after Mangan told him what happened.

'I get that. Barry humiliated Alex the other day and my mistake was to use an operational issue to try to restore her trust in the Force.'

'Well, I'd say you had a valid reason to think one of Barry's officers was in imminent danger,' Harry said, 'but I learned many years ago, never to mess with the UCs.'

'At least you've learnt something, Harry. Lately I've been feeling totally useless – after almost thirty years of service.'

Kosnich, realising from experience that this was a time

for him to listen rather than speak, said little beyond uttering the odd encouraging comment as Mangan unburdened herself.

'Twenty years ago, I helped to arrest the wrong man, thus allowing the true Beast of Hampton Court, as the press called him, to kill a girl he was holding captive. We still haven't caught the bastard, and probably never will. I've got two names and even a DNA profile but I'm no nearer the truth. In the meantime, while I thought I was helping to restore a good young detective's faith in the Met, I've only succeeded in making things worse for her. If she's right, there's a copper up in Manchester whose life is in danger and we're doing sweet FA about it because I cocked up. I should never have stormed into the Deputy Commissioner's office like that.'

When the tide of self-condemnation had ebbed, Harry Kosnich made what he hoped was a helpful suggestion. 'Look, why don't I wander up to Manchester and do a bit of poking around. It won't take much to find out where Grant is supposed to be based, and I could easily check up on him.'

'No, Harry. That's what Mark Barry should be doing. We dare not interfere in a UC operation.'

'Okay, understood, but I could at least go to see Alex. Make sure she understands that we will keep an eye on Barry and that we're in her corner not his.'

'She's on leave for a fortnight,' Mangan said, 'but that's not a bad idea. You two have always got on well and I wouldn't want today's little episode to fester over the next two weeks. It would certainly make me feel better if you had a word with her.'

They talked shop for a while longer before switching from the professional to the personal.

'How's the divorce going?' Louise asked.

Harry Kosnich had married a woman he'd lived with for seven years. Three years later, they were now in the process of divorcing.

'Hellish,' Harry replied. 'That's why I was late, been going through things with my solicitor. Thank God there are no kids to complicate things.'

After a few minutes complaining about divorce lawyers, each from their own perspective, Kosnich asked how things were going between Louise and her 'Greek boyfriend'.

'Boyfriend sounds so inappropriate for a woman of my age,' Louise responded.

'It's better than "manfriend" or "paramour",' Harry insisted.

'Doesn't paramour mean someone you're cheating with?'

'Not sure. All I know is that my problems began when I stopped being her boyfriend and became her husband. Anyway, stop ducking the issue. How's it going with Petros?'

'I'm not sure it ever was "going",' Louise said. 'But if it was, it seems now to have stopped.'

She described how the planned trip to Barcelona had been scuppered and told Harry that there'd been no contact since.

Kosnich scratched his beard in a ruminative way.

'I've always wanted to go to Barcelona,' he said eventually.

'So have I. But I don't fancy going there on my own.'

Kosnich shifted his large frame nervously before saying, 'You don't have to go on your own.'

'Harry Kosnich,' Louise exclaimed. 'Are you trying to chat me up?'

They both laughed, but Louise noticed how Harry's laughter stopped short of his eyes.

35

THE TAGG'S ISLAND RESIDENTS' ASSOCIATION

'If I had my time over again, I'd live in Venice, in a flat with a balcony overlooking the Grand Canal,' Rosemary Tillman announced as she ushered Detective Chief Superintendent Mangan into the narrow sitting room of *The Bounty*. 'A houseboat on Tagg's Island is a poor substitute.'

'And how long have you lived here?' Mangan asked.

'Twenty-five years in June. Believe it or not, I was once in great demand as an opera singer; always on a plane going somewhere. Basing myself here complemented my peripatetic lifestyle.'

'I keep telling her she needs to invest in bricks and mortar now that she's retired,' the Reverend Stephen Marsh remarked.

He'd agreed to meet Louise that morning in order to accompany her here and provide the introductions.

'Yes, Stephen is always trying to get me onto terra firma, and no doubt I'll be dragged off to a rest home for elderly mezzo-sopranos one day, but I'm perfectly comfortable here for the time being. As long as I can still get up the stairs I'll stay. Now, you must tell me how I can help you, my dear.'

The room was warm and comfortable, all elegant chintz and low lights. On the walls were a couple of tasteful murals and five framed posters from Rosemary's time with the Royal Opera. Not much of the mid-morning light was filtering in through *The Bounty*'s small oval windows.

'We need to know as much as you can tell us about Patrick Venn, who rented *The Great Gatsby* and lived there for a while in the 1990s with his girlfriend, Vicky West. I appreciate it was a long time ago, but the vicar here thought that as secretary of the residents' association, you may have records going back to that time.'

'Well, TIRA isn't a very sophisticated organisation, I'm afraid. And although most owners join, they don't always tell us who they are renting to. But let's consult the oracle, so to speak,' Rosemary said, pointing to an enormous ledger that was resting on a smooth walnut-laid desk at the far end of the living room.

She was a large woman whose bulk was shrouded in loose fabrics that spread out from her like the drapes of a Bedouin tent. Rising with difficulty from the low settee, she led her visitors across to the desk.

'This contains all the information the association has about each houseboat going right back to the 1930s. Now, I presume this Patrick Venn was a liveaboard, as we call residents, and not just a holiday rental?'

'That's right. Sage told me Venn was a permanent fixture,' Mangan replied.

'Ah, poor Sage. Stephen told me about your previous association around the time of all that trouble at *Navicula*. Now let's see what we have recorded here,' Rosemary said distractedly as she opened the tome and began to turn its thick pages. She adjusted a table lamp to better illuminate her scrutiny.

Mangan, looking over Rosemary's shoulder, saw that there was a section of the ledger dedicated to each of the sixty-two houseboats. The page for *The Great Gatsby* recorded that the boat had been in private hands until 1962 when it was purchased by a rental company. That company had changed hands three times with each change of ownership neatly recorded. The latest iteration was Nautical Homes Ltd based in Chiswick. Rosemary turned the page to where the occupants were listed together with the date they took residency, recorded in the handwriting of whoever was TIRA's secretary at the time. Her own neat copperplate went back as far as 2004 when she took over, but Mangan's interest was focused on 1999.

'I know you weren't the secretary of TIRA back then. But you were here during the period Patrick Venn was at *The Great Gatsby*, weren't you?'

'Yes, dear. I moved here in 1995, but I didn't know this Mr Venn. I knew Sage, of course. Indeed, I was friends with his aunt Jane. She was a member of our little congregation, wasn't she, Stephen?'

The vicar nodded. 'Her death was very sudden,' he said. 'She was in her mid-seventies so I suppose we shouldn't have been surprised, but as fit as a flea one moment and dead the next. So it was a shock.'

'Of course, she hated what she saw as a change in the character of the island when Mr Rockov purchased *Navicula*,' Rosemary said. 'Sage has always maintained that her battle to stop those security gates being built contributed to her illness.'

'I see the gates have gone now,' Mangan said.

'Yes, although like most residents, I never saw them as a problem, particularly as Mr Rockov put lots of money into the island to compensate for any perceived incongruity.'

'Who are the new owners incidentally?' Mangan asked.

Rosemary turned her attention back to the ledger, leafing through until she found *Navicula*.

'Not so new, it seems. It was in Mr Rockov's name for some years after his death, but a change of ownership was recorded in . . . Let me see now – 2009. Ten years ago.'

'But nobody lives there?' Mangan asked.

'Occasionally,' Rosemary replied. 'Didn't you say you saw someone there on the evening of the fire, Stephen?'

Mangan noticed how uncomfortable the vicar seemed when invited to elaborate.

'As I've already told you, I was visiting a very sick parishioner here on the night of the fire. A doctor had been called out to see him and I left the boat while he examined his patient. It was getting on for 3 a.m. About a quarter to, I'd say – very dark and very cold. My parishioner's boat is on the inner lagoon, so when I stepped ashore I was looking straight towards *Navicula*. I saw a man come out of the shadows and go through the gates onto the vessel. He didn't see me. I expected a light to go on, but *Navicula* remained in darkness. It was then that *The Inner Peace* burst into flames and I ran towards the fire.'

'And you didn't report this to the police?' Mangan asked.

'No, I didn't.'

'But why not? It can't have seemed normal for somebody to be creeping around at that time of night.'

'You're right, I should have reported it. But when I saw you last week, you confirmed that what happened to Sage was an accident, and that you were here investigating the events of twenty years ago. Anyway, I am reporting it now, I suppose.'

'So, who is the current owner of *Navicula*?' Mangan asked, turning to Rosemary who still held the ledger open at that page.

'It's a company called Makhanda Medicines based in South Africa.'

Mangan, taking a note of the name, asked the TIRA secretary to return to the entries for *The Great Gatsby*.

'There's no reference to Patrick Venn,' Rosemary said, running her finger down a long list of names.

'Are you sure?' Louise said, leaning over her host's shoulder to look more closely at the list. 'The period to concentrate on is early 1999.'

'I've gone right back to 1997 just to be sure,' Rosemary pleaded. 'If you follow my finger down through that year, 1998 and into 1999 you'll see . . .'

Mangan wasn't listening. One name leapt off the page she was looking at, from March 1999. It wasn't Patrick Venn, it was Ian Escreet – the man whose DNA matched that found on Tiffany Mordaunt's blanket. Her suspicion was confirmed – Patrick Venn was Ian Escreet, and Ian Escreet was a convicted rapist.

'We'll need a copy of this page,' she announced. 'I'll send somebody straight round. Thank you so much, Rosemary. You've been unbelievably helpful.'

The ledger was closed by its keeper, who hadn't the faintest idea why or how she'd managed to be so helpful.

Louise Mangan and the Reverend Stephen Marsh said their farewells to Rosemary before leaving *The Bounty* together. They had met that morning at St Mary's, and now Stephen drove them back to his church.

Louise had already called DS Din and asked him to get somebody to collect the ledger, copy the page with Ian Escreet's name and return the volume to Rosemary Tillman on *The Bounty*.

As they pulled into the church car park, Louise told the vicar about an idea she'd been formulating.

'Do you think it would be appropriate to hold a memorial service for Sage?' she asked.

'Well, it would be the only way to commemorate his life given that he can't have a funeral because we don't have a body.'

'Would you conduct a service here at St Mark's?'

'In normal circumstances the family would need to make the request and, of course, cover the costs.'

'But these aren't normal circumstances. And so far as I know Sage has no family. As for the costs, I suspect that if you ask Rosemary nicely, she'll contribute from the considerable assets of the Tagg's Island Residents Association.'

'Yes, I'm sure that all makes sense,' said the vicar, 'although I can't see many people attending.'

'There will be a substantial congregation if I have anything to do with it,' Louise said. 'I plan to get our press people on to it – "Memorial Service for Fire Victim With No Family" will be a great headline for the tabloids.'

'Bound to attract attention,' agreed Marsh, 'and I suppose you could get lots of strangers there out of sympathy, but why would the Met want to instigate a memorial service?'

'Well, first of all it's the right thing to do. Secondly, I'm really only interested in one potential mourner,' Mangan said, thinking of Vicky West.

36

ALEX GETS A LETTER

It was Monday morning and Alex was driving up the M6 towards Manchester. Deep in thought and careless of her speed, she'd covered half of the distance from London before Ken Bruce's 'Popmaster' came on the radio. She'd requested this break from work in order to restore her spirits, but had felt no better when she woke up that morning than she had after the confrontation with DCI Barry on Friday evening. The weekend had been spent worrying about Grant Traore, who she was convinced had been placed in mortal danger because of her stupidity in responding to Cutler's WhatsApp message.

During Saturday night, while she was out with friends, a vague idea had come to her. By the time she sat down to lunch at her mother's the next day it had taken shape, and that morning when the post arrived, it was consolidated – she would go to Manchester.

The letter from Grant should have reassured her that he was safe; it even said as much:

Dear Alex,

I'm not much good with words or keeping in touch with people but I really want to keep in touch with you, so these words are important. They're all I have to take

*your heart away (as Ronan Keating used to say). We
was having such a good time when that bloke came in.
I'm so sorry I had to leave in a hurry. I hope to get a
chance to explain it to you some day. I'd invite you to
Manchester but up here I'm Philip Geddes and I'm not
sure whether he'd be someone you like.*

    *So it will have to be when I'm back down there after
finishing this job, but in the meantime this note is the
securest way to let you know I'm okay and thinking
about you a lot.*

    Love and Best Wishes,
    Grant xx

It was undated. She'd examined the crumpled envelope for a date stamp. There wasn't one. But on the back,
written in the same hand was what looked to be a car
registration number – '*MA19 BXX*'.

    Alex had considered going into the Yard to search for
the owner of that number plate, but remembered that data
protection would make it impossible unless her request
was directly connected with an ongoing police investigation. Her concerns about Grant were obviously not shared
by his commanding officer, however, and this letter supported DCI Barry's version of events. Grant was telling
her he was fine.

    It could have been written under duress, she supposed,
or perhaps it hadn't been written by Grant at all. Weeks
had passed since their evening drink together in the Two
Chairmen; why would he leave it so long before writing?
And wasn't it a bit too much of a coincidence that it should
arrive so soon after the showdown with DCI Barry? Alex

wouldn't put it past Barry to write a letter himself and post it through her letterbox to prove that Grant was safe. No other letters had arrived with it and her post didn't usually come that early.

But she soon discounted this theory. The letter was so obviously from Grant – the diffidence, the humour, even the grammar. But why the car registration number? Barry had tried to convince her that the WhatsApp message was from Grant but she saw this as further evidence that it wasn't. If he'd already WhatsApped her, then why send a letter?

The revelation that Grant was a cocaine addict had shocked Alex, but hadn't diminished her affection for him. Indeed, this added vulnerability had enhanced her feelings. She wanted to be part of Grant's rehabilitation, part of his recovery, part of his life. She'd had lots of boy-friends, including what she'd considered to be a serious relationship at university. But nobody had impressed her so immediately and so profoundly as Grant – and they hadn't even kissed.

Having mulled all this over, Alex concluded that her choice was to spend two weeks in a kind of restless torpor or to act on the idea she'd been developing over the week-end. She would 'march towards the sound of gunfire', to use a phrase her father was fond of, although she hoped this wouldn't be literal in relation to her trip to Manches-ter. She had Martin Cutler's business address on the card he'd given her. Alex tapped Modernate's postcode into her satnav and commenced her private search for Grant Traore.

*

Alex's dark blue Citroën pulled into the car park at Modernate's two-storey HQ in Salford at one-thirty that afternoon. The building looked new, as did all the other low-rise offices on this small business park.

After refreshing her make-up and patting her hair into place, she walked to the reception desk, behind which was a middle-aged woman who was polite in a kind of superficial way that suggested courtesy didn't come naturally. Alex introduced herself as Ms Maddison from Her Majesty's Treasury – the same name and occupation she'd used in her conversation with Cutler at the Two Chairmen. She showed the woman Cutler's card.

'Mr Cutler asked me to come and see him whenever I was in the vicinity,' Alex said amicably.

She was wearing a business-like grey tunic jacket with matching skirt and a pale pink blouse arranged décolleté. A soft leather briefcase enhanced the sober, reliable bank manager impression that she'd hoped to make. The receptionist seemed unimpressed.

'You may be in the vicinity,' she responded, 'but I'm afraid Mr Cutler isn't – not today.'

'Is he at one of his other companies in Manchester?' Alex asked.

'I wouldn't know,' the receptionist said acidly. 'All I know is he's not due to be here until the Board Meeting tomorrow. I suggest you pop back then. If you're still in the vicinity, that is.'

Alex confirmed that she'd return the following day. She'd been expecting to stay over in Manchester anyway, reserving a room at a small boutique hotel in the Piccadilly district, but had decided not to check in yet.

She had two important pieces of information about Grant: his pseudonym that he had mentioned in the letter, and the name of the pub he frequented, which he'd talked about on their night out together.

Back in her car, she looked up the address of the Brickmakers Arms and decided to go there straight away.

There was a text on her phone.

> Hi Alex. Sorry to disturb your holiday but Louise told me what happened on Friday and I wanted to check that you were alright. Just tried ringing you but your phone is off. What do you say to a coffee? My treat. Be good to have a chat. Harry.

Alex adored Harry Kosnich. There was something about that big, hairy wreck of a man that screamed reliability. He'd been her friend and confidante ever since she'd been appointed to Mangan's team. Although she had no intention of confiding in him about her trip to Manchester, this did provide an opportunity to check that registration number. He was a better bet than their boss. DCS Mangan would ask lots of awkward questions – DCI Kosnich wouldn't.

> Hi Harry. Coffee would be great. Will have to wait a few days because I'm out of town visiting a friend right now. Will text you when I'm back. In the meantime, can you check out a car reg for me (will explain when I see you). It's MA19 BXX. Thanks mate. Alex

*

The pub didn't seem focused on lunchtime trade. There were none of the lavish laminated menus that most eateries seemed to favour these days. In fact, there were no menus at all. The culinary treats available were chalked up on a board above the bar: three varieties of sandwich, jacket potato with two types of filling or meat pie with chips.

Alex immediately sensed that the Brickmakers was about as female friendly as a Freemason's Lodge. Before setting out from Salford, she'd wondered if she should change out of her grey suit. She now wished she had. The outfit she'd chosen to overcome barriers at Modernate, was creating them here. It obviously wasn't a place that the business community frequented.

Four men were strung out along the bar drinking in studious isolation, as if the others weren't there. About a dozen more elderly men were scattered around, some playing the one-armed bandits. Others were at tables with newspapers open in front of them. A few more were checking their phones. All of them were silent.

But they didn't lack curiosity, each drinker looking up briefly to observe the incongruous stranger in their midst before returning to their pints.

Alex walked to the bar, high heels clicking on the wooden floor, to order a lime and soda. When the mild disturbance of her arrival had faded, she asked the young barman if Phil had been in lately?

'Phil who?' he asked.

'Phil Geddes.'

'He calls himself Philip. But no, he's not been in today – yet.'

As the barman moved away, Alex was aware of the drinker standing closest, albeit two metres away, looking her up and down. Eventually he spoke, as if addressing the spirit optics directly in his line of vision.

'Come up from London, have you?' he asked.

'Gosh, no,' Alex lied. 'I'm based here now. Have been for a while. What about you?'

The lone drinker ignored the question, preferring to ask another of his own. 'Based here for what?'

Conscious of how posh and out of place her accent must sound, and anxious not to cause problems for 'Philip', Alex had already invented a profession that she thought wouldn't be out of place here.

'I'm a solicitor,' she told her questioner, and via him, the rest of the pub.

'Right, thought so,' he said, nodding sagely.

The young barman, busy polishing glasses with a rancid-looking tea towel, sidled back over to where Alex was now perched on a bar stool. He was around the same age as Alex, of average height, with an unruly mass of dark curly hair. And, like Alex, he didn't look as if he belonged at the Brickmakers.

'My name is Liam,' he said quietly, 'and I'm pretty sure I know who you are. You have just come up from London, haven't you?'

'Some kind of mystic, are you, Liam?' Alex asked, sipping her lime and soda as nonchalantly as she could.

Liam told her that he was studying criminology, rather than mysticism, at Manchester University. 'I also know your name,' he whispered, 'and I'd be pleased to tell you how I know but not here. I'll be finished in fifteen minutes. Let's meet in the Costa at the top of the road.'

Alex was seated with a latte when Liam walked into the coffee shop twenty minutes later.

'You're Alex Cornelius, and you live in London SW1,' he announced quietly as soon as he sat down next to her. Alex could only stare at the barman, open-mouthed, thereby confirming the accuracy of his statement.

He introduced himself formally as Liam Cafferty, saying, 'I had a hunch it was you as soon as you asked about Philip – attractive woman, posh southern accent. Made sense,' he continued, stirring the coffee he'd brought to the table. 'The only surprise is that you got here so quickly. Philip only gave me the letter to post on Saturday morning.'

'Do you know where he is?' Alex asked.

'Look, he's a mate as well as a customer. I have to be careful who I'm talking to. I know you're the woman Philip wrote to, but in the pub you said you were a solicitor based up here. That's bollocks. You could be a copper for all I know.'

'What, you seriously think Philip Geddes has a police officer for a penfriend? Give over. No, me and Philip go back a long way. I was his lawyer once. Got him off a drug-trafficking charge. That's how we met. We had a relationship before his drug-taking became an issue,' Alex said, rehearsing the story she'd thought up on her way to the Brickmakers. 'I'm as unlikely to be involved with the police as Phil is. The letter you posted suggested he was in trouble. I need to find him. Who did he leave the Brick-makers with on Saturday?'

'A jumped-up little worm in a baseball cap called Clive who claims he's part of Blue Moon, the big criminal fraternity round here. I saw him throw Philip's lighter in the trash can. God knows what that was all about, but I retrieved it. Got it on me now, ready to give back to Philip when I see him. Didn't look like he was in any trouble to me. Clive and Philip seemed chummy enough.'

'Do they work together?'

'Never seen them together in here before but, yes, prob-ably. I think Philip is doing something with Blue Moon. He and Clive left the pub together but it's a bit weird that Philip hung back to ask me to buy a stamp and post the letter. Made me think that wherever they were heading off to there'd be no opportunity to pop to the shops on the way.'

'And nothing from Philip since?'

'No, he's usually in Sunday lunchtimes, but there was no sign of him yesterday. He must be running low on sup-plies. Unless he's found another dealer.'

'I know students are leaving university with huge debts these days, I've not long left myself, but I didn't realise they were having to trade drugs to make ends meet,' Alex said.

'It helps,' Liam replied, shrugging his shoulders. 'Never got hooked on them myself but I soon realised I was expected to do more than pull pints at the Brickmakers. And it pays well over the odds for a barman, although not many of my contemporaries would want to work there.'

Alex made a mental note to earmark the Brickmakers for a police raid at some point in the future. Right now, this barman's most important virtue was that he seemed to be one of Grant's few allies in a hostile environment.

'What do you know about a man named Martin Cutler?' she asked.

'Not much. Big cheese around here. Always in the local media. Bit of a philanthropist.'

'You don't think he's involved in Blue Moon?'

'Yeah, right. Along with Mother Theresa,' Liam snorted.

'Well, she's dead, so that's not a fair comparison. Cutler, on the other hand, is very much alive, and I'm certain he knows where Phil is. I'm going to see him tomorrow,' Alex said, scribbling her phone number on a Costa serviette and handing it to Liam.

'Call me if you see or hear anything interesting, oh and if you see a car with this number plate,' she added, inscribing *MA19 BXX* onto the extemporised notepaper. 'That was the car reg Philip wrote on the back of the envelope. He must have done it as an afterthought otherwise it would have been in the letter, not on the envelope. And that suggests it's the number plate of the car that picked him up.'

Liam was busy transferring the information contained on the serviette onto his mobile. Alex had a sudden thought.

'What are you doing tomorrow morning?' she asked.

'Nothing. A bit of revising, and then the evening shift at the Brickmakers.'

'Will you come with me to see Martin Cutler tomorrow morning? I could do with a hand, and you might learn more about criminology by coming with me than you would from your studies.'

37

GINGERNUT

Salford's skies were smoky grey when Martin Cutler parked his Bentley in its reserved space at Modernate HQ on Tuesday morning. The rain that had poured down all night was easing to a persistent drizzle. It was ten o'clock, an hour before the board meeting. Cutler breezed through reception calling out 'Good morning, Eileen' to the woman on reception.

'Oh, Mr Cutler, sir; a young lady called . . . Let me see – I wrote her name down somewhere. Ah, here it is! A young lady called Alex Maddison came in to see you yesterday. She's coming back today.'

The owner of Modernate was intrigued by this news. So Alex Maddison had driven all the way up to Manchester to see him. It was true that he'd given her his card, telling her to drop in any time, but with no expectation that she'd appear.

When he reached the privacy of his office Cutler called Stitch Maguire. 'I need you over here straight away,' he said bluntly.

'Can't it wait until tomorrow, boss?' Stitch pleaded. 'I've arranged to see a bloke who I think will be a perfect replacement for Geddes on the airport job.'

'How are things going?' Cutler asked, ignoring Maguire's request.

'Okay. The rest of the team are here now. I've told them all about that snake Geddes, so they're all aware.'

'Good. Thanks for the update. I still need you here as soon as possible. I've got his girlfriend coming to see me.'

'Who is she?' Maguire asked.

'The woman who was stupid enough to tell me that it was Geddes I saw in that London pub.'

'The woman you messaged?'

'Yes, name of Alex Maddison. Claims to work for the Treasury, and that she only knows our friend through being chatted up by him that night.'

'Bit strange she turns up now,' Stitch remarked.

'Exactly. Confirms my theory, don't you think?'

Although it seemed certain that Philip Geddes was a police officer, Cutler had voiced an alternative explanation for his suspicious behaviour, which was that he might be working for a rival gang. A London outfit was trying to muscle their way into the lucrative Manchester market, led by an East End gangster called Tavernier. Martin Cutler had floated a theory to Stitch that Geddes might be working for Tavernier rather than the police.

'Have you ever known the Met to employ a drug addict as a UC?' he'd reasoned.

He returned to his theory now. 'Suppose this woman is another member of the gang? I see them together in a London pub and reappear to talk to her the next day. Now that Geddes is incommunicado, she's been sent up to sus things out and, perhaps, initiate talks with me. Mark my words, this may open up the possibility of a lucrative alliance between Blue Moon and Tavernier.'

'What if she's a cop?' Stitch said acerbically.

'We'll know soon enough, because I've arranged to talk to Tavernier himself.'

'Didn't know you were pals,' Stitch said.

'We're not but we have mutual contacts, and he knows the importance of pooling information when our joint interests are jeopardised. He's calling me later on, but in the meantime, I need to ensure that this woman doesn't get away, like she did in London a few weeks ago. Bring one of the boys with a van. I'll make sure she's manageable.'

Alex drove into the Modernate car park at 10.45 a.m., having picked up Liam Cafferty from his student digs.

'Shall I come in with you?' he asked.

'No. It's best you stay in the car. You can drive, can't you?'

'Sure. Passed my test first time,' Liam said proudly.

'Good. I'll tell them I arrived by taxi. It will save me having to give my registration number to the hatchet-faced bitch on reception. I'm rather hoping Cutler will offer to take me to lunch, I'll say yes if he does, and you need to be ready to follow.'

'Great, just like in the movies. That must be his car with the personalised number plates,' Liam observed, pointing towards the Bentley.

'That's not the number plate we're looking for, unfortunately,' Alex said as she left the car and made her way to reception. Liam watched as she adroitly avoided some substantial puddles on her way across the car park. After she'd disappeared inside, he switched seats to be behind the wheel of the dark blue Citroën, like a racing driver on the starting grid.

Alex had to wait under the receptionist's disapproving gaze for a few minutes before Martin Cutler came out to collect her. Wearing a dark grey suit, and with his red hair cut very short, he was immaculately groomed and his manner wasn't as unwelcoming as his colleague on reception.

When he spoke, he was charm personified. 'I'm really pleased you dropped by, although you couldn't have picked a more hectic time – board meeting's due to start shortly, I'm afraid and every available bit of office space is taken. But it will be over by half-twelve and then I'll take you somewhere nice for lunch.'

Cutler had taken her past an office door with his name on it and some double doors marked 'Boardroom', into what was obviously a storeroom at the back of the building. Amidst the bric-a-brac, a space had been cleared and two chairs placed around a small Formica table.

'We'll be able to have a quick cuppa and a chat before my meeting starts, but it will need to be in here. Now, what can I get you?'

As her host went off to get the teas Alex thought through the story she had prepared for this occasion.

'I just happened to be up visiting our HMRC office in Manchester, and thought I'd pop in to see you,' she said when Cutler had returned.

'I hope you're free for lunch,' he said.

'Yes, that would be lovely, thank you. I don't have to do anything workwise until tomorrow.'

'And how long are you up here for?'

'That depends on how things go with the taxmen, but a few days at least.' She took another gulp of tea before asking, 'Have you ever caught up with your friend who you thought you saw me with in that pub?'

'I have, actually,' Cutler replied.

'In London, or here in Manchester?' Alex asked.

'Why in Manchester of course. Surely you know that Philip is estranged from the city of his birth.'

Alex said that she hadn't even known his name was Philip. She felt uncomfortable about the way Cutler had pulled his chair closer towards her and was gazing intently into her eyes. Alex was beginning to feel faint. It seemed as if she was floating away.

'Would you like a biscuit with that?' Cutler was asking. 'A gingernut, perhaps?'

It was the last thing she heard.

A steady stream of cars pulled into the executive spaces reserved for board members. Liam clocked the registration numbers, but none matched the one that had been scrawled on the back of the envelope.

It began to rain again, and the young barman had to switch the wipers on to clear the windscreen so that he could maintain an unencumbered view of the entrance to Modernate.

After half an hour his mind was wandering. The last board member had taken his parking space, after which all activity ceased. Liam rolled a cigarette and felt for Philip's lighter; the one he'd retrieved from the bin. It was too wet to smoke outside, and Liam dare not risk Alex's wrath by lighting up in her car. So he put the fag behind his ear for later, and the lighter back in his pocket.

He stared through the saturated windscreen, turning the wipers on intermittently – as much to relieve the monotony as improve his view. He was about to check his iPhone for messages to give him something else to do, when he saw a dark Mercedes pull into a disabled space close to reception.

A large, bald man got out, and walked with a heavy step towards Modernate HQ. Liam noticed him make a gesture of acknowledgement towards a small removals van which had found a space further back. Only by lifting his buttocks from the driver's seat and leaning to his left could Liam obtain a clear view of the Mercedes' number plate. His heartbeat quickened when he saw it was MA19 BXX.

He texted Alex, telling her to ring him when she could. There was no response.

Twenty minutes after the bald guy had walked into reception, he came out again from a side door, pushing a large green, four-wheeled rubbish bin. The white removals van started up and began to move towards him. When the van was in position the driver left his cab and went to the back to operate the hydraulic tail lift and manoeuvre the big wheelie bin onto the vehicle. On a wet Tuesday morning on a Manchester industrial estate this kind of activity wasn't unusual. But Liam sensed there was something wrong.

This was no rubbish collection, and what was the association with the Mercedes whose driver looked like a heavy? He tried contacting Alex again, but to no avail. The white van and the Mercedes were about to move off.

If he followed, Alex would have no transport when she came out. But she'd already said she planned to go to lunch with Cutler if invited, and she'd been desperate to find the car with that number plate. She wouldn't thank him for losing contact with it now. He started the engine and followed the white van and the black Mercedes – registration MA19 BXX – out of the car park.

38

LOUISE LEARNS A LOT

Louise Mangan's vague recollection of Olive Sabatini from their one meeting twenty years ago,was of a thin, timid girl in ill-matching clothes whose abundance of hair cascaded onto her shoulders.

The woman who accompanied Rushil Din into Mangan's office was a neatly coiffured, self-possessed, confident brunette who obviously cared about the impression she was making. Mrs Olive Burnett explained how she and Carl had begun a relationship shortly after Jenny Daniels died, and that what began as an office romance had developed into a strong marriage, cruelly ended by the grim reaper. Carl, who'd always had a weak heart, had suffered a massive cardiac arrest almost two months earlier.

'I'm sorry to hear about your husband,' Mangan said gently. 'The Commissioner also passes on her condolences, and her thanks for the invaluable help your husband gave us on the Daniels case.'

'Carl was devastated by Jenny's murder. She died on the doorstep of the house they shared. It was Carl who told the police about Colin Brown's totally illogical hatred of Jenny; how she'd got him a job at the BBC; how he'd attacked her on his bike, but she'd declined to press charges. But I'm not here to talk about the Daniels murder,' she concluded.

It was clear that Mrs Burnett had no memory of meeting Mangan at the offices of *Crimesolve* in BBC Television Centre; only of meeting two anonymous police officers. Mangan explained that she'd been one of them, and reminded Olive of the commotion when she and Ralph Harrison first arrived.

'You'd been having a heated discussion with that doctor who was going out with Jenny Daniels at the time and was in the programme you were making.'

'Oh, I remember him storming into my office. Jamie Templeman was such a dick. We needed him for the Jack Handysides exposé but he was more trouble than he was worth.'

'Whatever happened to him?' Louise asked.

'It turned out he was more deeply involved in Handysides' drug cartel than he let on. Served five years in Wormwood Scrubs and then left the country with one of his many girlfriends to start a new life in Argentina. Carl tracked him down to the extremely lucrative practice he now runs in Buenos Aires.'

'Wasn't he a suspect in the Jenny Daniels murder?' Din asked.

'No. Templeman was in police custody when Jenny was murdered. Carl had made sure Jenny knew all about Templeman's various affairs and that was that – end of engagement. It's not Templeman who I wanted to tell you about, but the man who he claims lured him into the drugs trade – a South African by the name of Jeremy Van Wyk.'

'Okay,' Mangan said. 'Why don't you go through it all while DS Din here takes some notes. You don't mind if we tape this as well, do you?'

Olive Burnett nodded her assent and began by telling Mangan and Din that Van Wyk was a pharmacist by profession and effectively Marko Rockov's deputy. He'd lived at *Navicula* on Tagg's Island, escaping along with his boss and Jack Handysides, when Operation Zeus, which Olive described as, 'the massive police operation that broke the biggest narcotics racket in Europe but failed to capture its boss', was unleashed in 1999.

'It was Carl who traced Rockov back to Belgrade and discovered he'd died there on the oncology ward of a hospital. Whilst there were strong rumours that Handysides had stayed in England, relocating to the north away from London, Carl was unable to substantiate them. He received no help at all from the Met. My husband had been willing to risk his career, and possibly his life, by exposing the Handysides empire on prime-time telly, but the Met treated his work as a slight on their competence. They claimed to know all about Handysides, and that Operation Zeus proved their point. Carl understood that. But what he couldn't accept was the Met's apparent disinterest in helping him find Handysides. His ambition – our ambition – was to make a TV documentary revealing how the most successful criminal mastermind of our time evaded justice. I've got all his papers and you're welcome to trawl through them. But it's fair to say we had no more idea where to find Handysides when Carl died than we had when the empty speedboat was discovered at St Katherine's Dock twenty years ago.

'But we did learn a lot about the third man in that boat – Jeremy Van Wyk. Carl traced his journey back to South Africa via Amsterdam and Rabat. He discovered that when Rockov died, it was Van Wyk who took over great swathes of the Serb's illicit drugs business. In the final few weeks of his life, Carl had a real breakthrough. The South African police had taped Van Wyk back in 2005, talking to someone he thought was a potential client. Here's a transcript of the conversation.' Olive paused her narrative to hand Louise an envelope. 'You'll see that he's offering to supply something that can be used for what he describes as "profitable euthanasia". He mentions using the drug on a woman whose nephew wanted the boat she owned. It had been left to him in her will, and it was in a prime position on the River Thames. That must be Tagg's Island. He goes on to say that he'd also been trying to deal with the same guy's sexual perversions.'

'The guy Van Wyk was dealing with must be Patrick Venn,' said Din.

'Except that we know who inherited a houseboat after his aunt died,' Mangan responded, 'and that was Sage.'

'Yes, that's the name of the guy that Van Wyk had a close association with, but they fell out over something. When this conversation was taped fourteen years ago, the chemist was talking about having a score to settle with this guy. Which must be one of the reasons he came back.'

'What do you mean he came back?' Din asked. 'You mean back in 2005?'

'No,' Olive said calmly, 'I mean recently. Carl discovered that Van Wyk had taken over Rockov's old property on Tagg's Island and had returned to live there.'

Mangan remembered seeing the name of *Navicula*'s new owner in Rosemary Tillman's ledger. Makhanda Medicines, based in South Africa.

'With all this evidence, why didn't the police in South Africa arrest Van Wyk?' Din asked.

'I only know what Carl told me. Van Wyk had friends in high places over there. In any case the crimes that this sting uncovered took place here, not in South Africa. Carl's theory was that Van Wyk could lead him to Handysides. Until then he was of more use to us out of jail than in. Of course, everything has changed now. All the evidence that Carl accumulated is now available to you and if you want to question Van Wyk you know where he is.'

Mangan remembered what the Reverend Stephen Marsh had said about seeing somebody skulking around *Navicula* just before the fire broke out. Her problem was that she had no grounds to raid *Navicula*. The fire that killed Sage had not been regarded as suspicious, and Surrey Police, who were dealing with the aftermath, were only awaiting the formality of the Marine Accident Investigation Branch report before closing the file. Her authority was to conduct a cold case review into the murder of Tiffany Mordaunt, not to question the accidental death of Sage, or pursue an inquiry into the death of his aunt Jane.

She escorted Mrs Burnett to the lift. 'I hope that Carl's work can be of some use to you,' Mrs Burnett said as they walked along the corridor.

'It's been of enormous help,' Mangan reassured her. 'Van Wyk is still wanted in connection with Operation Zeus. If he's back in the UK, we need to find him.'

'So you'll pay a visit to that houseboat that Rockov used to own?'

'I'll need a warrant to search *Navicula* and your testimony will help enormously,' was as much as Mangan could say. 'I'll arrange to have all Carl's evidence picked up.'

She could tell that her visitor, already dubious about the Met's commitment, wasn't convinced that anything would come of her revelation.

'This is my husband's legacy. I don't have his journalistic skills or his unflagging energy, and I'm finding it difficult to cope on my own. I'm relying on you to make all the effort he put into this worthwhile.'

With that, Olive Burnett, nee Sabatini, stepped into the lift. As the doors closed, Mangan looked into her sad, dark eyes and felt the pain of another lonely woman.

Mangan's phone rang as she walked back to her office. It was DCI Kosnich.

'I've tried to contact Alex like we said, but she's gone away.'

'Well, she is on holiday, Harry. Don't make it sound like some kind of dereliction of duty.'

'The problem is, I think she's gone to Manchester.'

'What makes you think that?'

'She sent me a text asking if I'd check out a registration plate.'

'Okay, that's a bit strange, but this is Alex we're talking about.'

'I'm not sure she realises that the first two letters denote the region the number plate was issued in. The one she asked me to check begins with MA, it's a Manchester plate.'

'Did she say why she wanted it?'

'No, and I'm getting the registration checked now, but if she's gone to Manchester, it's likely she's gone to try to find her boyfriend.'

'That's a very big "if", Harry. Let me know how you get on checking the car.'

Rushil Din was in the outer office talking to a uniformed policewoman when Louise returned to her office. The woman approached Louise as soon as she saw her.

'Are you Louise Mangan?' she asked. 'My dad said I had to see you. I'm PC Sharron Bennett – Basil's daughter.'

Mangan could see the similarity to the veteran safe-cracker: same eyes, same prominent chin. But there was no similarity in what they did for a living.

'Dad always says that you were the one who convinced him that I'd be okay in the police.'

'Yes, I remember him telling me that the last time we met,' Louise said, as if she and Basil had bumped into one another on a Saturday morning in Sainsbury's, as opposed to travelling in the back of a squad car together heading towards a custody suite.

Mangan asked after Basil's health.

'He's fine. I visited him yesterday. Mum won't go anymore, says he's too old to be carrying on like this and doesn't see why she should be punished by having to traipse across to whichever prison he's been banged up in.'

'I bet you had an interesting time going through the vetting process for Essex Police,' Mangan said.

'Why should I be punished for things my dad did? I didn't try to disown him or anything. I knew I wouldn't have been recruited if I'd failed to declare that my dad was a safe-cracker. I told them straight up.'

'You were a traffic cop, weren't you?' Mangan asked.

'Still am. I love it, to tell you the truth. Thought about applying to the Met but Essex Police is fine for now.'

'So, why have you come all this way to see me?'

'Dad told me I had to tell you, nobody else – just you. And I had to do it quick. You wouldn't believe the problems I've had just getting to your office – even though I'm a copper. Couldn't have done it without your boy here.'

'Do you two know each other?' Mangan asked, smiling at her embarrassed assistant.

'We do now, don't we, Rushy?'

Rushil Din explained that the reception desk had called him to say there was a PC who'd asked to see DCS Mangan but refused to say why. Just that she had some information for Mangan. 'I spent a bit of time downstairs with PC Bennett before deciding that she was someone you'd want to meet. Although I still don't know any details of what she wants to talk to you about. Only that she says it's a matter of life and death.'

'Well, fire away,' Louise said as they settled in her office. 'What's this life and death issue?'

'I went to see Dad yesterday,' Sharron began, 'like I do regularly. I never go in uniform, although it's nothing Dad's said. He's proud of me, I know he is, but I don't think it would do him any favours for me to be swanning around in my blues. Anyway, he hears a lot of stuff inside. You detectives should bug their cells.'

'We do,' Din interjected from his position next to his

boss, taking notes that he'd already assured Sharron would be for DCS Mangan's reference only.

'So, I'm sat there, opposite Dad when he leans forward and says, real quick like, that I'm to come and see you. You and nobody but you – to tell you there's a copper being held prisoner by a Manc gang known as Blue Moon. Dad reckons they're going to kill him.'

'Did he tell you the copper's name or where he's being held?' Louise asked, suddenly impatient to get the full details.

'Not the name, but the place is Peak View Farm in Derbyshire. Sorry, don't have a postcode.'

'That's alright. We'll find it,' Louise said, already fearing that the officer's name may be Grant Traore.

'There's one other thing,' Sharron said as Louise was leaving her office to act on the information she'd just been given. 'Dad says he's never grassed, but he'll not have anything to do with violence. With me on the force and everything, he's buggered if he's going to stand by when a copper's life is in danger. Anyway, the other thing is this – his old mate Arnold Spearing is part of this Blue Moon crew. Only for one specialist job at the airport but Dad says to tell you that Arnold's the one who got the message to him, so you're to go easy on him.'

39

STORING GRAIN

It was simple for Liam to follow his quarry through the city, from Salford across Manchester, and then towards Stockport. The traffic moved slowly and the white van remained prominent regardless of how many vehicles were around it. Wherever the van was, the Mercedes would be as well. It was when they hit the open road beyond Hazel Grove that the young student began to worry, not about losing sight of the two vehicles but about them realising they were being followed.

The cloud and rain had given way to some early spring sunshine. Alex's Citroën was metallic blue, and noticeable even before the sun began to glint off it. Liam remembered reading a detective novel by a famous American writer in which the hero had developed a method of following a vehicle from in front rather than behind. Those characters driving the white van and the Merc would be focused on what was behind them, not the cars ahead. He overtook on the A6 and was already tracking them comfortably via his rear-view mirror when they hit the A623 which stretched across the Peak District like the margin of a page, making his back-to-front pursuit even easier.

Liam was enjoying what he supposed could still be called the thrill of the chase, albeit from two hundred metres to the fore of the Mercedes which in turn was being followed by the white van. This was a doddle. Then he saw the left indicator of the Mercedes flashing. Fortunately, there wasn't much traffic, and Liam managed to manoeuvre across to the west-bound carriageway before doubling back to the narrow unclassified road that the two vehicles had turned onto. He was relieved to see the roof of the white van visible above the hedgerows for a mile or so before it disappeared. He backtracked – nothing.

Liam parked up and got out of the car, straining his ears to try to pick up the sound of an engine. Silence. He trudged along for a bit before coming to a stile on which he could stand to get a clear view across the landscape, looking for the white van. But the only thing of interest he could see was a sign strung across an even narrower track a little way down from where he was standing. He went closer to read the ancient lettering secured high up between two ash trees: 'Peak View Farm'.

This must be the turning the two vehicles he'd been following had disappeared into. Liam decided against going back for the car. It was parked close to the side of the road, allowing even the largest piece of agricultural machinery to get by, and he guessed that many a dogwalker or hiker would park where the Citroën was to access the public footpath that the stile he stood on was part of. So his parked car was unlikely to attract suspicion. He walked along the track for about half a mile until he was looking down an escarpment towards a farmhouse. In the yard was a white van and a black Mercedes with the number plate MA19 BXX.

*

While Din was finding out where Peak View Farm was situated and contacting Derbyshire constabulary, Mangan had gone upstairs to talk to Deputy Commissioner Statham. She was told he was in conference with his boss, Karen Dale, and not to be disturbed.

Ignoring the various underlings who tried to stop her, Louise entered the Commissioner's office, uninvited. The two senior officers looked up, startled and, in the case of Dale, obviously annoyed.

'Sorry to burst in like this,' Mangan said, 'but one of Mark Barry's UCs is in serious trouble. He's being held against his will, and his life's in danger.'

'Is this Grant Traore again?' Statham asked.

'Yes, the guy I came to talk to you about with DI Cornelius last week.'

'But I've been on Barry's back about that guy, as I assured you I would be. He's carrying a tracker. Mark showed me his whereabouts only yesterday – Traore was in the pub he normally frequents, having been out and about in the city over the weekend. In other words, he was precisely where he was supposed to be.'

'No, that's not right. Grant is on a farm in the Peak District. We need to get an armed unit there – now,' Mangan said, still breathless from the run upstairs.

'Have you had any involvement with DCI Barry's work?' Commissioner Dale asked icily.

'No, but I've received some reliable intelligence.' Mangan related what Sharron had told her, protecting PC Bennett's confidentiality by saying it came from a known informant.

'All very interesting, Louise, but you do have a bit of

a reputation for rushing into things and we need to speak to the officer in charge of this undercover operation before we do anything else.'

Mangan resisted the temptation to point out to Dale that, so far as she could remember, every time she'd rushed into things it had subsequently proved to be something worth rushing into.

Statham suggested that they establish DCI Barry's whereabouts before reconvening in his office to give the officer in charge an opportunity to react to this new intelligence. Mangan knew it was the best she could hope for, particularly with Commissioner Karen Dale silently nodding her agreement.

By the time Mangan got back to her office DS Din had not only located Peak View Farm, but also had details of its ownership.

'The farm is in a remote area of Derbyshire,' he told Mangan, 'and was purchased by a company called Cutler Holdings four years ago.'

'Martin Cutler is the man who followed Alex; the one who she says saw her in the pub with Grant. He's who sent her that WhatsApp message.'

'I've alerted Derbyshire Police,' Din said. 'All they're waiting for is the Deputy Commissioner's authority. They've been told that Statham's speaking to the officer in charge at this very moment.'

As soon as he'd said this Din could see that his boss was about to implode. It happened rarely but all the warning signs were there; her preternatural stillness to be followed by a supernova burst of activity. When Mangan left the office Din made sure he was close on her heels. The

Commissioner's offices were two storeys above them, on the top floor. Rather than wait for the unreliable lift, Mangan took the stairs, two at a time. Din followed. As they approached Statham's office one of the same junior officers who'd tried to keep her out earlier rushed across.

'Sorry, Ma'am, but the Deputy Commissioner left strict instructions that you mustn't be allowed to—'

Mangan, once again ignoring the attempted intervention, walked in without knocking to find DCI Barry with Statham in front of a computer studying a map.

'Just wondered if you'd established DCI Barry's whereabouts yet – oh, he's here. What a surprise.'

'I did say I'd give him a chance to react to your intelligence,' Statham said.

'Yes, but you forgot to tell me he was waiting in your office,' Mangan said calmly. 'The farm where I've been told DC Traore is being held is owned by Martin Cutler. Did you know that, DCI Barry?'

'What's eating you, DCS Mangan?' Barry sneered. 'Time of the month?'

'Thank you,' Mangan said, walking up to her antagonist. 'I can now add my serious complaint to the one that DI Cornelius is about to submit, and I have the Deputy Commissioner as a witness.'

'We'll deal with that in due course, Louise,' the Australian said. 'DCI Barry is demonstrating to me that far from being held prisoner, DC Traore appears to be free to travel at will.'

DS Din was looking over the Deputy Commissioner's shoulder at the map on the computer screen, its little flashing light indicating where its carrier was situated.

'But he's not travelling around now, sir. He's stopped,' Din said. 'I've just been studying the detail of the area on a map downstairs, and it looks to me as if the place he's stopped at is Peak View Farm.'

Martin Cutler wouldn't usually drive to the farm in his Bentley. He'd normally be driven there by somebody else, or, on the rare occasions he'd had to go under his own steam, he'd take one of his less conspicuous cars – one without personalised number plates. What went on at Peak View Farm was Blue Moon business, and Cutler had been careful to avoid any obvious connection with the criminal network he ran. His associate, Raymond Sillars, was the one primed to take responsibility for these nefarious activities, which allowed Cutler to expand the philanthropic reputation he'd cultivated over the years.

One of Cutler's companies had acquired Peak View several years ago, but that wasn't unusual. Cutler Holdings owned properties across the country which they rented out to various businesses and individuals. Indeed, the farm itself was rented out to an agricultural conglomerate. Only the farmhouse – the remote, concealed farmhouse – was used by Blue Moon.

The early afternoon traffic was light, which was just as well because Cutler didn't have a minute to spare. He hadn't had time to travel home for another vehicle, and he couldn't ask Stitch to come and collect him because Stitch had to stay where he was. He and that Polish psychopath, Eryk, had collected the blond woman that morning. She wouldn't have known much about it given the strong sedative he'd slipped into her tea, but by now she'd be awake, and none the worse for her ordeal, save for a few bumps and bruises acquired during transportation inside that wheelie bin.

Cutler had originally envisaged having plenty of time to interrogate the young woman and her coke-snorting partner, Philip Geddes, but that plan had changed after one phone call.

He had truly believed it would be possible to forge a lucrative partnership between Blue Moon and Tavernier's London operation. He was convinced that Geddes was working for Tavernier. So convinced, in fact, that he'd arranged a phone call with his rival to work out a way forward. That call had taken place an hour ago. Once upon a time, it would have been inconceivable for two bitter gangland rivals to have a civilised conversation about issues of equal concern. But in the modern era, the importance of communicating with – and even assisting – a competitor was becoming normalised.

For Cutler, however, there was an ulterior motive. His legitimate business interests had earned him the recognition and respect in the local community that he'd always craved. He'd originally become involved in serious organised crime because he'd needed to build up his personal wealth quickly. It had worked. He was now a rich man by anybody's definition and no longer needed to be taking the risks involved with Blue Moon. He'd been thinking about ways to ease himself out for some time, but it wasn't the kind of job where you simply handed in your notice. He'd brought in Ray Sillars as his deputy in the expectation that he'd take over one day, but the reality of working together and being from the same area was that it was impossible for Cutler to just walk away. There were too many ties, too much baggage, numerous interconnections. The only feasible solution was to engineer a takeover by a rival and forge a peaceful transfer of power to Tavernier.

The phone call had gone well. Tavernier was interested in a loose partnership, which Cutler saw as the first step towards his ultimate goal. They had even agreed to impose an immediate truce between their two organisations pending a face-to-face discussion about issues that couldn't be discussed, even over a satellite phone. The two men had established a relationship. It wasn't yet one of total trust and confidence but that would come in time; the foundations were now in place. Tavernier wanted control of Blue Moon, and Cutler was keen to relinquish it. Tavernier had even created a position for Raymond Sillars in the new organisation, if Sillars wanted it. The discussion couldn't have gone better, except for one thing. Tavernier had been explicit – Geddes was nothing to do with him. Ditto that Alex woman.

The one awkward moment in the conversation had come when Tavernier had tried to be jovial about it.

'Well, Martin my son,' he'd said, 'if this Geddes fellow is not one of mine and he's not one of yours – he must be one of theirs.'

And of course, he was right. Geddes was a cop, and the chances were that his girlfriend was as well. They'd both need to be disposed of, and Cutler had to ensure the job was done properly. His personal future depended on Geddes and Maddison not having any future at all. Nobody would know where they were. Stitch would have made sure there were no location devices on them.

And when it came to how they should be eradicated, he remembered a conversation from the time the farm was being rented out. Cutler had asked the manager of the consortium taking it over whether the enormous brick silo that cast its shadow over the farmhouse remained in use. He'd been told that it contained seventy tons of grain which needed to remain stored there for at least the next fifteen years or so, because by then prices would have risen and the company could extract maximum profit from their investment. In the meantime, Cutler had been told, it would need very little physical attention, which was just as well given the number of farmworkers killed by being buried or engulfed in grain stores.

'Moving grain acts like quicksand,' the manager had told him. 'It can bury a worker in seconds.'

Cutler had stored away this snippet of information rather as the grain had been stored in the silo – waiting for an opportune time to retrieve it. That time had now come.

Liam didn't know what to do for the best. Should he go back to his car and drive away to find help? How long would that take? He didn't know where to go or who he needed to convince, but was confident that even if he did succeed in finding someone, they would take a lot of persuading. He imagined how he'd begin the conversation.

'Well, officer, I'm a barman at the Brickmakers Arms and this cocaine addict I know . . .'

Besides, he could see that the drama unfolding below would reach its awful climax before he could even begin a 999 conversation. The skies were darkening, but from his position behind a dry-stone wall up on the escarpment,

Liam still had a perfect view. The farmyard below was illuminated by three powerful lamps positioned around its perimeter. The wind had swept some surviving remnants of a recent snowfall into little heaps of weather and grime. The yard looked like a film set being prepared for a major production.

Liam was still wondering what to do when he saw Alex being pushed out, her wrists tightly bound in front of her. Clive, the young thug in the baseball cap, followed behind, and was the one doing the pushing. Liam couldn't hear what was being said but he could see Clive's aggressive sneer.

Liam mapped a route down to ground level in his mind. He could see it was mostly shielded from view. The wall he was behind sloped down to some bushes and from there he could duck behind the rusting hulk of some agricultural machinery to enter the farmyard from its now deserted working end furthest away from the house.

A few minutes passed before Philip Geddes was pushed out to stand beside Alex. He was bound just as tightly, and Liam could tell by his shuffling gait and constant attempts to bring his arm as close to his face as he could to wipe his nose and eyes, that Geddes was in desperate need of a fix. His minder was a brutal-looking man with a gun in his hand.

The two captives cut pathetic figures; Alex looked disorientated, Philip shook uncontrollably, more from cold turkey than cold weather, Liam assumed.

Onto this dark scene came another car – the Bentley with personalised number plates that Liam had seen in the Modernate car park – Martin Cutler's car. Its owner emerged immediately, calling instructions so loudly that Liam could hear from his vantage point a hundred metres away.

'Turn those CCTV cameras off, you idiots,' he yelled.

Liam saw Clive disappear into the house to carry out this instruction and then heard the rumbling sound of another vehicle coming into the yard. He thought it would be another car but from the rear of the long shed on the perimeter of the farmyard came a bright yellow cherry-picker driven by the bald man with broad shoulders who Liam had seen driving the Mercedes.

'Okay, Stitch,' Cutler shouted, 'stop next to the silo and check that the platform reaches the top. Take Eryk up so he can open the hatch.'

The brutal-looking thug with the gun moved away from Philip to step onto the gated platform of the cherry-picker which then went slowly up until it reached the top of the silo where the process of opening the hatch began.

Looking down on the farmyard, discerning the horror that was about to unfold, Liam was finally spurred into action. He scrambled down to ground level. Soon the young barman was at the far end of the farmyard amongst a wreckage of old vehicles and bits of farm machinery housed in half-demolished brick buildings which, despite their decrepit state, still offered shelter. He saw some hay bales stacked in one dry corner under a thick canvas sheet, and suddenly knew what he had to do.

Liam tried the door on an ancient rusting Bedford truck, its tailgate open. He jumped in the cab and released the handbrake. The tyres had sufficient air for him to be able to push the old vehicle out into the yard. Two bales of hay, as dry as tinder, were thrown onto the back, and then Liam searched in his pocket for the lighter.

The two captives were near the farmhouse door, Clive watching over them. Eryk had stepped off the cherry-picker and was talking to Stitch who was still at the controls. Cutler was in the middle of the yard looking up at the brick silo that must have been around forty metres high. From his position up on the escarpment Liam had been practically level with the hatch that Eryk had opened at the top. Now he was at ground level, hidden from view watching through a hole at the back of one of the crumbling farm buildings; waiting to go into action.

He saw Eryk, the Polish psychopath, roughly manhandle Philip and Alex onto the platform of the cherry-picker and then step onto it himself, becoming a third passenger, eager to give the two prisoners a final push through the hatch that he'd opened and watch as the grain parted and the weight of their bodies took them down deeper and deeper, burying them alive in a silo miles from anywhere.

Liam understood the full horror of what was about to happen. Alex and the man she'd come to rescue stood side by side on the platform like two French aristocrats on a tumbrel being carried towards the guillotine. Eryk stood behind them and Stitch operated the boom lift that was carrying them up towards their terrible fate.

It was then that Liam lit the bales of hay using the lighter, and pushed the truck out towards the silo. He had his shoulder to the door frame on the driver's side, his left hand on the steering wheel, out of sight of the observers in the yard but not the three people above on the platform.

There was a slight downward gradient to the farmyard which helped the truck's momentum. The hay blazed fiercely, its black smoke rising in billowing clouds towards the top of the cherry-picker. Liam gave a last push and ducked away leaving the wheeled inferno heading straight towards Cutler in the centre of the yard.

The previously ordered – if gruesome – events dissolved into chaos. The Pole aimed his gun down towards the vehicle and fired, the bullet ricocheting harmlessly off the stone flagging. The platform had reached the hatch at the top of the silo but, distracted by the fire, Eryk didn't notice Philip coming at him from behind. The gun went flying as the two men struggled and Alex, like Philip still bound at the wrists, aimed a vicious kick at Eryk's groin. It put him off balance just as Philip attacked again from the other side, aiming a vicious double-handed swing at the Pole's head. Eryk, lurching to one side, tumbled through the hatch, his scream drowned out by the sirens of five police vehicles sweeping into the yard.

Stitch leapt out of the cherry-picker's cab and ran with Martin Cutler towards the Mercedes. They never made it. Five seconds later they were lying face-down on the cold cobbles of the farmyard as instructed by the six armed officers standing over them. Clive had run back into the house but was unlikely to escape the attentions of another five armed officers who followed him in. There they found William the Rastafarian and Arnold the safe-cracker sitting by the open fire in the lounge.

Nobody seemed sure how to operate the controls on the cherry-picker, so Grant – a.k.a. Philip – and Alex remained high above the skirmish with Liam down below trying to find a police officer who knew how to bring the boom lift down to ground level.

Alex and Grant didn't seem to mind too much. Holding each other's still tightly bound hands and gazing transfixed into each other's eyes, they seemed content to stay where they were.

40

REMEMBERING SAGE

Alex Cornelius returned to work at the end of her two-week break as originally planned, despite the exhortations of Louise Mangan to stay on leave for longer. Mangan's concerns for Alex's welfare were interspersed with vows to wring her fast-tracked neck if she ever did anything so stupid again.

Grant Traore wasn't yet ready to resume his duties. He was still at a private clinic that specialised in the treatment of drug addiction. He was also suspended pending an investigation by the Independent Office for Police Conduct (IOPC) into the death of a Polish national, Eryk Szymanski, at a grain silo on Peak View Farm.

Harry Kosnich was waiting for Alex when she arrived at New Scotland Yard on her first day back, anxious to take her through what had happened. This task had been delegated to him by Louise Mangan, who was attending the memorial service for Sage, which had been organised by the Reverend Stephen Marsh at her request. Detective Sergeant Rushil Din had gone with her.

Having settled his young friend down with a cup of coffee, Kosnich commenced his explanation. 'Louise was in with the Deputy Commissioner and DCI Barry when I called in to tell her that the number plate on the car you'd asked about was registered to Martin Cutler. She'd already been tipped off about Peak View Farm, but that was the final bit of information she needed to convince Statham to overrule Barry and authorise the armed unit to go in. Even so, we would have been too late if it hadn't been for your young accomplice.'

'Thank goodness I took Liam with me,' Alex exclaimed.

Kosnich told Alex about Liam having the tracking device in his pocket ready to give it back to Grant when he next saw him.

'Mind you, he just thought it was a cheap lighter and was carrying it around central Manchester. Which was why Barry was able to convince Statham that everything was okay.'

'Now, tell me what happened to DCI Barry,' Alex pleaded eagerly.

'Sacked on the spot by Statham for gross misconduct.'

'I wish I'd been there to see it.'

'You and me both. Apparently, the DC had already discovered Barry had two convictions for assaults on women in his private life.'

'And yet he'd still been promoted to Detective Chief Inspector,' Alex stated incredulously.

'The Commissioner has got some awkward questions to answer,' Kosnich responded. 'It was Karen who insisted that his record as a copper shouldn't be discredited by non-police issues.'

'Gosh.'

'Gosh indeed. Mind you, aside from all that, he completely cocked up in Manchester. Any UC in Grant's position should have had a team ready to facilitate an emergency rescue. Barry had redeployed them to carry out surveillance on a guy called Raymond Sillars, who he was convinced was Blue Moon's big chief. To cap it all, another UC – Detective Sergeant Roger Neil – reported Barry for making a racist remark about Grant. Apparently, he'd been heard saying that if he had to lose an officer at least it wasn't a white one.'

'Excuse my French, Harry, but how the fuck do men like that get to even be in the Met, let alone promoted?'

'Search me, Alex. There's always been a strand of thought that as we deal with some nasty, evil people, we need to have a few equally nasty and evil people in our own ranks to even things up. Heard the same thing when I was in the military. It's a warped definition of masculinity that I've never understood, but it's there.'

St Mary's Church at Hampton, close to the Thames, was packed. The Met's press and publicity department had done its job well, encouraging the tabloids to take a morbid interest in the 'Memorial for Fire Victim with No Family'. One paper, the *Daily Candour*, had been particularly helpful. Its readers could be forgiven for thinking that Sage was a candidate for canonisation. The paper had even carried a front-page colour portrait of the 'recluse who died a lonely death'. Rosemary Tillman had found the photo amongst her voluminous papers, and an enlarged copy had been placed on the altar of St Mary's along with a model of a houseboat that passed for a miniature of the *Inner Peace*. In the absence of a coffin these formed the centrepiece of the service.

When Louise Mangan arrived, she found it slightly disconcerting to have Sage's eyes staring out at her from the photograph. She no longer felt any posthumous affection towards him; not since she'd read the transcript that Olive Burnett had passed to her. It may be unprovable now but this evidence, formed of Jeremy Van Wyk's own words, suggested that he'd provided the drugs for Sage to conduct 'profitable euthanasia' on his aunt Jane. No wonder that, by all accounts, she'd deteriorated so quickly.

Whilst Louise was now retrospectively critical of her own feelings towards Sage, she still had a murder to solve. She not only needed to find Jeremy Van Wyk, but she was also searching for Ian Escreet/Patrick Venn. The person who could best help her do that was Vicky West.

The details of the memorial service had taken a while to determine. In the end, Rosemary had agreed to say a few words about the Tagg's Island community in general, leaving the Reverend Marsh to say what he could about Sage specifically. He complained about not having much to go on, having failed even to establish his subject's given name.

'Sage can't have been his Christian name,' the vicar had said to Rosemary, 'and even if it was, he must have had a surname to go with it. Only pop stars and Brazilian footballers have a single epithet.'

Rosemary couldn't help. She pointed out that every reference in her records since the day he'd arrived to take up residency on his aunt's houseboat hadn't varied. He was simply Sage. In desperation, Stephen Marsh had established that Aunt Jane's surname had been Cridland and so, whilst he knew that she'd been Sage's mother's unmarried sister, he nevertheless ascribed this surname to the man he was memorialising. Thus 'Sage Cridland' was the heading on the little four-page commemorative programme that the Residents' Association had financed.

The vicar may not have had much to say, but by the time the service began he had a substantial audience to say it to. Thanks to the *Daily Candour*'s coverage, the little church was almost full. Mangan worried that this would inhibit her ability to spot Vicky West amongst the congregation – thereby scuppering the entire point of this exercise. Whilst there were two doors into the church, she insisted that only one be used, narrowing the points of entrance and egress to assist the surveillance. She also ensured that a memorial book be placed there for mourners to record their names. It was hoped those attending would assume the two plain-clothes police officers were church helpers.

Mangan and Din both carried an enlarged version of Vicky West's passport photo from over twenty years ago, despite realising that it was unlikely to be of much practical assistance.

Mangan was worried that the whole event would be a waste of time. Even if Vicky West saw the press coverage, would she still be living in or around London? And if she was, would she travel to Hampton for a service that wasn't even a proper funeral for a man she'd probably lost touch with anyway?

It wasn't as if Mangan had nothing else to do that day. She'd have liked to have been in the office to welcome Alex back after her ordeal.

Alex, Mangan thought, needed some tough love. She shouldn't have gone to Manchester full stop, and she certainly shouldn't have gone without telling her mentor. Even though, as it happened, the outcome of her actions was that one of the most formidable criminal gangs in the country had been destroyed, a police officer's life had been saved, and an odious senior officer disgraced and dismissed.

Not a bad result, Mangan had to admit, but it had almost cost Alex her life.

There had been an interesting development subsequently. One of the Blue Moon gang had offered to provide some important intelligence in exchange for a less severe sentence.

Stitch Maguire claimed to know the assumed identity of Jack Handysides, the legendary mastermind who'd evaded arrest in the massive police operation against his criminal empire two decades ago. When Mangan heard about this attempted plea bargain, it bolstered her determination to see the unredacted file on those events.

Her team were trying to track down the South African chemist, Jeremy Van Wyk, who'd escaped the clutches of Operation Zeus along with Handysides. Olive Burnett was convinced that Wyk had returned to England and Mangan's unit had already established that Makhanda Medicines, the company that now owned *Navicula*, was founded by Van Wyk in his homeland. She didn't yet have enough to justify a warrant to break into the biggest and poshest vessel on Tagg's Island, but the case was building nicely. Stitch Maguire's intervention made her wonder what secrets lurked in the depths of that heavily redacted file.

And that afternoon, after the service, she was due to meet the Chief Inspector of the Marine Accidents Investigation Branch who was travelling up from Southampton, hopefully to produce the long-awaited report into the fire on the *Inner Peace* that had killed Sage. Mangan thought it strange that the head of the MAIB should ask to speak to the police before submitting their report. She knew the organisation usually reported directly to the Department of Transport, but it was clear that it's lead official had something that he thought was of more interest to the Met than the Minister.

So Louise Mangan had plenty of things she could have been doing rather than hanging around this church in the hope that somebody vaguely resembling Vicky West might turn up. But she was here anyway.

By the time the service began nobody had recorded that name in the memorial book but many in the congregation had ignored it and most of those who did register their attendance did so in handwriting that was almost indecipherable. With the service about to begin, Mangan and Din stood on opposite sides of the church facing out towards the assembled mourners. The Reverend Marsh commenced his eulogy, and it was then that Vicky West revealed herself.

The vicar had asked a rhetorical question.

'Why,' he began in a stentorian manner, 'are we here to mark the passing of Sage Cridland?'

'That's not his name,' a woman shouted from the fourth row of pews. 'Why are you commemorating him under a name that isn't even his?'

Stephen Marsh was understandably flustered by this early intervention in a speech he was already nervous about making.

'I do apologise, madam,' he said to the woman who remained seated. 'Could you possibly enlighten us as to his real name?'

The woman stood and although time had eroded those delicate features both Mangan and Din knew immediately who she was.

'His name,' Vicky West said firmly, 'was Sebastian Andrew Gregory Escreet.'

The woman who'd revealed that Sage's name was an acronym was being interviewed by the two Metropolitan Police officers under caution. Amongst the congregation, only Mangan and Din knew that Ian Escreet – as with many a Sebastian, he'd shortened his first name by adapting its last three letters – was the convicted sex offender whose DNA had been found on Darcy Kramer and on the blanket covering the dead body of Tiffany Mordaunt.

When DCS Mangan reminded Vicky West of the conversation they'd had on the *Inner Peace* long ago when Louise was a Detective Constable and Vicky was supposed to be the girlfriend of Patrick Venn, she admitted that Venn had never existed, that he'd been invented by Sage as an elaborate decoy.

'Having got away with creating one alter ego,' Vicky said, 'he had the idea of creating another more disposable one and rented *The Great Gatsby* under that name, as somewhere to base it.'

'He rented it in his real name,' said Louise, remembering the name in Rosemary Tillman's ledger.

'Yes, well, his problem was that he had to show his birth certificate as proof of identity so that was the one place where he'd had to use the name Ian Escreet. He figured it was safe enough buried away in the records of Tagg's Island. But it was you who forced him to bring Patrick Venn to life. Sage never thought the police would find him. For a start he didn't think they'd be interested in what he regarded as low-level crime and even if they conducted a proper investigation, it was unlikely they'd discover him on Tagg's Island. He was really spooked by the concerted attempt to catch him on that Friday night.'

'You knew he was attacking women?' Louise asked.

'Yes. I was living with Sage and, I'm ashamed to say, knew all about the little sexual adventures he had when he went out on his bike on a Friday evening.'

'They were a bit more serious than "little sexual adventures", wouldn't you say?' DS Din remarked.

'I knew nothing about the murder. He always said that Tiffany Mordaunt was nothing to do with him, and I was stupid enough to believe that – at first. These urges of his seemed to me to be more delinquent than wicked – but I was enthralled by this man and yes, I did love him once.'

'So everything you told me about meeting Patrick Venn in a pub, coming to Tagg's Island to live – it was with Sage on the *Inner Peace* rather than Patrick Venn on *The Great Gatsby*?'

Vicky nodded.

'And all those delicate problems that emerged in your love life, were with Sage?' She nodded again before explaining how, after he'd got back on that Friday evening, word had spread quickly about the commotion just along the road from Tagg's Island, where the Beast of Hampton Court had apparently been apprehended.

Sage immediately changed out of his cycling gear to join the crowd of onlookers. He'd seen Mangan and her colleague as they waited for a police van to collect the bike that the man they'd wrongly arrested had been riding.

'Sage was already concerned that the police had come so close to catching him and was making plans to divert suspicion when you turned up on the island about a week later.'

Mangan remembered the moment well; Sage appearing as if from the mist coming off a wintery Thames.

'But he told me he'd just arrived in a taxi; that he'd been hiking round Argentina or somewhere,' Mangan said. 'He had a knapsack on his back.'

'Sage always kept a backpack ready for a swift departure. When he saw you, he grabbed it to mislead you into thinking he'd been away when the attacks happened. He couldn't have gone abroad. He didn't own a passport. He knew it would have to be in his real name.'

'Shame I didn't check out his story.'

'Why would you? You had no reason to believe that he was the attacker, particularly after he'd diverted your attention onto the fictitious Patrick Venn. The Met thought they'd caught the 'Beast of Hampton Court' anyway. That morning when you came to Tagg's Island I'd gone to an office temping job I was doing in the City. He told me how you'd come aboard, and that you'd spouted some nonsense about being a biker. Having rented the *Gatsby*, he insisted that I go there that evening to play the part of Venn's imaginary girlfriend. He moved his bike and all the associated paraphernalia across, close to the *Gatsby*. It was important for me to tell you Patrick wasn't home from work yet. Sage had concluded that the police would eventually figure out that Darnell Thomas was the wrong man and that the right one was somewhere on Tagg's Island. He was puzzled, however, as to why you went there alone and pretended not to be a police officer. He thought you might be working undercover as part of a team.'

'But it was Sage who attacked the last victim, Darcy Kramer, wasn't it?' Louise asked. 'Why do that when Darnell Thomas had been charged and was likely to be convicted? Surely it was in Sage's interests to stop the attacks now that he was off the hook?'

'Oh, that was the bit that went badly wrong,' Vicky explained. 'Sage didn't know how strong the evidence was against the guy you'd caught, and with you apparently still on the case, he hit upon what he thought was a brilliant idea. To put another alternative in your sights.'

'Colin Brown,' Louise said.

'Yes, exactly. If he attacked again that night, firstly it strengthened his Patrick Venn deception because so far as you knew, Venn had been out on his bike when it happened. But even more importantly, Colin Brown – who he knew had convictions for assaulting women – could be put in the frame as another suspect. After you'd gone, that evening he put on all the gear and cycled into town but Colin Brown came back for the coat he'd left behind and so Sage inadvertently provided him with an alibi. I'd returned from the *Gatsby* by the time Colin called for his coat and pretended Sage was upstairs which, half an hour later, he was. He'd seen Colin's bike outside, sneaked in via the fire escape and came down as if he'd been there all the time.'

'And his other big blunder was leaving DNA on Darcy Kramer that matched that of Ian Escreet.'

Vicky said she knew nothing about the fingernail, and was sure Sage didn't either. But he did know he'd been too clever by half and wished he'd never carried out that last attack.

'Why didn't Sage seek any medical help for his "urges"? Louise asked.

'He did. He'd already done time for a sexual assault, which was one of the reasons he was determined never to go back into prison again. He'd had an awful time inside. When he got out, he tried to erase this dark episode by becoming Sage. He came from a very well-to-do family, but his father died when he was little, and his mother when he was sixteen. The only relative he knew was his mother's sister, who lived on a houseboat on Tagg's Island. It was the perfect location for him to start afresh. I don't think Aunt Jane knew anything about his prison sentence. She'd known Ian Escreet as a child, so when he reappeared as an adult she was pleased that her nephew was keen to forge a relationship with her. She told Sage that he'd inherit the *Inner Peace* when she died.'

'And you were telling us about the medical help he sought,' Din reminded her.

'Oh yes, he didn't want to go to a doctor because his medical history was under the name Ian Escreet. He knew a man who said he could provide him with drugs to sort out his problem. He'd provided medication for his aunt Jane when she fell ill. That's how Sage got to know him.'

'And this man lived on the island?' Louise asked. 'At *Navicula*?'

'Yes. But I forget his name.'

Louise knew she was referring to Jeremy Van Wyk, the South African chemist. She reminded Vicky West once more that she was speaking under caution, and asked what she knew about the murder of Tiffany Mordaunt.

The woman immediately broke down in tears. 'I don't know why I came here today. I think that subconsciously I wanted confirmation that Sage was dead. After you'd gone that day, I went back to *The Great Gatsby*. We were due to leave for Scotland the next day, and Sage said I should have a last tidy-up before locking the boat down for the summer. When I went out onto the island there were lots of police around, but their attention seemed focused on that huge place where the gangsters lived.'

'*Navicula*,' Louise reminded her.

'Yes, *Navicula*. They hadn't found Tiffany's body yet.' More tears flowed as Vicky West struggled to keep control of her emotions. 'When I went on board the *Gatsby*, the door leading down from the galley, which had always been locked, was open. Some stairs led down to a low room in the belly of the boat. I'd heard noises from there on the few occasions I'd been on board, but Sage told me they were the natural sounds of the river and, as that was the only bit below the waterline, it wasn't unusual, or anything to be worried about. So, seeing the door was open, I went down there with a torch to check it was clean and everything. I saw something lying in a crack between the wooden planks. It glistened in the torchlight. It was this.'

Vicky reached into her handbag and brought out a gold chain with a heart-shaped locket containing a photograph of Tiffany Mordaunt's mother.

It took a while for Mangan and Din to piece everything together. How Vicky had heard Jeremy Van Wyk and Sage discussing a different way to deal with his 'urges', and how she knew instinctively that the locket she'd found had belonged to Tiffany Mordaunt. How she'd heard later that the girl's body had been discovered on the marshland behind *Navicula*. How Sage said that it must have been one of Rockov's men who'd held Tiffany captive before killing her. How Vicky, who said nothing about finding the locket, was already planning her escape.

She was sure that Sage and Van Wyk had conspired to keep Tiffany Mordaunt as a sex slave, killing her when they knew the police were coming. Vicky had believed that she may well be drugged and kept prisoner for the same purpose if she didn't escape.

The couple travelled to the Hebrides the next day. Their original plan had been to lay low for at least a year. As the beneficiary of Aunt Jane's will, as well as inherited wealth from his parents, Sage had enough for them to live on, but by now Vicky was terrified of him and worried about the consequences for her if she went to the police.

'Even if I wasn't arrested as an accessory, I knew I'd never be safe so long as he could get to me. So on the second night in Scotland, I ran away; caught a train to London and then down to the West Country to live with an old school friend.'

This friend was the only person who knew that Vicky had once lived on Tagg's Island. She still lived with the woman – their relationship, Vicky hinted, was now more intimate than friendship – and it was she who'd read about the fire and the *Daily Candour*'s campaign to commemorate Sage.

Mangan knew that the Met would also have known that Vicky West had lived on Tagg's Island if they'd read her report. Operation Zeus and the murder of Jenny Daniels in nearby East Molesey would have distracted their attention, but none of that was an excuse. A proper investigation would have taken DNA samples from everyone who lived on that island to check against the DNA found on the blanket that Tiffany was wrapped in. The failings were serious, and Mangan hoped they wouldn't occur in any modern investigation of this kind, and certainly not on any under her watch.

Mangan couldn't tell Vicky if she'd be prosecuted for withholding this vital information about the murder of a young woman twenty years ago. The evidence of the locket certainly solved the murder she'd been assigned to reinvestigate. She hoped that the prosecuting authorities would go easy on Vicky. Mangan had been deeply impressed by the woman's dignity and stoicism. She'd come to London with the locket to finally hand over this evidence to the police now that she knew Sage was dead.

Vicky West had wasted her life on a murderer, a man whose gentle charm was directly at odds with his violent nature. Louise recognised that her sympathy for Vicky was compounded by her own gullibility. She had once looked into those same green eyes and been similarly beguiled.

41

NAVICULA

When Mangan returned to her office, the man from Southampton was already in the waiting room. The Chief Inspector of the MAIB was a neat, military-looking man, wearing a double-breasted suit. When Louise thanked him for taking the trouble to come and brief her personally, he raised a hand, as if to hold up traffic.

'Please don't mention it. Whilst we provide our reports to the Department, we always inform the police first if any foul play is suspected. It doesn't happen often but it's important to get the process right.'

'Foul play?' Louise repeated in surprise. 'You mean the fire was started deliberately?'

'No doubt about it, I'm afraid.'

The Chief Inspector went on to tell DCS Mangan that there was no indication of any accidental cause for the blaze; no paraffin on board, the Calor Gas cylinder was empty and the *Inner Peace* had no heaters, either electric or gas.

'The resident of this houseboat seemed to be impervious to cold – probably wore lots of flannel underwear,' he added unnecessarily. 'There was a carbon dioxide fire extinguisher on board, but no attempt had been made to

use it. So we had our suspicions even before the incontro-
vertible evidence emerged.'

'And what was that?' Mangan asked, keen to move
things along.

'As you know, most of the vessel and its contents were
swept away, but by some divine intervention a chunk of
the *Inner Peace* turned up in the nets of a trawler that was
fishing in the North Sea close to the Thames Estuary. A
sturdy piece of ribbed steel. The safety rail on the stairs
leading to the upper deck.'

'How do you know it's from the *Inner Peace?*'

'Because some of the steel rail was amongst the little
that was left of the vessel, and it matches exactly.'

The conversation was paused while the Chief Inspector
rooted around in his briefcase, emerging with some photographs.

'And how does this rail indicate there was foul play?'
Mangan asked once she had regained her visitor's attention.

'Sorry, should have explained. It wasn't the rail that
told us there'd been malicious behaviour. It was the object
handcuffed to it,' he said, handing Louise an A5-sized
photograph depicting one of the most macabre sights that
Mangan had seen in a long career of dealing with macabre
sights. Handcuffed to the rail was a hand. The manacle
was tight enough to secure the wrist bone but most of the
flesh had gone along with the body that was once attached
to the hand.

'Before you ask, these remains have been under-water
for too long to yield any DNA, but this must surely be the
chap who's missing. I'd say this was conclusive proof that

somebody went aboard that boat, secured its owner to the rail and then set fire to it.'

The cold case review was over. The man who had murdered Tiffany Mordaunt was now known to be Sebastian Andrew Gordon Escreet. But this man was now a victim of murder as well as a perpetrator. What was previously considered to have been an accident now had to be investigated as a crime – as murder.

For Mangan, there was no doubt as to the chief suspect. Olive Burnett had been certain that Jeremy Van Wyk was back in England; he was the owner of another houseboat on Tagg's Island; he had a clear motive given all that Sage knew about his poisonous activities; the Reverend Stephen Marsh had seen somebody enter *Navicula* just before the fire broke out on the *Inner Peace*.

Who else could that have been but the owner, Jeremy Van Wyk? And what else could he have been doing skulking around the island at two-thirty in the morning?

Mangan had all she needed to obtain a warrant to search *Navicula*. There must be at least the possibility that Van Wyk was still there. Nobody was yet aware of the MAIB's conclusion of foul play. As far as the media was concerned, the fire on Tagg's Island had been an accident. The Met would ensure that the report was embargoed until the police search was completed. Mangan's thoughts were already focused on leading that exercise the same evening. She'd asked Din to arrange for her to see Deputy Commissioner Statham to get the necessary authority, as soon as she got back to the Yard.

There was something else she wanted authorisation for. Van Wyk had been one of the three leading figures who'd escaped the clutches of Operation Zeus twenty years ago. It was known that he had connections with Jack Handysides and Marko Rockov, as well as Sage. Now he'd become a suspect in a murder case that she was heading up. Mangan felt that she was now fully entitled to see the unredacted file on those events of twenty years ago.

She made this point forcefully to Deputy Commissioner Bob Statham when she entered his office an hour later.

'I'm not sure why you want to see it,' Statham responded. 'I'll authorise the warrant for you to search Van Wyk's houseboat. If you catch him there, fine. If not, we'll pull out all the stops to find him. I've already alerted the National Crime Agency and they'll be working with their buddies in Interpol to nab him, wherever he—'

'Why shouldn't I see that file?' Mangan interrupted abruptly. 'I'm senior enough; it has information relevant to an investigation that I'm leading, and preventing me from seeing it doesn't change the fact that our combined forces of law and order have already let Van Wyk slip through their fingers once. There was no intelligence that he was back in the country until I provided it.'

It was unusual for Louise Mangan to sing her own praises in this way, but it had the desired effect.

'Okay, okay, I get your point. I needed to assure myself that you weren't being influenced by this nonsense coming out of Manchester.'

'The Handysides stuff?' Mangan asked.

'Yes. The theory about Jack Handysides operating in

Manchester that's being put around by one of Cutler's thugs in an attempt to get a reduced sentence.'

'Let me assure you, sir, I haven't the slightest interest in anything other than Jeremy Van Wyk, and the investigation that you put me in charge of.'

'I'm not sure how seeing the unredacted file will help you, but you've done a great job, and as you well know, I rate you very highly, Louise.'

Mangan thought the Deputy Commissioner seemed a bit embarrassed by this little paean of praise or he may have just needed time to think. Whatever the reason, he broke off from the conversation to wander round his substantial office, pausing by the big central window that overlooked the Thames.

It was late afternoon, and the river was rising towards its second high tide of the day.

'Sweet Thames, run softly, till I end my song,' Statham murmured just loud enough for Louise to hear. She allowed his lapse into poetry to pass unremarked, deciding to leave him with his thoughts for a few moments longer.

Eventually, Statham returned to his seat.

'Okay,' he said, 'you can see the unredacted file, but on one condition.'

'Which is?'

'That you sit in this office and read it under my supervision.'

'Will you help me with the big words?' Mangan asked facetiously.

'Very funny. If you accept my proviso, I'll arrange to have it here tomorrow. Goodnight, Louise.'

'Goodnight, Bob,' Mangan said, calling the Deputy Commissioner by his first name for the first time.

'Now get out there and search that bloody houseboat,' Bob responded.

The unmarked police car containing DCS Mangan and DS Din drove across the little bridge onto Tagg's Island at 5.30 p.m. Behind them was a people carrier with an armed unit – just in case. Behind that followed a third vehicle containing a forensics team.

Everything on the island looked familiar to Louise: the big 'Welcome' sign beneath which were details of where each vessel was berthed, the flora and fauna, the onshore clutter around each dwelling; the sense of complete separation from the city. As usual there was little activity, aside from the police units getting themselves organised; preparing to move on foot to the inner lagoon and board *Navicula*.

An elderly woman was walking her small dog, a workman packed away some plumbing equipment, his job finished for the day. To Louise's amusement, a cyclist came past them, complete with helmet and goggles, heading towards the wider cycling horizons of the A308. She remembered how she'd only discovered Tagg's Island because she was looking for just such a cyclist at the tail end of the previous century.

The police procession having now arrived at *Navicula*, Mangan pressed the bell and shouted the obligatory warning.

'Police. Open the door or we'll remove it.'

A trio of armed officers panned out to cover all angles of the vast houseboat, aiming their guns at the galley and the glass expanse of the upper deck. Two more approached the front door with the 16-kg manual battering ram referred to as Enforcer. Three blows, and there was no longer a door or anything else to prevent them going in.

Navicula was empty. After a sweep by the armed unit, the forensic team got down to work. Mangan was outside looking across the river with Din, telling him how, during the still legendary Operation Zeus, the speedboat carrying Handysides, Rockov and Van Wyk had left from this very spot, only to be found empty at St Katherine's Dock next to Tower Bridge.

Her narrative was interrupted by the head of the forensics unit coming out to tell her that the man they were after had only just left.

'How do you know?'

'The drink of tea he made himself was unfinished, the cup still hot. There's a full wardrobe of clothes but no personal artefacts, no wallet, keys or money. He was travelling light, but he was certainly travelling. And you'd better come and see something else.'

The forensics man led Mangan upstairs, to the lounge area.

'He would have seen us coming,' he said, pointing to a screen displaying the small bridge that they'd crossed; the only route onto the island. 'He must have fixed a camera up somewhere to give himself a perfect view.'

'It was the cyclist,' Mangan exclaimed. 'That was Van Wyk. He went past within touching distance as we were preparing our approach.'

DS Din was ordered to put out an alert but there was little optimism that one nondescript cyclist would be discernible amongst the thousands on the roads at that time of the evening.

'Are we sure it was Van Wyk who was here?' Mangan asked.

'Not yet,' said the man from forensics. 'But we'll know soon enough – once we examine the DNA from the cup he was drinking out of.'

Louise Mangan sat at the conference table in one corner of the Deputy Commissioner's office, a file open in front of her.

At first, Bob Statham had sat with her, but this close proximity soon became uncomfortable for them both. He'd gone back to his desk and was working his way through a pile of paperwork, looking across to Mangan at regular intervals, but saying nothing. Louise, too, was silent as she read through the file. She was too absorbed to speak.

She read how the police and the security service, alarmed at the spiralling level of crime associated with the growing market for recreational drugs in London had devised an audacious plan.

They decided to enter the crime scene themselves, inventing the persona of Jack Handysides and giving the MI5 officer playing that role access to millions of pounds, worth of seized narcotics, much of which would be redistributed into the market to bolster Handysides' credibility and to draw in the major players by convincing them that by pooling their efforts they would be invincible.

The true reason for consolidating and combining these

criminal networks was to better enable their destruction
– and it worked. The file revealed how Jack Handysides
succeeded in welding together a phalanx of previously
disparate gangs with him at its head. It required him to
not just pose as a criminal, but to actually be a criminal,
contributing to the rising level of drug abuse in London
and the Home Counties. For this reason, the operation
required clearance at the highest level, signed off by the
Prime Minister as well as the Home Secretary in two suc-
cessive administrations, on the strong recommendation of
the Commissioner and the Director General of MI5. The
file revealed that, at one stage, eighty-five percent of all
drugs crime in London was carried out either directly or
indirectly by someone associated with Jack Handysides.

There was a fascinating section about a TV programme
called *Crimesolve* which came close to ruining everything
by naming Handysides. The TV people had no idea that he
was an undercover officer. Neither did Dr Jamie Templeman, *Crimesolve*'s main source of information, who'd
studied Handysides' activities in great detail, and was said
to have been writing a book about him. The prospect of
a TV exposé had led to the final phase of the deception,
codenamed Operation Zeus, being instigated two weeks
earlier than originally planned.

Using all the information accumulated through Jack
Handysides over four years of painstaking work and in
the biggest operation ever launched by the Metropolitan
Police, organised drug-trafficking in the capital was all but
destroyed.

Louise found herself reading the file as if it was a thriller.
She'd been too gripped to break off for tea or coffee, or to

say anything to the Deputy Commissioner. She was aware of his presence but refused to allow it to break her concentration.

She was now on the final few pages, which recorded the escape of the three men in a speedboat. The file expressed disappointment at Rockov and Van Wyk's escape, but relief that Handysides had not only survived the ordeal but also enhanced his reputation by evading capture. Nobody was to know that the Handysides empire had been constructed as an enormous honeytrap, or that the man who destroyed it was also its creator. False stories were circulated in the criminal underworld about Handysides being betrayed by informers within the ranks of his organisation. The full story was only ever revealed to some very senior people who were either members of the Privy Council or signatories to the Official Secrets Act, the file suitably redacted.

There was nothing about where Handysides had come from. Only a single, final annexed page about where he'd gone to after handing himself in to New Scotland Yard on the same evening as his escape in the speedboat.

Louise read the page, gulped, and spoke for the first time to the man whose office she was occupying.

'It was you,' she gasped. 'You were . . . are . . . used to be Jack Handysides.'

42

A HAPPY OCCASION

Alex Cornelius and Grant Traore were married that August. Even many of those who wished them well worried that they might be rushing things. Alex pointed out to such people that she and Grant had been through more in six months than most couples experienced in a lifetime. Grant just shrugged, saying that he'd never met a woman like Alex before and never would again, so what was the point of delaying things? His parents were delighted. Hers were less so.

'But isn't he a drug addict?' Alex's mother had asked when her daughter relayed the happy news.

'I told you, mother, he became a cocaine user as part of his police work, and now he's been weaned off. You are more likely to snort cocaine, now, than he is.'

Alex's father, ever the High Court Judge, pronounced his view as if summing up for the jury. 'Marriage for me and your mother was always a precarious exercise, but that doesn't mean it will be for you. Have fun, retain your sense of curiosity and do not, under any circumstances, sacrifice your career.'

Alex had no intention of leaving the Met, although her period working with Louise Mangan was due to end at Christmas. The two women pledged to stay in touch. As

Mangan had remarked once to Harry Kosnich, she looked upon Alex as a third daughter.

Grant was back at work, but kept away from frontline policing for a while. It was felt that his role in destroying Blue Moon made him vulnerable, at least in the short term. He was determined to go back to undercover work eventually, but was happy to work at Hendon on the Detective Degree Holder Entry Programme in the meantime. Being a non-graduate himself somehow added to his job satisfaction.

The date of the wedding was 17 August. Mangan had hoped that Captain Petros Diamantapoulis would be able to come over from Athens and attend as her plus one, but she had always known it was an unlikely prospect. The phone calls between them had all but stopped after the Captain pulled out of their planned trip to Barcelona. Nevertheless, Mangan had convinced herself that the relationship was worth preserving, and had emailed Petros to see if he was free to attend.

Sadly, he wasn't, explaining in his reply that he'd already agreed to remain at work throughout August when many of his colleagues would be on holiday. He also mentioned in passing that he was about to be promoted to Police Major. There was nothing else – no news, no gossip and, most tellingly, not even a suggestion of when they might next meet or even communicate. Mangan couldn't help but conclude that it was the end of a beautiful friendship. Yet she so wished they could talk as they used to, exchanging information about the latest cases they were involved in. She would have loved to confide in Petros about Sage and the events on Tagg's Island. Most of all she wanted to tell him about Jack Handysides. She certainly couldn't tell anybody else.

Information about Handysides' true identity was classified. Petros was far enough removed for her to give him the bare bones, but even she didn't know that much. All she knew was that an MI5 agent had assumed the identity of Jack Handysides and after the success of Operation Zeus, been given a new identity on the other side of the world, joining the Victoria State Police. His 'legend' – as Grant would have called it – was that he'd emigrated from England looking for a new adventure. Thinking this through, Louise knew that 'joining' was the wrong term. What was the phrase that Statham had used in his office that day?

'Blending – that was it.

He'd been 'blended' into the VSP at Melbourne, returning to England as Deputy Commissioner Bob Statham. Was Statham his original name? She didn't know. All she was told was that he'd wanted to come home after twenty years down under and this route had been devised as the channel through which it could happen.

'I've no idea how long I'll be doing this, Louise,' he'd said as she left his office that morning. 'Probably for a year or so, until I retire. It will be a nice way to end a career that was sometimes a little bit too exciting, if you know what I mean. But of one thing I'm sure, in the battle between good and evil I was always on the right side – and so are you.'

Mangan went to the wedding alone. Many of her team were there, including Harry Kosnich and Rushil Din. Harry took Mangan onto the dance floor and asked where her 'Greek chap' was.

'Oh, that's all over, Harry,' Mangan said, admitting it to herself for the first time.

'Ah, so there's a chance for me yet,' Harry said, pulling her a little closer as he did so.

'There's always a chance, Harry, but I wouldn't want you to get your hopes up.'

They both laughed.

Alex introduced Louise to Liam Cafferty, who was there with his girlfriend. Liam was beginning his final year at Manchester University and no longer worked at the Brickmakers Arms, where he'd also studied criminology a little too closely for comfort.

Cutler's trial would begin in the autumn. It was expected that he'd be in prison for a very long time, as would his acolytes in Blue Moon.

Everyone had been up dancing to 'Hi Ho Silver Lining' when Rushil Din took Louise to one side.

'The protection guys need to know what time you're thinking of leaving so that they can plan your journey home.'

Mangan had been given protection immediately following Jeremy Van Wyk's escape from *Navicula*. It wasn't the Full Monty protection given to the Commissioner or the Home Secretary, just a couple of armed officers who accompanied her whenever she was out and about. The Deputy Commissioner had insisted upon it immediately after Van Wyk's escape. The South African was known to have murdered at least once.

Mangan was considered to be in even greater danger when the DNA found in *Navicula* matched that of Sebastian Andrew Gordon Escreet. It was then that they realised that the man who'd died on the *Inner Peace* was Jeremy Van Wyk.

The man who'd escaped from *Navicula* on his bike just before the police arrived, brushing so closely to Louise in the process, was Sage – murderer of Tiffany Mordaunt, Jeremy Van Wyk, and, in all probability, his aunt Jane. The man with green eyes was a serial killer, and he remained at liberty.

ACKNOWLEDGEMENTS

This is a work of fiction, although the murder of Jenny Daniels is based on something that tragically happened in 1999. John McVicar's *Dead on Time* helped me to with the detail of that crime.

Liam Thomas, author of *The Buyer* told me much about undercover policing that I didn't know.

As always, Alex Clarke at Wildfire was a patient commissioner and wise advisor. My agent Clare Alexander was a constant source of encouragement. Jack Butler at Wildfire, like all good editors, improved the book, and I was privileged to have Russel McLean, an expert in this genre, as my copy/line editor.

My wife Carolyn read it before anybody else and gave it her seal of approval. The book is dedicated to Carolyn's father.

Alan Johnson's childhood memoir *This Boy* was published in 2013. It won the Royal Society of Literature Ondaatje Prize, and the Orwell Prize, Britain's top political writing award. His second volume of memoirs, *Please Mr Postman* (2014) won the National Book Club award for Best Biography. The final book in his memoir trilogy, *The Long And Winding Road* (2016), won the Parliamentary Book Award for Best Memoir. *In My Life – A Music Memoir* was published in 2018 and his highly acclaimed first novel, *The Late Train to Gipsy Hill*, was published in 2021. The second 'Mangan' novel, *One of Our Ministers is Missing* was published in 2022.

Alan was a Labour MP for twenty years before retiring ahead of the 2017 general election. He served in five cabinet positions in the governments of Tony Blair and Gordon Brown, including Education Secretary, Health Secretary and Home Secretary. He is Chancellor of the University of Hull.

He and his wife Carolyn live in East Yorkshire.